I Was Made to Love You

I Was Made to Love You

Jessica Wren

www.urbanbooks.net

Urban Books, LLC
300 Farmingdale Road, NY-Route 109
Farmingdale, NY 11735

I Was Made to Love You
Copyright © 2018 Jessica Wren

ISBN 13: 978-1-945855-39-9
ISBN 10: 1-945855-39-8

First Trade Paperback Printing September 2018
Printed in the United States of America

10 9 8 7 6 5 4 3 2 1

This is a work of fiction. Any references or similarities to actual events, real people, living or dead, or to real locales are intended to give the novel a sense of reality. Any similarity in other names, characters, places, and incidents is entirely coincidental.

Distributed by Kensington Publishing Corp.
Submit Orders to:
Customer Service
400 Hahn Road
Westminster, MD 21157-4627
Phone: 1-800-733-3000
Fax: 1-800-659-2436

Dedication

Bernice Johnson,

Words cannot express the pain I felt the day you left me. I know you're in heaven cheering for me. I love you, Grandma! May you continue to rest beautifully in peace.

Acknowledgments

Mom, you are my rock! Thank you for pushing me and standing behind me. You believed in me and always told me to follow my dreams. You are the best mother a girl could have. When I have children, I hope my children will look up to me with the same admiration. I love you! Ashley, I don't know what I would do without you. You and I have a bond like no other. I have never met a person I argue with, then burst out laughing with ten minutes later. I love you, and I could not have asked for a better sister. Daddy, thank you for always guiding my footsteps. You taught me to protect my self-esteem, and because of your love and patience, I grew into a humble, grounded woman. I love you, Daddy! To my nephew Jaylen, words cannot express what you mean to me. To see you grow every day, learning new things and seeing your little imagination is such a blessing. I love you! Grandma, I can't even type without crying. You are my rock! I love you so much! Your wisdom and spirit have gotten me through. Your laughter and jokes always brighten my spirit. You are the best grandmother a girl could have. I love you, Grandma! Kim, I don't know what I would ever do without you. You are more than my cousin. I love you so much. Kitu, Charmain, Ayesha, and Arie, you women rock! Your warmth, encouraging words, support, and love throughout the years have made me understand the true meaning of sisterhood. I am so thankful for all of you. I love you ladies. To my family members: I love you all. To my supporters: I'm humbled by all those I've come in contact with. Your belief in me and kindness means more than words could ever express. Blessings!

Introduction

The Beginning of Our Love

"Damn," I yelled in frustration as the sensor to my 2017 Silver Chevy Tahoe blinked, alerting me to low tire pressure.

Making a right turn, I pulled into a Tiger Mart gas station, driving toward the air pressure machine and parked vertically in front of it. Stepping out of my truck, I frowned as I was greeted by the unbearable Texas heat.

"Got damn!" I yelled while removing a small white washcloth from the back pocket of my white linen shorts. Sweat beads began to form on my forehead.

Quickly surveying my surroundings, an uneasy feeling came over me as I glanced across the street and saw the Justice of Peace Building. Honestly, I didn't care for this part of town. The Austin Police Department stayed trolling up and down MLK just to harass black men. I didn't have time for their shit that day, so I hurried to remove the tire valve stem caps from my two front tires.

Just as I was about to place quarters in the machine, a custom-made, candy-coated, purple Tahoe came zooming through the parking lot. The bass booming through the speakers, along with the black matte rims, piqued my interest. The vehicle stopped and parked on gas pump number four.

I watched for a second trying to get a look at who was driving the truck. The mirror tint prevented me from being able to see inside. As the car door opened, a full-figured woman emerged, leaving me smiling with the dancing eyes of an optimist.

"Fuck, who is that?" I whispered while biting my bottom lip. I locked my truck and dashed across the parking lot, not paying attention.

Beeep!

"Hey, man, watch where you're going!" an older Hispanic man yelled.

"My bad!" I yelled, startled, throwing my hands up.

I rushed inside the gas station and spotted the beauty over by the beverages. I stood over by the row of chips and watched as her neatly arched eyebrows eased up and down concentrating as she gathered different snacks. *Yes,* I inwardly chuckled seeing that she and I had the same taste in snacks. Ranch sunflower seeds, gummy bears, and a peach soda.

As she made her way to the checkout, I followed behind her and mugged a short, ugly-ass dude with dreads that had also been eyeing her. *Too late, she's all mine, playboy,* I silently thought.

"May I please put thirty-five on pump four?" the beauty asked the cashier while she placed her items on the counter.

"Sure, that will be forty-one dollars and fifteen cents total," the cashier smiled.

As the stunning woman proceeded to dig in her Coach purse for her wallet, I stepped behind her and passed the cashier a fifty-dollar bill.

"Don't worry about it, Ms. Lady. I got you! Keep the change, man." I smiled at the cashier, whose name tag read José.

"Hey, thanks, man! *That's* what I'm talking about," José said excitedly.

"Thank you so much! I appreciate you, mister." She turned around and stuck her hand out to shake mine. All I could do was stare. I was speechless.

Our eyes met and locked like magnets. Her gray eyes with a hint of brown gazed at me. We stood there, she and I, and I felt this instant chemistry of love and understanding.

I continued to stare, noticing her long, midnight-black curly hair that flowed over her shoulders. She stood at five feet nine, a perfect match for my tall, lean six-foot-three frame. Her skin was chocolate and smooth. A pair of deep dimples greeted me when she smiled, showing off her halo-white straight teeth. I was enticed by her shapely size 24 full figure. She had a sweet voice that matched her ladylike personality. Our stare was rudely interrupted.

"Ahem, excuse me, shit, but people do have places to go," some rude-ass female from behind me said.

The beauty's smile quickly faded, turning into a frown. Her upper lip curled, and she threw her head back slowly. She took a deep breath and then pinched the brim of her nose. "You know what, bi—?" She paused and looked me in my eyes once more. "Never mind, you ain't worth it. Thank you again, mister!" She smiled at me briefly and walked out of the store.

I turned to look at the chick behind me and shook my head in disgust at her appearance. *Damn, at least put some lotion on and comb yo' head,* I silently thought before I left the store.

As the beautiful woman pumped her gas, I couldn't help but ogle. The long, wild orchid and white Emily Stripe wrap front maxidress she wore hugged her curves in all the right places. Her ass twerked and jiggled on its own with every movement she took. *Daaaaamn,* I wanted to scream.

"Do you always stare, mister?" She turned around and smirked.

"My bad, you caught me red-handed." I laughed and licked my lips.

"What you did back there was sweet, and I appreciate you; but you know I could've paid for my own gas. What's your name anyway?" she asked while she leaned up against her truck.

"It depends on who you ask, but my government name is Avantae."

"Avantae, huh?" her eyes widened. "Wait, aren't you Big Tae's son, the one who used to own Big Tae's Barbershop and the clothing store?"

My jaw clenched, and I took a deep breath. Hearing my father's name almost made me tear up. Five years ago, he was found murdered in his barbershop. There were no witnesses or evidence, and his murder remains a cold case. Having someone mention his name and old businesses hurt. I often felt shame for closing his businesses, but I needed time to heal. Before I answered, I swallowed the lump of emotions that wanted to spill out.

"Yeah, I'm his son. How do you know him?" I placed my hands in my pockets.

"My father used to speak very highly of Mr. Avantae. I met him years ago, and he was one of the sweetest men I have ever met. He joked about me meeting his son one day." A sad expression covered her beautiful face. "Tae, I mean Avantae, I'm sorry about your dad. How have you been holding up?" she asked, piercing my soul with her beautiful eyes.

"I'm good, and you can call me Tae. I like that." I smiled while winking at her. "What's your name, beautiful, and who is your pops?"

"Ceanna! Ceanna Black and Calvin Black was my father. He passed away a couple of months ago from cancer." Her eyes watered.

"Damn! I'm sorry to hear that."

"It's okay! I'm dealing with it. Day by day, right? Moment by moment. I miss him and my mother so much. Without their guidance, I feel lost most days. I just hope they are proud of the woman I've become, you know?" she openly admitted while blinking away tears. Conversation with her was so natural.

"Your pops was a good man. I'm sorry for your loss. If you ever need to talk, I'm here. Word is bond! Look, let's get out of here and go get us something to eat. I know this dope Mexican restaurant, and I would love to continue our conversation."

"That really sounds inviting, but I'm involved. You know how small Austin is. That won't go over so well. You know how things can be. You seem like a really nice guy, though, and if our paths had connected some other time, I would have definitely taken you up on that offer. I'm sorry, but I have to pass, love. It was nice meeting you, Avantae, and you take care. Oh, and thank you again for paying for my gas and snacks. I really appreciate you!" She kissed me on the cheek, and I opened her truck door for her. I couldn't let her leave, though, without shooting my shot one last time.

"I understand, but at least give me your number. I mean, being friends can't hurt nothing," I pouted, feeling a little rejected. She halted from getting into her truck and turned to look at me.

"Honestly, you and I both know that is *not* a good idea. Other than the obvious, the conversation with you is so natural, and I can tell you're a good man. I just don't believe in placing myself in situations where boundaries end up crossing. You're definitely trouble for me. I'm a loyal woman, and I want to stay that way. I'm sorry, Tae!" She kissed me on the cheek again, but I quickly turned my head instantly, being greeted by the softness of her lips.

"Damn, Ce, I was outta line. Please forgive me. I just see something I want. I know you got a nigga and all, but I'm checking for you." I spoke sincerely while looking Ceanna in her eyes. We stared at each other a few more moments before she hopped in her truck and pulled off, taking a little piece of me with her.

I couldn't shake Ceanna or get her out of my thoughts. As time passed, she was all I thought about. I respected her relationship, so I held back, but that didn't stop me from inquiring and doing my research on her.

Ceanna Black definitely had my full attention. I learned she had degrees in fashion marketing and fashion design. She didn't have any children; she dated one lame-ass nigga name Marcus from the East Side, went to Huston-Tillotson University, Austin Community College, was a low-profile chick, her best friends were Asia, Keisha, and Tonya, she was the daughter of a kingpin, and owned her own boutique for curvy women.

Her shop was located in the Springdale Shopping Center. She was easy to find, and I could have approached her on numerous occasions, but after I kissed her briefly, I didn't know what to say or even how to approach her. I wondered if she would run from me or be mad at me. I prayed that one day our paths would innocently cross again, and it did months later, but not the way I'd hoped.

Gina, who was married to my father, called and stated that her son Jaceyon wanted the entire family to come over to her home so he could introduce everyone to his new love interest. I didn't really fuck with Jaceyon like that, but since Gina asked me to come over, I did.

That night I sat on the brown and tan sectional Googling on my phone. The clock read 7:20 p.m., and I remember thinking that if they didn't arrive by 7:45, I was bouncing. As soon as those thoughts entered my mind, the doorbell rang. Uncle Samuel, who is Gina's brother, drunkenly answered the door and smiled.

"Well, my my my, aren't you beautiful," he said loudly as he stumbled to the side to allow Jaceyon and the young lady entrance. I continued to Google on my phone, not looking up.

"What's up, Unc? This is my baby, Ceanna. Ceanna, don't mind him. This is my crazy-ass uncle, Samuel," Jaceyon laughed.

At the mentioned of her name, I looked up and made eye contact with her. She smiled at me, and there I was, stuck again. *Damn, what the fuck is she doing with his ass? I thought I did my homework thoroughly on her,* I silently fussed.

"Ceanna, this nigga here," Jaceyon pointed at me, "is my stepbrother Avantae." Jaceyon and I mean-mugged each other for a second, and the hate couldn't be missed.

Ever since Jaceyon and I were young kids, we shared a silent beef with each other. I couldn't stand that nigga, and the day my father saw Gina's high-yellow, tall, slender frame with green eyes stroll into the barbershop with Jaceyon in tow for a haircut, my life changed. I knew she and her son would become a permanent fixture in our lives.

From day one, Jaceyon stayed competing with me. If sharing my father with him wasn't enough, he competed with me over females, style of dress, and as we got older and deep into the streets, he tried to steal my clients. The nigga was disrespectful. Period. That wasn't what my real issue with him was, though. Deep down, I always felt Jaceyon knew what happened—or had something to do with—my father's death. I just couldn't prove it.

"Hey, Tae!"

I stood up and gave Ceanna a friendly hug. She smelled so good.

"Tae? You giving this nigga nicknames and shit already?" he frowned. "You two know each other or something?" Jaceyon asked in a hostile tone while trying to square me up. He looked me up and down.

"What's good, homie?" I asked while mugging him.

"Relax, Jace." Ceanna placed her hand on Jaceyon's chest. "This is the nice guy I was telling you about who paid for my gas. Thank you again. After I left the gas station, I realized I left my card in my jean pocket. So I *really* appreciate you!" She rubbed my right arm, winked, and smiled.

There was something in that moment about Ceanna. She understood me and knew what to say and do to calm me. Had she not winked or smiled, Jaceyon and I probably would have had more than words. It was brewing inside me, and I knew a day would come that he and I would go blow for blow.

"It was good seeing you again, Ceanna. Take care of yourself, beautiful, and enjoy your night." I kissed her on her cheek and left. I had to get out of there—and fast.

"Ho-ass nigga!" Jaceyon shouted loudly as the door closed.

I jumped in my whip hitting the dashboard. Seeing Ceanna with Jaceyon had me *tight*. She was too good a woman to be with him. *Aaaargh!* The way she was looking at him made me sick. I knew then that Jaceyon had her wrapped around his finger. He was no good.

Although Ceanna wasn't mine, there was something about her that made me want to protect her heart. She was loyal, pure, and down-to-earth. She didn't deserve the bullshit that was sure to follow by being with him. I knew he was going to hurt her. I've seen him over the years play so many women and toss them aside like they weren't shit, and I just didn't want Ceanna to be on the receiving end of that.

It wasn't my place or business, but the more I tried to forget about Ceanna, the more she crept into my thoughts. The shit was weird. I hadn't even made love to her yet, and I was pressed, checking for a woman that wasn't even mine.

Months went by before I built up the courage to go visit Ceanna. I sat in the parking lot of her boutique going over a speech in my head. I was nervous. I had never felt so nervous in my life about approaching a female. There was just something about her. *Nigga, get a grip. You're tripping. Just go in there and tell shorty how you feel,* my inner voice encouraged.

I would have sat in my truck longer, trying to find the proper words, but it began not only to rain but to thunder. I grabbed the BBQ food I brought from the passenger's side and made it to the front door of the boutique just in time before the rain came pouring down.

"Oh my God, Avantae, hi. What a pleasant surprise. What are you doing here?" Ceanna greeted me while smiling and giving me a big friendly hug.

"I was in the neighborhood and brought you something to eat. Is it a bad time? Can you talk right now?" I asked while looking around. This was my first time at Ceanna's shop.

I inhaled the sweet scent of vanilla and admired glossy white swirled with purple marble floors. Hues of purples, gold, and white danced across the luxurious boutique. Thick, white, luxuriant plush lounge chairs were surrounded by the dressing room. A soft jazz version of Aaliyah's "Rock the Boat" played in the background on the loudspeaker as the sounds of the aquarium-blue waterfall pounded against the soft-textured rock wall. A crystal chandelier hung high on the ceiling. Fierce, plus-sized bodice dolls posed throughout the boutique with plus-size clothing adorning the many racks. Accessories of shoes, scarves, shades, makeup, perfumes, purses, and any other items to bring out the style of a perfect outfit were present.

"Sure, come on back to my office. It's kinda slow today, so I let my staff leave early. With this rain, I'm sure I won't get much business today. I'm just going to go ahead and lock up. Besides, we're under a flood watch. I should have left earlier. It looks really bad out there," she said as she put the closed sign up and locked the door.

"You got it decked out in here. This shit is nice," I complimented as we made our way back to her office.

"Thank you! Go ahead and have a seat." She sat behind her desk and smiled. "I'm curious as to what brings you by. I haven't seen you in so long. I mean, other than seeing you at the hood crayfish boil, and then briefly when Jaceyon introduced me to the family, but that didn't go over so well." She frowned.

"What happened?" I raised my eyebrows.

"Shit, I wish I knew. Everyone was friendly, but then once he introduced me to Gina, she was rude. I was so hurt by her rude remarks and stares that I told Jaceyon my job was calling me and left. It would have been nice if you would have stayed. At least I would have known someone or felt a little comfortable, but I take it you don't really deal with your people like that, or should I say, Jaceyon?" She looked at me for confirmation.

"You would be correct. I don't really get into the dramatics of everything, I'm a low-key kinda nigga, but I don't fuck with him at all. I stay cordial, and that's about it."

"Noted! Not to switch the subject, and I hope you don't think I'm out of line, but I wanted to talk to you about something personal."

"Okay, shoot."

"The day we met at the gas station, I mentioned your father, and I saw the pain in your eyes. I often wondered why Mr. Avantae's son closed his businesses. I know what you do for a living. I'm not judging you in any way. My father was a drug lord, and I get it, but for the life of me, I can't understand why *you're* in the game. At least open your father's businesses back up. The hood needs that. It meant something to the black community. Besides, I just don't wanna see you go down a destructive path. Maybe I shouldn't care so much, but I do. I've been wanting to say that for some time now. I thought about you and prayed often for your safety. I just don't want anything to happen to you. We have enough of our black men in prison and six feet under," she expressed with so much compassion while looking into my eyes.

"I hear you. I really do! Damn, I never really thought of that. When my pops was murdered, I was lost, you know. I've been kinda lost ever since. This drug shit is really all I know. I ain't going to lie, though. I'm tired. If I make to see thirty, at the rate I'm going, that will be a miracle."

"I mean, what are you *really* doing it for? Whatever you do in this life, you need to have a plan. You're out here taking penitentiary chances, and for what? You're not hurting for money, so it's not like you're hustling to eat. Your father and my father made so much bread, so I know you're sitting on money. The question is, what are you doing with all of it? Don't you want more? Don't you want to go places you've never been and one day get out of the trap? Don't end up dead or in jail. You're worth so much more. Where do you see yourself in five years?" she asked as she took a bite of her brisket sandwich. I almost drooled watching her lips.

"To be honest, a nigga don't think of shit like that. I move weight and hope a nigga ain't tryin'a jack me, or worse, get a fed case. I don't think about tomorrow. I'm just existing and living day by day," I sadly admitted. Ceanna had me feeling some kind of way. No woman ever challenged me mentally or ever had me questioning my life. She was rare. Most females around here only wanted money and bundles of hair.

"Please stop addressing yourself as a nigga." She looked at me sternly.

"Why are you with Jaceyon?" I changed the subject. "I mean, how you even met that nigga, I mean, fool?" From where I was sitting, Ceanna was with the wrong man.

"I love Jaceyon, but lately, things have been distant between us. I found out he's been cheating on me with some chick name Monique. He says he only slept with her once, but I don't believe that. I forgave him, and I'm trying to move past it. I'm hurt, though, and I don't trust him anymore. I've been really unhappy lately too." A lonely tear slid down her left cheek. She hurried to wipe it away.

"Wow, I can't believe I just told you that." She smiled sadly.

"You can tell me anything. Don't ever feel like you can't talk to me. You don't deserve that shit, and you know it. Give *me* a chance. You know our chemistry is strong. You knew it the day you met me. I know you felt it, because I did too," I admitted.

"Things are complicated, and it's not that easy. I mean, that's your stepbrother."

"By marriage! That nigga's blood ain't running through me, so *fuck* him." I slammed my fist down.

"Tae!" she yelled.

"What? I'm for real. Give *me* a chance. I'll *never* hurt you. Word is bond."

"You barely know me. I mean, you don't know anything about me. What if you get with me and don't like the woman I am? What if things get too rough, and you leave? What if I bore you? What if my weight bothers you like it does Jaceyon? I'm not the female you think I am. I'm flawed and deeply affected by a lot of shit in my life. Besides, it's just not right. I may be hurt by what Jaceyon has done, but that doesn't change my loyalty. I'm not a cheater or a disloyal woman." She bit her lip, trying to hold back the tears that were threatening to fall.

"Man, what? Fuck all of that. Jaceyon is a fool if he can't see you for the woman you are. As far as your weight, I love BBW. You're a beautiful person, and you're worthy of love. I can give that to you. Jaceyon is a clown. You don't know him, and you don't deserve the bullshit he's putting you through. He's got you feeling all down, depressed, and shit. Let *me* be that man to make you smile and build you up. I can love you the way you deserve."

"I gotta go." She pushed her chair back from the table.

"So, just like that? A nigga pour his heart out, and you just shit on me?"

"*Uuuugh!* What do you want from me?" she cried. I was finally getting through to her.

"I want *you*. I can't help it. I've been thinking about you since the day I met you. You're *always* in my thoughts, and I need you in my life." I stood and walked around to where she was sitting.

Ceanna wrapped her arms around my waist and cried. "He hurt me so bad. It hurts so badly. Why would he cheat on me like that?"

As Ceanna cried, I played with her hair. I ran my fingers through her scalp impressed that no tracks were there. I lifted baby girl's chin up to look at me.

"Come with me, Ceanna," I whispered while biting down on my bottom lip.

"I can't, Tae!"

"Why not?" I backed away, frustrated and hurt. I proceeded to walk back around to where I was sitting and gathered my things.

"Wait, where are you going?" Her eyes pleaded for answers.

"Look, I ain't with the games." I turned to walk off.

"We're *married!*" she shouted.

Hearing the word *married* knocked the wind out of me. I felt played and stupid for putting my emotions on the line. I was confused. *Married?* When did that shit happen? I didn't mean to walk away from Ceanna the way I did, but I had to.

She called me a couple of times, but I ignored her, eventually blocking her altogether. I needed time to process shit, and the rejection fucked with my pride as a man. I felt weak and emotionally wounded.

The more I fought to block Ceanna from my thoughts and heart, the harder I pushed in the streets. Sometimes I would see Ceanna at Gina's or family gatherings. She would smile at me, but I ignored her while still somehow feening to be in her presence. I couldn't have her; yet, she still had this hold on my heart and emotions. I wanted to hate her, love her, protect her, and secure her—all at the same time. I was confused.

I never thought a time would come where my position in Ceanna's life would be solid or secured as her man. The way shit brought us together was crazy, but I wouldn't change a thing. I smiled, looking back on how it all came together.

It was Thanksgiving Day, a day of laughter, good food, and football. It was a hot day, but once the sun hid behind the clouds, it gave off a chilly breeze.

As the family piled into the small, brown, three-bed-room home of Gina's, they drank, played rounds of dominoes, and socialized. I found myself outside on the back porch smoking a blunt that relaxed me.

Songs of the legendary DJ Screw and the Screwed Up Click played loudly as laughter from children playing in the street could be heard. BBQ pit smoke mixed with weed lingered throughout the air. I felt most comfortable outside.

The inside of the home was occupied by Ceanna, Jaceyon, our cousin Donte, his wife Keisha, who is also Ceanna's best friend, Tyler, Donte's baby mother of twin girls, Cheryl, Gina's sister and Donte's mother, Uncle Samuel, and his son JR, Gina, and a few more family relatives. I was out of place honestly and only came to show Gina respect.

I would have stayed outside a little longer until I heard a commotion and argument around the front of the home. I listened to the female's voice and became outraged that she had the audacity to show up here.

The high-pitched voice could never be mimicked or mistaken. It definitely belonged to Mia Symone. I knew Mia Symone well. In fact, she and I had a brief encounter long ago, leaving me burning with two sexually transmitted diseases.

Mia Symone was Ceanna's first cousin. She was beautiful. Long weave, light-skinned, colored eyes, and had a body like Keyshia Ka'oir with a K. Michelle's ass. She was Austin's notorious slut, so I wasn't surprised that she was secretly sleeping with Jaceyon behind Ceanna's back.

At the crayfish boil, I noticed Mia Symone giving Jaceyon those same "come fuck me" eyes she once gave me. I put two and two together. So, there was no reason she should have showed up at Gina's home uninvited. I knew it was going to be trouble.

Everyone wore faces of disbelief at Mia Symone's presence and her boldness. Most side chicks knew their places, but Mia Symone was different.

Donte and Keisha silently battled with eye rolls and hand gestures while he told her to mind her business. He felt like everyone else. The truth was right in front of Ceanna's face, but she didn't see it.

Blinded by love, Ceanna was out of the loop on what was going on, and she silently became the laughingstock of everyone else. Whispering back and forth along with head shakes of disapproval filled the tiny space.

As Ceanna helped with cooking, unaware of what was going on, Mia Symone was clever enough to get Jaceyon to show her the upstairs bathroom. I was sick to my stomach as my male cousins all gossiped and laughed at how player they thought Jaceyon was. They referenced Ceanna's weight and stated that if Mia Symone wanted to have sex with them, they would have cheated too.

I had to calm myself from acting irrationally and remind myself that Ceanna wasn't my woman. Still, though, I was in love, and I couldn't continue to sit back while everyone laughed and gossiped.

The tension in the home was messy and thick. Between Keisha's and Tyler's "the wife verses baby mama" slick remarks toward each other, and Mia Symone and Jaceyon's disrespect, I couldn't take it anymore.

I snuck up the stairs, noticing the hall bathroom light on and the door closed. "Fuck me harder, baby," I heard Mia Symone scream, followed by powerful thumps that hit the wall. The noise was coming from Gina's bedroom.

I saw a bobby pin on the floor, picked it up, and picked the lock. Rage consumed me when I saw Mia Symone riding Jaceyon butt naked like it was nobody's business. My eyes widened when I saw that she had a tiny bulging stomach that I missed earlier and couldn't see well through the Alexander McQueen dress she wore.

Shocked with disbelief from being caught, Mia Symone quickly dressed and looked away from me with shame.

I couldn't believe they actually were fucking upstairs while Ceanna was downstairs.

"Mia Symone, here, baby. Wait for me at the house. I'ma be there in a few," Jaceyon said, naked, while handing Mia Symone the house key to his and Ceanna's home. She jetted out of there so fast, leaving Jaceyon and me.

"The fuck is your problem? Ho-ass nigga! What if my bitch Ceanna would have came up here? Yeah, and, nigga, I see the way you be looking at her too. She's mine, and she belongs to me. You could never be me, bitch. Ole hating-ass nigga," Jaceyon yelled, slamming Gina's bedroom door while pulling his pants up.

That was the last time Jaceyon would ever disrespect me again. I fucked him up with no mercy. I tried to kill him and probably would have if Gina and Samuel hadn't broken us up.

Shit was everywhere. Gina's bedroom was destroyed. Words of hate that Jaceyon and I had been wanting to say to each other spit out like poisonous venom. Gina and Samuel both attempted to calm us down, but my anger flared toward Samuel as well. I didn't trust anyone in the room. They all were snakes. Fuck them.

Jaceyon left, while I went into the tiny bedroom that was mine over the years. I sat there trying to cool off, knowing damn well I should have left too, but the weed and alcohol I consumed earlier still had me feeling fuzzy.

I stared at a photo on my dresser of me, my pops, and mother. It brought me comfort in the moment, and I smiled, reminiscing about how things were before my father married Gina.

I missed my mother and father, and I felt lost. I didn't belong here. These people weren't my family. I resented my father for introducing Gina and her family into our lives. I felt he just gave up on my mother when she needed him the most. I was eight when we left Houston, Texas, to move to Austin. My mother became addicted to heroin and infected with HIV. A nigga didn't know if she was dead or alive.

My pleasant mood was replaced with anger when Uncle Samuel entered my room and closed the door.

"How long you and Jaceyon going to keep this beef up, son? I mean, y'all been at it since y'all were youngins."

"No disrespect, but fuck Jaceyon. If you or Gina have any love for that gay-ass nigga, keep him away from me. You know what? I ain't feeling this shit right now. This conversation is dead, my nigga." I opened the door so his ass could leave. I couldn't stand him. I could feel his snakish vibe. I dismissed him with a quickness.

I grabbed my keys and left the room moments later, but I halted when I heard Ceanna's light cries coming from the upstairs' hall bathroom. I knew that cry from the first time she broke down in my arms. It was stored in my heart.

I rushed to the bathroom about to barge in when Ceanna and I ended up crashing into each other as she was walking out. For a moment, we stared at each other. It felt as though time had stopped, and with each passing minute, I felt the coldness in my heart flutter with warmness and melt for Ceanna. My body temperature began to rise.

"Damn, Ce, my fault, ma. You good? I was coming in here to check on you."

Piercing my eyes with hers, I stepped into the tiny bathroom with her as she backed up and closed the door with my foot. It was time. Our time to lay this shit to rest between us and for good.

"Why you keep running from me? I want you, and one day I'ma make you my wife, and when I do, them tears that you're in here shedding over that ho-ass nigga will *be replaced with joy and happiness. Your love don't have to run; it's safe with me. Let me show you, Ceanna."*

More tears escaped from her eyes as she listened to me speak to her soul. I handled her with so much love and care as I gently took my thumb to wipe away her tears. I began to speak but was silenced once Ceanna's lips met mine. Her lips were so soft. Our tongues danced around while I gently ran my strong, masculine hands over her body. She could taste the weed mixed with Peach Paul Masson alluring off my tongue, while hers tasted like cinnamon that left me hungry for more.

Her fingertips went under my shirt as she gently caressed my lean, muscled, toned abs. Curiosity got the best of her, and she took her right hand and fumbled to unbuckle my jeans. My manhood sprang out, coming to life through the slit of my boxers.

The space was filled with light moans from both of us. She played with my manhood, gently stroking it. Taking her thumb, she ran it over the tip as sweet precome oozed out. "Ceanna," I moaned as I sucked her big, double-D melons. We were so far gone and into each other.

"I got your bitch, bitch!" we heard, followed by sounds of rumbling and tussling. We quickly fixed out clothing and ran downstairs.

Gina, Cheryl, and other family members laughed and found pleasure in Tyler delivering blows to an unsteady Keisha. Ceanna had enough, and when she saw that her friend Keisha was injured, she began attacking Tyler, causing Donte and me to exchange words. I was so pissed off that I ended up leaving not only my phone, but I left Ceanna too.

When I finally cooled down and decided to make my way back over to Gina's, it was too late. I learned Tyler was rushed to the hospital by the hands of Ceanna, and Uncle Samuel took Ceanna to the home she shared with

Jaceyon. *The awful truth about Mia and Jaceyon's betrayal was exposed. They were caught!*

Brokenhearted, Ceanna blacked out. In a rage, she lost all sense of control, especially when she learned that Mia was five months pregnant with her husband's child. If it had not been for Ceanna's nosy neighbors who called the police, Mia Symone and her unborn child would have met a deadly fate.

Ceanna was arrested and taken into custody, while Mia Symone was transported to the same hospital Tyler went to.

I worked quickly, and with my connections, I was able to bond Ceanna out the next day. She gathered a couple of her items from the home she shared with Jaceyon, and we settled into her condo.

I stayed with her and comforted her. For the time, I felt complete and whole with her in my arms. We made love to each other and experienced passion on another level. We had been so engrossed with each other, that we were disconnected from the outside world, unaware of the tragic incidents that had taken place the night before.

Unanswered phone calls left us unaware that Zylan, Keisha's son, had passed away. He had a heart disease called hypertrophic cardiomyopathy that suddenly took his young life.

I thought maybe that would be the end to the ups and downs Ceanna and I experienced in one day, but I was wrong. Ceanna found out that she was carrying Jaceyon's seed.

That was too much for me. She was beginning to make me feel like this weak-ass man. It was one thing after another with her. First married, and then a baby. I told myself, I was done with her, Jaceyon, and the entire situation.

I stayed away from Ceanna a couple of days. She called and texted. I ignored her and felt bad, even guilty. She needed me, and I needed her. I set my pride and ego aside when she broke down crying on my voice mail. She left a message that Tonya, her best friend, wanted to come clean. Ceanna's goddaughter Jalisa was Jaceyon's.

I knew that was going to happen. I knew he would hurt Ceanna. Jaceyon wasn't shit and never was. I just couldn't leave her now. I had to protect her.

With everything Jaceyon had put her through, Ceanna was done. So done, that she wanted no part of him, including the child that was growing inside of her. She found herself at an abortion clinic, but there, she learned she was expecting twins and was too far along for the procedure. She left confused and dumbfounded. She had irregular cycles, and her size withheld the naked truth from her.

Her being pregnant with twins by Jaceyon, wasn't something either of us planned. I could have run like I did the first time, but something about us felt right. I loved Ceanna, and although we both were wrong, the heart wanted what it wants.

Our first unapologetic outing together as a couple was Zylan's funeral. There were a lot of frowns and displeased looks. I admit, maybe that wasn't the right time or place; but with our situation, there would never be a right time or place. I was in a relationship with my pregnant stepbrother's wife.

Words were exchanged between family members leaving Ceanna so emotional that she began telling everyone how out of order they were at Zylan's funeral. I tried to calm her down, and that rubbed Jaceyon the wrong way. He and I began to shout insults at each other, still fuming from the fight on Thanksgiving Day.

I was ready to kill him, but I had to ignore him out of respect for Keisha. It was time to go, though; we needed to go. I kissed Ceanna on the cheek and whispered to her that we should leave. The display of affection enraged Jaceyon and hurt filled his voice.

"Bitch-ass nigga, I told you not to address my bitch. Ceanna is my woman. You can never replace me. Fuck you!"

Boom, Boom, Boom!

Jaceyon riddled my body full of bullets. He shot me. I mean, he actually shot me.

Blood gushed out of me as pain filled my entire body. When my eyes closed, all I heard was police sirens, screams, and Ceanna's cries for me to please not leave her.

I fought to stay alive; I had to. I finally got her, and she's mine. I was made to love Ceanna, and that's exactly what I planned to do.

The question now was . . . Could I?

Chapter One

Avantae

Three Months Later

"Tae! Avantae!" Ceanna yelled while nudging me.

"Huh?" I jumped up out of my sleep. Ceanna and I were laid cuddled on the love seat. I must have dozed off while watching *Fridays*.

"What you over there dreaming about? You're snoring all hard and shit, talking to yourself, with yo' mouth wide open. Hell, I can't even watch the damn movie," she laughed.

"Man, you tripping, girl. I don't snore. If you must know, though, I was dreaming of the first time we met," I said while kissing her on the forehead.

"Oh, Lawd! I love you, crazy boy." She kissed me on the lips.

"I love you too, baby! What time is it? A nigga is starving," I yawned.

"There you go with that *nigga* word. Anyway, it's a little after eleven. I don't know what's still open. All I know is I've got a taste for a bunch of shit," she laughed.

"Don't yo' greedy ass always do?"

"Oh, shut up, Tae! I can't help it. These babies make me hungry as hell." She mushed the side of my head.

"Do you have an idea of what you want?" I smiled, knowing damn well with Ceanna, she was about to send me on a damn food chase at eleven at night. Her little greedy ass stayed snacking and always eating mixmatched shit. She always wanted me to try whatever it was she was eating. I didn't mind, though, because the way Ceanna loved me, this girl could have whatever she wanted.

"Yep, I sho' do, and you got to try this too."

"Man, Ceanna, I ain't eating hot fries, mustard, and sour cream again. Yo' ass is throwed off for real," I laughed. "That shit was nasty, and I can't believe I be letting yo' ass talk me into eating shit."

"No no no. So here's what I want. Are you listening?" She playfully tapped my hand.

"What, crazy-ass girl?"

"Don't laugh, but I want some Taco Bell, watermelon, hot fries, and Cookies and Cream ice cream. Pleeease. You know I can eat that every day, all day long, with fried pickles, oh, and ranch dressing." She smiled, placing both her hands together pleading.

"Man, you going have a nigga shitting all night. I got one request, though, if I do all of that," I smirked.

"Oh, Laaawd!" she laughed.

"I want that ass tooted in the air when I get back." I licked my lips seductively at Ceanna.

"Just nasty."

"You make me that way." I kissed her on the lips, grabbed my keys off the bar, and set the house alarm for her.

As soon as I cranked my vehicle, Big Moe, "I'll Do It," blasted through the speakers. I vibed with the song and bopped my head.

A young soldier was blessed. After I was shot, I was rushed to Brackenridge Hospital. There, I was reunited with my mother. She worked there as a CNA and had been clean and living in Austin for the last six months.

Two of the bullets were removed, but the third near my collarbone was too risky to move. Other than losing a lot of blood and a blood transfusion, I was okay. None of the bullets hit any main arteries. I stayed in the hospital for a week. Ceanna and my mother nursed me back to health.

We had a couple of scares with Ceanna's pregnancy. She would have high spikes in her blood pressure that would result in hospital stays. Her pressure was finally stable, and both of our health was on the right track.

Jaceyon went to jail for unrelated charges to my shooting, and Ceanna filed for divorce and placed their home up for sale. He wasn't signing any paperwork, even after being served in jail.

We had another curveball thrown our way with Ceanna's friend Tonya. She had been suffering in silence and dying. She could no longer care for herself or Jalisa and asked if Ceanna would raise her.

Sometimes I would sit and think that I selfishly wished Ceanna and I could go back to the beginning. I wished like hell that she would have given me a chance before she got so caught up with Jaceyon. I wished it was just me and her. I wished those twins girls she's carrying were mine. I know that's selfish, but I can't hide my feelings. I had to change the song, because realistically, as selfish as I wanted things to be about us . . . they weren't. Our relationship had many variables.

Sigh. Just that quickly, my high of happiness faded. My mood drastically soured thinking of Jaceyon. The music began to annoy me, so I turned it off and continued to drive in silence. I couldn't believe that Jaceyon shot me. I wanted to kill him, but deep down, I knew that would only cause Ceanna more pain.

The phone rang loudly through my Bluetooth speakers. It startled me. For a minute, I thought it was my baby Ceanna calling me. I just knew she was about to add some extra things to the list.

"Call from private caller," the computerized voice stated.

"Private caller? Who the fuck is calling me this late from a blocked number?" I fussed loudly.

"Yeah!" I answered dryly.

"Tae, this is Za. I've been trying to get ahold of you. Why you keep ignoring me, baby?"

"Look, Zaria, what is it that you want? You know I got a whole woman at home, so it's nothing you can do for me, baby girl."

"That's real cute, Devin. Stop the bullshit. You don't want Ceanna. Anyway, her fat ass might not want you after I say what I have to say." She called me by my middle name.

"Man, get the fuck off my line." I hit the "End" button and ran my hand over my face.

Ring, ring, ring.

"Zaria, you're trying my patience. You, of all people, know how much of a savage nigga I am. Quit playing on my line. Say what the fuck it is you need to say and don't hit my line no more!" I yelled.

"The results are in, and little Avantae is your son. Looks like I'll be around a lot more, baby daddy. Oh, and don't worry. They're sending the results to your address as well." She laughed and hung up the phone.

"Fuck!" I yelled while hitting the dashboard over and over again. I didn't need this shit.

Other than Ceanna, Zaria was the only other woman who had my heart at one point. She was my first love.

I remember spotting Zaria, walking with her back-pack through some apartments I was trapping out of. I could tell she was different. She wore a black plain shirt with white shorts that showed off her long, pretty legs. *On her feet, she wore black flip-flops. Her hair was braided in cornrows, showing off her two sparkly silver-studded earrings. She had long eyelashes and a complexion of cinnamon brown. Dark purple lipstick rested on her full lips. She was beautiful, and I smiled as she ignored all the dope boys that tried to holler at her.*

A week later, I spotted her at the 37 bus stop. I pulled over and took her out to eat. She was fun, down-to-earth, and the more time I began to spend with her, I fell in love. She was my peace to the insane world I was in.

Zaria didn't come from a good home or environment. Her mother was a typical welfare abuser and an angry drunk. The apartments she was living in was drug infested and dangerous.

I had to protect her, so I moved Zaria into her own apartment. I bought her clothes, food, furniture, and supplied her with everything she needed. My only request to her was to stay in school, be loyal, and make good grades.

Zaria and I were together for about two years before I began hearing little rumors here and there about her. Even my boys were telling me that she was a ho. I didn't believe that, though . . . until I saw the shit for myself.

On a video, there she was; the love of my life, sucking and fucking on another nigga in the same apartment I put her in. That shit broke me. I put Zaria out and cut her off completely.

I became a coldhearted, ruthless person after that. Matter of fact, it wasn't until that day I saw Ceanna at the gas station that my feelings for a female softened.

Two weeks ago, I received an unexpected call from Zaria. She stated that Mia gave her my phone number, and that I had a five-year-old son named Avantae.

Shocked, I set up a paternity appointment two days later. Zaria didn't have a vehicle, so I stopped by her mother's place to pick her and Avantae up for testing.

The entire time, Zaria was disrespectful and tried to push up on me. She kept stating how she knew little Avantae was my son and how we could be a family. I tuned her out. She was making a complete fool of herself.

Once the testing was over, Avantae was hungry. I took them to Mickey D's, and as he ate swinging his legs, I studied him. I knew he was mine. He had my same dark complexion, long hair, and mannerisms. I didn't need a DNA test to confirm it.

"You know he's your son, Tae. Baby, please! We can be a family." Zaria whined and made a scene. I wasn't with the extra shit, so I got little man a happy meal to go, gave her some money, and dropped them off.

I know I should've told Ceanna. Now I'm sitting here afraid of what this would do to our relationship. She and I made a promise to always be honest . . . and I went against the code. I don't know how I'm going to break this news to her. I pulled over to the side of the road to collect my thoughts. *I should just call her,* I silently thought.

I sat for a minute trying to find the words to tell Ceanna. The longer I sat there, I drew blank on what to say. I was pissed! Avantae will be taken care of, no doubt, but I wasn't about to play these "bitter baby mama" games with Zaria.

Instead of calling Ceanna, I ended up hitting up my fam Semaj. If anyone had a clear head and great advice on how to handle this, it would be him. He'd already dealt with a similar situation with his first baby mama.

Semaj was at the studio and told me to come holla at him. Within fifteen minutes, I pulled up and rushed down the hall to the booth he occupied.

As soon as I opened the door, Kwency, his assistant, jumped up from her seat. I mugged the chick and shook

my head. Man, these females today be so pressed. Semaj
did not want this chick; yet, she was steady in his face.

"Ayo, get yo' stank ass up out of here, Kwency, and find
something to do. Ain't you supposed to be answering the
front-desk calls or some shit?"

"Avantae, you better watch yo' mouth in my daddy
studio. For the record, I do what I want," Kwency popped
off while rolling her neck with her hand on her hip.

"That nigga don't put no fear in my heart, ma. Now gon'
on." I pointed toward the door.

Kwency smacked her lips, rolled her eyes, and swished
out of the room. I just shook my head at her.

"That girl's crazy, yo, but what's up with you?" Semaj
asked and gave me a brotherly hug.

"Say, man, dig these blues! It's this chick I used to deal
with back in the day name Zaria. Two weeks back, she
confesses she has a five-year-old son, and that I was the
father. We took a paternity test." I hung my head while I
took a seat in the chair Kwency just occupied.

"Tell me you not about to say what I think you are,"
Semaj said with raised eyebrows.

"Yeah! She just called and told me the results are in,
and he's mine."

"Damn! Does Ceanna know?"

"Hell, no, and I don't even know how to tell her," I
frowned.

I began to panic. After everything Ceanna and I had
been through, I just didn't know if we could handle
another storm. Telling her I had a five-year-old son
might break us. I was scared of losing her.

"I hear you, fam, but you need to tell her. This Zaria
chick sounds like a cold piece of work. You need to tell
Ceanna before *she* does."

"Damn, you're right! Anyway, what that next single
looking like, though?" I asked as I rubbed my hands
together and changed the subject.

"The shit is hot, boi. You ready to fuck with it?" Semaj asked excitedly.

"Shit, put me on, boi."

"All right, all right! I just need to add a few more effects, and I got this bad shorty coming in to sing the hook. You going to love her, Avantae. Tasha can sing her ass off. I want to set up a date to get you two together soon."

"Man, I'm ready, fam; good looking!" I dabbed Semaj up and ended it with a snap.

"Aye, though, make sure you tell Ceanna, man. Sometimes, these females be on that bullshit. If you tell Ceanna, y'all can talk through it together; but if she hears that shit elsewhere, shit can get ugly. You don't ever want to place Ceanna in a place to where she can't trust you. You feel me?"

"Yeah, man, I hear you. Thanks, man for the advice, and the track is dope. I'm definitely fucking with it. I'ma get up with you soon. Ceanna's ass done sent me on a food chase," I laughed.

"All right, boi!" Semaj said, and I left.

As I made my way down the hallway, I spotted Kwency at the receptionist's desk. I just shook my head at her and kept walking.

"Avantae, wait!" Kwency rushed toward me.

"What, girl?"

"What's your problem with me? I mean, why we can't be friends? Do you have to be so mean and cold to me every time you come around? What have I ever done to you?" Kwency asked with a hurt expression on her face.

"You hurt the woman I love."

"Who? I know you ain't talking about Ceanna. Oh, please! I'm so sick of her ass. Y'all niggas around here act like her big wide ass is something special. How am I wrong when Jaceyon is the one who is married and came on to me? Why am *I* the bad person? He knew he was married. I have no commitments to Ceanna. So, whatever, Avantae." Kwency rolled her eyes and placed her hands on her hip.

"Typical side bitch shit."

"Yeah, whatever! I'm sick of you judging me and sticking your nose down on me. You ain't no better than me, Avantae, nor is Ceanna. She's still married to Jaceyon and pregnant by him. Y'all riding around the city like a happy little family. That shit y'all doing is foul!" Kwency yelled.

"Say what you want, but you could never compare yourself to Ceanna. You're a ho and will always be one. As far as Jaceyon is concerned, he never deserved her to begin with. It just took a nigga like me for Ceanna to see that." With that, I left. I would never respect Kwency or women like her. They were only good for a washcloth to wipe their wet ass.

I jumped in my ride, heading to the first food place. Kwency struck a nerve with me by her comments. Calling me foul was something I wasn't. Hell, I didn't like the fact that Ceanna was still married, or the fact we were raising Jaceyon's daughter Jalisa. I felt some type of way every day knowing those twin girls were his. I knew shit wasn't right, but I loved Ceanna, and the truth was, I couldn't let her go even if I wanted to. I needed her like air. She completed and complemented me, so fuck who didn't like it.

Kwency honestly had no room to judge Ceanna or me. She was another one of Jaceyon's jump-offs. She and Mia were good friends, but Kwency didn't have any respect for herself, let alone anyone else. She began messing with Jaceyon behind Mia's back.

Jaceyon wasn't loyal to anyone. He was married to Ceanna, still dipping around with Monique, sleeping with Tonya, messing with Mia Symone, Kwency, and the nigga took it up the ass. He was no good. He had Ceanna and three other women pregnant at the same time.

Ceanna found out about Kwency the day she went to the abortion clinic. She and Jaceyon sat in the lobby like a couple. When Ceanna saw them, she and Kwency exchanged heated words. Ceanna left the clinic feeling even more hatred toward Jaceyon.

Kwency ended up changing her mind about the abortion, and when Mia heard of her friend's betrayal, she literally followed and ran Kwency over in the parking lot of her father's studio. Kwency lost the baby, and Mia was arrested. She is currently serving time and expected to be giving birth to Jaceyon's son soon.

Shaking Kwency's negative remarks out of my thoughts, I made all the food stops. When I arrived home, my baby Ceanna was snoring lightly in the same spot I left her in.

"I'm back!" I kissed Ceanna on the forehead and placed the bags of food on the sofa next to her.

Ceanna sat up and smiled. She ate a little bit of everything and placed the rest in the refrigerator.

"I'm so full! Thank you, baby." She took a seat next to me.

"Baby, anything for you. I need to talk to you about something," I said in a serious tone.

"Shh, wait. Hold on. Oh my God, I got to pee. Ohhh, I'll be back. Lawd, these twins keep me running to the bathroom." Ceanna jumped up and wobbled down the hallway.

I waited ten minutes for Ceanna before I realize she wasn't coming back into the living room. I turned off the television and lights and made my way to the bedroom. I shook my head at Ceanna. She was knocked out. *I guess I'll tell her some other time,* I silently thought before I joined her in bed.

Chapter Two

Ceanna

Ring, ring.

Avantae's phone rang out loudly, instantly awaking me out of my sleep. *That's that shit I don't like,* I silently thought.

"Eeeew, phew, stanky ass," I frowned.

Blowing out a sigh of frustration, I sat up on my elbows and looked at the alarm clock on the nightstand. The clock read 7:00 a.m.

"I just know ain't nobody that damn crazy enough to call this early in the morning. Disrespectful ass!" I fussed loudly while turning my body and rolling my eyes at a farting, snoring Avantae. *Ugh, he gets on my last nerves with that shit.*

"Really, Tae? Really? Answer the damn phone. It's right by you. Ole stanky booty ass. You stink, man!" I yelled while I lightly play pushed him.

Avantae opened one eye, smirked, passed gas again, and rubbed his left hand over his toned abs. "Man, chill out! Crazy-ass girl. Take yo' ass back to sleep. You always ready to pop off and fix your head rag looking like Cleo." He busted out laughing.

"It's not funny, Tae. It's too early for the bullshit. I just got comfortable. I'm tired, and you're up in here farting and carrying on. Smelling like rotten eggs. Just foul!" I fussed while holding my nose with one hand and fanning the air with the other hand.

"Man, it's all your fault. All these crazy-ass cravings you be having is rubbing off on me. You had a nigga eating Taco Bell and Cookies and Cream ice cream. You know that shit don't mix." He frowned while rubbing his hand over his stomach again.

"You know how I get. Now, silence that phone before I flush it down the toilet. You know I will too." I smirked at Avantae while giving him an evil glare. I dared him to say something else smart. Playfully, I thumped his forehead and pulled his pillow from under his head. I fluffed the pillow and placed it on top of my other two pillows, then repositioned my body and fell back into a deep sleep.

Avantae ignored his phone. He was too comfortable to answer the phone or silence it. Instead, he smiled, shook his head, and spooned behind me while rubbing my belly. The twins began to kick wildly responding to his touch.

"Daddy loves you," he whispered before dozing off.

Not long after getting into another comfortable sleep, another unbearable stench hit my nostrils. *Hell to the nah,* I silently thought as my eyes shot open. It was war now. Avantae knew I didn't play about my sleep. I threw the covers off of me and wobbled to the kitchen.

"Avantae got me so fucked up, he gon' learn to stop the madness while I'm sleeping!" I yelled.

I grabbed the mop bucket out of the kitchen closet, then opened the freezer and pulled out the ice cube holder. A wicked laugh escaped as I filled the mop bucket with ice. Next, I turned the sink faucet and filled the bucket halfway with cold water.

"This should do the trick. Avantae's gon' learn today," I laughed.

As soon as I made my way back to the bedroom, Avantae was cutting loose loudly. *Splash!* I threw the entire bucket of cold water on his ass.

"Aaaah, what the fuck?" Avantae jumped up yelling, coughing, and fighting dead air.

"Oh yeah! Ceanna, *that's* how you feel?" he grinned.

I knew that grin all too well and knew Avantae was about to get my ass. He stood there wet and chocolate with a bare chest. His print was semihard through his boxers, and all I could think about now was getting some early-morning loving. Avantae continued to smile and wiped the wetness from his face. He knew what I was thinking, but he wasn't about to let me off the hook that fast.

"You know it's war now! Ceanna, yo' ass is nuts, for real. Come here!" Avantae began to run toward me.

"Wait!" I put my hands up and turned around quickly. I wobbled as fast as I could. I laughed so hard that I was out of breath, not to mention my bladder was ready to explode.

"Stop, Avantae, gon' on somewhere. I told you to stop farting, man. You need to go get yo' ass checked. That shit ain't normal. Stanky, booty-ass nicca." We play fought until Avantae got me on the floor. He began tickling me all over. I rolled and hollered so loud until I peed all over myself.

"Girl, you play too many games," he laughed, and then kissed me on the forehead.

"Baby, don't forget we got to pick Jalisa up at ten from over at Tamara's house. I want to take Jalisa to see Tonya later."

"Damn, how is she doing?"

"Not too good, baby. The doctor says any day now. Last time we went, she was barely hanging on. I dread that call, baby, because I know it's any day now." My eyes misted.

"Damn! I know that shit hurts. It's messed up how she and Jaceyon did you; yet, at the end of it all, you're the only one she can depend on. It's reasons like that, that I love you. You got a good heart, Ceanna. Don't ever let what people do to you change you." Avantae kissed me passionately.

Ding dong, ding dong.

"Baby, are you expecting anybody?" I frowned while breaking our kiss.

"Nah, I mean, unless it's my T-Lady; but she normally calls first." Avantae got up off the floor and reached to pull me up.

"Tae, I'm saying I know that's your mom and all. I love her and please don't take this the wrong way, but sometimes she can be a little overbearing. I know she means well, but look at what time it is." I rolled my eyes and pointed to the wall that housed the clock.

Ding dong, ding dong, knock knock knock.

"Avantae, open up, or I'ma use the key. I brought breakfast," Barbara Jean, Avantae's mother, sang through the door.

"You gave her a key?" I asked in a highly annoyed tone with my hands on my hips.

"Come on, baby! Don't act like that. Be nice, baby! She cooked breakfast." Avantae kissed my lips and headed toward the closet to throw on a long white tee before heading to the front door.

There was so much more I wanted to say, but instead, I sucked my teeth loudly and walked back to the bedroom. *This that shit I be talking about. I mean, damn,* I fussed while I took off my soiled panties and nightgown.

I checked the clock on the nightstand again and frowned once I noticed that I wouldn't be getting any extra sleep. Carrying twins was taking its toll on me. I was exhausted, and I had to pick Jalisa up from Tamara's home at ten and meet with my attorney later on today.

Shaking my negative attitude, I grabbed a plastic bag from under the bathroom sink to place the soiled clothing in until after I showered. I had begun doing my oral hygiene before I heard Avantae's phone go off again. I stopped and debated on whether I should answer it. Since I trusted him, I decided against it and continued brushing my teeth, when it rang again. *Ugh,* I sighed while spitting the toothpaste into the sink.

Hurrying over to the phone, I looked at the screen and was pissed when it said: private caller. I'm not a morning person, so I couldn't hide the anger that was brewing within. "Hello," I answered with a slight attitude.

No answer!

"Hello, who is this, and why the fuck you keep calling this early in the morning? Rude ass! Who raised you?" I snapped.

"Put Avantae on the phone and stop playing these little petty-ass games. You shouldn't be answering his phone in the first place. I didn't call his phone to speak to you," the chick had the nerve to say.

I snapped my neck so hard. *Breathe, Ceanna,* I coached myself. I was doing my best to change my ways. After almost killing Tyler and Mia Symone, I enrolled in anger management courses, and I was trying to use other words besides curse words to express my thoughts. I had promised myself that I would learn to handle these females accordingly and not be so quick to put my hands on people, but it was females like this that made me nut up.

"Obviously, you forgot about me and how I get down. Just in case you have, I'm known for dragging a bitch or two. I will hate to come out of retirement, but believe you me, I will. With that being said since you got this number, I know that you must know where he stays and where *we* lay our heads. You're talking real reckless on this phone, but if you about that life, come see me." I hung up and threw the phone on the bed.

"Mmmm hmmm," I moaned loudly, while I paced back and forth. I was hotter than fish grease. I had already gone through bullshit recently with my soon-to-be ex-husband Jaceyon, and I wasn't about to go through it again.

Ding, ding

Avantae's text message sounded off.

Picking up the phone again, I opened the text message box. A screenshot of a paternity test, reading that Avantae was 99 percent the father, jumped out at me. My heart became heavy as it broke into a million pieces.

Another message came through with a laughing emoji, along with naked photos of a female and a video of her playing with herself. My eyes grew wide once I recognize the chick. "Zaria? He's fucking with this bitch Zaria?" I whispered. A steady flow of tears ran down my cheeks. I was numb and unable to move.

"*Really,* Tae? That's how you're going to do me? After everything! I thought you were different," I cried, hugging myself, as I rocked back and forth. I felt so stupid.

I had so many questions that ran through my mind. Had Avantae been cheating on me the entire time? When did they meet to take the test? Why didn't he tell me? How old is the child? My mind took a test of its own.

My right leg shook. I couldn't believe that Avantae was messing around on me with Zaria. I knew exactly who Zaria was. I met her through my cousin Mia Symone when we attended high school.

Another fifteen minutes had gone by. Internally, I was boiling. I listened to Avantae's loud voice carrying on from laughing, cracking jokes, and eating breakfast with his mother.

"Devin, where is that daughter-in-law of mine?" Barbara Jean asked, calling Avantae by his middle name.

"I don't know, but she's missing out on this good-ass breakfast, and you know my little ass can eat, so she better come on." he laughed. "Let me go check on my baby."

I could hear Avantae's footsteps getting closer to the door. My right leg continued to shake as I gripped his phone tighter in my hand. *Avantae got the right one all right. He's about to find out today,* I silently thought.

"Ceanna, girl, what you in here doing? The food's getting cold and my mom—" He stopped walking and stuffed the last bite of food in his mouth. He had a confused look on his face when he saw me crying with his phone in my hand.

"Baby!" he softly called out while shutting and locking the door behind him. "What's wrong? Why are you crying?" he sincerely asked.

"*Really,* Tae?" I threw his phone at him as hard I could. "A baby! You've got a baby by that bitch Zaria. Do you see that, Avantae? You are 99 percent the father of Avantae Devin Wallace the motherfucking Third. Oh, I can't hear you! Don't get quiet on me now. On top of that, this bitch sending your ass pussy shots. I thought you were different. I thought we said no secrets or lies. How would you feel if you saw Jaceyon's big dick in my phone?" Avantae's jaw muscle tightened, and his eyes turned to slits.

"All you had to do was be honest with me, but, nah, you chose to hide a whole child! You got me out here looking fucking stupid. I can't do this anymore. It's too much for me." I turned to head toward the restroom. Avantae stopped me and grabbed me from behind and placed me in a bear hug.

"Ceanna, baby, we can talk about this. Don't do this. Don't leave, baby. Hear me out! I promise I never fucked that girl or responded back to any of her messages. I did pick her and Avantae up to do the DNA test two weeks ago, but that was it. She just called me last night to confirm the results. I was waiting on the right time to tell you," he pleaded.

"Let me go!" I fought. "There's nothing to talk about. Maybe this is a sign that we don't need to be together. There's too much in the way of us being happy. I just need some time," I confessed.

I turned around to face him and looked him in his eyes. I was breaking inside. I didn't understand why I had to find out this way. He had all morning to talk to me. When was he going to tell me? The way Avantae went about things was sneaky and not sitting right with me.

The ringing of his phone broke our eye contact. We both looked at the phone as it continued to ring.

"Answer it! Yo' nothing-ass baby mama might need something," I spoke coldly. I broke away from him and began to gather my things around the bedroom.

Avantae continued to stare at me, not knowing what to say. The phone continued to ring, and he finally answered it.

Chapter Three

Avantae

Man, what the fuck just happened? This shit is all my fault. I knew I should have told Ceanna sooner, but things were good between us, and I wanted to keep it that way, at least for a little while longer.

Seeing Ceanna gather her things pissed me off. Her ass wasn't going anywhere until we talked about this shit. I answered the phone heated.

"Why the fuck you call my wife and phone with that bullshit?" I snapped.

"Oh, I'm sorry, Mr. Wallace, for disturbing your morning. This is Doctor Maridati."

Biting my bottom lip, a long pause of silence filled the air. Ceanna rolled her eyes and turned her back. I watched as she walked into the restroom and slammed the door.

"Hello, Avantae, son, are you there?" the doctor calmly asked.

"Yeah, Doc, my bad. How can I help you?"

"I'm sorry to have called so early. I tried calling Ceanna's phone, but it kept going to voice mail. I don't have good news for you or Ceanna. I wish I was calling with better news, but sadly, Tonya passed away this morning," he expressed sadly.

"Damn, man," I whispered. A lone tear ran down the side of my face.

"Thank you, Doc, for calling. I'll tell Ceanna, and we'll be on our way shortly," I said, ending the call.

"Tell her *what?*" Ceanna yelled, naked titties swinging with her hands on her hips as she walked out of the restroom.

I bit my bottom lip again and lustfully stared at Ceanna. The pregnancy put a little more weight on her, but her belly bump, juicy thighs, and swollen breasts turned me on. Damn, I know this ain't the right time, but seeing Ceanna in her natural glory just did something to me. My eyes scanned over her entire body. She was prefect!

"Avantae, do you care to share who you were talking to on the phone?" Ceanna interrupted my thoughts.

"Ceanna, baby, that was Doctor Maridati. It's Tonya. She passed away."

Ceanna held her chest and took a seat at the foot of the bed. A loud sob erupted from the pit of her soul.

Tonya was Ceanna's best friend. Around the time I was shot, Tonya found out she had the silent killer of women, which was ovarian cancer. She also had Graves' disease.

By the time Tonya was aware, the cancer had already metastasized to her bones, lungs, and breasts. There wasn't anything the doctors could do but make her comfortable.

Tonya's condition began to get worse. She couldn't breathe on her own and had a hard time moving around. Ceanna agreed to raise Jalisa, and Tonya went into hospice under the care of Doctor Maridati.

"Avantae, nooooo! Nooooo! My best friend is gone. Why does everybody I love always die on me? It's not fair! It's not faaaair! I knew it. I knew this day was coming. She looked so bad last time." She continued to cry.

"Shh, it's going to be okay, Ceanna."

I sat next to her and wrapped my long, muscular arms around her. She lay her head on my chest and sobbed uncontrollably.

"I'm sorry this is happening. Baby, you got to be strong. Jalisa is going to need you now, more than ever. Ma, you got to calm down so you don't upset the babies." I spoke with love and authority.

Throughout the pregnancy, we had been dealing with dangerous spikes in Ceanna's blood pressure. It was finally stable, but as hard as she was crying, I didn't want her to be admitted for too much stress on the babies. Her health would always be a priority of mine. I began to wipe her tears and kissed her with so much passion. I loved this girl, and if I could take away her pain, God knew I would.

"Hey, guys, is everything okay?" My mother knocked loudly while trying to twist the locked knob.

"Yeah, Ma, chill. We're good. I'll be out there in a minute."

"Baby, I'm going to go take a shower and get dressed. Can you call Tamara, Tonya's neighbor, and tell her we'll be on the way shortly to get Jalisa? I was supposed to be picking her up at ten this morning, but we'll be getting her a lot earlier." Ceanna rubbed her nose against mine, hugged me, and whispered that she's still mad at me, but that she still loved me.

I did as Ceanna asked and was about to place a call to Tamara when the phone ended up ringing in my hand. I frowned when I saw that it was a private caller. I knew that it was none other than Zaria playing on the phone. Now was not the time for her bullshit. I sighed!

I didn't understand what she wanted from me. Now that I know I have a son, that's all the communication I will have with her. I've already given her money, and I told her that once my household is settled, I'll get to know my son.

As the phone continued to ring, I battled with myself on whether I should take the call. I knew if I didn't, Zaria would be a problem later, but I just didn't feel like dealing with her now. I purposely ignored the call.

Once the phone stopped ringing, I placed a call to Tamara and informed her of the situation. Afterward, I placed the ringer on silent, removed the wet bedding to wash, went into the closet, and pulled Ceanna out a comfortable maxidress, along with her undergarments, and went to join her in the shower.

When I entered the restroom, Ceanna was hugging the toilet bowl. She was throwing up violently. "Baby, I'm here," I whispered as I rubbed her back with one hand and held her long hair with the other.

"I miss my friend. How am I going to tell Jalisa?" Ceanna cried while throwing up again.

"Baby, I got you. That's why I'm here. You're not in this shit alone."

"You got a baby, Tae. A babyyyy! That's supposed to be meeeeee. Everything is so fucked up. Aaaah!" She continued to cry.

"Fuck all of that, Ceanna. My home is with you. That girl doesn't mean shit to me. I didn't cheat on you. The little boy is five years old. I didn't even know about him. I would never hurt you, and you know that, baby," I pleaded my love. Seeing Ceanna cry like that was eating at me.

Ceanna began to calm down. She continued to vomit another five minutes, and it brought me great concern. The shower water was a little hot, so I turned it to a cooler temperature. I reached for Ceanna's washrag and ran cold water from the sink.

"Baby, come on, lift up." I helped her off the floor.

I let the toilet lid down and flushed it. Then I took the cooler washrag and began to wipe her face and mouth. She kept her eyes closed as silent tears fell.

"Thank you, Tae!" she whispered while opening her eyes. She slowly turned toward the sink and began to take care of her oral hygiene.

When she was done, I held my hand out for her and guided her into the shower. Ceanna pressed her back against the wall. I know my baby was exhausted from the weight of the twins, so I reached for her body wash. She turned around with her backside facing me. I lathered up her wash sponge and began to wash her back. Silent tears continued to run down her beautiful dark cheeks. Ceanna was heartbroken, confused, and devastated—all at once.

After I washed her backside, I positioned my tall, lean body in front of hers to wash the front of her body. I bent down and placed a kiss on her belly as I always did, and she smiled at me. Ceanna took my right hand and guided it to where one of the twins began kicking. My eyes lit up with joy, and I began to rub her belly while I talked in baby talk.

"That's right, little mamas, it's your daddy," I continued to speak while I rubbed her belly.

Every time I came near Ceanna's stomach, the twins would always respond to my touch. Just the thought of them being here in sixteen more weeks made me extremely nervous and happy, all at once. I wasn't ready for the drama, though.

Anytime I thought about the birth of the twins, a sadness came over me. I had been there since day one. I hadn't missed one appointment, and I had saved every photo of them. Those are my girls in my heart, but I had this fear.

I had a lot of questions. I knew Ceanna and I would need to have a heart-to-heart, and soon. I needed to know, will *I* be the one to cut the umbilical cord? Will she want Jaceyon in the room as well? Will she give Jaceyon another chance and want to be a family? If we stayed together, will she accept my son or hold this shit against me? So many thoughts ran through my mind. My heart tells me Ceanna loves me and wouldn't hurt me, but my mind conflicted with my heart.

"Damn it, Tae!" Ceanna whispered while she bit down on her bottom lip.

I looked her in the eyes and mouthed the word *sorry*. She looked away from me, grabbed my washcloth, and began to gently wash my chest. Her lips began to tremble, and I couldn't help but kiss her. Ceanna deepened the kiss, and our tongues danced awhile. Then I rested my forehead against hers.

"Baby, we're going to get through this. I promise, baby!" I spoke sincerely.

"I'm scared! We have so much to discuss."

"I know, baby! Just know I'm a solid nigga, and I ain't going nowhere."

"You chose for me, though. You didn't give me a chance. You kept the fact you have a son from me. That hurts." She looked up at me.

"I was afraid of losing you." My eyes misted.

"So you thought by *not* telling me would keep me?" She raised her eyebrows.

I lowered my head in defeat. No matter how I spin this shit, Ceanna was right. Semaj told me that I needed to tell her before Zaria did. I should have listened. Now, no matter what I say, Ceanna's trust level with me won't be the same.

Chapter Four

Zaria

Ugh! I yelled frustrated. I had just gotten off work from a long overnight shift. I attempted to call my child's father, Avantae, twice, and I was sick of him ignoring my calls. *The least he can do is return my calls. I'm sick of how he's treating us,* I angrily thought.

I stopped by Tamara's to get my son and chill for a bit. I was thankful for my cousin being able to watch my son for me at night. Most times, Tamara would also take him to school in the mornings with her four children.

"Aha, you can't get me!" Jalisa yelled, running through the condo with little Tater Bug chasing her. Tater Bug was the nickname I gave little Avantae.

"What I tell y'all about running through the house? Go back in the room to play," Tamara fussed.

"Yes, ma'am!" Jalisa and Tater Bug replied and went into the room.

I propped my feet under me on the love seat, and my mind became heavy with thoughts of Avantae. I wanted him badly, and there wasn't anything I wouldn't do to get him. My mind began to wander when all of a sudden, a sinister laugh escaped from my lips. Tamara looked at me funny.

"Tamara, damn, when is Ceanna coming to get Jalisa?" I needed to know when Avantae was going to be alone. *He's always under that fat bitch.*

"Will you knock it off! Damn! That man doesn't want your ass. Why are you so pressed behind him? Anyway, they'll be here in a little while."

"Whatever!"

"Listen, Zaria, whatever little scheme you have running through your mind, dead that. That man is in love with Ceanna. Just let them be." She grabbed a broom.

"Let them be? Now, all of a sudden you wanna act like you're for Ceanna. I mean, whose side are you on?"

"Look, I'm just saying, Z, Avantae does *not* want you. The man said to give him some time and he'll introduce his son into his life."

"Why does my son have to be introduced to any-fuck-ing-thing? I've been raising him by myself for five years, and I'm tired. He's over there playing daddy to Jalisa. That ain't even his seed!" I yelled.

Tamara's home phone rang, and she excused herself toward the back. I stayed seated thinking of ways to get Avantae back. I couldn't believe he would turn his back on me and ignore me the way he had.

I sat fuming at the thought of Ceanna and Avantae being together. I didn't understand what he saw in her. What puzzled me was the fact that Avantae would put Ceanna before our son. Not to mention the fact that he's helping her raise Jalisa and going around like a proud father of twins that ain't even his. I mean, what about our little Tater Bug? Is my son not good enough for his love, attention, and time?

Just the thought of my son placed a huge smile on my face. I remembered when I found out I was pregnant with him, and how close I was to aborting him. When I attempted to contact Avantae to tell him the news, he cut me off and wouldn't even speak to me. I knew I had made a mistake sleeping with that other guy, but in my mind, it was Avantae's fault. He was always too busy in the streets.

I only cheated that one time and couldn't believe that guy recorded me.

I saved all the money Avantae gave me through the course of our relationship. I was happy I did. After Avantae found out about the video and my unfaithfulness, he had one of his crew members put me out of the apartment.

I refused to go back to my mother's apartment in the hood. I didn't even want to stay in Austin if I couldn't be with Avantae. With nothing to lose, I caught a Greyhound bus to Houston and decided to start over and make a home there, for me and my unborn son.

I rented a room at the Motel 6 and began searching the White Pages for jobs. Within a week, I was able to find employment at a call center. I worked extremely hard, and within four months, I was able to get an apartment, vehicle, and items to prepare for my son's delivery.

Within two years of working at the company, I secured myself a management position. Things for me were going well until my company downsized. I wasn't picked for my company's new contract, causing me to start back at ground zero.

I stayed in Houston awhile and lived off my savings. I continued to apply for jobs, to no avail. I had no choice but to suck up my pride and come back to a place I didn't want to be. I moved back in with my mother and had to start over again.

I applied for three call center positions in Austin, but the pay sucked. My only other option I felt was getting a job as a care tech. I worked through a contract company, and wherever they needed an extra body at the hospitals, they would assign me. I was beyond sick of the low-paying job, but other than call center positions, that was all I could find. I wanted to quit most days and felt I had come too far in life to end up here. I felt like a failure for not being in the position to get my son the things he needed and wanted.

The day my car was repossessed, I cried like a baby. I hated my life, and I needed a plan to get out of my mother's apartment. Not only that, the long days and hours took a toll on me, and riding the city bus drained me. The days I hated the most were my off days, where I was always called in and had to fuss with my mother to watch my son. *"That little bastard ain't my responsibility. I wish you would hurry up and get stable so y'all can get the fuck out,"* my mother would yell often, leaving me questioning myself on why I even came back.

I never had interesting days . . . until the day my supervisor asked me to assist a female patient that was being discharged from the hospital. Whoever would have thought that assignment would lead me to Avantae?

There sat a pregnant, beaten, and abused Mia Symone. I hardly recognized her from the bruises and two black eyes. We chatted awhile about our journeys, pain, and the things we had been through. Both of us had one common enemy: Ceanna.

Mia Symone told me everything that had taken place that led her to the hospital. She was a bold bitch. I mean, who fucks their cousin's husband, gets caught, and also gets pregnant by him? I would have tried to kill Mia Symone my damn self. Ceanna beat the shit out of her.

One thing I respected about Mia Symone, though, was her raw emotions. She loved Jaceyon, and she didn't care about what anyone said or thought. Even after the ass whooping, she still went after him and held him down.

Mia Symone gave me Avantae's new phone number and information. Having his personal number in my hands made me feel mixed emotions. I still loved him.

In the beginning, I didn't want to hurt Ceanna. However, after I talk with Mia Symone, it made me realize that there is nothing wrong with going after what you want. Besides, in all honesty, I had Avantae first. I shouldn't have to raise our son alone. It's time for us to be a family.

Ding dong, ding dong.

Tamara walked quickly from the back of the condo to get ready to answer the door. Before she did, she turned toward me with a *don't start no shit* look.

"Zaria, this is Avantae and Ceanna. This is *my* house. Do *not*—I repeat—do *not* act an ass up in here. I ain't got time for the extra bullshit."

"Yeah, whatever!" I replied, pissed off.

I brushed my hands over my head to make sure my hair was lying straight. Tamara answered the door, and there he was. Avantae. He stood there for a moment staring back and forth between Tamara and me.

"Come on in, Avantae. Is Ceanna with you?" Tamara asked nervously.

"Nah, ma, she's next door at Tonya's gathering some things," Avantae said, coming through the door.

"Okay, well, I'll be back. Let me go get Jalisa and her things together." Tamara hurried down the hallway.

"Funny we meet here, baby daddy." I licked my lips, walking toward Avantae. He looked so fucking good in his white tee and red sweatpants.

"I ought to fuck you up for that bullshit stunt you pulled this morning. Let this be my last time telling you this. Ceanna is my woman, and she will be my wife. I don't want you. When I'm ready to see Avantae, I will, but until then, stay the fuck in your lane," Avantae warned in a low, aggressive tone.

"Or *what*, Deviiiin?" I took it a step further and boldly kissed his lips. In one motion, Avantae flung me around and placed me up against the wall with his hands around my neck.

"You of all people know I'm a hood nigga. You had better respect who the fuck I am. Now let that be your last attempt. This daddy dick belongs to Ceanna."

"Avantae, you're hurting me," I whispered while trying to remove his hands. He was applying too much pressure, and I felt myself getting weaker.

"Daddy Tae! I'm ready now," Jalisa cheerfully sang walking toward us.

Avantae released my neck quickly. His entire demeanor changed once he saw Jalisa. He picked her up and kissed her on her forehead. When our son came down the hallway, Avantae placed Jalisa on the floor and stared at him.

"Hi, Mr. Tae," our son innocently said with a smile.

"Hey, what's up, little man? Come here!" Our son ran to him, while he picked him up and kissed him.

Tamara watched at the end of the hall, and I could see her shaking her head at me in disgust. I didn't understand what her deal was with me. I mean, what woman doesn't want to be a family with their child's father. Oh, but she wouldn't know shit about that since all her kids got *different* daddies.

The doorbell rang and caught everybody's attention. Everyone knew it was Ceanna. Avantae placed our son on the floor, and Tamara motioned for Tater Bug to come in the room with her. Tamara looked at me and tilted her head for me to hide in the bedroom, but I refused. Fuck that, and fuck him. Avantae is going to learn to fall in line. Either he's going to do things *my* way, or *I'm* going to make his life a living hell.

I made my way to the front door with a smirk. Avantae's eyes widened, and he shook his head mouthing the word *no*.

"Well, hello, Ceanna!" I busted out laughing while opening the door. Ceanna stood there and shot daggers. If looks could kill, I would have died on-site.

Avantae grabbed Jalisa and brushed past me. "Bye, baby daddy. I love you, baby! Oh, don't forget to wipe my lipstick from your lips," I laughed and slammed the front door in Ceanna's face.

"*Really,* Avantae?" I could hear Ceanna yelling. I looked through the peephole.

"Ce, chill. It ain't what you think," Avantae pleaded.

"You know what, Avantae? Let's just get to this hospital, and then you can drop me and Jalisa off at my condo. I don't need this shit." Her voice cracked.

"*Got 'em!* Po' tink tink," I said out loud.

I couldn't help myself, so I opened the front door and stood on the porch. The lovebirds were still going at it, and I enjoyed every moment of it. They didn't even notice me standing there.

Barbara Jean got out of the vehicle and grabbed Jalisa. She put Jalisa in the car seat and walked to where Ceanna and Avantae were.

"Avantae, baby, when are you going to get your son? He's been dying to spend time with you!" I shouted while I crossed my arms over my C-cup breasts, causing everyone to look in my direction.

"Son?" Barbara Jean asked while looking at Avantae. "Wait a minute! Don't I know you from somewhere?" his mother asked, walking toward me.

"Mama, come on. That broad ain't shit," Avantae coldly yelled.

"Oh, I ain't shit, Avantae? Well, since I ain't shit, why don't you tell Ceanna the truth about us? We made love in that truck. Look under your seat. I bet the condoms and my thong are still there," I smirked.

"Ho, quit fucking lying. I never touched your broke ass. I took you and little man to McDonald's after the test because he was hungry!" Avantae shouted harshly.

"You and this no-edges-ho got me fucked up!" Ceanna yelled, looking between Avantae and me.

"Nah, I know your little trick. You work at the hospital. Listen here, I don't know what kind of games you're playing, but you need to leave my son and daughter-in-law alone," Barbara Jean pointed at me.

"Mommy, what you doing out here?" Tater Bug asked, peeping his head through the door.

Barbara Jean came up the three stairs and up onto the porch. She looked at Tater Bug for a brief moment with eyes of recognition. At that moment, I knew that she knew that my son was indeed her grandchild. She stared a few more moments and then turned to walk off. I hurried back into the condo and quickly closed the door. A frowning Tamara greeted me.

"Here you go!" Tamara held my purse and keys. "Look, Za, I asked you not to start any shit in my place. Please go! You're really messing with the wrong people. Don't let Ceanna's calm demeanor fool you. You keep fucking with her if you want to and see what happens."

"Yeah, whatever, Tamara," I yelled and yanked my keys and purse out of her hands.

"Whatever is right, and since you want to play these little bullshit-ass games, find somebody else to watch your son!" Tamara yelled.

"So it's like that, Tamara? I thought we were family. Tater Bug has nothing to do with this," I replied in disbelief. Tamara knew I didn't have anybody else to watch him.

"Yeah, not now, but sooner or later, you'll be using him as a pawn in your little games. I ain't with that shit. I got my own issues and problems, and I don't need yours. You didn't even think about that little girl who just lost her mother. Jalisa and Tater Bug, along with my children, are her little friends. By this little stunt you pulled, I doubt Jalisa will be coming over anymore. I wish you would think about the things you do, Za, *before* you do them. Ever since you came back, you have changed. You don't even act the same with your son. You're too busy running around after Avantae."

I didn't have a comeback for what Tamara said. It was all true, but to me, being a single mother was too hard and depressing. Seeing Avantae with Ceanna, catering to her and treating Jalisa like his own, bothered me. My feelings were hurt, and I am not running this time. Avantae *will* pay.

Chapter Five

Ceanna

It was going on day three, and I was not accepting any of Avantae's calls. I even changed the locks. I left whatever little stuff I had at his place and comfortably settled back into my own condo. I was sad, but it was something I felt I needed to do for me.

Zaria was on some case of the ex-type of mess. She was obsessed with Avantae. I knew in my heart that Avantae was telling me the truth, but right now, I couldn't handle it. Mentally, I felt that I needed to seek professional help. I felt I was on the verge of snapping again the way I had on Thanksgiving Day.

Sitting in my comfortable purple chair, I thought about everything I had been through the last couple of years. I was the only child of my mother and father. I lost my mother a few years back to a car explosion, and my father to cancer last year. Mia Symone and I were first cousins. We had been very close, almost like sisters, which is why when Mia Symone called and asked if she could come live with me, I said yes. Now I was shaking my head at how naïve I was, to allow another woman to live under the same roof as my husband.

I blamed myself for everything. I thought about the girl Monique who Jaceyon cheated on me with. That was the beginning of our downfall. I knew I should have left Jaceyon then, but I stayed.

My mind drifted, and my thoughts landed on my ex, Marcus. I briefly smiled, followed by a lonely tear that ran from the corner of my left eye. I was once madly in love with Marcus. I met him in college.

Marcus was a man I thought I would one day marry. I even carried our son. My world came crashing down the day I checked in for a scheduled appointment. The doctor informed me I had an STD. I remembered confronting Marcus, and he confessed that he had been seeing a woman name Melondy. I tried to forgive him, but the pain was too great. I gave birth weeks later to our still-born son. Burying my child is something I never really got over.

I left Marcus, and I later learned that he married Melondy and had two children, little Marcus and Courtney. I shook my head at how small Austin was and how everyone seemed to be related in some way. I would later learn that Marcus and Tonya were adopted by the same family and that Melondy and Donte's baby mother Tyler were sisters.

I placed my legs under me, and my mind drifted back to Jaceyon. He was so perfect and made me forget about Marcus and the pain he had put me through. I really had no clue just how much of a ho my husband was, though.

Monique was one thing, even Kwency; but Tonya and Mia Symone, they were my inner circle. Tears flowed freely down my face. The betrayal was something I didn't think I could forgive. I wiped my tears, upset that I was always so emotional and couldn't seem to move past the pain.

I was so unhappy in my marriage to Jaceyon; yet, I stayed. I endured many sleepless nights, tearstained pillows, and worst of all, insecurity that I never had before.

I had so many unanswered questions. When did Jaceyon and Mia Symone start messing around? Did he really love her? Who was this Kwency? The questions in my mind went on. It wasn't as if I wanted to be back with Jaceyon or anything, and as far as Mia Symone was concerned, I really didn't have anything to say to her. Sometimes, though, I felt I needed closure, but then again, a "sorry" wasn't going to heal my wounds.

It made me sick to know that my first cousin Mia Symone and Jaceyon's son will be here soon. I had no clue Mia Symone was five months when I fought her Thanksgiving Day. To make matters worse, I heard through my aunt Monica, who is Mia Symone's mother, that Mia Symone was getting out of jail soon. Kwency had refused to press charges and was actually paying for Mia's legal fees and everything. I guess she felt bad. Who knows, they're both disloyal.

Aunt Monica began calling me, in hopes that I would forgive Mia Symone. She would defend Mia Symone's actions as if *I* was wrong for how I felt. It angered me because I felt that I wasn't being given the space to heal and deal with one issue at a time.

Maybe I could pretend that things were okay if I didn't have Jalisa's well-being and the twins' well-being at stake. It wasn't just me, and as much as I wanted to hate Jaceyon, I couldn't erase the fact that he was their father.

Sometimes I could barely stomach Jalisa. I loved her to death and would do anything for her, but honestly, this isn't what I signed up for. I never thought being a godmother would alter my life. It was hard raising an active school-age child. I had to rearrange everything in my life to fit Jalisa in. I didn't regret it, but I just felt like it was one thing after another.

My timer on the oven broke me out of my thoughts. I got up from the sectional and checked on the roast. My friend Keisha was coming over to help with the planning of Tonya's funeral. Keisha loved my cooking, so I decided to cook pot roast, with collard greens, yams, and corn bread.

The food had the house smelling so good. Everything was almost ready, so I tightened up and made my way to Jalisa's room.

Ever since I told Jalisa about Tonya, Jalisa had been really sad and withdrawn. Today was a normal school day, but I informed her principal of everything that was going on. I wasn't really good at speeches with a child, so I made sure to shower Jalisa with lots of hugs and kisses. I knew I couldn't replace her mother. Nothing would bring Tonya back.

I walked into Jalisa's room and shed silent tears. She was sleeping so peacefully with the bear her mother had given her. She had drawings of her mother lying on the floor with crayons. I struggled to pick them up and then sat down lightly on Jalisa's bed.

Grabbing one of Jalisa's pillows, I buried my head inside of it and cried. "This is too much, God!" I wasn't ready to see Tonya go. Although my best friend hurt me to the core, Tonya's passing is something I could have never prepared for. I knew the day was coming because just last week, Tonya appeared so weak when we went to visit.

Blowing my nose, I looked up and smiled at a photo of Tonya, Jalisa, and me. Little Jalisa was throwing up the peace sign while Tonya stuck her tongue out and crossed her eyes. That day, Tonya was feeling okay from the chemo and asked me to bring Jalisa to see her.

I remembered Tonya being a little fragile that day, but she held the biggest smile on her face. It was one of the saddest visits, and at that moment, I knew that visit was possibly our last. I remembered Tonya sitting Jalisa down to let her know that she may not see her for a while.

***

"Jalisa, come sit with Mommy for a while," Tonya whispered.

"Okay, Mommy." Jalisa came and lay on Tonya's chest.

"Mommy, your stomach sounds funny." They all laughed as Jalisa continued to crack up laughing at the sounds coming from inside of Tonya's body.

"Jalisa, you know Mommy loves you very much," Tonya whispered while wiping a tear.

"I love you too, Mommy," Jalisa said.

"Mommy is going to go away for a long time. I don't know when, but Mommy is very sick. God is going to need Mommy soon in heaven, and Mommy is going to need for you to be strong. Ceanna is your new mommy now, and she's going to take good care of you. Promise me you'll be a big girl and do as Ceanna says."

"Mommy, I promise, but you can't leave me. When will I see you again?" Jalisa cried.

"Oh, baby! I'll always be right here in your heart. You remember, look at me, baby."

"Roses are red, violets are blue, but as long as I touch my heart, I'll always have you," the two sang in unison as we cried.

Drying my eyes from the sad memory, I placed the pillow back in its rightful spot. I straightened up a little more in Jalisa's room, kissed her on her cheek, cracked her bedroom door, and went to freshen up before Keisha arrived.

Right on time, the doorbell rang. I hurried to answer it, and there stood my friend Keisha. I needed Keisha right now more than ever. There was no way I could plan Tonya's funeral alone.

"Hey, sissy, boo!" Keisha greeted me as we hugged.

"Hey, boo! Come on in here. Where's Asia?" I asked. Those two were always together.

"Giiirl, don't even get me started on her. Can you believe she asked me when Mia Symone has her baby and gets out of jail, if she can stay with us?" Keisha frowned with her hands on her hips.

"Bitch, get out! Wait! What do you mean 'live with us'? What am I missing?" I asked while pouring Keisha a glass of sweet red wine. This was news to me.

It had been a minute since we hooked up, but I had heard that Asia and Keisha were an item. I never went off hearsay though, since it hadn't come from Asia or Keisha. They were close friends, so to me, maybe people just assumed they were a couple.

"I'll get to that in a minute."

We took a seat at the table, and I could tell that Keisha was visibly upset. "I just can't believe Asia. She, of all people, knows how I feel about Mia Symone. I mean, come on. She slept with my husband Donte all the while smiling in my face, and you think I care to help her? I don't need that around me. I hate the day I met all of them," she went on. Maybe giving her wine was a bad idea. Keisha was on ten.

"Nah, Asia is tripping. With everything that happened and how Mia Symone betrayed us all, I can't even believe she suggested that. Asia has always been the peacemaker. She just wants everyone to forgive and move on. That's easy when you're not the one going through the situation."

"That's what I've been telling her, Ce, but it's like she acts like I'm wrong for feeling the way I feel. She's making this about her, honestly. I think she forgets that this is deeper for me. I lost my son, and although I am grateful for her love and friendship, this isn't about her."

"I know, Key. I'm so sorry for everything you've been going through. I haven't been a good friend. I miss Zylan so much, Keisha, and I'm sorry that I wasn't as present the way you needed me to be. I pray every day that you forgive me and hold no ill will in your heart toward me. I just wanted to be woman enough and apologize for being selfish and thinking only of myself. I didn't know how to process everything, and I still don't, but I vow to be better. I love you."

Keisha stood up and came around to where I was sitting. We hugged, and both sobbed. I knew she was still hurting over everything and having Asia insist on bringing people around who meant her no good opened up old wounds.

"I forgive you, Ceanna, and I love you," Keisha whispered while placing a kiss on my cheek.

"With our crybaby asses." We both busted out laughing.

"Okay, babe, let's get this funeral organized, and afterward, we're going to talk about how you just left my boy Avantae. Giiirl, his ass is sick without you, Ceanna. He came over the other day begging for my ass to call you. That man loves him some, Ceanna." She smiled.

"I love Avantae too, but you know I drag hoes, and I already went to jail behind Mia Symone. Zaria is gonna make me reach out and touch her. You know I don't be playing with these silly little girls. Hunny, I had to take anger management classes and all."

"Don't forget how folks was recording you, and how you went viral for beating Mia Symone's ass. You're a mess, Ceanna! Well, you're better than me. I learned my ass can't fight. Tyler whooped my ass, and then some on Thanksgiving, but I had a trick for her ugly ass."

"Dawg, and she did. I was like Keisha done talked all this shit and let this girl tag her ass."

"Just sad, ain't it? To be honest, though, since Donte got locked up with that charge and we're no longer together, I haven't had to deal with fistfights from his bitches. It's been calm with Asia." She smiled.

"You still tap-dancing around the subject. I heard some thangs," I laughed.

"See, Austin too damn small and nosy as fuck. Yes, we're a couple. I moved out of the home Donte and I shared, and we have our own place."

"Wait! Pause! I'm still confused as hell. When did you and Asia become an item? I know I've been out of the loop for a minute, but when did you get a lick-a-license? You know I don't care either way, though. I'm just sayin' that shit came out of nowhere. How long had y'all been seeing each other, and when was you going to tell me?" I asked as I pulled photos of Tonya out of a box.

"Ceanna, honestly, Asia was just there for me. I'm not really gay, and I've never been into women. She just happened to be there when I needed someone. I was vulnerable. She expressed to me that she was in love with me. It just kinda happened. I didn't tell you or anyone because, to be honest, this just doesn't feel right. I don't love Asia that way, and I feel like shit because Asia really loves me. I'm torn, honestly, on how to end things with her. We're all friends, and I don't want to hurt her. Besides, do you remember Wykeith from the North Side?" she smiled.

"Hell, yeah, I remember fine-ass Wykeith. Girl, that man right there, Lawd. You know I don't even like light-skinned men, but that nicca there is so fine, with his dimples and gold teeth."

"Well, I ran into him a couple of weeks ago at the tattoo shop on 290. We exchanged numbers and have been on a couple of dates. I really like him, Ce," she confessed.

"Keisha, don't do it. Look, if you not sure about your sexuality or love for Asia, then let her go. She does love you, but I understand your reservations. I know you, though, Keisha, and Asia was just something to pass the time. We both know what it feels like to be heartbroken.

Don't let what Donte has done to you change you into the person he was to you. Asia doesn't deserve that."

"Yeah, you're right! Enough of all of that. What colors will the funeral be?" Keisha asked, looking away. She was feeling Wykeith, and I knew she was going to do what she wanted to do.

"Yellow, pink, purple, and white. Those were all her favorite colors."

Keisha and I sat and planned the funeral. We ate most of the day and reminisced about old times. I checked on Jalisa often, even waking her to eat. She hung out with Keisha and me for a little bit and then went back to drawing more pictures for Tonya.

Avantae called on and off, but I sent him to voice mail. I even smiled when he called Keisha's phone and poured his heart to her about me. It was cute, and my anger about the Zaria issue was fading. I loved him, and I couldn't lie. These last couple of days without him had been hell. I needed Avantae, and I missed him. It was time for him to come back home.

Chapter Six

Jaceyon

"What's up, Jaceyon? How are you and your wife, Ceanna, doing? The streets are talking." Mina, the front-desk clerk, smirked.

"Man, gon' on with that shit. Messy ass," I bellowed while signing in my name.

I took a seat in the waiting area of Lab Corp and waited for my name to be announced. A permanent vein was etched across my forehead, as a worried feeling filled the pit of my stomach. I shook my head trying to push aside the anger, hurt, and bad memories. My life was spiraling out of control.

After I shot Avantae at Zylan's funeral, Donte and I were arrested. The charges were unrelated to me shooting Avantae. Nevertheless, being locked up was one of the worst things that could happen to me.

My past had caught up with me. An old lover of mine name Boog ended up being my cell mate. I had framed him, and he had been serving time for a crime he didn't commit.

They found a loophole in his case, and Boog was set to be released soon and was transferred to the jail I was in. At first, it was nice having someone on the inside I knew. I felt comfortable. I should have known, though, that Karma would catch up with me.

Boog sought his revenge by letting other inmates know I was up for grabs. I was beaten and raped by three big niggas, including my old lover.

Even after all that, I still had to fight. I was only released because they didn't have shit on me, and I was being blackmailed by this dirty-ass detective name Rick. He needed me out to get to Avantae. I wasn't the only one who hated that nigga.

I shifted in my seat. I was nervous about testing HIV positive. Boog had that shit, and I just prayed I wasn't infected.

I looked up briefly and locked eyes with Mina. She was ogling at me with the same smirk. I had slept with her a couple of times in the past, but she wasn't anything special. Just another piece of lame Austin pussy. She's for everybody. I rolled my eyes at her and stood to move to the corner of the waiting area out of her view.

My mind was all over the place. I thought back to Thanksgiving Day and sighed loudly. I can't believe the way that shit went down. I had no clue that Mia Symone would show up at my mother's home.

The night before Thanksgiving, I dipped by her place, had sex with her, and told her that I needed to fall back. She felt used and hurt. I understood her position, but she knew what our relationship was from the start. Even though we both caught feelings, I was clear and honest. I would never leave my wife, Ceanna.

I knew about her pregnancy, and I did what I needed to do. I provided Mia Symone with everything she needed, including a new vehicle, condo downtown, and the nicest shit money could buy. That was even after I had already told her to get rid of it.

The stunt she pulled popping up unannounced was fucked up. I wanted to tell her to leave, but when I saw the lust from my male relatives and their stares, my ego got the best of me.

I had felt this unexplainable rush that led me to make a stupid decision. The possibility of getting caught by Avantae never crossed my mind. *I should've killed that nigga.* I sat fuming before returning back to my thoughts.

I don't know what made me give Mia Symone the key to Ceanna's and my home. I could have easily met up with her later at her condo. *Damn, man!*

Ceanna showing up and catching Mia Symone and me was one of the worst feelings. I never expected her to witness anything. I had planned to return later to my mother's and pick her up.

Now that everything was out in the open, I was confused. I had a decision to make. I don't know why I chose Mia Symone over Ceanna, but I did. Now I'm regretting everything. I just want my wife back.

I couldn't believe how one mistake of sleeping with Ceanna's cousin would cause so much turmoil. I know I was wrong, but damn, Ceanna turning her back and sleeping with Avantae never crossed my mind. Then to see her actually at the abortion clinic to abort my seed after she tried to hide the pregnancy test, thinking I wouldn't find out, was fucked up.

I sighed loudly, causing other people in the waiting area to stare at me. All this shit was my fault, man. If I had just been faithful, none of this shit would have happened the way it did. *Man, fuck!*

My phone buzzed in my pocket, pulling me away from my thoughts. I pulled it out and rolled my eyes when I saw the display screen read I had a new message from this dirty detective named Rick. "Ho-ass nigga!" I whispered before I placed the phone back into my pocket.

"Jaceyon Thomas, we're ready for you," the lab tech called out into the lobby.

Once I had completed my testing, I returned back to my mother's home. On the table, sat another large envelope from Ceanna's lawyer.

I was getting really sick of her games. She had already placed our home up for sale, repeatedly sent divorce paperwork to the jail, blocked my calls, and ignored me completely. I ain't signing shit. Ceanna is my wife, and I'll kill her before she thinks she can divorce me. She had me fucked up.

I sat on the back porch and fired up a bleezy. I was so stressed out. I was broke, Mia Symone was close to having my son, my plug wasn't supplying me anymore, and I was back living with my mother.

Truthfully, I just didn't know what to do anymore. I was so jealous of this nigga Avantae. He left the game and reopened his father's businesses. That nigga ain't hurting for shit. I even heard this nigga's single while I was in the joint. I can't front, that shit bangs. The little nigga always had advances over me. I hate that nigga, and I'm pissed those three bullets didn't kill him.

"Baby, are you hungry?" my mother asked, stepping out on the porch.

"Yeah, what you cook?" I passed her the blunt. She puffed twice before responding and taking a seat in a nearby chair.

"Nothing yet, but I was about to fry some pork chops, yams, skillet cabbage, and I made a turtle pecan cheese-cake earlier," she smiled. "How you holding up, Jace?"

"I don't know, Ma, I just know shit is all fucked up. Ceanna won't even talk to me. I want my wife back, and Tonya's death just hit a nigga out of nowhere. I ain't ready for tomorrow."

"Yeah, well, Jace, son, maybe you should just let that go. What we need to focus on is getting custody of Jalisa. What about these twins Ceanna is carrying? I know that bitch is not about to try to keep me from my grandkids."

"That's exactly what she's doing. She keeps sending divorce papers and shit. I ain't signing shit."

"Well, I got something for Ceanna's ass. She is not about to keep me from my grandkids. Anyway, let me go cook. You know I can't stand that girl. Oh, do you have your suit ready for the funeral tomorrow?"

"Yeah."

My mother kissed me on the cheek and left me to my thoughts.

The next morning was a blur. It was the day of Tonya's funeral, and honestly, I couldn't bring myself to go. I was sick without Tonya being here.

My mother had never really seen me in a weak state, but I was tired of being strong all the time.

"Let it out, Jaceyon," my mother hugged me as I welled like a little child. I couldn't believe Tonya was really gone.

I stayed in my mother's embrace like I did the day I found out my father was murdered. I had so much pain in me, and I was so confused. I really needed my wife right now. Ceanna was always a calmness to my spirit.

"Are you better, baby?"

"I will be," I assured her while I dried my face with the back of my hands.

"Well, come on, baby. We got to get to the funeral. We're already extremely late."

When we made it to the church, we had to circle around twice. There was literally no parking at all. It saddened me that we weren't called to ride with the family. We finally parked a block away and had to walk. The church was packed, and luckily, I spotted a bench that had enough room for the two of us.

*I've had some good days/I've had some hills to climb/
I've had some weary days/And lonely nights/*

*But when I look around/And I think things over/All of
my good days/They outweigh my bad days/*

So I won't complain

"Yasss! You better saaang, Brother Roberson," one of
the many members shouted out that was in attendance
at the funeral.

I looked around the church that was now standing
room only. I had to give it to Ceanna and Keisha. The
church was beautiful. It was adorned with many colors of
yellow, soft pinks, purple, and white.

There were many photos of Tonya displayed throughout the church. Some of her alone, others with Jalisa,
some with Ceanna, Asia, and Keisha, and there were
even some at her beauty salon with her clients. The
flower arrangements were beautiful, and the environment was uplifting with great song selections from the
choir. It felt more like a musical than a home-going
service.

I smiled. That's what I loved about my wife, Ceanna.
She had a good heart, and when she loved you, she loved
hard. The fact that Ceanna forgave Tonya and agreed to
raise our daughter Jalisa gave me hope that maybe one
day she'll love and forgive me again also.

"Baby, you okay?" my mother whispered. I shook my
head no, followed by a lonely tear. She lay her head on
my shoulder.

I took another glimpse around the large church. I
didn't recognize most of the people, but I knew Tonya
was loved by many.

As one of the youngest, Tonya was a well-respected
hairstylist. She had clients who came from all over and
was known for her annual hair shows.

Tonya was a really beautiful, sweet, talented, person. She really loved me, and all I did was dog her. I even shitted on her and Ceanna's relationship. I made Tonya feel unloved and unworthy and even compared her to Ceanna at times. I knew I was the one responsible for the betrayal role Tonya played toward Ceanna.

All that was behind us, but I missed Tonya deeply. Before Tonya took her last breath, I sat with her for a while. I wished the visit was pleasant, but it wasn't. Tonya was so small and sickly. All her hair was gone, and her face was sunken. The chemo and meds did more harm than good. She was just a shell of who she used to be.

Selfishly, though, I couldn't hold my anger and disap- pointment. I felt some type of way about all of this shit. Tonya gave Ceanna control over everything. That was a slap in my face. I knew Ceanna was her best friend, but, damn, *I* was the one who bought Tonya that shop, condo, SUV, and *I* was Jalisa's father. Why the fuck would she do that?

Even in Tonya's weakest state, I couldn't respect none of it. I felt used and betrayed. I was hurt about everything. I hated the fact that I no longer had control over Tonya. She had grown a backbone toward the end, and I couldn't gaslight her like I had many times before. Still, though, to give Ceanna custody over our child was an insult. Jalisa had a father and a grandmother. What about us?

"At this time, if anyone would like to take a minute to speak on their memories of Tonya and how much she means to you, now is the time," the heavyset, forty-year- old-looking pastor's wife stated.

I stood up and made my way toward the front. I could see Ceanna crying, wrapped in Avantae's arms. My blood began to boil. *That should be me,* I angrily thought. I balled my fist wanting to punch Avantae in the back of his head when a hand grabbed my wrist. I looked down and saw Asia looking up at me from her seat. She was shaking her head. I yanked my hand away. Fuck waiting in line to speak about my baby mama. I cut my way in line, took the microphone, and let it rip.

Chapter Seven

Ceanna

I exhaled, not even realizing that I had been holding my breath the entire time of the funeral. The service was beautiful. Keisha, Asia, Jalisa, Mama Barbara Jean, Avantae, and I were all seated in the front row. We all wore white with either yellow, purple, or soft pink accessories.

Even though I was still angry with Avantae, he was my rock and soul mate. He was always there for me when I needed him. If it hadn't of been for Avantae and the help of his mother this morning, I wouldn't have made it.

Jalisa cried for Tonya all night long, and I couldn't do anything but hold her and rock her back and forth until she fell asleep.

I cried and had a mini meltdown this morning. I had attempted to wake and dressed Jalisa, but she started back up crying again. I was stressed, and I couldn't take much more. As always, Avantae just knew when I needed him. He and his mother came knocking on the front door.

I fell into Avantae's embrace and cried. He rubbed my back and told me things would be fine.

Avantae had a special bond with Jalisa. He was able to calm her down, help her with her bath, make her eat breakfast, and dressed her. He was able to place a smile on Jalisa's face and dry her tears.

I also appreciated Barbara Jean. She could be a tad bit overbearing at times, but I knew it came from a loving place.

The service wasn't long at all. Keisha and I had a talk with the funeral director and pastor as well. We wanted the viewing and service on the same day. Our directive was to have the casket open once. That way, people could come around and view Tonya's body before the service, and during the service, the casket was to be closed. We didn't want a long, drawn out service or have the casket opened over and over just to bring back overwhelming emotions.

I had it arranged that Jalisa and I were the first to view Tonya's body, and I allowed Jalisa to place her drawing in the casket, kiss, and hug her mother. The pastor's wife even took time to explain heaven and God's will to Jalisa. I couldn't help but sob when Jalisa told the pastor's wife the poem she and Tonya shared. She was such a brave little girl.

"Baby, we're gonna get through this," Avantae whispered while wiping away my tears. I was heartbroken. Tonya looked so beautiful in the soft pink dress that we picked out.

The church was packed. Some faces I recognized, and many I didn't. I smiled when I saw Janair and Semaj. Semaj was a good friend of Avantae, and I had met his wife Janair recently. We hit it off, and it was beautiful to see them there supporting us during this time.

A shocked expression registered on my face when I saw WyKeith's fine ass coming around to view Tonya's body. I couldn't help but ogle at him. He had this boss air about him that made you respect him. He was humble and down-to-earth with a tad bit of aggression and roughness to him. I laughed because I could see Avantae's tight jaw muscle and him giving me the side eye. Okay, okay, maybe I was staring a little too hard, but, damn, it don't make no damn sense to be that handsome. He put you in the mind frame of the rapper Ball Greezy from Miami. He was average height, gold grill, dreadlocks, had a full goatee, and had the prettiest moist mix of black and pink-toned lips.

WyKeith played it so cool when he came around and gave everyone a hug. I caught Keisha smiling a little too hard when WyKeith came toward her. I shook my head. I wasn't the one to judge as a friend, but I could see a train wreck a mile away. I was just happy Asia hasn't caught on to the flirting and love connection between Keisha and WyKeith.

I turned back toward Avantae, kissed his lips, and nestled back into his arms. Another man could never replace him, and I wanted him to know that. He kissed me on the forehead and whispered he loved me in my ear. Then his crazy ass actually took his tongue and licked the inside of my ear. He knew that shit drove me insane and would place a smile on my face.

As everyone walked around to view Tonya's body and take their seats, I frowned when I didn't see Jaceyon or Gina present. I wasn't actually checking for him or Gina, but I heard he had gotten out of jail and by this being the mother of his child, why *wouldn't* he be here?

The Word was really good and inspiring. I was happy we chose Pastor Jeremiah to deliver the sermon today. I looked toward the end of the row and saw a sleeping Jalisa in Keisha's arms. I smiled! Jalisa loved her aunt, Keisha.

As the service began to wind down, the pastor's wife asked if anyone would like to speak about Tonya. I stayed nestled in Avantae's arms. There was so much I had to say about her, so I would go last.

"Nawl, this is fucked up! Give me the microphone!" Jaceyon shouted.

I jumped out of Avantae's arms and turned slightly. *Where did he come from?* I silently thought. I felt Avantae applying pressure to my thigh. He knew I was about to set it off. Thankfully, Keisha carried Jalisa out of the church.

"How the fuck you going try to take my daughter, Ceanna? On top of that, you didn't even allow a nigga to plan my own my baby mama's funeral. You got my mama and me walking a block and shit just to attend. Then you got this nigga raising my seed! A nigga been trying to call you shit the last past week," Jaceyon yelled loudly into the microphone.

"Fuck outta here," Avantae stated. He was so cool and calm. I prayed he remained seated.

"Uh, son, this is the house of the Lord. This is *not* the time or the place. We are here to celebrate Sister Tonya. Now, I'm going to have to ask you to leave," Pastor Jeremiah stated as four ushers began to walk toward Jaceyon.

"The fuck y'all going do? I ain't going nowhere without my daughter."

"Jaceyon, this is not the time for this shit!" I yelled out. I had a face full of tears; this was so disrespectful.

"Ceanna, bring your ass outside now!" Jaceyon yelled while throwing the microphone on the ground, causing a loud screeching noise that caused everyone to cover their ears.

"Nawl, playboy, that ain't happening. Anything you got to say to Ceanna, you can say it to me," Avantae stood up and said.

"Bitch nigga, this doesn't have shit to do with you. This is between me and my wife! Nigga, I should have killed you. That's *my* wife, and those are *my* daughters she's carrying, *not* yours. Ceanna belongs to me, nigga, *not* you. You will *never* have her, because I ain't going nowhere." Jaceyon pointed at Avantae.

"Is that right, playboy?" Avantae asked, smirking while he rubbed his hands together.

I stood up as well and grabbed Avantae's arm. "Come on, baby, let's just go," I pleaded.

"Nawl, ma, sit down. We not going nowhere. This is your friend's funeral, and we are here to honor Tonya's memory," Avantae spoke in an authoritarian tone.

I turned to look around the church. Some were looking on in amusement with smirks on their faces, while others were visibly upset, crying and wiping their eyes. I hung my head.

"Say, though, check this out, Jaceyon, either you can carry yo' ass on up out of here by choice or get thrown out. The choice is yours," Semaj, Avantae's friend, spoke up. He came and stood by Avantae's side.

"Who the fuck are you, lame-ass nigga?" Jaceyon questioned Semaj with his fist balled.

"It don't matter who he is. You're real disrespectful, blood. Tonya was my homegirl, and I don't appreciate you upsetting Ceanna, Keisha, or all these people who came today. So like this man said, either leave on your own or get fucked up. The choice is yours, blood," Wykeith advised, also taking a stand next to Avantae and Semaj.

"Nigga, is that a threat?"

"It's a *promise,* blood. My pistol game is official. Ask about me, blood." WyKeith stepped in Jaceyon's face.

"Jaceyon, I didn't come here for this. Let's just go now!" Gina cried while grabbing his arm.

Jaceyon stood still, looking between Avantae, Semaj, and WyKeith. I said a silent prayer that he would just go. I couldn't believe this shit.

"Ceanna, this shit ain't over. I'm getting custody of my daughter, Jalisa, too. You got me fucked up. This is how you do me, Ceanna? I mean, damn, I know I fucked up, but a nigga trying to make shit right with you. You steady sending divorce papers and shit. Damn, we ain't even talked. What happened to 'for better or worse'? You're just going to let this nigga come in between us? My brother at that. What about *my* seeds, Ceanna?" Jaceyon screamed with a face full of tears. His mother was pulling his arm trying to get him to leave.

I made eye contact with Jaceyon. I had no words or love for him. My heart was on ice. I mean, what does he expect for me to say? Did he think his actions were forgivable? He has a baby on the way with my first cousin Mia Symone. Nah, I ain't over that. It should have never happened. Then to find out he was actually fronting her entire lifestyle, got her friend Kwency pregnant as well, and hid the fact that my goddaughter Jalisa was actually his daughter is just too much. Jaceyon's been cheating and lying from the jump. I was just too smitten with him to see the smoke and mirrors. Avantae was right. I don't deserve this shit.

Gina was finally able to drag a shouting, yelling Jaceyon out of the church. Avantae dabbed up and hugged Semaj and WyKeith. The two men nodded their heads at me. Semaj went back to sit next to Janair, and Wykeith went to go find Keisha.

"I got you always," Avantae whispered in my ear.

"Brother and sisters, the devil is busy!" Pastor Jeremiah shouted.

"Amen!" the church sang out.

"Let us remember why we came together today. Sister Tonya was a beautiful sister, and we will all miss her. The family has asked for privacy at the burial grounds, and there won't be a reception. We thank you all for coming to send Sister Tonya off to glory. If there isn't anything else, let us all stand, hold hands, and pray."

Chapter Eight

Avantae

This nigga Jaceyon's time is almost up. I've let him make it long enough, but after today, it was time to get rid of him. I see now he's going to be a major problem. He had shit twisted if he thought for one minute he was getting custody of Jalisa or the twins. Those are *my* girls.

After the church service, Ceanna hung around for a minute to greet guests. She decided against having a reception and just wanted the service to end. While she stayed and talked to people, Keisha, Asia, and Janair stayed in the church with Jalisa. Semaj, WyKeith, and I waited around outside. We were waiting on Ceanna so we could head to the burial grounds.

The three of us stepped off the church grounds and passed a blunt back and forth, tripping off of the incident that just took place. I didn't know WyKeith too well, but I knew his brother who was killed awhile back. The way WyKeith stepped to Jaceyon made me proud. The nigga was his brother through and through, and I respected his gangster. The cat was all right with me.

"So, WyKeith, what's up with you and my girl, Key?" I asked, switching the tone of the conversation.

"Shit, hopefully, she'll be my girl and stop playing. Naw, what I'm sayin'? Dig these blues! On some real shit, I'm digging Keisha. I've been digging Ms. Lady for a long time. Even when she was with that ho-ass nigga Donte." He rubbed his goatee.

"I dig that, but you do know about Asia, right?" I chuckled.

"Yeah, I know! That shit ain't going to last. That's just a phase. You know after li'l man died, Key been kinda gone. Asia's a cool chick and has been helping Keisha through her issues, but Key ain't comfortable with their relationship. I'm just sitting back. When she's ready, I'll be here."

"That's what's up," I smirked. This nigga was tryin'a play cool, but love was written all over his face.

"So, my nigga, what are you going to do about this Zaria chick?" Semaj asked.

"Man, I don't know, but she straight bugging, yo," I yelled, getting pissed off. Ceanna ain't gave me none in almost a week behind her ass.

"Aye, though, what y'all niggas about to get into?" WyKeith asked.

"Shit, Ceanna talking about cooking and shit at the house. That ain't happening, though. She needs to stay off her feet."

"Yeah, the twins are almost here," Semaj said, smiling.

"So have y'all planned the baby shower or anything yet?" WyKeith asked.

"Nawl, we ain't done shit yet. I'ma get up with Keisha sometime within these next two weeks to plan the baby shower. I have a feeling they going to come early," I frowned.

"You all right, my nigga?" Semaj asked.

"Nawl, man, I can't even front. That shit Jaceyon pulled has me tight. I should have put one in his dome. I've just been holding back because my pops was murdered, and I know what it feels like not to have your father. Then it's like on the other hand, eliminating this nigga sounds good. The shit has been eating at me. I need to talk to Ceanna. I really don't want this nigga around, and I want the girls to have *my* last name. I want to marry Ceanna too."

"You know I kill niggas for breakfast. It ain't shit to dome that nigga, son. Give me the word. That shit was mad foul he pulled. Besides, Keisha speak so highly of you. You're a good nigga! I got a plug in the mall in H-town too. Don't worry about baby clothes and shoes. Your little mamas is going to be decked the fuck out. I'm talking the newest shit," WyKeith said excitedly.

"*That's* what's up! Good looking and I'll let you know about that nigga Jaceyon. His time is ticking. I've been playing shit cool too because this ho-ass Detective Rick keeps snooping around. So I've been chilling," I replied, coughing hard as fuck from the weed.

"A detective?" they both asked in unison.

"Yeah, man! I believe him and Jaceyon may be working together."

"They got something on you, bro?" WyKeith asked.

"Nawl, I cover all bases, but Jaceyon got out too quick. Ain't no way you get locked up and outta the joint within three months unless it's some major paper floating around or you're a snitch. Some shit is going on."

I chopped it up awhile longer with the fellows. We laughed and joked around more about WyKeith trying to hide his feelings, Zaria, the babies, and Jaceyon. The beautiful ladies finally came out, and we all headed to the burial. Jalisa slept the entire time. Baby girl was drained.

Afterward, we all said our good-byes. My mother decided to take Jalisa back to my crib so Ceanna and I could work some things out. I was grateful for that. I kissed my mother on the cheek and thanked her. Besides, Ceanna and I have a lot of making up to do.

Ceanna and I made it back to her condo, and I whipped baby up a quick bite to eat. She sat down on the sectional, and from the kitchen, I could hear her snoring.

"Ma, wake up!" I nudged Ceanna, handing her a bowl of watermelon.

"Avantae, your ass plays way too many games. You had me thinking you were really in the kitchen doing some shit. Watermelon?" She cracked jokes.

"Man, you tripping, girl. Shit, cutting that watermelon was hell," I cracked up laughing.

"Oh, Laaawd, I can just see it now. Please tell me you did *not* make a mess in the kitchen."

"Man, girl, chill out. I got this," I laughed.

Ceanna and I sat in silence for a little while, both enjoying the sweet taste of the watermelon. I didn't like the distance we had between us. Conversation with us was always so natural and raw.

"I'm going to go draw us up a bath, baby. We need to talk, Ceanna." I pulled her up from the sectional.

Ceanna hugged me and gazed into my eyes. Her eyes were lustful and low. I kissed her deeply. Her light moans began to turn me on, and I couldn't take it any longer. I began lightly biting Ceanna's neck and licking her left ear.

"Ummmm, Tae! Tae, please, baby, I *need* you," Ceanna moaned.

She began pulling on my belt and unzipping my pants. My manhood sprang freely through the slit of my boxers. Ceanna softly grabbed my tool, massaging it. She kissed me hungrily while moaning the sexy tune.

"Ah, fuck, Ceanna. That shit feels so good. I missed you. You hear me, baby? Daddy missed you," I whispered in a low, sexy growl.

Ceanna pulled my pants and boxers all the way down. I removed my shirt, and Ceanna ordered me to sit down. My manhood began jumping with anticipation. I swear Ceanna had my ass whipped.

She slowly lowered herself on her knees and took my tool whole in her mouth. "Ah, fuuuck!"

"Ssshhhh, be patient, baby," Ceanna softly spoke as she began sucking and flicking each one of my balls.

"Got damn, ma! What the fuck are you doing to a nigga? Aaaah, that shit feels so fucking . . . aaaah, fuck!" She began slurping and using some trick with her ton-gue. She then placed my whole sex and balls in her mouth and started vibrating her tongue.

"Ceanna, aaaah, Ceanna! Let me feel that pussy, baby. Come on, baby. Come sit on daddy's dick."

Ceanna stood and removed her dress and bra. Once I saw her big, round melons jiggle freely, I stood up and started sucking them aggressively. She was so fucking sexy. I took my tool and started rubbing it up against the folds of her sweet womanhood.

"Fuck, you're so fucking wet. Can I enter you, baby?"

"Please, Tae!" she screamed.

I turned her around with her ass facing me and sat back on the sectional. She sat on my manhood taking its entire length. I gently grabbed her softly around her neck and began sucking her ear. She began popping and bouncing her wet, tight pussy with a dancer's rhythm. As I was sucking her ear, I took my right index and middle finger and began rubbing her clitoris. She began squirting everywhere.

"Yeah, gimme that shit. Let that shit out. Aaaargh, Ceanna. Fuck, baby, fuck!" I growled.

"Devin. Fuck me! Fuck me, baby! Yes, right there. Oh my God! Avantae Devin Wallace. Aaaah, *papi, i m corriendose, me coge por favor!*" Ceanna screamed at the top of her lungs in Spanish. That shit turned me on. I couldn't hold it any longer.

"Aaaah, fuck, baby." I released deep inside of Ceanna's walls.

"I'm soooo sleepy," Ceanna lazily moaned.

"Nawl, girl, you been blasting Beyoncé all got damn week, so yo' ass gonna take me to Red Lobster, 'cause I slay." We both fell out laughing. Moments later, both of us were knocked out.

Chapter Nine

Mia Symone

"You're writing your cousin again?" my cell mate Kellie asked in a high-pitched voice while frowning.

"Yeah," I replied sadly while I rubbed my belly. I had been having pains on and off today. I've been writing Ceanna letter after letter hoping one day to hear from her. I had even tried calling her cell, but she blocked me. I couldn't count how many time I had my mother Monica, Gina, and even Asia attempt to call Ceanna on three-way. She would hang up every time. The truth was, I needed Ceanna.

"Look, Mia Symone, have you ever thought about just letting things go? I mean, I can't lie and say I blame your cousin. What you did to her is kinda unforgivable," Kellie shrugged.

"Don't you think I know that? Ugh! You wouldn't understand anyway," I fussed. This bitch is always in my business. I tuned my cell mate out and continued to pour my heart out to Ceanna.

"Have you thought of a name yet?" Kellie asked.

"Yeah, I'm going to name him Jaceyon Jr."

"Oh, okay, cool. So do you know when you're getting out of here, and who's going to raise him until you do?"

"Yeah, my mom is going to raise him for me. She has an apartment for the baby and me as well. I should be getting out soon. The girl I ran over was my friend, and she didn't press any charges. The only reason I'm in here is because the child she was carrying died, so I got charged with that. I should be home soon, though. I have a good lawyer."

I sighed and thanked God that Kwency hadn't filed charges against me. I thought back to the day I ran over my friend.

I was released from the hospital a couple of days after Jaceyon's arrest. He had phoned me and asked if I could take care of all his affairs. I agreed! We were a family, and according to Jaceyon, as soon he got out, he was going to divorce Ceanna and marry me. I had no clue all of that was lies.

It wasn't until Tonya and I got into it in an argument. Tonya was cleaning the shop and preparing for her transition. I was an employee, and although Tonya and I never had beef, I was extremely hurt that she packed all my things and boxed them by the front door of the salon. We got into a shouting match and started hitting each other below the belt. I thought I won the argument . . . before Tonya ripped my heart out. She informed me that Jaceyon was playing me and that he had been sleeping with my friend Kwency, got her pregnant, and that Kwency had also been going up to the jail to visit Jaceyon.

I didn't believe Tonya. I had to see this for myself. I went up to the jail during visitation hours. I waited for a parking space when, lo and behold, Kwency came walking out of jail, heading to her vehicle. The pain I felt was indescribable.

I pondered on what I wanted to do and how I would handle confronting Kwency for two days. On the third day, I headed over to her home just as she was leaving. I followed her a good distance across town.

Kwency pulled up into her father's recording studio. I sat for a moment wondering how I would approach her and what I would say. I couldn't believe my friend out of all people would betray me this way.

Moments later, Kwency emerged from her vehicle. The blue jean denim one-piece fit her toned body like a glove. Her fire-red hair was freshly curled, and the prostitute-red lipstick she wore gave her a fearless look. I admired her body as she walked across the parking lot. She was indeed a bad bitch. I was so focused on her that when she rubbed her tiny hand over her belly and smiled, something inside of me broke.

Quickly reversing my vehicle, I threw my car in drive. I drove full speed ahead. Kwency turned and looked in my direction. A wave of fear and shock registered all over her pretty face. She let out a loud scream and attempted to run. Her right ankle buckled due to her losing her balance in her high wedge shoes.

Thump, thump; my vehicle rose high, causing me to almost lose control of it. I swerved just in time before hitting a parked car. Witnesses screamed who had just come from the inside of the building out into the parking lot. A smile appeared on my face seeing Kwency lie on the ground.

In the rearview mirror, I caught a glimpse of people pointing toward my vehicle. I hightailed it out of there and rushed home. "Oh my God! What have I have done?" I screamed rushing into my condo. Hours later, I was arrested.

"You okay?" Kellie asked, noticing that I had a frown on my face.

"I don't know! I just got a sharp pain, and I just urinated on myself. I'm really uncomfortable. Maybe if I just lie down, it'll go away. Ooooouuuuch!" I screamed in tears.

"Mia, that is not pee. Your water just broke! Oh my God, the baby is coming today!" Kellie yelled excitedly.

"Guard, guard!" she screamed.

"What is it, Kellie?" a female guard asked.

"She-she-she-her water just broke. She needs medical attention," Kellie stuttered.

"Ohhh please hurry. Kellie, it hurts so badly. Owwwooo, Owwwooo," I breathe heavy in and out.

"Hold on, Mia!" Kellie yelled in a panicked tone.

"I can't. I feel like I have to doo-doo, there's so much pressure. I got to push, Kellie."

Kellie pulled my pants off, and I slightly sat up and began to push. Kellie was pushed to the side as the correctional nurse came.

"Mia, you're doing good. I see the head," Nurse Franny said.

"Oh Gooood, it hurts," I cried. I pushed one last time and felt light-headed. Something was wrong. My heart slowed down, and the room began to spin. I heard the faint sounds of my son before I passed out.

Beep, beep, beep, beep! I woke up to sounds of a beeping alarm. In my right arm, an IV was placed, and on my left arm was the blood pressure monitor cuff. Around my neck sat a heart monitor machine with different wires plugged up to the sticky connections placed on my body. The room was dark, and I knew I had to have been at a hospital.

I was so hungry but extremely exhausted. I wanted to see my son, but truthfully, I couldn't keep my eyes open. I tried to picture my son. Did he have my green eyes? My eyes began to roll. All I remembered was the smile on Kellie's face and the cries from my son before I blacked out. I drifted back into a deep sleep.

"Mia Symone," my mother Monica called out, kissing me on the forehead.

I stirred in my sleep before finally coming to. It felt good to touch my mother. The entire time I had been locked up, I could only communicate with her through a video chat during visiting hours.

"Hi, Mama! How did you know I was here?"

"Your lawyer informed me." She smiled, taking a seat next to me.

"So what is he saying? Can I go home now?"

"No, baby, not yet. You shouldn't be in there much longer, though. Kwency is doing all she can."

"Can I see the baby now? Oh, Mom, did you call Jaceyon and Ceanna?"

"Jaceyon, Gina, and Asia are on the way. Ceanna and I had a falling out."

"A falling out? Why? What happened?" I frowned.

"I asked the bitch to raise your son until you got out, and she basically said no. Ugh! She is just like her mother!"

"But what about what you promised? Why would Ceanna need to raise him? I thought you had a place for the baby and me. I thought you were going to watch him until I get out."

"Look, Mia Symone, I'm leaving. I met someone. I'm sorry, but I can't take him," she confessed flatly while replying to a text.

I couldn't control the pain that was easing its way out. I cried. My mother always turned her back on me. I began retreating back to my younger self. All the old pain resurfaced. My pain turned to anger.

"Bitch, fuck you! Get out! You were *never* there for me. You always turn your back on me. I fucking hate youuuuuu!" I screamed at my mother as tears rolled.

"Little bitch, I know you ain't screaming at me. If you really want my opinion, you should have never had the little bastard. You're not capable of love, and I feel sorry for that baby," she laughed.

Beep, beep, beep! The machine began beeping loudly. The red number on the machine rose. The door opening got both of our attention.

"What's good, Mia Symone?" Jaceyon asked dryly while taking a seat in a chair that was sitting in the corner.

"Well, that's my cue to exit. You know I don't fuck with Gina or her kind. I'll be in touch," my mother said, blowing an air kiss and leaving.

"That's fucked up!" I cried uncontrollably.

I continued to cry for another ten minutes. I was hurt that Jaceyon didn't even reach out to hold me like old times. Gina sat next to me rubbing my leg, and Asia smoothed my hair. Jaceyon flipped through the channels as if he was ready to leave or had more important things to do.

"May I speak to Jaceyon in private for a moment?" I looked at Asia and Gina.

Jaceyon sighed loudly as if he was annoyed. Asia and Gina shared a weird look between the two of them. They both stood and walked out the door.

"Jaceyon, why you treating me like this?"

The door opened, and a nurse with red hair walked in.

"Mia Symone, are you okay, dear?" she asked while checking the monitor. I nodded my head, wiping away my tears. The nurse left and closed the door behind her.

"You betrayed me, Mia Symone. You let your emotions get in the way. I love you, and I never denied it, but I also told you I would never leave Ceanna for you. I love my wife. Shit is all fucked up now, and I really ain't got shit to say or do with you. I'm just here for my son and to sign the birth certificate," he said coldly with dark eyes.

"What about meeeeee? What about uuus? I have nobody, Jaceyon. What I'm I going to do when I get out of here?"

"That's something you gotta figure out. I'm trying to get my wife back. I should have never fucked with you in the first place. That was my bad. You could never be or even compare to Ceanna, and what we did was foul. What I felt for you was real. You're a cool chick, and when it comes to my son, I promise to do my part, but as far as *us,* that's a dead issue. I can't take back what we did, and we had some wild, crazy times, but we could never build together. I'm sorry! That's just what it is," he shrugged.

"So, in other words, fuck me, huh? That's fucked up, Jaceyon. You used me all this time. I betrayed my own cousin for you. I thought you loved me. What am I supposed to do without you? I thought we were going to be a family! Now I have nobody because of you. *Nobody!*" I screamed.

"Check this out . . . You're fucking delusional if you ever thought I would leave my wife for you. Besides, you let yourself go. I should have never betrayed Ceanna. I mean, what the fuck was I thinking, cheating on my wife for a stripper bitch?" Jaceyon spoke with his hands.

"*Bitch?* So *that's* how you view me, Jaceyon? After *everything?*"

"I don't have time for this shit, yo. Fuck outta here, being all dramatic and shit. You know what it was. I just came to see my son, and I'm out, shorty. Look, I spoke to your mother already. She told us she was leaving, so I worked it out with your lawyer, and the baby will come home with Ma and me. Take care of yourself, Mia Symone." Jaceyon stood to leave.

"Nooooo, wait, Jaceyon, wait. Please don't leave me like this. I love you, Jace! Can't you see that?" I sobbed.

"I'm sorry, Mia Symone, but it's over for us. I gotta try to get my wife back. I'm dying slowly without Ceanna." He turned and walked out.

"Fuck you! Fuck you, Jaceyon! I fucking hate youuuuu! I fucking hate you! You lied to me. You said we would be a family! Fuck you. That's why she left you for Avantae."

"Get out!" I yelled when Gina and Asia walked into the room. "Just leave me alone!"

I sat crying to myself for over an hour. Jaceyon crushed my hopes, spirit, and heart all at once. I finally released my soul from all the pain, and now I was ready to be with my son. I pressed the intercom and asked the nurse to please bring my child.

After waiting ten minutes, Asia walked into the room with the baby in her arms. A nurse walked behind her wheeling in a baby bed and set it next to me. I wanted to scream at Asia to get out again, but seeing my son brought me the biggest joy.

When Asia placed little Jaceyon in my arms, calmness and love came over me that I had never felt before. I had always heard of love at first sight, but this was a different kind of love. A flow of tears continued to run down my cheeks. I was so in love, and when little Jace opened his eyes, I cried harder when I saw my same green eyes staring back at me. He was absolutely perfect.

Chapter Ten

Ceanna

The next morning I woke up and smiled at Avantae's snoring ass. He was laid back on the sectional, butt-ass naked, with his mouth wide open. I wanted to video record him so he could see for himself just how loud he snores.

I spotted my purse on the dining table and searched through it to grab my phone. I frowned when I saw over seven missed calls. There were three missed calls from St. David's Hospital, another missed called from my aunt Monica, two missed calls from Keisha, and one from Barbara Jean.

"Ssshhhh, oh, I got to pee," I whispered, crossing my legs, and then hurrying down the hall with my phone still in my hand. I barely made it. Catching my breath, I decided to place the first call to my aunt, Monica.

"Ceanna, I've been trying to get ahold of you. I'm at the hospital, and I need you to get to the hospital. Mia Symone had the baby last night. She's at St. David's out South."

It felt like someone had stabbed me a million times. My head began to spin. Everything was happening so fast that I hadn't had a chance to cope with any of this. *She had the baby,* I whispered to myself as tears began to freely flow.

Raw emotions filled my heart. The feelings of betrayal, jealousy, and insecurity. How can Jaceyon hurt me like this? I did *everything* a wife was supposed to do—and more. I helped my cousin when she had nobody, and *this* is how they both do me? A baby, though? Would I be wrong to keep my girls away from their brother? Would I be wrong not to accept this child? I battled inwardly. So much pain was going through me. I couldn't stop the tears from flowing.

"Ceanna, look, baby, I know my daughter did you wrong, but, Ceanna, I can't raise this baby. I've met someone, and I plan to leave as early as next week."

"Leave and go where? Uh-uh, and what about Jaceyon? I can't raise that baby. I refuse, and furthermore, I don't want to see the baby either."

"You're the stepmother to that child, and he has done nothing to you. I can't believe you're acting like this. Damn, Jaceyon ain't shit but dick. Mia Symone is your *family.* You've moved on, Ceanna, to Avantae, so why the fuck you mad for? Mia Symone needs you!" she shouted.

"You know what? I'm going to go ahead and hang up now. Mia Symone has a mother, but I guess you wouldn't know shit about that since you were always leaving her on my mother and father growing up. That's *your* grandchild. I don't want shit to do with Mia Symone, Jaceyon, or the child that *they* created!" I yelled and hung up. She was not about to guilt-trip me. Nope!

"Baby, you okay?"

I jumped. Avantae startled me. I wondered how long he had been standing there. I looked up at him shaking my head.

Without any words, Avantae began to run bathwater. When it was filled halfway, he turned the water off and reached for my hand. I stood up from the toilet and closed the lid while flushing it.

Avantae stood behind me and guided me into the tub. I gently sat down, and he got in and sat down as well. We stared into each other's eyes and knew it was time. We both had been dreading this conversation that needed to take place.

The love between Avantae and me was real, but the fact of the matter was, we didn't start this thing right. I was still married, carrying another man's babies. Avantae had a son now, and I had my husband's daughter. There were so many questions and uncertainties between us.

"What's on your heart?" Avantae asked as he gently rubbed my cheek.

I stared at him for a few minutes. Finding out he had a child by Zaria was eating at me, and I knew Avantae could sense that. We had so much in the way of us being happy. So many outside influences trying to tear us apart.

"Look, Ce, I ain't going to lie. I've been really tight lately. Shit has been fucking me up on the inside. I don't want to argue, and I haven't been as open with my feelings because we both know shit is fucked up. I want you to hear me, though, on everything. From the moment I saw you, I had to have you. I craved you mentally. You are my best friend and soul mate. Yes, there are times, though, that I wish those babies were mine. I hate the fact you're married and carrying that ho-ass nigga's name. Lately, Ce, I've been uneasy. I love you more than you know, but I need to know. Do you ever think about being back with that nigga? And what about when the twins are born? Are you giving them *his* last name? Will you allow me to cut the cord or will that bitch nigga? When will you divorce? Will you marry me? Will you allow me to adopt Jalisa as my own? When the twins are born, are you allowing Jaceyon to be there? I got so many questions, but the main question I have is . . . Do you trust me?" He paused and stared deeply into my eyes.

"Ceanna, you low-key hurt my feelings. I hate sounding like a bitch or a weak nigga, but communication is key. I should have told you about Zaria. That was my bad. Things were so good with us, and I just didn't want this distance we have now. I swear on everything I never fucked that girl nor have I been doing dirty shit behind your back. You're it for me. No other woman tops you. I ain't playing head games with you; yet, you treat me like I'm this ho-ass nigga. I know Jaceyon fucked you over, but have I not been there? Not one time have I neglected you or turned my back, but yet, you believe this bitch Zaria over me? I'm fucked up behind this shit too, Ceanna. This bitch had my son for five years and didn't even tell me. That's *my* seed, Ce, and I will be in his life. I need to know, will you accept him? Will you trust me? I want us to have a future. I gave that street life shit up for us. I'm in the studio tryin'a make this shit happen for us. So, baby, I need you to stop fighting us and give us a chance. Can you do that, baby?" Avantae expressed with so much passion.

"Avantae, I love all of you, so I never want you to question that. It is hard to trust when everyone you have loved betrayed you in some kind of way." A tear began to roll.

"We all have had pain, and without it, Ce, I wouldn't even be the man I am today."

"Tae, I don't even know where to begin. There's so much on my heart," I spoke sadly. "For one, I don't think I have fully forgiven Tonya or Jaceyon. I don't want to take it out on Jalisa. She's innocent. However, sometimes when I look at her, it reminds me of all the betrayal. Then too, nothing." I paused and looked away.

"What?" Avantae turned my chin to face him.

"Nothing, just forget about it." I lowered my eyes. I knew this was going to lead to an argument.

"Man, spit that shit out. I ain't with the games." Avantae looked at me intensely.

"Promise me you won't get mad."

"Mad about what?"

"I should have just gone ahead and told you. As you know, I was taking Jalisa to see Tonya every day. Before she passed, she told Jalisa the truth about Jaceyon. Jalisa wants to see him."

"Nawl, ain't happening next. I don't wanna hear that shit," he yelled.

"Tae, why do you always do that shit? *You're* the one that kept saying we needed to talk. 'What's on your mind, Ce?' Then when I tell your ass, you tell me you don't want to hear that shit. I wish things were different, baby, but I can't ignore the fact that Jaceyon is going to be around, regardless of whether we like it. Not to mention the nigga won't sign the divorce papers, so I'm still married," I cried. All this shit was upsetting me. I'm already emotional and uncomfortable as hell.

"The nigga tried to kill me, Ceanna. Do you *really* think I care to hear his name? The only reason that nigga breathing is because of you, but don't push me. I don't want Jaceyon around you, Jalisa, or my babies. The fuck you on? Keep fucking playing loaded, and you gon' fuck around and find that nigga in a body bag!" he yelled loudly, causing me to jump.

"Now wait a damn minute. I just know yo' ass ain't got all loud yelling at me. You act like this is *my* fault. Well, it's *not*. Do you think I want this? Huh? Every day I try to find reasons to love these babies and to get ready for their arrival. How do you think *I* feel to know that my children have siblings? You don't know the pain I feel. And there's the fear that one day, this will be too much for you, and you'll leave me. I love Avantae, and I don't want Jaceyon." I stood. "Stop coming at me like that. You make it hard to be honest with you when this is your solution to conflict. If this is too much for you, I understand, because, trust me, it's a moment-by-moment thing for me. You said you were made to love me, and if that's true, show me and quit running away."

"Damn! Please don't go, Ceanna. Sit back down, baby. Me and my ego. I apologize, I'm tripping," he whispered, and I sat back down.

"One thing I am sure about is the love I have for you. To answer your questions, I don't know about a lot of them. I haven't thought that far. I won't lie to you. I've pretended in my mind that none of the other elements matter. I guess at the funeral is when things got really real. I knew then that I can no longer ignore what's evident. I'm trying to get divorced from Jaceyon. Yes, I want to be with you and marry you. As far as Jaceyon is concerned, he is their father. He wasn't here the entire time, though, so you have earned the right to name them and cut the cords. You have been at every doctor's visit and been there through it all since day one. I would never take that from you, baby. However, he *is* their father, so, yes, I will not keep this man from his children. Also, because I love you, yes, I will accept your son. I want you to know I *will* drag your baby mama if she steps on my toes. I don't like the bitch and don't ever force her on me. As far as your son, though, he is welcomed, and I will never mistreat him. I love you, Tae, but I need to say one more thing. Ever since Jaceyon has been out of jail, you have been insecure about me. It's like your heart and mind are in conflict. I know you, and I know you're questioning shit. I want you to know that when you see me crying, it is me releasing pain. I'm not crying because I love Jaceyon or want to be back with him. That part is over," I smiled.

"I love you, Ceanna. Word is bond. Come here." Avantae opened his arms widely. I turned my back and scooted between his legs.

"Put it away, Tae." I laughed because Avantae's manhood was always hard and ready for me.

"You feel that, girl?" he whispered in my ear. I turned around too fast and head butted him. "Got damn, Ce, with your big-ass forehead!" Avantae laughed while holding his head. I fell out hollering while holding my head. Avantae was always tryin'a crack jokes and shit.

"Man, you the one that wanted to sit in this little-ass tub. I can't hardly move and shit. This shit is made for one person. My ass is about to hop in the shower," I laughed while standing. "Oh, your mother called too. I didn't get a chance to call her back." I slowly stood, getting out of the tub, careful not to fall.

Crash! My bedroom glass broke. Shocked, we looked at each other. Next, we heard a car burning rubber pulling off fast. *Argh, can't I just have one night?* I inwardly screamed.

Avantae jumped out of the tub, slipped, and fell on the floor. If this hadn't of been a serious situation, that would have been funny. *Dick slinging everywhere.* He hurried off the floor and ran into the bedroom turning on the light. I was right behind him. Someone threw a brick through my window with the word *"Bitch"* written on it.

"Ceanna, go take your shower. I'm going to board up the window, and we're leaving. When you get out of the shower, pack whatever it is you and Jalisa need. I'll call my homeboy to fix the window tomorrow. You already know I ain't calling the law. I'ma get to the bottom of this shit."

I wanted to argue with Avantae. I didn't want to go anywhere, but in my condition, if anything popped off, I wasn't no good. I hurried and showered as Avantae asked and grabbed the items we wanted and needed.

Avantae had secured the window and dressed. We made our way to our vehicles. When we did, I thought I was going to have an anxiety attack.

Someone had sliced all four of my tires and scratched my paint on my truck. *Ugh,* I held my stomach feeling as though I would start vomiting. I was so upset. I took a seat on the ground and watched as Avantae inspected my truck further.

I placed my head in my hands and began to cry. I wanted to physically harm whoever did this to my truck. That truck was a gift given to me from my father Calvin before he passed. It was more than a vehicle; it was my heart.

"Ayo, what the fuck?" Avantae yelled. I looked up and saw him accessing his truck. Whoever did this had destroyed both of our vehicles.

"I just texted Keisha, and she's on her way to get you. She's going to take you to my crib. I'm waiting on my nigga Elijah. He has a tow truck that can tow both of our trucks. I'll be home later on tonight, and tomorrow, I'll get us rental cars." Avantae kissed me.

I stayed nestled in his arms until Keisha pulled up. I was pissed off and wanted to know who the fuck did this shit. They violated, and they *will* pay. *I hope Avantae's baby mama ain't got shit to do with this, because if so, I will not spare her from the ass whooping she has coming,* I silently fumed.

Chapter Eleven

Zaria

"Bitch, go, go, go, go, go, go!" I yelled at Kwency, laughing extremely hard. "Oh my God, I can't believe I just threw a brick through Ceanna's window and fucked up both of their vehicles."

"Tasha, you're a trip, girl," Kwency called me by the fake name I gave her. Tasha was the name I gave when I met new people, especially in Austin.

I wasn't going to let Avantae get away with putting his hands on me like that. He had another think coming. Ever since that day, I had been plotting on ways how I was going to get him back. Just so happened Kwency and Semaj was perfect pawns in my game.

At first, I was chill. I heard what my cousin Tamara was telling me. She was right, and I hadn't been focused on myself or Tater Bug since I found Avantae. I tried to let him go, but I loved Avantae, and seeing him with Ceanna was eating at me.

Avantae really hurt my feelings that day. He disrespected me and called me a broke ho. How could he diss me like that in front of Ceanna and his mother? The Avantae I knew used to love and adore me, and he would have never spoken to me like that. Then the fact that he actually put his hands on me completely floored me.

Not only that, I had been going through a lot. I lost my job, was damn near homeless, and officially, another chick caught up in the system, thanks to Avantae's mother, Barbara Jean.

I didn't understand what Barbara Jean's beef was with me. *Petty ole bitch!* She even went as far as to get me written up and then fired. Other than my little petty arguments with Avantae and me being obsessed with him, Barbara Jean had no right to stick her nose where it didn't belong.

I was sick of her. Every time I had to work a shift with Barbara Jean, there was always some shit. The patients' beds weren't made correctly, the vital signs weren't logged in on time, and she was always clocking my times when I went on break or to the restroom. She made the work environment hell for me.

I couldn't understand how a grandmother to my son never took the time to get to know me. It's not like I was keeping Tater Bug from Avantae. It was Avantae who acted as though his precious little Ceanna and Jalisa were all he cared about. All I wanted was to be included and be a family again. I couldn't understand why everyone was acting as though *I* was wrong.

After all Barbara Jean had done to me, even though I had vowed to myself that I wasn't going to reveal the information I had on her from four months ago, now that I lost my job, I was going to tell it all. The gloves were off. I thought back to the time a patient died at the hands of Barbara Jean.

I checked the hallways to make sure they were clear of any nurses. Once I saw that the coast was clear, I quickly made my move as I had done many times before. I headed toward the medication closet. I was addicted to muscle relaxers and Tramadol.

I grabbed the pills and had just placed the medication in my pocket when I heard the doorknob being twisted. My heart began to race, and I quickly took cover behind a file cabinet praying that no one would come that far back into the room. I stood there panicking, trying to control my breathing. I prayed that my phone wouldn't vibrate. I had a clear view of the door, and I watched intensively as the door opened wider.

In walked a nervous Barbara Jean. She moved quickly. I saw her grab a syringe and insulin. My eyes grew wide in shock. Through past private conversations with Avantae, I knew of her HIV status, and the fact she used to be addicted to heroin. Maybe she's on the shit again.

As quickly as Barbara Jean came, she was gone. I hurried from behind the cabinet and carefully exited the room.

As I made my way back down the hallway, I briefly got a glimpse of the back of Barbara Jean's head. I saw that she was in Samuel's room. I didn't understand why, when I had just checked on him thirty minutes prior.

I brushed it off, grabbed my purse, and clocked out for the day. As I was leaving the hospital, a Code Blue was called over the intercom. The next morning when I came to work, I got the news that Samuel had died.

I didn't think much of it until an investigation began. Apparently, Samuel's sister Gina had the hospital investigated for a suspicious death. The report stated that Samuel died of insulin overdose and that he wasn't a diabetic. Therefore, insulin should have never been given to the patient.

All the staff members, including me who worked that day shift and floor were all being investigated. Once the official report came back, it was determined that not only had Samuel been given the wrong meds, but that he also was murdered. It didn't take long for me to put two and two together.

Samuel was brought in for a gunshot wound to his foot. I recognized him immediately. Whenever I would work at that location, I would always treat Samuel kind as he had to me when I was younger. I had a liking for him, but I could never understand Avantae's disdain for him.

I knew a little about Avantae's past, but not too much. He was very private about his mother and rarely spoke of her. I knew deep down, Avantae and his entire family had dark secrets, which is why I pretended I didn't see what I saw that day.

I was going to let things ride. Even after the ugly things Barbara Jean had done, but Avantae ignoring me was the icing on the cake. I wanted him to hurt like he had hurt me. So I placed a call to Detective Rick Miles and informed him that Barbara Jean is a person of interest in the murder case of Samuel Thomas and hung up.

"Tasha, damn! What are you over there thinking about, bitch? I done called your name three times," Kwency laughed.

"Girl, nothing. I just can't believe I did that," I laughed.

I looked over at Kwency and admired her lovely glow. She was beautiful and reminded me of Jessica Dime from *Love & Hip Hop.* My mind drifted back to Avantae. I couldn't shake him for some reason.

Deep down, I envied Avantae and his lifestyle. I had to change my entire life for five years, with no help. I always had aspirations to be a singer, but when I found out I was pregnant, my dreams were placed on hold. It was a bitter pill for me to swallow.

Now that I was back in Austin, not only was Avantae ignoring me, but I felt jabbed at the same time.

Avantae's new single was blowing up around Austin, and every time I heard his single, all I could think about was how he needed my dope voice on the hook. The single made my passion come back, and when the radio announced one morning that Avantae would be performing his single at a local popular nightclub, I knew I had to go.

I showed up at the club careful not to be seen. I secretly watched Avantae all night from the first floor. I saw him with a guy who I would later find out was Semaj and a girl who I would later meet as Kwency.

Avantae seemed a bit annoyed with the girl. They even looked like they had a few choice words between them. The girl was pissed off, and once I saw her coming down the stairs making her way toward the restroom, I followed.

"Girl, that's a cute-ass dress," I said, being extra fake.

"Thanks, love! You're rocking that purple matte lipstick," she replied.

"Oh, really? Thank you. Sometimes I don't like it, though, because after a while, my lips peel."

"Oooh shit, that's my fucking jaaam," Kwency said, throwing her arms up and grinding her hips.

The girl was bad and sexy as hell. If I were into girls, I would bump clits with her, for sure. She had fire-red hair and a sexy body. Her ass was huge.

"Hell, yeah, mines too, but I was really digging ole boy Avantae's single too," I said.

"Oh, Avantae? That nigga all right, but I think he needs more, like maybe a female singing a hook. I don't know; it's just something about that rap singing shit that turns me on." She smacked her lips and rolled her eyes while checking herself in the mirror.

"Well, shit. It sounds like he's missing me," I blushed.

"Can you sing?" she asked.

"Bish, whaaat? Check this out. Soooon as I get hoooome oooomee," I began singing a Faith Evans song.

"Damn, bish, you can blow. Why the fuck you ain't known yet? Here is what I can do. My father owns a studio; his name is Quincy."

"Bish, get out. Oh my God, that's your father? Yeeees, I know Quincy. Well, I don't know him, but you know everybody tries to get on with him. Yo' pops is a fucking legend!"

"Yes, I'm his daughter. My name is Kwency, and I'm Semaj's assistant. He's a producer, and he also produced the song Avantae just performed. Maybe I can hook y'all up," she smiled.

"Oh my God, bish, you just made my night!"

"Here's my number and the number to the studio. Give me a call tomorrow, and I'll set something up. Maybe we can do lunch or something." She smiled, passing me a business card out of her purse.

After that night, I kept Kwency close but not too close as to where I was exposing my hand. Kwency had revealed to me all about her brief affair with Jaceyon and how Mia Symone's crazy ass ran her over and made her lose her baby. Every now and then, I would throw caution to the wind and ask about Avantae.

Kwency kept her word and introduced me Semaj. They both knew me as Tasha, and Semaj loved my voice, so much so that he told me he was working on some new music for his homeboy and that he thought I would be a wonderful addition to his new single.

I had been to the studio four times, careful not to run into Avantae or expose myself. I always had an excuse or made up a lie anytime Semaj wanted Avantae and me to meet. I almost got caught recently when I pulled into the studio parking lot. Avantae was just leaving.

I decided to follow Avantae that evening. I had been plotting and plotting on how to get him back, and seeing him leave the studio gave me the perfect idea.

We drove a good fifteen to twenty minutes. He didn't stay far from the studio. A twinge of jealousy and anger filled me when I followed him into these nice-ass condos. Here I was jobless and living with my mama in Masa Manor Apartments.

When I saw Avantae pull up next to Ceanna's truck, I yelled in anger, "That should fucking be me!" My head began to spin, and all I could think of was the living condition my son and I were living in. It was war now.

I watched the condo for a couple of days before I decided to make my move. I didn't have anyone to confide in, so Kwency would do. I didn't mean to tell her everything about Avantae, but my anger wouldn't allow me to shut up. I told Kwency everything but my real name.

Kwency hated Ceanna just as much as I did, but her real bone to pick was with Avantae. She told me how Avantae coldly spoke to her one night and how he was always judging her. So when I asked Kwency to ride with me today, she was down.

"Bitch, I got some news for you," Kwency stated excitedly as we exited her vehicle heading into her nicely laid condo.

"What, spit it out?" Zaria yelled, sitting on the love seat.

"There's this club in Dallas that wants Avantae to perform his single and any other music he has." She smiled, passing Zaria a glass of red wine.

"So I told Semaj, and he's going to inform Avantae. It's set for next Saturday, and I'm responsible for the hotel rooms. Guess what, though?" she smiled.

"Giiirl, what?"

"Semaj wanted me to inform you that you'll be coming too. He wants Avantae and you to perform the new single and freestyle it. The song is complete now with your vocals on it, and Avantae completed his part last week. Although he hasn't been able to get y'all to rehearse it, he wants to see how y'all vibe together and how the audience receives you and the song. So, bitch, this is your opportunity to kill it. The killer part about all this is, Avantae has no clue you're coming."

"Bitch, I know where you're going with this." I was about to jump off the sofa.

"Sooooo, next Saturday, bitch, you'll be in Dallas performing with your baby daddy. Can you imagine Avantae's face when he finally sees you? Guess what else?" she laughed.

"You're going to make me have a heart attack, girl, if you don't spill the tea, hunny."

"*I'm* responsible for the hotel rooms, rental cars, and dinner reservations. Your bitch hooked you up. Your room is right next door to Avantae's, and I will get two room keys. I also got some Rohypnol from my homeboy so you can drug Avantae, or I will. I want you to fuck the shit out of him while I record it. I'll make sure to send the tape to little Ms. Wifey." We both fell out laughing.

"That's why you're my biiish." I jumped up, hugging Kwency.

Chapter Twelve

Avantae

It's been a couple of days since the incident at Ceanna's. I still haven't tracked down who threw the brick through the window, but as of right now, I have more important things to do. The time is nearing for the twins' arrival, and we are going to need a bigger space.

I haven't told Ceanna this, but I've been secretly meeting with a realtor and interior designer named Denise. She came highly recommended.

I had us a home built, and I put it in Ceanna's name. I planned to marry Ceanna, and if anything was to ever happen to me, her security as a woman would always be taken care of. I didn't ever want her to lack anything.

The home I had built was one story. It had a large family room, game room, a large dinner area that fits sixteen guests at a table, an office for Ceanna to run her boutique from home, Jalisa had her own room and bathroom, and the twins had a room. I made sure to make their room larger, so when they get older, a wall could be built to separate their rooms, and it had three guest rooms.

I knew Ceanna was not going to want my mother to stay with us, but for Ceanna's safety and help with the babies, it was best. Therefore, I built my mother a room. She had her own washer and dryer connection, bathroom, and kitchen. I also made a door where she could come in and out separately from us. Of course, now that I had a son, he had to have a room with his own bathroom.

We had a master suite with an attached living room, huge walk-in closets, and a grand bathroom. The garage was large enough for eight vehicles and fun adult toys that I planned to get us. I had a playground and sandbox built outside for the children to play and a gated pool with a cover. I even had the home childproofed with covered plugs, higher locks, alarm systems, and cameras all around the house. I even built a panic room and a secret stash spot for our guns and money, since I was a street nigga.

Even though I was not in the streets anymore, I still had street instincts and mentality. If this music shit I was building, or the storefronts ever failed, I knew one thing I could always do was push weight. I had a family now, so going broke was never an option. I just wanted baby girl to rest and be happy.

Ceanna's favorite color was purple, so I made sure to incorporate a sexy purple theme. As of now, some of the walls were still bare. That was only because I had a special day set up for Ceanna. I hired a makeup artist, hairstylist, and photographer. I knew Ceanna hadn't felt as sexy lately with the weight gain and changes to her body. I wanted to set her up a beautiful maternity photoshoot, and I wanted us to take family photos.

"Okay, Mr. Wallace, this is our final walk-through. Let me know if there are any last-minute adjustments that you want to make before you guys move in. I have one more piece that will be delivered for the twins' room. I hope you like the designs and concepts I came up with," Denise smiled widely.

"Everything looks good. I appreciate you for making this shit happen for my wife and me. My baby is going to love this shit. I could not have done this shit without you. You are a lifesaver. Oh, and I sent your PayPal card an extra five grand as an appreciation gift from me and my wife. Every single room is perfect. My baby girl Jalisa is going to love her room. The photos of Tonya were a beautiful addition to her room. Man, and the twins' room is absolutely perfect. My wife isn't going to have to do anything but rest and take it easy. My son is going to freak out when he sees his room. I love the Teenage Mutant Ninja Turtle theme and all the pieces you got to match. I just can't thank you enough," I expressed sincerely while biting my bottom lip.

"You're absolutely welcome. I'm going to use the restroom real quick, and I'll be out of your hair," she said as she walked toward the guest bathroom.

I stood frozen in the spot I was in and silently thanked God. My life was finally coming around full circle and blessings were falling out of the sky for me. I had everything to be thankful for. Ceanna and I were back to being one with each other. Jalisa is doing really good. I'm healthy, my single is still doing good, my money is looking right, I'm sleeping good at night without worrying about a fuck nigga tryin'a jack me or a dope case, and my mother is back in my life, and her health is doing good. I could go on, but I'm just a thankful young nigga right now.

I jumped when I felt a pair of arms go around my waist. I turned around and was speechless when I saw Denise butt-ass naked. She turned around and began clapping her ass cheeks.

"What the fuck is you doing, yo?" I yelled.

"Avantae, I know you want this pussy, baby," she moaned while rubbing her hairy-ass pussy. That shit looked nasty. I thought all women shaved down there.

I stood quietly for a second, trying to collect my thoughts. I was wondering, did I ever say or do something that would make Denise get the impression that I wanted her? The answer was no. I had never flirted with this chick, I never told her she was beautiful, I never spoke to her about anything other than furniture or colors for the walls and shit like that. I always spoke of my wife and let it be known from the jump I was unavailable. So I'm really fucking confused right now.

"Look, ma, you playing yourself and you being really disrespectful. Go put your fucking clothes on and get the fuck out now!" I yelled.

"I just wanna make you feel good, baby. Nobody has to know, Avantae. I just wanna fuck you so bad. From the moment I saw you I started fantasizing about you." She grabbed ahold of my dick.

"Yeah? You feel that, Denise? My shit is soft as fuck. The only woman who can fuck the shit out of me and get me hard is my wife. Now, get the fuck on. I swear, y'all hoes want a nigga to talk bad to y'all." Normally, I'm not a disrespectful man. Calling women out their name ain't really my style, but females like her don't understand when a nigga tell them no.

"Whatever, Avantae! You going to wish you hit this. I know that whale you call a wife ain't fucking you right with her big disgusting ass," Denise yelled, pissed off while putting her clothes on.

Typical. I shook my head at Denise. Granted, she was a beautiful woman, but can't no other female make me want to stroke her with the death stroke but Ceanna. I valued that I would never hurt her, and truthfully, being faithful and one hundred is easy to do with Ceanna.

"Have some class about yourself. We good here, and I appreciate your services, but they are no longer needed, and lose my number." I opened the front door waiting for her to leave.

Denise smacked her lips and twirled her tacky-ass, long weave around her finger while smacking her gum.

"Whatever!"

I see my fam Semaj pulling up, and once he got out of the car, he looked at ole girl and me with a perplexed look.

"Nawl, fam, it ain't even like that!" I shouted out.

"Oh, Denise!" I yelled.

"What, nigga?" she yelled in a hostile tone.

"You might want to go see a female doctor. You smelling tart, baby girl. Stanky-ass pussy," I laughed.

"Avantae, you a fucking fool, boiiiiii." Semaj laughed while dabbing me up. I stood to the side and allowed him entrance.

"I got you a gig, are you down?" he asked.

"Hell, yeah, I'm down, but when is it? You know I be trying to stay close because of the babies. My baby already having a lot of discomfort, and I need to be within reach if she goes into labor with my girls."

"It's next Saturday, in Dallas. They're feeling the single, fam, but I figured you and Tasha can go ahead and introduce the new single. I had Kwency book rooms, a rental van, and dinner reservations. The club is paying you ten grand just to perform. I think we should go. As far as Ceanna is concerned, I can ask Janair to come over with the baby; that way, she won't be alone."

"Hell, yeah, that's a great idea. I'll ask Keisha and Asia too. That way, they can do some shopping and bonding."

"So when are you moving in here? Man, Ceanna is going to love this shit. This shit right here is the shiiit," Semaj yelled excitedly, walking around the house.

"Shit, I'm trying to get baby girl in here tonight. I need to ride out to Sam's and get food. You wanna ride? Shit, we can even do a get-together later on. Janair and the baby can come hang out with Ceanna and Jalisa. We can put some steaks on the grill and shit."

"Hell, yeah, that sounds like a plan. Besides, I've been working so hard lately, so this would be a good way to get baby out of the house."

"How is she liking Austin so far?" I asked.

"You know, Janair is a content type of woman, and she doesn't complain or ask for much. So I'm not too sure. I know she be shopping her ass off, though." Semaj busted out laughing.

"Shit, Ceanna ass too. I be like, damn, baby, you think you got enough shit?" We laughed some more.

"Come on, fam, let me show you the rest of the home. My nigga, wait until you see the baby girl's room." I smiled widely.

After I gave Semaj a tour around the home, we headed over to Sam's and went bananas shopping. We were excited getting our women together later on and cooking for them. It was only nine in the morning when we were done shopping.

I dropped Semaj back at the home, and he left in his vehicle. I put all the food up and seasoned the steaks. Once I was done, I showered in my new shower, dressed, set the alarm, and headed over to my old home.

As soon as I entered the home, I smiled. My three favorite girls were cooking breakfast together.

"Daddy Tae!" Jalisa screamed, running toward me with pancake mix on her little cheek.

"Hi, baby! Are you cooking for Daddy?" I asked while picking Jalisa up and kissing her on the cheek.

"Of course, Daddy," she giggled.

"Guess what, Daddy? I felt the babies moving and kicking, and Mommy Ceanna showed me her stomach, and it looked crazyyyy." Jalisa made a funny face. We all laughed.

"Devin, come on in here and sit down," my mom said. Ceanna smiled at me and winked her right eye.

"I love you, baby!" Ceanna smiled while sexily licking her lips at me.

"I saw that you two. Get a room."

Ceanna was glowing so beautifully this morning. I could tell her spirits were lifted, and she was in a better place. She's going to be in an even better mood when I give her the keys to her new home.

"Baby, what are you over there smiling about?" Ceanna asked.

"This is just a beautiful sight to see, all my queens in one room. After we eat, y'all, I need everybody to pack a bag and get dressed for the day. We won't be coming back here tonight," I smiled. The ladies all looked at each other and smiled extremely hard.

"Deviiiin, what you got up you sleeve, boy?" my mother asked with her hands on her hips.

"I can't tell y'all, but is the food almost ready? A nigga is starving," I laughed.

"Daddy Tae, you're always hungry." Jalisa laughed, causing us all to laugh. Her little ass is funny, yo.

We all ate and cracked jokes. Today was a good day, and I was happy to see my mom and Ceanna getting along the way they were. They always had a good relationship, but I know at times my mother can be overbearing. I appreciate Ceanna for being the bigger person and not being petty about the situation.

"I'm finished now!" Jalisa yelled out, causing us to bust out laughing once again.

"Me too, baby girl. Come on and let's get you a bath," Ceanna laughed.

Ceanna stood, and I wanted her right then and there. I needed a release, so I asked my mother if she could help Jalisa. Ceanna smiled at me and shook her head. She already knew I needed to slide in between her good ass loving. We couldn't even make it all the way in the room before I was attacking her.

"Avantae, nooooo, put it away," Ceanna moaned while play fighting me.

"Come on, baby. Just let me stick the head in," I moaned while rubbing my sex against the folds of her wetness.

"You're so fucking sexy, ma. Mmmmm I need you, baby. Toot that ass for me," I continued to moan in a low voice.

"Okay, baby, but don't be making so much noise. You know your mama is nosy as hell," Ceanna smiled while getting in position on the bed.

Whap, whap, whap! "Avantae, ouch! Shit, you're going to make me kick your ass. That shit hurts," Ceanna said, rubbing her ass.

"Your ass is so big, baby. I love the way the shit shakes," I growled.

Ceanna and I made love for thirty minutes straight. I love being between her warmth, and truthfully, if we didn't have anywhere to go or a child in the home, I would have made love to her all day and night long. However, that could wait because I couldn't wait to see the expression on Ceanna's face.

I helped her shower, and I packed her a bag. Once she was done, we met my mother and Jalisa in the living room.

"Y'all ready?" I asked my mother and Jalisa, smiling.

"Boy, we've been ready. *Um-huum*, is *y'all* ready is the question," Mama smiled.

Ceanna and I looked at each other and spoke in unison. "Ready."

I made sure everyone was seated comfortably in the new rental I had. Ceanna's and my vehicle had been shipped to Houston. We both had a special candy-coated paint on our trucks, and my nigga Elijah knew who could get us right. I paid Elijah fifteen grand for his services, and to get our vehicles repaired with new tires and rims as well.

The ride to our new spot was filled with laughter and joy. I could live like this forever. Finally a day with no

drama. I mean, well, Denise's stank ass tried it, but
other than that, today was beautiful. I drove another ten
minutes before we pulled up to our destination.

"No fucking way! I mean, no way. Avantae, tell me you
didn't? Whose house is this? This is fu—I mean this is
absolutely beautiful," Ceanna yelled, damn near jumping
out of the car.

I didn't even respond. I just smiled. Jalisa screamed
joyfully while jumping up and down, and my mother
had tears flowing down her dark, beautiful face. I held
my mother for a second and kissed her on her forehead.
Ceanna was already at the front door, and Jalisa was
right behind her. As soon as I made it to Ceanna, I gave
her the key.

Ceanna's eyes widened, and tears began to flow down
her beautiful face. She gave me a big hug and just started
bawling her eyes out. Jalisa was so dramatic, so she
grabbed Ceanna's leg and started crying too.

"Baby, this is all for you. It's in your name. If anything
ever happens to me, you and all my children will be well
taken care of. I love you, Ceanna," I whispered in her ear,
and then licked it.

"Stop, boy!" Ceanna smiled, and then kissed me.

Seeing Ceanna's, Jalisa's, and my mother's facial
expression as they ran through the home brought tears to
my eyes. I ain't an overly sensitive nigga, but until I met
Ceanna, a nigga had no purpose. Being here today, in this
moment, made me feel like a man. I was proud and felt I
had something to live for.

The night was beautiful. Semaj and Janair came over
with their little baby. We ate, played cards, and sat
around and talked. I told Ceanna about Saturday, and
baby girl was cool with the arrangement. I looked forward to more days like this and the day Ceanna officially
became my wife.

Chapter Thirteen

Mia Symone

"Mia Symone, let's go. You're being released," the heavyset black female guard yelled.

I brushed my hands over my hair and took a quick glimpse in the mirror. Gawd, I was so fat now and feeling other than myself these days.

"Oh, girlie, you look good." Kellie smiled while standing to give me a hug.

"Bye, Mia Symone! I'm going to miss you. You take care of yourself and write me once you get settled," Kellie softly whispered.

"I will, boo. I promise!" I kissed Kellie on the cheek and rubbed her big round belly one last time.

The guard opened the cell door. I turned back and looked at Kellie one last time and smiled. She truly was kind to me the entire time I was in there.

As I made my way down the hall, I purposely kept my head down. I ignored the ugly remarks from all the other female inmates. Let's just say Austin isn't a big place, and I had my share of men, even some of theirs. I wasn't a well-liked female.

The guard handed me my belongings, and I changed. I was so embarrassed with the way my clothes were fitting.

I was thankful for Gina picking me up. I waited outside, taking cover under a building. It was pouring down extremely hard. "Damn, where the fuck are you at?" I fussed under my breath.

After waiting twenty minutes for Gina, she finally showed up. I was beyond annoyed with the fact I had to wait that long. I plastered on a fake smile and got into her truck. Since I didn't have anywhere to go and Jaceyon had my son, she offered me Avantae's old room. Her home was so tiny, but I guess it could be worse.

Honestly, I'm thinking of just going back to Houston and stripping again. Maybe I can find me another sucka-ass nigga. Besides, I still have my old furniture in storage and a lot of clothing, purses, shoes, and shit like that in there. Well, it's not like I can fit in the clothing anymore, but another reason I want to go back is because there is a man there who really does like me. He always did. It's just I got so caught up with Jaceyon.

I shook my head while looking out the window. It's crazy how we always love people who never loved us back, and the ones who love us we run from and never give them a chance. I should have never taken up with Jaceyon because he was never mines to begin with.

This shit is sad, man. I can't believe I ended up here. This time last year, I was at the top. I had a bad car, a condo downtown that was fully furnished, and expensive clothing. I guess none of that means shit now since it's all gone and I have a child.

I never thought the day would come that I, Mia Symone, would have to apply for assistance. That shit just don't sit well with me. I know them little stuck-up state bitches are laughing at me. That's okay, though, because this shit will only be temporary.

Damn, a part of me still envies my own cousin. I thought I had a winner in Jaceyon, but this nigga is, in fact, broke, living with his mama; his name ain't ringing no mo' bells in them streets; all the while, Ceanna has the winner in Avantae.

Avantae, hmm. I was shaking my head. That nigga was a straight boss. He came and scooped Ceanna up and made her whole again. Nothing that Jaceyon and I did to Ceanna broke her one bit. She has gone on with her life, and Avantae really loves and respects her. I guess that was something I thought I was going to get out of Jaceyon. I was so stupid, though. Like most side chicks, you think you're winning, but when the shit hits the fan, you realize you really are just an escape from a man's reality and basically, just something to do to pass the time. It's a hard pill to swallow.

"Mia Symone, how are you feeling?" Gina asked.

"Numb. I'm just trying to figure things out," I sighed.

"Well, I don't have much, but I'll help you and my grandson any way I can."

"Thank you, Gina; that means a lot. So I guess your son is really done with me, huh?" I asked.

"Yeah, he is. He wants to mend his family back together, but Ceanna doesn't want him. She has sent divorce papers, but he won't sign them. He's been really stressed out too. He can't seem to find work either. It's been really hard for him. Anyway, have you given any thought as to how you're going to support your son?" She turned her body to face me once the light turned red.

"Well, I'm hoping to find a job really soon and my own place." I frowned. I really wasn't in the mood for this type of talk.

"Well, I know one thing you can do."

"What's that?" I answered drily.

"Since Jaceyon is still married to Ceanna and the baby is in our custody, you can file for child support. Jaceyon doesn't have a job, so they'll go after Ceanna. With the money she makes from the boutique, you're liable to get a good four grand a month and some change," she smirked.

In Gina's eyes, I saw greed. I wasn't going to put my cousin on child support, nor am I going to go out of my way to harm her. I've done enough damage. I bit the hand that always fed me, and now Gina's small-ass home and a broke-ass baby daddy who doesn't want me is all that I have to look forward to.

"Besides, it's not like that wide bitch is hurting for money. I know Calvin Black left her ass money and prop-erties. I told Jaceyon's ass he needs to sue her ass too for trying to go behind his back and sell the home they shared. He needs to ruin that bitch instead of mopping around here. He's going to have to do something, 'cause I can't take care of him, you, and a baby. Something has got to give. Shit, rob a nigga or something." She fired up a blunt and then continued to drive.

I just looked at Gina. She was a typical hood bitch. I tuned her out and closed my eyes. All I know is I can't wait to take a bath and get rid of this musk smell I have. It's like no matter how many times I shower, I always have this musky smell. I feel so dirty most of the time.

"Oh, before I forget to tell you, Asia came by and brought you clothing, shoes, undergarments, hygiene products, a phone, and a six-hundred-dollar Walmart card."

"Oh, wow, that's really sweet of her," I smiled.

"Have you spoken to your mother?" Gina asked.

"Nope! But let me ask you this, do you know her or something? At the hospital, I noticed a weird look you two exchanged, and the last time I saw you at the post office, you brushed me off quickly when I mentioned her." I frowned.

"Yeah, I know that bitch. We have old history!" she said coldly.

"Old history like what?" I asked, now looking at her.

"Look, Mia, just leave it alone. I don't feel like traveling down throwback memory lane. Some shit should just stay in the past."

"Why you so mad, though?" I frowned.

"I ain't! It's just a lot of shit you don't know about your mother, or father, for that matter." She coughed deeply from the weed smoke. "Shaaat! This is some good-ass weed. You sure you don't wanna hit this?" she asked.

"Nawl, I'm good. I'm waiting on you to tell me about my parents, though. Like, I knew my pops was murdered and sold drugs, but did he do more?" I asked, and Gina laughed.

"Oh, did he!" She shook her head. "Okay, so I see you're not going to just let things be. Long story short, your father Carlos, Calvin, and Teddy ran an underground sex trafficking ring. When my parents died, your mother and father took me in as a foster child. Your father drugged me and had his way with me. When your mother saw him touching me, instead of standing up for me, she kicked me out on the streets. I was pregnant with his child and had an addiction. I did any and everything to feed my habit, including killing your father. Asia is his daughter. Happy?" she yelled, taking two more puffs off the blunt.

I sat there speechless. My mother was young and pregnant with me when my father was killed. Her greed growing up kept us in a bind. My mother did any and everything for status. She ran the streets most nights and even brought the streets in our home.

I knew all too well Gina's pain. I too was a victim of one of my mother's men. Instead of being there for me, she dropped me off at Ceanna's home. Her parents were more of parents to me than my own mother. It's funny because people always call me a ho, but how can I value myself or worth when it's always been taken? Underneath this cold interior is a little girl's soul reaching out.

My heart couldn't be mad at Gina for what she had done. Hell, my heart wouldn't even feel for a stranger I never met. I never had a father, so Carlos was just a part of my DNA. The only man who showed me love was my uncle, Calvin.

We pulled up to Gina's home, and my heart jumped with joy when I saw Jaceyon walking up the sidewalk with our son in his stroller. Little Jaceyon seemed like he grew so big in just a short time. Being without my son almost killed me.

I ran up to the stroller and picked up my son. I began crying extremely hard, kissing all on his beautiful face. I stared at Jaceyon for a moment wishing this moment would last.

"Well, y'all, let's get in the house. Mia Symone, I hope you're hungry. I made enchiladas, Spanish rice, beans, and corn bread for dinner," Gina smiled.

Man, that sounds so good. That jail food was so nasty. I used to dream of home cooked meals.

As Gina warmed up the food, I settled into Avantae's old room. I had little Jaceyon with me, and I wanted to give this breastfeeding thing a try. A flow of tears ran down my face when little Jaceyon attached on to my left nipple. I can't explain the love and joy I felt. I couldn't stop staring at him. My son was so beautiful and perfect in my eyes. I hadn't noticed before, but he had dimples. His caramel complexion was finally coming in, and he had a head full of black, curly hair. He was definitely going to be a heartbreaker one day.

Once I was finished breastfeeding, I burped little Jace and rocked him to sleep. Thanks to my sister Asia, I had a little baby bed in the room with me. I smiled! Asia has always been more cordial to me than Keisha and Tonya. Ever since she found out we had the same father, Asia has been there for me more than anyone else. I made a mental note to call her later on.

After I put the baby down, I went through the bags of things she had brought me. I found a pajama set and settled on that since I wasn't going anywhere. I grabbed my clothing and hygiene products and headed toward the bathroom.

As I passed by Jaceyon's room, I heard him on the phone. His door was slightly ajar to where I could see in. He didn't notice me standing there, but I could see him lying across the bed. He was on the phone whispering, but I heard him make reference to killing Avantae numerous times. In my gut, I had a feeling something bad was about to happen.

Before he noticed me, I headed to the shower. Once I undressed, I stared at myself in the mirror. I was so disgusted with myself. I was so fat, and my face was now round. This weight looked horrible on me.

The warm water felt so good, though. I stood under the water and enjoyed the scalp massage it gave me. I wanted to stay in longer, but this wasn't my home, and besides, the water began to turn a little cold.

Even though I brought my clothing in the bathroom with me, it was too small in there. So I wrapped a towel around me, grabbed my belongings, and headed toward my room.

Jaceyon was sitting on my bed. I was confused about why he was in there. The baby was still sleeping so there was no reason for him to be there; besides, the way he crushed my heart at the hospital is unforgiveable.

"Jaceyon, what are you doing in here? Please leave!"

"Mia Symone, look, I apologize for how I came at you."

"Cool, now you can leave." I turned my back toward him while dropping my towel.

Jaceyon stood up, came, and wrapped his arms around me. He began kissing on my neck. I turned and pushed him away. "Not this time, Jaceyon."

"Why not? You know where we stand."

"You one confused-ass nigga. I can't do this with you anymore. I heard you loud and clear at the hospital. It's time I start taking responsibility. What I did to Ceanna was wrong. Loving you is wrong." I tried to control my shaky voice.

Jaceyon leaned in to kiss me, and I know I should have stopped him, but I couldn't. I deepened the kiss with him, and he grabbed my ass. He began sucking on my neck, and then he pulled away. I opened my eyes, staring at him, wondering why he stopped.

"Damn, I'm tripping. My bad, and you're right. I got a lot shit on my mind. Truth of the matter is, Mia, I should have never fucked with you. Forgive me." He turned and walked out of the room.

Once again, I fell for his bullshit. I knew Jaceyon never loved me. He just saw me as an object and something to pass the time with. Ceanna had his heart, and that is something I could never compete with. I'm just sad that it has taken me this long to finally wake up.

I closed and locked the door behind him. Then I sat down on the bed, lotioned up, and dressed. I kissed my son on the cheek and then headed downstairs.

"Mia Symone, the food is ready. Make yourself at home. I'm on my way to church," Gina informed me.

"Church?" Jaceyon and I said at the same time.

"Yes, church."

I fixed myself the biggest plate and sat at the dining table. I was so into my food and enjoying it when Jaceyon came and sat at the dining table. I rolled my eyes. I just wanted him to leave me alone and let me be.

"I need your help, ma," Jaceyon said while taking a piece of my corn bread and eating it.

"I'll pass. I feel horrible for setting Boog up like that, and you know what's funny, Jace? I loved you so much; I would have done anything for you. Still to this day, I have no clue why we set Boog up, but because I loved you, I did as you asked. However, now, I'm trying to change my ways. I'm a loose cannon, and I have a son now. I'm done with the streets. All my life I've been doing underhanded shit, and to be real, I just got out of jail for running over a bitch I thought was my friend. Luckily, she didn't press charges on me. At least she did all she could to help get me out. You, on the other hand, don't give a fuck about me. So, nope, I ain't doing it."

Jaceyon glared at me with the coldest eyes. He scared me a little, and I really didn't feel too safe being here with him. I prayed God would get me out of this situation and fast. Maybe Ceanna will feel sorry for me and help me. I didn't know, but I did know I wouldn't be staying here too long.

"Fuck you," he barked and stood up.

I started to respond, but the look in his eyes told me that he wouldn't hesitate to do me harm. I looked away from him and continued to eat my food. I was happy when he left the kitchen. Something had changed in him. He was different and not the Jaceyon I used to know.

"Nawl, fuck that," Jaceyon yelled, coming back around the corner.

I jumped and grabbed my fork tighter. If this nigga tried anything, I swore I was not going down without a fight.

"I lost everything because of you, bitch!" He threw my plate of food on the floor.

"Bitch nigga." I threw my drink on him. Jaceyon charged at me, pushing me out of the chair.

"Get off of me, Jaceyon. Stop!"

Whap, whap, whap. Jaceyon punched me over and over.

"Bitch, you'll do as I say. *I'm* the reason you got a roof over your head. You made my wife leave me. You told Boog I set him up and had them niggas pin me down in jail, bitch. I'm going to fuck you up, bitch. Don't *ever* fucking tell me no. Ho, I *own* you." He ripped my pajama pants with force.

I fought to get from under Jaceyon, but it was no use. He was much bigger than I was, and I was a little disoriented from the blows he delivered. I reached for my fork and jabbed it into his arm. I then spit in his face. He didn't flinch one bit.

"I see you wanna play games, Mia Symone, but *I* run *you!*" Jaceyon yelled while ripping my pants further.

I stared at Jaceyon wondering who this person was. I knew what he was about to do to me, and I didn't have anything left in me to fight. I was tired.

When Jaceyon was finished, he stood up and just looked down on me. We locked eyes, and I knew I was going to kill him. He was going to pay for this. I was done being a victim to men. Enough was enough.

Chapter Fourteen

Jaceyon

"Ceanna, it's me, Jace. I guess by now you heard about my son. I need to see you, and I would like to see my daughter. I know I fucked up by fucking Mia. I regret that shit every day. I'm sorry about the scene I caused at Tonya's funeral. It's just seeing you with that ho-ass nigga bothers me, Ceanna. Can you please call me back? I don't want to go through with this divorce either, so you can stop sending papers because I ain't signing them," I spoke into Ceanna's voice mail.

I was beginning to feel like Ceanna's bitch. That's probably the thirteenth message I've sent her. I don't understand why she just won't talk to me. She just can't end things with me like this. I won't let her.

My life is so fucked up, man. I had everything with Ceanna, and I ruined it. I can't stand the ground Mia Symone walks on. This bitch has ruined me. I don't have shit anymore because of her, and now I got to look at this fake ho every day.

My T-lady is foul, man. She knows I've been trying to get my wife back. I couldn't understand why she did some underhanded shit and offered Mia Symone a place to stay here. Low key, that was messy as fuck, and if Ceanna hears about this, it's definitely a wrap.

Mia Symone doesn't have a job, a car, or nothing to offer, so she shouldn't be staying here. She ain't my fucking problem. Every time I look at her, I just want to kill her.

When I asked Mia Symone to help me, and she refused, something in me snapped. The bitch tried to buck me, so I broke her ass down. Hell, why not? She was the last piece of ass I had before I went to jail and now the first piece of ass since I'm out.

I don't know what's wrong with me, but jail changed me. The way those big niggas ripped my ass apart makes me feel worthless and like a piece of shit. I don't like the way I feel, and the fact that I was exposed to HIV scares the shit out of me. My mind can't rest, and even though the lab techs have told me over and over that I'm negative, I can't help feeling like I'm not.

Mia Symone fucked me up. I don't know why she would write Boog and tell him everything. I thought she was my gutter bitch, my ride or die, but she flaked on me. She was so pissed about me fucking her friend Kwency and getting her pregnant that she turned on me. I mean, damn, I'm a dog, so what did Mia Symone expect from a nigga? Did she really believe I didn't want no other pussy besides hers? Did she really believe I was going to leave Ceanna for her? I mean, why would I respect Mia Symone or want to build anything with her? I met the bitch in a strip club. Everybody has seen her shit, and on top of that, she was fucking Donte, Samuel, the judge, JR, and some female cop. I guess she thinks I didn't know about all of that, though.

I heard Mia Symone in the kitchen crying, and I just left her there. I gave her what she wanted. Shit, just minutes ago, she was begging for the dick and wondering why I stopped. So she got what she wanted, and then some.

I hopped in my truck to go meet up my homeboy Rick. Rick was this dirty-ass detective. We had a common interest, which was Avantae. I was going make this nigga Avantae pay for fucking my wife.

"Ayo, Rick, my nigga, where you at?" I yelled through the vacant building.

"I'm right behind you, nigga. I caught your ass slipping, fam." He and I hugged.

Rick passed me a bottle of water, and we walked over to a side room and sat down on a sofa. He was sitting a little too close for comfort.

"I got some information I think you may wanna hear." He licked his lips.

"Okay, let's hear it," I frowned, trying to catch this nigga's drift.

"Well, first, word on the street is that you're breaking niggas' back in." He rubbed his hands together.

"Fuck outta here. I ain't gay!" I yelled while screaming and standing.

"There's no need to get tight, Jaceyon, I believe you. I ain't gay myself, but a nigga can do what no female can. So you scratch my back, and I will scratch yours," he said, eyeing my semierected print.

"I don't get down like that, homeboy."

"I tell myself that too, Jace." He stood.

Rick began removing his clothing until he stood before me naked. He took a condom out of his pocket and began to roll it on his piece. Sweat began to form on my forehead. I tried to fight these demons and look away, but I couldn't.

Rick was tall and slender. His yellow body glistened in the shadows of the dimly lit room. I could smell his Creed cologne, and it began to tickle my loins. I even felt my own sex getting harder as I stared at his body.

"I'm not a bottom, and I don't have any condoms," I finally spoke.

"I know all about you, Jaceyon, and you *are* a bottom. Take off your clothes!" he ordered.

I wanted to leave and tell Rick he was wrong about me, but I couldn't hide eleven inches of a hard-rock piece, so I did as he asked.

For two hours straight, Rick and I head banged. It was some of the best sexual aggression and sex I've ever had. I was beat and on a high. We still had business to tend to, though.

"So what you got for me?" I asked, relaxing lazily on the sofa.

"Well, for one, I got a voice mail from Avantae's baby mother, Zaria. She said that Barbara Jean is a person of interest in Samuel's death. I've been watching her lately, and she had access to the medication supply room as well. If everything pans out, I'll be booking Barbara Jean for the murder of your uncle, Samuel. Second, Avantae just brought Ceanna a new home in the city of Manor. I have the address for you. I heard he has a performance coming up next weekend in Dallas. So that means Ceanna and your daughter Jalisa will be alone. Through a valid source, I also heard that your plug ain't fucking with you because he's cool with Avantae. He also heard about you getting down with men, and he couldn't fuck with it," Rick shrugged.

"Damn, man." I had so much shit running through my mind, but being broke wasn't one of them.

"You down for two robberies?" I asked, shocking my own damn self.

"Who are we talking about?" he asked.

"Keisha and Avantae on the same night," I smiled.

"Whooo, don't you think that's a little too far?" Rick asked while frowning.

"Nah, so dig these blues. If Avantae has a show, he ain't going to leave Ceanna alone, so more than likely, Keisha will be with Ceanna. There's a secret stash under the home of Avantae. I used to see his father bag up money and drugs. I'm almost positive that shit is still there, and as far as Keisha, I know that bitch found the money out of one of the secret trap houses. The bitch thought she was so smart!" I yelled, getting pissed off.

"Only if I get half of the take and nobody gets hurt."

"Deal." We shook hands.

"All right, I've got to get out of here. I've got an appointment with the lawyer."

I went to the restroom to clean myself. Placing my hands on the sink, I stared at my face in the mirror. *What the fuck did I just do?* I silently fussed. I thought I had rid myself of homo thoughts. I can't believe I just let this nigga fuck me down. Is it *that* obvious now? Is word *really* on the street that Boog and I used to get down? If so, it all makes sense now why everybody's acting funny toward me. Even my own damn mama looked at me differently.

It's funny how I killed a nigga to set Boog up to keep my secret from getting out on the streets. I felt bad every now and then for my past demons, but, shit, Boog was taking things too far. The nigga was all in love and wanted us to be this happy gay couple. I wasn't with that shit and did what I felt I needed to do.

I had to get out of there, so I hurried out of the restroom and got in my truck. As I was on my way to the lawyer's office, my gas light came on, and my truck began to jerk. "Fuck, come on, not now!" I yelled and pulled over to the side. I am officially a broke nigga. I don't even have ten dollars to my name.

I sat on the side of the road like a jackass for ten minutes. I didn't have too many people to call. I attempted calling Rick, but he didn't answer. Mia Symone didn't have a car, Asia didn't answer, and my mama didn't answer either.

Placing a call to my lawyer, we sat on the phone and discussed how I wanted to handle things. Since Ceanna wanted to avoid me and play hardball, I was about to make her suffer. Not really, but she made things this way between us. You can't just *x* me out like you don't have a piece of me growing in you, and you can't just take my daughter from me.

Even though I am broke now, one thing I'm happy about is the relationship I have with my lawyer. He's been my lawyer for years, and he gets his hands dirty too. I gave him so much bread back in the day that whenever I call, he answers. After I spoke to the lawyer, I called Ceanna.

"Hello." I heard my daughter Jalisa's voice. A huge smile came on my face.

"Hey, baby, it's me, your daddy."

"Hi, Daddy! What you doing?"

"Jalisa, who is that on the phone?" I heard Avantae's ho ass.

"Nigga, don't be calling my wife's phone, bitch-ass nigga!" Avantae yelled.

"What, bitch? That's *my* daughter and wife, little bitch!" I yelled while punching my horn.

"Yeah, ho-ass nigga, we'll see." Avantae hung up.

I punched my horn eight times, causing people passing by to stare at me. I wanted to kill Avantae for stealing pieces out of my life. I was so pissed off and ready for whatever that I locked my truck up and started walking.

"I don't even got money for gas!" I yelled, walking, punching the air.

"That nigga got me fucked up, fam. On my daddy, I'ma kill that nigga."

"Bitch!" I yelled to myself.

"The *fuck* y'all looking at, blood?" I yelled at some kids that were staring at me. One of the little girls started crying. I guess I scared her.

Up ahead was the 37 bus stop. I dug in my pocket and sighed. "At least a nigga got bus fare," I whispered to myself and shook my head.

Chapter Fifteen

Ceanna

My little family and I had been in my new home for three nights now. I smiled while stretching. Avantae was snoring away, so I left him sleeping. It was five o'clock in the morning, and since having Jalisa, I've been getting up early to cook breakfast and get her ready for school. I normally set the alarm for six, but for some reason, I'm wide awake today.

I smiled while roaming the home, stopping by the twins' room. I entered the room, and a sense of peace came over me. I loved the strawberry shortcake theme. Everything was so pretty with vibrant colors.

A host of different shades of pinks and greens covered the room. Even the color of gold was incorporated. I also loved the diamonds and pearls that were included in the decorations.

I sat down in a soft rocking chair that reclined and lay my head back. "Aaaaw, shaaat!" I sang out, impressed that the rocking chair was also a massage chair. I began rubbing on my stomach when one of the twins kicked.

Tears ran down my face, and I began humming one of my favorite songs my mother used to sing. *"With all my heart, I love you, baby. Stay with me, and you will see . . ."* I sang Anita Baker's "Sweet Love" song.

I could hear my mother as clear as day singing that song to me. I missed my mother so much it hurt. She was my best friend. Her death was so tragic. I still remembered the day when I got the terrible news that she died in a horrible car accident. Her car ended up blowing up, so we had a closed casket funeral. The last thing she said to me was she loved me. I only hoped to be the mother to my children that my mother was to me.

I was ashamed, though, because this was probably the first time I've smiled about this pregnancy. I can honestly say my pain is slowly fading, and I'm blessed to have a man who loves me past my flaws, insecurities, and who helps me through the healing process. It feels really good, and I never want to run Avantae away.

"Ceanna, baby, wake up." Startled, I opened my eyes. The chair was so relaxing that I had drifted off to sleep.

"What you doing in here, baby? Did you sleep okay?" Avantae asked.

"I slept so well, but when I awoke I couldn't get back to sleep, so I started roaming the home and ended up here. This room is so peaceful and beautiful, baby," I smiled.

"Yeah, it is, isn't it? It's actually one of my favorite rooms in the house. How you feeling, ma?" Avantae kissed the side of my cheek.

"I'm feeling really good, baby. Today was the first time I've bonded with the babies. I think I've finally let go. I'm sorry for everything I put you through. It was just my pain and insecurities. I want you to know I heard you the other day, and I never want you to feel that I don't trust you, because, honestly, I do. I love you, Avantae," I spoke softly. Avantae sat on the floor in front of me.

"I know, baby. Just know I got you, baby, and you will never be alone. So we haven't talked about baby names yet." He smiled.

"Well, my king, I was thinking about letting you name them." I blushed while taking Avantae's hands and kissing them.

"Wow, Ce, that's an honor, and that means a lot. What about Aariah Nicole Wallace and Aaniah Nichelle Wallace?" he asked excitedly.

"You think you slick, Tae. You probably already had names picked out. Yo' ass came up with that too fast. Aariah and Aaniah . . . I actually like that, Tae."

"Okay, you got me, but me too. Is that okay, though? If not, I mean, we can do an A name for me and a C name for you, like Aariah and Ciara with both the middle names being Nicole," he suggested.

"Nah, I kinda like Aariah and Aaniah. It's different, and Nicole is perfect because that was my mom's middle name," I smiled.

"I know, baby. So are you ready?" Avantae asked in a serious tone.

"Honestly, I'm scared, Tae."

"Of what, ma?"

"I mean, honestly, your music is taking off, and with three kids, I'm going to have to run the boutique from home. I just don't want to lose sight of my dreams or feel overwhelmed. What if you have to travel a lot? You know the seasons are changing, and I normally do the annual plus-size fashion show. I just feel that everything I've worked so hard for is being placed on the back burner. But the real reason I'm scared, Tae, is because I don't want to fail as a mother. I have no clue what I'm doing," I sadly expressed.

"We're in this together, though, and you are the best. I can't wait until you have my seeds because I know to have you as a mother will be a blessing. Motherhood comes naturally. I mean, the way you treat and love Jalisa warms my heart, not to mention how you love me. I was broken until you came into my life, Ce. As far as traveling, you and the kids can always travel with me too. I'll do whatever I have to, baby, to keep your boutique running. Hey, maybe we can even work together. I can perform at the fashion show, baby, and bring in more clients. We can even work on a shoe line and a men's line. Not to mention we can do clothing for children, baby. Ce, baby, you've just got to look at things from a positive angle. I'll never make you do all the work, baby," Avantae sincerely expressed.

I couldn't do anything but smile. Maybe I was being selfish. A part of the reason I didn't want the twins was that my entire life was about to change, but having Avantae by my side made me feel so much better about things.

"So, baby, before I get Jalisa ready for school, I want to run some things by you."

"Shoot, ma."

"Well, I was thinking about keeping Tonya's condo for Jalisa. That way, when she gets older, she'll have her own. Tonya placed the condo in my name in case I wanted to sell it, but I'm going to transfer it to Jalisa's name. I'm also going to keep Tonya's vehicle because it's new. I feel Jalisa can decide what she wants to do with it later. I'll just keep the vehicle in good condition. As far as the shop is concerned, I'm going to ask Keisha to run it. If she says no, I'll keep the building, and if Jalisa decides later to follow in her mother's footsteps, she'll have a location already. Tonya also left me with half a million dollars and her gun. I put the money in a safe for Jalisa at the bank. She can't get the money until she's twenty-one."

"Okayyyyy, that sounds good, baby; but you're telling me this like you won't be around or something," he frowned.

"Baby, life is short, and I might not be around. However, I wanted to let you know so that you'll be informed, baby. Jalisa is set for the rest of her life. I would never touch a dime of the money her mother left, but in case something happens to me, you'll know my wishes for baby girl."

It always bothered me how, we as a people, never had our affairs in order. Death is something that we all will face. Having policies, life insurance, burial insurance, and making sure our children's future is set up should be a priority. Imagine how stressful it is when a loved one passes. Who will raise your children? Do you have anything left behind to ensure their future if you pass? I always found it unfair and selfish to leave the family with the burden of raising your children or trying to bury you. You can't properly grieve, which is why I'm so proud of Tonya. She made sure Jalisa's future was set up, and she knew I would give her child the best. I wanted Avantae to know, just in case anything happens to me. When I have my girls, I will ensure their future as well.

"That's what's up, baby! Speaking of Jalisa, baby, what are we going to do for her birthday?" Avantae asked.

"I don't know yet," I shrugged.

"Ceanna, would you have a problem if I got my son and invited him? I really want to get to know him, and I want you to get to know him too," Avantae expressed with pleading eyes.

"Avantae, I don't have a problem with that at all. However, I'm not dealing with the fuckery from his mother. As long as she stays in her lane, we won't have any issues. All that calling and doing extra shit is a dead issue," I spoke sternly.

"I got you, and every time I get him, I want you to be with me, baby."

"Tuh, you damn right about that. You know I ain't playing that shit or them type of games. Come on, baby, it's time to wake Jalisa."

"I'll cook breakfast," Avantae volunteered.

"Negative, Tae. You play too much and ain't nobody about to eat watermelon or a sandwich," I busted out laughing.

"Girl, you just mad because my watermelon be the shit." He pulled me up from the chair.

I cooked breakfast while Avantae got Jalisa ready for school. Barbara Jean joined us in the kitchen, and we all ate and laughed.

My phone ended up ringing, and it was my doctor's office. The assistant was wondering if I could come in early this morning due to the doctor going out of town next week.

I asked Barbara Jean if she would like to come, and Avantae smiled at me. It would be her first time joining us at an appointment. I'll admit that although she can get on my nerves at times, Avantae's mother has been extremely kind to me. She is always helpful. Sometimes too much, but if I have to be honest, I can say that I had placed a wall up at first.

After everything, I just didn't trust women, and honestly, I was jealous of her and Avantae's relationship. I wanted my mother too, but the blessing of it all is Barbara Jean never treated me like an outsider. She welcomed me with open arms, and I love her for that.

We all piled into the rental car to drop Jalisa off at school. I wasn't about to update our address to the school, because Jalisa loved her school and had many little friends. I think that would be too much to uproot her to a new school so soon after her mother's passing; besides, my little princess is adjusting well.

As soon as we pulled up to the school, the unthinkable happened. Avantae got out of the vehicle and came around to open my door, then Jalisa's door. We were about to walk Jalisa in the school, when Jalisa screamed out, "Tater Bug," while taking off running to a beautiful little chocolate boy.

I knew just by looking at him he was indeed Avantae's son. He was so handsome and tall for his age. He had

Avantae's complexion and his long, wavy hair. I looked at Avantae, and his eyes confirmed what I already knew.

"Avantae!" Tae called out to the little boy. Jalisa and little Avantae came running toward us hand in hand.

"Hi, Mr. Tae! Is it okay if I call you dad? All my friends have dads," he asked innocently, bringing tears to my eyes.

"Come here and give me a hug." Avantae scooped the little boy up.

I frowned, pissed off. I wanted to beat the shit out of Zaria. As Avantae was hugging his son, I looked closely at his appearance. Now I know damn well Avantae gave this bitch a couple of bands twice, so why are this little boy's shoes all dirty? His hair is matted and hasn't been combed. His backpack was dirty, and his clothing had stains on them. *Chill, Ceanna,* I coached myself. Laaawd knows I wanted to snap.

"That's more than okay, and from now on, call me Dad, okay?" Avantae placed his son on the ground.

"I want you to meet someone very special to me. This here is my wife, Ceanna." Avantae rubbed my huge belly.

"Tater Bug, that's my mommy Ce Ce, and she is soooo nice. She loves me, and she reads to me every night before bed," Jalisa bragged.

"Really? Can you be my mommy too? My mommy is mean to me, and I hardly see her anymore," he expressed solemnly.

I wanted to cry. This little boy was so loving. How could you *not* love him? I love him already, and if Avantae wanted to bring him home, I would take him in, no problem. I could see Avantae's jaw muscles flexing. He was pissed. I knew he was just now taking in his son's appearance.

"Hi, baby! May I have a hug?" I asked little Avantae, and he ran into my arms.

"I want you to meet someone else, little man. This right here is your grandma," Avantae pointed to his mother who had just stepped out of the vehicle with a face full of tears. Barbara Jean picked up little Avantae and placed kisses all over him.

"Grandie ma, don't forget about me," Jalisa said, causing us all to laugh.

"Tater Bug, that's my Grandie ma, and she can cook, and she makes me whatever I want, and she the best Grandie ma in the whole wide world," Jalisa sweetly sang while using her hands. The class bell rang and got all of our attention.

"Avantae, who brought you to school?" Avantae asked his son.

"Well, my grandma dropped me off at the corner, and I walked the rest of the way," he said.

"Where is your mother?" Avantae asked, flexing his jaw.

"I don't know. Her don't come home in two nights, Daddy."

"Are you eating, taking a bath, and got clean clothes?"

"No, sir! I eat bread, though."

"Come on; I'll walk you and Jalisa to class. Ceanna, you and Mom wait here. I'll be back, baby." Avantae shook his head. He grabbed Jalisa and little Avantae's hands and walked them to their class.

Barbara Jean and I got into the car, and I became lost in my own thoughts. I was so angry at Zaria. I hated females like her. We've got to do something and fast. I'm going to have a long talk with Avantae. I know he hates the courts and shit, and I do too, but Avantae needs to get his son. Hell, I'm already raising Jalisa; might as well add one more. Besides, that little boy needs his father.

"Ceanna, baby, are you okay? How are you feeling?" Barbara Jean asked.

"Mama, I'm okay. Very uncomfortable but I'll make it." I put on my seat belt.

"I don't mean to pry or overstep, but we're going to have to get my grandson," she expressed.

"Yes, we are, Mama. I was just thinking that." Avantae's mother placed her hand on my shoulder. I grabbed her hand and squeezed it.

"You're heaven-sent, baby, and I'm happy my son is with you," she spoke sweetly. The car door opened and a pissed-off Avantae entered inside.

"Ceanna, man, Zaria been missing two nights straight. Did you see my son's clothing?" He sighed.

"*Shhhhh*, Avantae, we have to get your son. When I pick up Jalisa later and if I don't see Zaria, I'm going to bring him home with us. I've got to go the court next week to get the paperwork process started too." I grabbed his hand.

Avantae stared at me shaking his head while biting his lip. I reached over and touched his face. I knew it was coming. Avantae leaned over and pressed his forehead against mine. Tears flowed from his eyes, and I knew seeing his own flesh and blood like that was tearing him up inside.

Once Avantae composed himself, I smiled and winked. He reached his hand back and squeezed his mother's knee. I passed him some tissue from the glove box. He wiped his face, and then cranked the vehicle and drove to our next destination. *Today is just full of surprises*.

We finally pulled up to my doctor's office, which was on the side of the hospital. I loved how they had everything all in one building. When I have the twins, I can bring them here also for their shots and checkups as well.

I checked in, and we waited in the lobby. After about ten minutes, I excused myself to go use the restroom. I washed my hands and heard this baby hollering at the top of his little lungs. "Whew, that baby got some lungs on him," I said aloud to myself.

I exited the restroom and ran right into Jaceyon. He had the screaming child. My heart dropped as I stood there speechless. *Oh, Lawd, where did he come from?* I silently thought.

"Ceanna, can I please talk to you?" Jaceyon asked in a cordial manner.

"Is that him?" was all I managed to say.

"Yes, this is my son, Ceanna, Jaceyon Jr." Jaceyon lowered his head.

The little baby stopped crying and yawned. He then began sucking on his fist. He opened his little eyes wide and looked right at me. Tears started flowing down my face. He was perfect and had Mia Symone's green eyes.

"Baby, I'm so sorry. If I could take it all back, I would. Please forgive me," Jaceyon cried.

"Jaceyon, I-I-I-I-I gotta go," I stuttered. I wasn't ready for this.

"Ceanna, please talk to me. Let me explain, baby. I never meant for none of this to happen. I'm a mess without you."

"I can't do this with you." I walked away.

"When can I see Jalisa? What about my babies? I have a right to be in their lives. Don't shut me out," he pleaded. The door on the other side of the clinic opened, and my eyes grew wide.

"Ceanna, baby, I was just coming to—" Avantae paused when he saw Jaceyon.

"Nigga, what the fuck are you doing here?" Avantae shouted while walking toward him.

"Tae, come on, baby. He was just leaving." I grabbed Avantae by his arm.

"Come on, Ceanna, and you stay the fuck away from my wife." Avantae pointed at Jaceyon.

Avantae and I went back inside the waiting area. He hadn't said one word about Jaceyon, but I knew this was far from over.

"Ceanna Black!" the nurse shouted. We all stood and headed toward the back.

After seeing the twins, Avantae's demeanor softened. He held on to the 3-D pictures staring at them in amazement. Barbara Jean smiled the entire time while holding my hand. I felt so loved.

"Doc, how is her blood pressure?" Avantae asked the doctor.

"It's actually okay today. I would like that bottom number to be a little lower, but she's doing okay," the doctor replied.

"Do you think the twins are going to come early?" Avantae's mother asked.

"Oh yes, definitely, which is why Ceanna needs to be very careful. You should be taking it easy and stay off your feet as much as possible." The doctor smiled at me.

"Can we still fu—, I mean, can we still get it in?" Avantae asked seriously, and we all busted out laughing.

"Tae, you are a nut, you know that? Wow, you and that thing of yours is going to drive me nuts."

"Well, I see you two are a fun bunch. I would advise Mr. Wallace to be careful. Also please wait six weeks after the babies are born, sir," the doctor laughed.

"Cool, that's all I wanted to know, 'cause, Doc, I got to be up in that thang." Avantae did a little dance.

"Boy, hush." His mother play popped his arm, and we laughed again.

"Ceanna, have you made up your mind yet of where you will be delivering the babies? I know you spoke of a water birth, but if something were to go wrong it would be best to have the babies at the hospital," the doctor spoke seriously.

"Ayo, Doc, do y'all have private suites? We don't want certain people to know where we are or feel like they can just come up to the hospital."

"Sure, that can be arranged."

"Well, my favorite patient, give me a hug. I'll see you both back in two weeks, and remember, Ceanna, if you start to feel too much pressure, see bleeding, your water breaks, or you feel pain, call me personally," the doctor informed her.

As Avantae, his mother, and I walked out of the doctor's office and to the car, I spotted Jaceyon staring in our direction. Panic rose in me because I was unprepared if he tried anything.

I can't believe he sat in his car and waited until my appointment was over. Once I saw Jaceyon's car door open, I alerted Avantae by squeezing his hand.

"Ho-ass nigga, that's my wife. Ceanna, let me see the ultrasound pictures!" Jaceyon shouted coming our way making yet another scene.

"Baby, please, let's just go, Avantae," I pleaded with Avantae, but he wasn't having it.

Avantae let go of my hand and ran toward Jaceyon. The two fought right there on the grounds of the hospital. Barbara Jean and I screamed for the both of them to stop, but the two continued to go at it.

I could hear sirens getting closer, and I guess Avantae heard them too because the next thing I knew, he ran toward us and yelled for his mother and me to get in the car. I did as he said, but my heart went out to Jaceyon and that baby he had in his car.

"Ceanna, are you crying over that ho-ass nigga?" Avantae yelled at me while driving crazy out of the parking lot.

"Nooooo," I cried extremely hard.

"What the fuck are you crying for, ma? You think I'm just going to let that ho-ass nigga disrespect me? I just told that nigga to stay away from you, and he violated." Avantae hit the dashboard.

I didn't say anything else because Avantae would never understand. This rage he has toward Jaceyon is only going to take him away from us. He is not thinking clearly. I feel in my spirit that this is far from over between those two. Someone is going to end up dead, and I can't go through that again.

Chapter Sixteen

Avantae

Seeing Ceanna cry pissed me off. I didn't mean to snap on her the way I did, but I didn't understand why she was over there bawling her eyes out.

I had errands to run, so I dropped her and my mother off at the house. I also needed to clear my head, and I just needed to be alone for a minute.

"Mama, gon' on in the house and let me holla at my wife for a sec."

As soon as my mother safely entered the house, I turned and faced Ceanna. She was so beautiful when she was mad. Her bottom lip was poked out, and her little spoiled ass was looking straight-ahead with her arms crossed.

"Ce."

"Nawl, fuck that, Avantae. I don't know who you think you are, but you gon' stop snapping off on me like that." She stubbornly stared straight-ahead.

"My bad, baby! Look at me." I rubbed her arm trying to hold my laughter. Man, this girl is nuts.

"What, Avantae? Nawl, I don't appreciate that shit," she yelled while rolling her neck.

"I apologize for going off like that. Look, Ce, I know you tied to this nigga, but, baby, I can't promise you that the next time this nigga violate I won't dome him."

"That's the problem, Avantae. I sat there and told you nights ago that when you see me crying, it is not because of Jaceyon. You just don't get it!" she yelled while speaking with her hands.

"Get *what,* Ce?" I asked.

"Avantae, when you got shot, that almost killed me. I thought I lost you. Now that I have you, I have this fear that this rage and hatred you have for Jaceyon is going to take you away from me. I love you too much!" she cried.

I unbelted Ceanna's seat belt and pushed up the armrest. "Baby, come here." Ceanna did as I asked and slid closer to me.

"I ain't going nowhere." I kissed the side of her head.

"Baby, this beef the two of you have going on has got to stop. We have got to be mature for the children. I know you don't want to hear what I'm saying, but it's true. Jalisa is Jaceyon's daughter, and he does have a right to see her and these twins. I know you're uncomfortable with this, and so am I, but it's the right thing to do. What type of woman and mother would I be to keep any child away from their father? I wouldn't do you that way either, Avantae."

"You got to understand; my job is to protect you and my girls. I'm not denying that; he's their sperm donor. What I'm saying is Jaceyon is not to be trusted. This nigga's world has fallen apart. His wife left him, he's broke, the plug isn't supplying him anymore, and he is ass out. A broke nigga is a dangerous nigga. Jaceyon wants you and will do anything to have you, including *murdering* you. He does *not* want to see you happy with me or any other man. It's deeper than what you think. I know him. You also need to understand that just because I'm outta the game and ghost in the streets, niggas think I'm sleeping. They will try me by trying the ones I love."

"I know you're up to something. I know this is far from over with you and Jaceyon. I've said my peace, Avantae, and I'm going to leave it alone. I'm going to head inside. Go ahead and handle what you need to do. Be back here by three so we can get the kids. You don't have too much time left. We need to take Tater Bug shopping too, and I guess we can take the kids to Gatti Land or something. We're also going to have to talk to Zaria about Tater Bug too. I'm sorry, but your son is coming home with us. I don't trust her, and when I have these twins, I owe your baby mama an ass whooping. The only reason I'm being cool is because I'm pregnant, and I promised you I'd do better with my mouth than my fists, but that one right there is going to make me come out of retirement. You better talk to her ass and soon, 'cause you know my communication skills is nonexistent when I have no understanding."

"Tater Bug, huh? I see Jalisa got you calling him that too. I hear what you saying loud and clear. Your ass ain't going to be fighting or shooting, for that matter. I got to watch your little crazy ass." I smiled and exited the vehicle to come around and help Ceanna out of the car.

After I walked her to the door and kissed her one last time, I made my way over to Zaria's. I know I promised Ceanna that whenever I dealt with Zaria, I would bring her or inform her, but this was some shit that didn't concern anyone but my son.

I can't believe Zaria would do our son that way. I mean, what the fuck, yo? I gave this chick more than enough bread, so there was no reason for my son to be dirty or hungry. That shit ain't sitting well with me. I needed answers now.

When I arrived at Zaria's mother's place, the house was dirty as fuck. Dirty clothes, old food, and dishes everywhere.

"Where is Zaria, Mary?" I yelled while I looked around the dirty apartment in disgust.

"Her sorry ass just walked in about an hour ago. She back there in the back. You need to get yo' son. This ain't a fucking day care center, nigga." Mary puffed on her cigarette.

"Bet." I made my way to Zaria's room.

Zaria attempted to play asleep. She was naked with her legs spread open. That shit pissed me off.

"Zaria, wake the fuck up," I yelled. She rolled over on her stomach, giving me a view of her ass. *Pfffff! Pffff! Pffff!* She jumped. I was so heated I shot through the roof three times. The next time will be her.

"Do I have your motherfucking attention now, ho? Get the fuck up and get dressed. I'm taking my son home with me when he gets out of school. You got me fucked up. Look at this fucking room, yo. Dirty muthafukka!" I began kicking clothing and trash around the room.

"You fucking disgust me. What the fuck is this shit?" I lost it when I saw a small bag of white powder and pills.

"Nooooo, give it here!" She leaped off the bed.

"You fucking junkie, bitch. Is *this* the reason my son looks like shit? The nigga had on dirty clothes and shit. What the fuck did you do with those two bands I gave you, Zaria, huh?" I poured the bag of white powder out.

"Gimme my shit." *Whap!* She slapped me.

"Bitch, are you fucking crazy? You gonna fuck around come up missing fucking with me!" I growled angrily while choking her.

I almost choked the shit out of Zaria. I had to get out of there. I made up my mind right then and there that little Avantae was coming home with us. I didn't take anything from there. I'll buy my son everything new.

Once I left from Zaria's, I jumped back into my whip and made my way over to my old home. I had a secret stash spot that my pops built under the house. He had gotten the idea to do that one day when we were watching the movie *Training Day* with Denzel Washington.

Under the house, I had two million dollars in cold cash, over sixty guns, bullets, and even bombs. If a street war ever came my way, I was always prepared. This was just one of my stash spots, but honestly speaking, even though Ceanna hasn't said anything and she is humble, I know this ain't shit compared to what Calvin left her.

I grabbed a mil five and placed the money in some duffel bags along with some guns and bullets. I was going to move that to the new home.

After I straightened up a bit, I set the trigger wire up. If a nigga ever tried to rob me and stepped in a certain spot, it would be lights out for that nigga. I grabbed the three duffle bags and made my way over to Keisha's house. I had texted her earlier this morning to let her know I was coming through and needed to holler at her about some shit.

"Pause! What's all of that?" She pointed at the three duffel bags I placed on her floor.

"Shit my cash, some bombs, and guns. I couldn't leave that shit in the car."

"Nawl, bring that shit over here and place it behind this secret wall. You know how shit goes."

I smiled because Keisha was street smarts. Donte taught her well. If the laws were to kick in the door, they wouldn't be able to trace shit.

"Nigga, I know your ass is hungry too, so here." She placed a plate of chicken Alfredo, Caesar salad, and three pieces of cheese garlic bread on the table.

"My nigga! That's what's up, fam." I smiled and began digging in.

"What's up, Tae? What brings you by?" Keisha asked as she sipped on her drink.

I ate another bite of my garlic cheese bread and sat back for a minute. I took in the home and smiled. It was very cozy and peaceful. I see why my nigga WyKeith was digging Keisha.

Keisha is good peoples. It's a shame Donte dogged her all those years. In her eyes, you can see a broken woman who was now coming into her own. I respect Keisha because she is a real woman and friend. I hate how Zylan passed away. I know that shit still eats at her every day.

"Key, first, I just wanna say thank you for being a good friend to Ceanna. That shit is so rare these days." I sipped on my drink.

"On some real shit, I don't know what I'd do without Ceanna. She has been there for me in ways I can't even explain. I hate that so many people have betrayed her in some way or another. I'm happy she has you, Tae. So thank you for loving my girl beyond her pain. You make her happy, and I see her tears fading. She smiles because of you, and that confidence that was broken is now back. She's stronger than ever," Keisha smiled.

"You deserve that too, Key. So what's up with you and WyKeith?" I asked.

"Damn, Avantae, yo' ass is nosy as hell. If you must know, though, I'm feeling him a lot, but I don't want to hurt Asia. I'm not really comfortable, and Asia wants to be this proud upstanding, in the front; let everybody know we're a lesbian couple, but that ain't me. I mean, don't get me wrong. I love Asia as a friend but not like that. I was lost and hurt when she expressed her feelings, and I needed anything or anyone to help ease the pain. I know that's selfish, but Asia has helped me heal in many ways, and I'll forever be grateful to her for her friendship through that storm. I just can't do it anymore, but I don't want to hurt her either," she expressed.

"Well, have you tried just talking to her and letting her know how you feel?" I asked.

"I have tried. She is low-key unstable, and I'm starting to see that now. She is crazy and superjealous. I feel like I'm in another relationship like the one I had with Donte without the physical scares and hoes. WyKeith, on the other hand, is for me, I believe. I'm digging him so much, his style and his peace mentality."

"So you're Jill Scott now?" I busted out laughing.

"Shut up, Tae." Keisha play hit me. "Anyway, big head, what did you need to holler at me about?" she asked.

"I need you to do a couple of favors for me. It's for Ceanna, but you know with her nosy ass, I can't get shit by her, and it's a surprise."

"Sure, Tae, anything for my girl."

"Well, for one, next Saturday, I need you to stay over at the house with her. I have a show in Dallas. I'll leave y'all funds to shop and do whatever it is y'all females do. But the real favor I need is the baby shower."

"Yeeees, I can't wait. I got all these ideas already, and I know the perfect spot too. What are the names? Oh, I'm soooo excited," she smiled.

"We're naming them Aaniah Nichelle and Aariah Nicole Wallace."

"That's so pretty, and the Nicole for her mother. That just makes my heart melt."

"Appreciate it! So what about the Saturday after next, or the Saturday after that? Is that enough time and will fifty grand be enough?" I asked.

"Fifty grand is way too much money."

"Well, use whatever for the baby shower and keep the rest for yourself as a thank-you gift. I'ma present Ceanna with a custom van I'm having made. I know she still has her Tahoe her dad gave her, but she'll also have this one too. On the day of the shower, I'm going to have it delivered to her." I smiled, thinking of ways to surprise her.

"Ceanna is going to be so happy. Wait, though, not to change the topic, but how are things with your son? How are Ceanna and your son adjusting?"

"Actually, Key, I feel like a dumb ass. I literally could have lost her behind not being one hundred when I found out. I chose for her and didn't want to tell her for fear of how she would react, but when I tell you how my son just latched on to Ceanna earlier . . ." I smiled.

"Who wouldn't latch on to Ceanna? That's what I love about her, though. She is so loving."

"What amazed me the most was when Ceanna told me my son was coming home with us after she saw his appearance. Man, Zaria ain't feeding him, and he was dirty. I almost killed her earlier, Keisha." I shook my head.

"Damn, Tae, that's fucked up because I know damn well you gave her ass some ends for him." She frowned.

"Yes, but she's a junkie now. You should have seen her room, yo, but, aye, baby girl, I gotta run and go get Ceanna. We got to pick up the kids. You good, though? Do you need anything?" I rose from the table and gave Keisha a hug.

"No, you've done so much for me already. I am so thankful and thank you for stepping up and checking on me when Zylan passed. That truly touched my heart, and your mother will always be my guardian angel," she smiled.

"Anytime and just talk to Asia. I know WyKeith is feeling you too." I walked to the secret wall.

"Here's fifty grand for the baby shower. Oh, and don't forget to invite Vera from the jail too; that was Ceanna's mother's friend."

"Sure, Tae! It's going to be beautiful. You got a theme, or you want me to just do something with purple since that's her favorite color?"

"Yeah, that sounds good."

"All right, bye, Tae, and thank you again." Keisha hugged me, and I exited the house.

It was going on 2:15 p.m., and I rushed home to get my woman. She was already standing on the porch when I pulled up. Ceanna was always on time and ready. I loved that about her.

"Hey, baby, where's Mom at?" I greeted Ceanna with a kiss once she sat in the car.

"She's lying down. I set the alarm for her. She's not feeling too well. Maybe later we can stop and get her some soup and orange juice," she suggested.

"Damn, babe, that worries me. I just don't want—" I began when Ceanna grabbed my hand.

"Don't do that, baby. She'll be fine. Have faith," Ceanna smiled.

"Faith." I smiled and pulled out of the driveway. For the first time in my life, my head was clear, and I was at peace.

Chapter Seventeen

Zaria

Avantae put his hands on me for the last time. But that's okay! He can go ahead and take little Tater Bug. Let Ceanna's wide ass watch our son, because next weekend, I got something for Avantae's ass.

Once Avantae left, I washed up and got up for the day. I looked at the clock, and although I should have been on my way to get my son from school, I linked up with Kwency to go shopping for our Dallas trip. I knew Avantae wasn't playing when he said he'll take my son, but this nigga was *not* about to mess up my food stamps, child tax credit, or housing list.

My room was a complete mess, and I was embarrassed that Avantae saw it looking that way. I've always been a neat freak, but as of lately, getting high had been my only motivation. Ever since Kwency introduced me to coke and X-pills, I've been hooked. I really need to get it together, and truthfully, I need to be searching and looking for a new job.

Finally, I received a text from Kwency letting me know that she was outside the gate parked on the street. She refused to drive into these ghetto-ass projects. I didn't blame her, though.

I grabbed the fake Coach purse that I had purchased from Citi Trends and checked my appearance one last time. Then I walked to the front door and rolled my eyes at my mother.

"You've been here too fucking long. When you getting out?" she asked in a bitter tone.

"Soon," was all I managed to say. I was so sick of this bitch riding me. Damn, it ain't like she wins the mother-of-the-year award.

"Well, you need to hurry up. This wasn't the arrangement, nor was it the arrangement for me to wake and take your son to school."

I stared at her briefly. A piece of me wanted to respond to what she had just said, but sadness is the only thing that came over me. A hug sometimes would do, but for as long as I could remember, my mother hated me. I'm a product of rape.

In these very projects I was raised in, she became a victim. Instead of aborting me or giving me away, she kept me. She used to do all she could to break me.

My love for Avantae was deep because at a time when I had nothing, he was my something. Avantae kept money in my pocket and food in my belly. He taught me how to drive, how to care for myself, how to be a lady, how to shoot and recognize game. He was my sanity to my insane world, my protector from my unstable environment, and my love when I had no self-love or -worth. It was always supposed to be Avantae and me against the world. I'm hurting without him, and seeing him with Ceanna tortured my soul.

"I lost my job, and I'm planning to get another one. We shouldn't be here too much longer." I turned to leave.

"Bitch," I heard my mother say loudly.

I fought back the tears and made my way through the crowd of aggressive men. A couple of gropes and disrespectful name-calling lasted all the way until I made it out the front gate. I hated living here, and honestly, my son and I were better than this.

"Hey, bish," I greeted Kwency getting into her car.

"You okay?" she asked.

"Nah, Avantae is threatening to take my son. He even showed up earlier and put his hands on me. Look at my neck." I showed Kwency the red marks.

"That's all right, bitch, 'cause we got something for that nigga. You should file charges on him and put a restraining order on him. That way, if he does try to take Tater Bug, it won't be so easy."

"Nawl, that's a little too far, and Avantae will kill my ass for sure."

"Bitch, I'm saying, though, until this music shit for you pop off, you're going to be broke and miserable. Don't let Avantae and Ceanna live all lavish while you struggling and rocking knockoff shit. I'm just saying, boo. Oh, and, bitch, you need to slow down. You starting to like that powder shit a little too much. It's supposed to be for fun, not a habit," Kwency shrugged.

I wanted to argue with her, but she was right. Damn, is it that obvious? I ain't going to lie. I have been liking the powder a little more than I should, but I don't consider myself a junkie, though. It just gives me a rush I can't explain.

"Wait, Kwency, before we go shopping, run me by the school real quick so I can see my son. He should be getting out."

We drove up to the school, and Kwency parked in the parking lot. A number of cars lined up behind one another, as each vehicle waited for their child. The way we were parked gave me a full view of the front doors of the school.

I spotted my Tater Bug and Jalisa laughing and holding hands. I was about to hop out of the car and call out to him when he and Jalisa ran full speed ahead down the long sidewalk.

"Look, Tater Bug, there goes Mommy Ce. Come on, Tater Bug, you're coming home with us, and wait until you see your room!" Jalisa screamed, running toward an SUV. He followed while smiling and asking her about his room.

I swear the wind was knocked out of me. My blood began to boil when I spotted Ceanna. My son went right into her arms, and she smiled while kissing him on the cheek. Tears ran down my face. Ceanna had me fucked up. Now she's trying to turn my own son against me. I started to jump out of the car when Kwency grabbed my arm. Ceanna couldn't see us from where we were parked, and Kwency's windows were tinted.

"Don't do it. At least you know where your son is, and he'll be taken care of. You know yo' mama ain't going to watch him or feed him."

She was right.

After Kwency and I went shopping, we headed back over to her place. I was thankful for her allowing me to crash there until I got myself together. I sat on her lavish sofa and ran my hand over it. The material felt so good.

"What you over here thinking about?" Kwency asked, handing me a glass of wine.

"I was thinking about what you said earlier."

"Which part, 'cause you know a bitch be on it, and I say a lot of shit, hunny," she laughed.

"The part about filing a police report on him," I shrugged.

"Oh, bitch, hold on." Kwency jumped up and ran to her bedroom.

I sat there wondering what she was up to. She always had something up her sleeve. She came back into the living room with her phone and a bag of makeup.

"This is what you call 'My baby daddy beat my ass so bad' makeup kit. Stand up real quick."

"Okay, let me see. Hmmm." She placed her index finger to her temple while she tapped her right foot.

"Oh, I got it," she excitedly announced while pulling out a black makeup pencil and purple, blue, and red lipstick.

For the next hour, Kwency did bruising makeup, cut up my shirt, and made me look as though I was severely attacked. When she was all done, I looked in the mirror in amazement. She was really good at this.

Kwency began to take several photos of me posing in different ways. I was tired, to say the least, and a bit worried about all of this. Truthfully, I just wanted my family back, but the way Avantae had been treating me, I know I have no chance to be with him again.

"Listen, Zaria, I know this is something you may not want to do, but you have to. I mean, you can't just allow Avantae to put his hands on you like that. On top of that, why are you struggling the way you are while Ceanna has it all with your baby daddy? This bitch is paid, and have you seen her boutique? Oh my God, it's nothing but class. If I were a big bitch, hunny, I would be on fleek. She's got some shit in there. Meanwhile, your ass is a part of the struggle. Uh-uh, hunny, couldn't be me," Kwency said as she belittled me.

"Can you send the pictures to my phone please?" I asked.

She was right, but damn, did she always have to put it in my face? I couldn't take any more, so I called it an early night and went to take a shower.

In bed, I tossed and turned thinking about my son and Avantae. I couldn't take it anymore.

Jumping out of bed, I grabbed my phone that was on the computer desk. I sat on a nearby sofa and began scrolling my contacts.

I landed on Detective Rick's contact information and placed a call to him. He's the detective that had been investigating Samuel's death. He also had this hard-on for Avantae.

After speaking to Detective Rick awhile back, I learned that he had been watching Avantae for years to bring a case against him. However, he could never find anything on him. So when he learned of Barbara Jean being Avantae's mother, along with the little piece of information I gave him about Barbara Jean stealing insulin out of the med supply closet, his interest began to pique.

I informed him of the fake bruises and sent him pictures. I also told him about Avantae having my son. He thanked me, expressed his concern for me, and told me not to worry.

Once I got off the phone, I thought I would have been feeling happy, but the truth is, this shit is going to get really ugly—and fast.

"Oh my God! What have I've done?" I whispered to myself.

Panic began to rise in me once I thought about the things that may . . . or may not happen. I wasn't thinking smart for sure, and when everything hits the fan, I know I won't be the last man standing. I'm liable to be thrown to the crocs for supper. Avantae is a savage, and I know for sure messing with his mother, Ceanna, or even my son is going to wake up a sleeping beast in him.

"I don't know why I allowed Kwency to talk me into this shit," I fussed.

Chapter Eighteen

Avantae

"Daddy, Daddy Tae! Wake up, wake up, wake up!" Jalisa and Tater Bug yelled while they jumped up and down on the bed.

"Mommy Ce said to come wake you up, and if not, you're going to be in *biiiig* trouble," Jalisa sang.

"Okay, here I come," I groaned.

"Nope, we were given instructions not to leave until you're up. Don't shoot the messenger," Jalisa said with her hand on her hip.

"Huh?" I looked at her confused and laughed.

"Maaaan, hell, nawl, I ain't going have you being a mini-Ceanna." I grabbed Jalisa and started tickling her.

"Beat him up, Tater Bug! Get him!" Jalisa laughed.

"Oh, you want some too?" I played boxed my son, and he laughed.

"Hey, guys!" Ceanna and my mother yelled at the same time.

"Coming," the kids and I laughed.

"Okay, Daddy, you got to close your eyes."

I did as Jalisa asked and the kids grabbed each one of my hands. "Okay, Daddy, open your eyes!" Tater Bug yelled excitedly.

"Surprise!" they all sang in unison.

Ceanna and my mother had a beautiful cake with candles lit. I smiled and bit down on my lip. I didn't even remember the last time a nigga had a cake. I had to have been a small youngster. I low-key forgot today was my birthday.

"Make a wish, baby," Ceanna smiled.

I looked around at all four of their beautiful faces, and my wish was already complete. My mother is here, and Ceanna finally gave me a chance. Not only that, I have two of the smartest kids on the planet.

"My wish has already been granted." A lonely tear slide down my left cheek.

"Can I blow out the candles? Please!" Jalisa asked.

"Me too," Tater Bug smiled.

"Y'all can blow them out with me. Ready . . . 1, 2, 3." *Whew* the three of us blew.

"Morning breath cake!" Jalisa yelled, causing us all to holler in laughter. Balloons were spread throughout the living room, and the kids went wild throwing them and playing.

"Devin, go freshen up, aye. I'm going to cook your favorite," my mother smiled.

"Ma, are you sure? I can cook," Ceanna asked.

"No, baby, you need to stay off your feet. They are already swelling, baby. Go ahead and tend to my son. I see it in his eyes. Seems like you're readyyyyy," she sang, and we laughed as she shook her head.

Ceanna and I wasted no time. I was horny and needed to feel my baby. It was going to be a long weekend without her. Truthfully, I was dreading this performance in Dallas and leaving her.

I tried to dig Ceanna's guts out. I don't know if it's the pregnancy or what, but I can't get enough of her. *"Whew!"* I smiled, coming out of the shower with a towel wrapped around my waist.

Wham! I hit Ceanna's ass hard. Her ass started moving like a big-ass wave. Ceanna got that oooweeeemane. "Ouch, shit! I done told your crazy ass about that."

"Ass is so big, girl." We laughed.

I was about to try to go another round before I saw little hands sliding under the door and banging on the door.

"Are y'all done? Come on!" the kids yelled on the other side of the door.

Ceanna and I looked at each other and shook our heads. I guess I now know what to expect when these twins get here.

My T-lady prepared a feast for a king. She cooked bacon, eggs, potatoes, pancakes, and sausage patties. We all dug in, and I was amazed at Tater Bug's appetite. His little ass can eat, and Jalisa was right behind him.

"Daddy, can we go play laser tag later?" Tater Bug asked.

"Yeah, little man, sure. You good, though, little man?" I asked. His happiness was all I cared about.

"Yes, I'm good, and thank you, Daddy. You, Mommy Ceanna, Grandma, and my sister Jalisa treat me so nice. I love it here." He blushed.

Out of the corner of my eye, I could see my mother shedding tears. Ceanna grabbed her hand and lightly squeezed it, while Jalisa smiled and swung her legs.

"I told you, Tater Bug, these are my people here."

"Huh?" Ceanna laughed.

"Little man, I am your father, and you don't ever have to thank me. I love you, son, and I'm sorry it has taken five years for us to meet. I missed a lot, but, Avantae, I promise to be there for you here on out. You're my son, and when I'm gone, you are the man of this house. Always protect your sister and never let anything happen to her. Always respect Ceanna and your grandmother. We love you, son." I choked back emotions.

"I love you too, Daddy." Little Avantae hugged each one of us.

After breakfast, we all gathered inside the rental and headed to the San Marcos outlet. I wanted to buy Tater Bug and myself some shoes and hats. I also needed a fit for this weekend, but the real reason I went there was to check on the progress of the ring I had custom made for Ceanna.

We shopped most of the day and then took the kids to play laser tag. I was tired as fuck. Jalisa and Tater Bug wore me out. I let them continue to play and tapped out. I saw Ceanna and my mother laughing and talking and went to join them.

"I see those two wore you out," Ceanna laughed.

"Hell, yeah! A nigga is tired. Jalisa's ass kept killing me off."

"Have you guys thought about maybe having her birthday party here?" my mother asked.

"That wouldn't be a bad idea, baby," Ceanna agreed.

"Cool, then, let's do it. Y'all ready to get out of here? I still have to pack for tomorrow, and I'm hungry as hell." I rubbed my belly.

"Tae, you're *always* hungry. Yeah, let's get out of here. I got a taste for fried pickles," Ceanna laughed.

Chapter Nineteen

Zaria

Kwency decided that we would head to Dallas a day early. I was game, and besides, it's not like I had anything else to do. Low key, I missed my son, and I had regrets that I called that detective. I couldn't let Kwency down, though.

There was something about Kwency that made me want to put on all the time. I was drawn to her and found myself trying to get her approval most of the time. I was acting other than myself, but I was enjoying the ride and rush I felt at the same time.

The ride to Dallas was a smooth ride. The three-hour drive kind of tired me, but I knew we didn't have time to relax.

Kwency checked us in our rooms, and I smiled when she handed me the second key card to Avantae's room. We made our way to our rooms, and the setup was really nice. Kwency checked out her own room, and then she came over to my room ten minutes later.

"Bitch, what I tell you? Don't worry about shit when you with me. Oh, and here you go." Kwency passed me a bag of roofies while she entered my room.

The thought of Avantae's big, long, juicy-ass dick excited me. To make matters even better, I'm ovulating, and who knows, I might have another little Tater Bug by my baby daddy.

"You told me, and what about you and Semaj?" I asked.

"Oh, there's plenty of time to get him. Right now, I'm focused on Avantae. I can't stand his ass." She smacked her gum.

The rest of the day Kwency and I shopped and were pampered. I felt so alive and beautiful again. The beautician hooked my hair up, and my face is so beat.

We settled in the rest of the night, and I enjoyed a nice hot bubble bath. I was in heaven and wished I could live like this more often.

The next morning, Kwency and I went out to breakfast, and then we went to Medieval Times. I loved things like this. I wish my little Tater Bug was with me. I used to be able to afford to take him to places like that.

As the show came to an end, Kwency got word that Semaj and Avantae were in town and had just checked into their rooms. I couldn't wait until Avantae saw my face.

When we made it back to the hotel, I showered and got cute for tonight's performance. Just as I applied my lip gloss, Kwency knocked on my door.

"Bitch, you ready? The guys are downstairs in the front lobby waiting on us. Wait until Avantae sees your pretty little ass," she laughed.

"I'm ready! Wait, am I getting paid to perform tonight 'cause you know a bish need ends?"

"Yes, you are. Now come on, let's go," Kwency stated.

As the elevator doors opened, a wave of nerves hit me. I could see Semaj and Avantae by the bar nursing a drink. Semaj was the first to spot us. He walked toward us smiling.

"Ayo, Avantae, this is Tasha, the girl I was telling you about. She's the one that I had sing the hook to the new song," Semaj smiled.

"Tasha? Her name ain't Tasha, fam. This is Zaria, the chick I was telling you about." Avantae held a cold, hostile tone while he pointed his finger at me.

"Zaria?" Semaj and Kwency asked at the same time.

"Hey, baby daddy. You ready to make this money tonight?" I busted out laughing.

Semaj stood there with a perplexed look on his face. He didn't know what to think, and truthfully, he really didn't know what was going on. Every time he tried to get us together for rehearsal, I would always make an excuse. I was actually surprised Semaj still wanted Avantae to introduce the new song. Either way, I wasn't going to pass up a weekend to be with Avantae. I didn't care if we performed the song or not. His single was hot with or without the new song.

"Aye, fam, I swear I ain't on no fuck shit. You know I would never disrespect you or my sis, Ceanna. I've been working with this chick for a minute, and she told me her name was Tasha. I can't believe this shit," Semaj spoke with his hands.

"Aye, check this out, Kwency. If I find out you had something to do with this entire little setup, I promise you, you're fired!" he yelled at Kwency.

"Whatever, Semaj, and for the record, I know her as Tasha too."

"Look, Avantae, we can just call this shit a rap and head back home if you want," Semaj suggested.

"Nawl, fam! I'm doing this shit for my family. I ain't turning down ten grand. Besides I have a son to raise now."

"Ayo, Zaria, check this shit out. I don't know what you're on, but I have already warned you," Avantae glared with low dark eyes.

"Come on, then, let's just do this show and get the fuck outta here." Semaj walked away shaking his head.

Kwency and I followed behind Semaj and Avantae and sat at the back of the rental van. She finally caught on to why I had told her my name was Tasha to begin with. "Clever bitch!" she whispered to me.

The ride over to the venue was extremely quiet. Kwency silently tapped me on my leg, and I saw where she had opened a bottle of Patrón liquor. That was Avantae's favorite. I smiled as I watched her secretly put the drugs in the drink. When she was done, she gently shook the bottle and placed it back on the floor.

Inside, I was screaming for joy. This girl *always* had my back. Even though she had given me pills earlier, I kept wondering when I would have the perfect opportunity to use them.

The venue was superpacked. We were supposed to do a sound check, but due to the timing and technical difficulties, we couldn't.

Semaj went on the stage to introduce Avantae, and the crowd went crazy. Avantae walked past me and mugged me. I watched as he took his place on the stage.

The audience went wild, and they knew all the lyrics to his song. Seeing Avantae on stage made me so wet. I couldn't wait to fuck him later. Once he was done with the single, Semaj went back on the stage to introduce his next single.

"Oooh, bitch are you ready?" Kwency asked excitedly while jumping up and down.

"Hell, yeah, I'm about to kill this shit," I replied cockily.

"All right, all right, all right, Dallas, I got something for y'all. Now, this little shorty right here can sing her ass off. Tasha, hit them with something, girl," Semaj excitedly yelled.

"*Oooh aaaah a haaaa oooh,*" I sang in a high Mariah Carey pitch voice. I was still standing backstage.

"What I tell y'all?" Semaj boasted.

"Ayo, check it, so here's how we about to do this joint. My man Avantae has a new little joint for y'all, and Tasha's going to sing the hook. Since this is Texas and we known for doing some throwed off shit, I'ma have them free style this for y'all. I want y'all to give Tasha a warm welcome. So when I say Tasha, y'all say come out. Y'all got that? Let me here y'all say 'heeell, yeah,'" Semaj hyped the crowd.

"Heeell, yeaaaah!" the crowd mocked.

"Tasha!"

"Come out!"

"Tasha!"

"Come out!"

"DJ, drop the fucking beat!"

"*Aaaah ohh ohhh ohhhh oooooo yeah aaaa,*" I sang coming on the stage.

The audience went wild. Whistles from the thirsty men could be heard, and I zoned out. Avantae looked at me shocked. He hadn't heard my vocal skills in years. He rapped his part, and I did sexy groove dances as I worked the stage left to right. The beat from Fat Pat's *Ghetto Dreams* was used, and the crowd was feeling the new song.

When the song ended, I looked over at Avantae and smiled. We told the audience thank you, collected our money, and left the club.

Just as Kwency suspected, Semaj stopped by a gas station and bought 20-oz white foam cups and a bag of ice.

It was so late at night that we stopped by Jack in the Box and grabbed us something to eat. The drive-through line was so long that Semaj asked Kwency to pour him a cup of Crown Royal Apple and Avantae a cup of Patrón. My insides began to stir when I saw Avantae down the cup of Patrón. I tapped Kwency on the leg and smiled.

Our food was finally ready, and Avantae was now on cup two. By the time we pulled up to the hotel, he was good and sleepy.

"Wake up, boiiiiii, we're here, fam. I know your ass ain't tapped out already, my nigga," Semaj joked, shaking Avantae.

"Got damn, fam. This Patrón got me tripping. A nigga can barely focus. I'm fucked up, fam." Avantae lay his head back.

"Ayo, Kwency, help me get this drunk-ass nigga to his room." Semaj laughed.

"Damn, boi, you're heavy." Semaj talked shit while he and Kwency both helped assist Avantae to his room.

I walked behind them and pretended to go to my room. I waited for the knock from Kwency that let me know that it was time.

"Bitch, Avantae is fucked up," Kwency beamed with joy.

I covered my body with a robe that had nothing on underneath. Kwency and I opened Avantae's door and heard him moaning. He tried to sit up to see who was coming through his door, but the roofies had his mind in another world.

"Get oouut, Za Za Zariaaa!" he slurred his words.

"Hey, baby daddy. Are you ready to give me this dick now?"

"Geet oouut." Avantae tried to fight while moaning in discomfort.

I looked over at Kwency, and she began recording. I unzipped his pants and pulled his long tool out through the slit of his boxers. Avantae tried to fight, but the drugs ended up relaxing him. He ended up falling into a deep sleep, but his dick was brick hard.

I began slurping on Avantae's manhood. It tasted so good and brought me back flashbacks. I couldn't hold it any longer, so I slowly sat down on it and began grinding my hips.

"Damn, bitch, you look so fucking sexy," Kwency said in a low, mellow voice. I began giving her a show, bouncing harder on Avantae's dick while moaning loudly.

"I'm about to coooome uuuum, Avantae!" I screamed out.

I felt his dick swelling and pulsating inside of me. I tightened my muscles around his width and went into overdrive. I hadn't had dick this good in years. Once I was done, I rolled off of him and lay next to him.

"Say hi to the camera," Kwency laughed while getting a close-up.

"Hi, Ceanna, bitch, I told you this was my dick. I guess Avantae didn't tell you that I was coming along with him to Dallas. His dick was so good. Oh, and thank you for watching my son. Tell him his mama and daddy loves him." I placed Avantae's dick into my mouth and sucked it so Ceanna could see it.

"Oh, bitch, you is something else. I'm going to send this to Ceanna's phone right now. Don't worry, this is a throwaway phone, so she can't track it," Kwency confirmed. We chatted another twenty minutes before Kwency left and went to her room. I stayed lying next to Avantae. This is the way it's supposed to be.

Him and me.

Chapter Twenty

Ceanna

"Baby, I'll be back early in the morning. I love you," Avantae spoke on the phone.

"Boy, bye, I'll be okay. Keisha, Janair, and Asia are on the way over, and the kids are outside playing in the yard. Your mom is watching them. You just focus on your performance tonight, baby, and I'll hold everything down here." Avantae had only been gone three hours, and this was the fourth time he had called.

"How is little Avantae adjusting, baby?" he asked.

"Baby, he's fine. He and Jalisa are having the time of their lives, and, baby, I really do enjoy your son. He is so helpful and sweet," I stated sincerely.

"That means the world to me. Thank you for accepting my son, baby. I swear that only makes my love for you deeper."

"Baby, I ain't going to lie. At first, I didn't think I could handle this, but after seeing him like that, my heart wouldn't let me hold any ill will toward him. He is innocent, and I had to realize that this situation was news to you too. It's not like you cheated on me or knew you had a son all this time. In the beginning, I was angry with you for not telling me initially when you found out, but we're past that now. Your son is welcome here, and I will never mistreat him, Avantae. Besides, I can't ask for what I'm not willing to give. You treat Jalisa and these twin girls as if they were your own. You love me past my flaws and all, so I would be less of a woman if I couldn't open my heart toward your son and love you past your flaws too."

"You just focus on getting that divorce, Ceanna. I wanna marry your little pretty ass now," Avantae said in a serious tone.

"Trust and believe, baby, I am. Now enough of that; have fun, and I'll see you tomorrow, baby. I love you, Tae!"

"I love you too, baby!"

I looked out toward the yard and smiled. I couldn't see how Zaria could mistreat this little boy. He was so beautiful and reminded me so much of his father. I opened the back door and joined Barbara Jean on the patio.

"Hey, baby!" his mother greeted me.

"Hey, Ma! How are you feeling?" I asked.

I learned that Barbara Jean was infected with HIV through a violent rape years ago. We didn't speak of it or mention it unless she brought it up, but lately, she can't seem to shake this cough she had. I was really worried about her. I didn't know what I would do if I lost her.

"I'm feeling okay. The doctor told me my T-cells were a little lower and gave me another medication. This new medication has me tired more, and the meds don't sit too well with my stomach at times."

"Is there anything I can do?" I asked.

"Oh, baby, you do enough, Ceanna. You're a blessing, baby. I know that I can be a bit much, Ceanna, and I don't ever want to overstep my boundaries, baby. This is your home, and you're the woman of this home. I thank you for putting up with me and welcoming me the way you have. I see the way my son loves you, and it makes me proud to know that he has someone who loves him," she smiled.

"I do love Avantae so much. Can I ask you something?" I said, turning to face her.

"Sure, baby."

"I feel so convicted at times. Do you think our relationship is wrong? I'm trying to get a divorce, but Jaceyon won't sign the papers. He's really making things difficult for me. Sometimes I get scared because I know this isn't fair to Avantae either. He wants to marry me, and he speaks of children all the time," I expressed with a worried look on my face.

"Did Avantae ever tell you what happened in the past? I'm asking because I need to share something with you, and then it will lead me to answering your question," she said.

"Yes and no. I mean, he told me you were on drugs, and he and his father moved here, and his father married Gina, but that's about it."

"Well, he might get upset, but this is something you should know. Years ago, my son and I were home alone. His father was a big-time drug dealer. He moved us to the outside of Houston thinking we would be safe. He was wrong, Ceanna. While his father was out there in the streets fucking down hoes, Avantae and me were held at gunpoint. Three men busted in our home looking for money and drugs. I guess they didn't find what they were looking for, and they decided to take it out on me. Avantae had to watch as three men beat and brutally raped me. His little eyes had to witness shit no child should have to. I was later diagnosed with HIV, and my husband made me terminate a pregnancy. I fell into depression and began shooting heroin. Then my husband left me and took my son with him. I told you all of that to say this: When my son looks at you, Ceanna, I no longer see a broken little boy. You are his joy and light. Everything, baby, will work out the way it's supposed to.

You and Avantae came in each other's lives for a reason," she said as tears ran down her face.

I held her hand and cried with her. I never knew she had to endure so much pain. This is the reason I wanted Avantae out of the game. When niggas can't get at you, they go after your children and wife. I knew Jaceyon dabbled in the streets, but he wasn't on the level Avantae was. Avantae was pushing that real weight, and the type of money he made would only bring him enemies, death, or prison. I couldn't have that.

"Mommy Ce and Grandie ma, look at Tater Bug do his flips!" Jalisa yelled out in excitement.

We looked on in amazement as Avantae flipped backward six times, did a cartwheel three times, and then a headstand. Barbara Jean and I looked at each other and began clapping. Avantae smiled, and I could tell that he was really enjoying himself.

"Mama, I'm going to go ahead and get dinner started. The girls should be here later." I stood.

"Okay, and, baby, I'm going to take the kids to Dave and Busters and a movie in a little bit. That will give you and your girls some time to unwind and catch up," she winked.

"Ma, that's okay, really. Besides, it is about to storm soon, and I don't want you guys to get caught in it. I hope the girls get here soon. According to the news earlier, the weather is going to get really bad. The kids can just go in the game room and play and watch movies. Plus, Keisha is coming, and you know she loves her some you. You really helped her when Zylan passed, and she speaks so highly of you." I smiled while I headed inside.

I began surfing through the refrigerator and debated on what to cook. Avantae's ass loved to eat, and he had all kinds of food in the refrigerator. We even had a deep freezer too. I finally decided on a honey-pineapple-glazed steak on a bed of steamed rice with shrimp, seasoned steamed broccoli, corn on the cob, corn bread, and a homemade lemon strawberry cake. I was making a meal big enough for ten people. I was so happy that Tater Bug and Jalisa liked whatever I cooked, especially Tater Bug. That boy was just like his father and could eat you under the table.

I placed my phone on the counter, then turned on my Pandora to the Syleena Johnson station. My boo Brandy "Sittin' Up in My Room" came on, and I began jamming around the kitchen. As I was placing my cake in the oven, the doorbell rang. I was a little puzzled and caught off guard because this is a new home and nobody other than my circle knew where we lived. Although Keisha, Asia, and Janair were on their way shortly, I still wasn't expecting them for another hour or so.

I viewed the camera that Avantae had installed and saw a nice, older model dark blue Cadillac out in the driveway. At the doorbell stood a rather short, bald, caramel-complexioned man with a full beard and a beige Cole Haan suit. By his stance, mannerisms, and the large yellow envelope he had in his hands, I knew right off that he was either a private investigator of some sort, a detective, or something like that.

Checking the back door, I made sure Barbara Jean, Jalisa, and Little Avantae were secure. I'm happy Avantae had higher gates built where you couldn't see in our backyard. He also had an area out back that led to the panic room with guns in secret places. Avantae spared no expense when it came to our safety.

My sixth sense went up, and I grabbed two of my nines and placed them behind me. My first mind was not to answer the door, but I did anyway.

"Ceanna Black-Thomas?" the man announced.

"Who wants to know?" I asked in a hostile tone.

"You have been served. Have a good day!" He tossed the envelope into the house.

He turned quickly, walked off, and headed toward his vehicle. I slammed the door and picked the envelope off the floor.

"What the fuck is this?" I shouted aloud to no one in particular.

"Aaaaw, Mommy Ce, you said a bad word," Jalisa giggled.

I placed a fake smile on my face and made my way back over to the kitchen. I hadn't even heard them come in from out back.

"Baby, are you okay?" Barbara Jean asked. I shook my head no and told the children to go play, while I talked to her.

"A man just gave me this, talking about 'I've been served.'" I leaned up against the counter.

"Well, what is it?" she asked.

"The hell if I know. Let me open it now." I tore the seal from the envelope. My eyes widened when I saw a legal document.

"No, the fuck Jaceyon didn't!" I yelled.

"What?" Barbara Jean asked.

"Can you believe Jaceyon is suing me for damage to his property and half of the sale from our home? Wait, though, it gets even fucking better. This nigga right here is even trying to take me to court for 'emotional distress' and custody of Jalisa. Maaaan, he's got me so fucked up. Mmmm-mmmmmm," I bit my bottom lip while I paced back and forth.

"Does Jaceyon *really* want to go there? I'm so sick of him. Baby, you just calm down. We'll handle this. You know I have no issues putting him in the grave. I already killed off Samuel's ass and Jaceyon on my list too for shooting my baby," Barbara Jean confessed as she fired up a blunt.

"Wait! Hold up. When did your ass start smoking? Let me find out, Gangster Jean," I teased. "Oh, and rewind. So *you're* the one who killed Samuel? But why?"

"Because he was one of the men who raped me. I will never forget the darkness of his eyes and how he beat me. Ceanna, it used to haunt me, and I never thought my day of revenge would come. I used to sit and think for hours what I would do if I ever saw him or heard his voice again," she choked.

"You know Samuel was Zylan's father, right?" I asked.

"I didn't know that until recently. That's why I was trying to leave when Keisha comes over. I feel horrible. She loved Samuel, and I took away someone she loved," she expressed.

"Was he the one who gave you HIV?" I asked curiously.

"No! He raped and beat me first. He even came pre-pared, like raping me was something he planned on doing. He had a condom ready and everything. That nigga was sick," she frowned.

"Well, Keisha doesn't know and that ain't my place to tell. I'll give you the space to tell her on your own time. Oh, and can you please smoke outside?"

"Thank you! I'm about to toss this out anyway. That's not a habit I want to pick up, if you know what I mean."

"Oh shit, my cake!" I wobbled quickly over to the stove.

"Man, it smells so good in here. Let me go check on those two. That little Avantae is sneaky just like his damn daddy was at his age. Avantae's ass stayed into everything. From eating rolly pollies, playing in his own shit, getting bit up by ants, playing with bees and stung all over his body. He was a headache. He stayed at the damn hospital. Broken bones here, shots here, antibiotics there, so get ready, Ceanna," she laughed while leaving the kitchen.

I began to prepare my special sauces and made my homemade lemon frosting. I kept trying to ignore the envelope, but I just couldn't do it. I picked up my phone and dialed Gina's house phone. I wanted some answers now.

"Hello!" a female answered, and I rolled my eyes because I knew it was none other than Mia Symone.

"Mia Symone, where is Jaceyon's bitch ass at?"

"Ce-Ceanna," she stuttered.

"Surprised, ho? Now, where's he at?" I yelled.

"He's not here, Ceanna."

"Oh, so you over there living in the house now? So what, y'all just one big happy fucking family, huh?" I asked.

I don't know why hearing her voice put me on ten. I was livid all over again. Damn, that anger management class didn't do anything 'cause I feel like 1-800 slapping this ho through the phone.

"Ceanna, it's not like that. My son and I had nowhere else to go. I have nothing, Ceanna, and I don't want to be here. I'm not sleeping with Jaceyon, and we barely speak at all. Ceanna, I did a horrible thing to you. Please forgive me and help me. I need you, Ceanna!" she cried.

"Giiirl!" I yelled. "I just wanna know why, Mia. I did *everything* for you. I gave you everything I had. What was mine was yours, and I never turned my back. Why would you hurt me like this?" I choked up.

"Ceanna, I fell in love with him. I don't know when or how, but I did. You know I used to be a stripper, and that's how I met Jaceyon. I should have told you then, but the day you introduced me to Jaceyon, I was with him the night before. For the longest, I tried to ignore him, Ceanna, but he came on to me. I knew it was wrong, but, Ceanna, you were so happy, and I wanted what you had. I've always wanted what you had. From the time we were little, you had your mother and father, and I just had y'all. I always borrowed pieces of your happiness, wishing it were me. With Jaceyon, it wasn't to hurt you. I fell in love, and he promised me the world. He was a good time and gave me a love I never had. At least I thought so. Now, he wants nothing to do with me. I'm so lost. I'm sorry for everything I've done to you. Can you please forgive me? I need you, and I know I have no right asking you for anything. I'll leave, Ceanna, I promise to never bother you again, but can you give my son and me some financial backing? If not for me, then for him? He's innocent, Ceanna!" she cried.

"Did you know about Jaceyon trying to sue me?"

"No, I didn't, Ceanna, but I do know this . . . Jaceyon and Gina have it out for you and Avantae. He knew Tonya had money, and if he gets Jalisa, then he knows he can fight for the will Tonya left. I even heard him on the phone mentioning killing Avantae a couple of times. Y'all need to be careful. I want no parts of it. Just please get me and my son out of here," she pleaded.

"On some real shit, Mia Symone, I forgive you for me. I know you aren't really sorry, and if Jaceyon wanted to make you his wife and be with you, you would jump at the opportunity. I always knew you were jealous of me, but I didn't understand why. I knew your pain because I was the one consoling you through it. I loved you like my sister, and I would have done anything for you. You hurt me so bad, but I thank you too. Because of you and Jaceyon, I'm experiencing a love I never had. I have a man who loves the ground I walk on. He walks with me and helps me in ways that only God knows. I wouldn't wish even on you the pain you've caused because you couldn't handle it. I almost killed your ass behind a man who disrespected me. It wasn't worth it.

"The only reason I'm going to help you, Mia, is because when I saw your son, he looked at me with those big green eyes. I thought of the little innocent girl you once were before those boys gang-raped you. A piece of you died, Mia Symone, and you were never the same. You are my first cousin, and I will always love you, but I ain't fucking with you like that. You showed me who you were. You'll never be happy bringing misery to other people. You really need to get help and find ways to heal," I spoke sternly.

"Ceanna, I know. I'm an ugly person. I do need help. I'm so lost," she said.

"Well, I have to go now. Asia told me she brought you a phone. Text me your number, and I'll hit you with the code for Western Union. Take care of yourself, Mia Symone." I hung up.

Hot tears ran down my face, and I couldn't stop myself from feeling this heavy emotion. Not speaking to Mia Symone is a heavy burden. It's a loss. I love her with everything in me, and it hurts to know that she hates me that much. I do hope she heals and finds the strength she needs. I can tell I'm growing as a person. I really wanted to tell Mia Symone where to go, but I guess since I'm a mother now, a piece of me really wants her to get her life in order for her son.

Chapter Twenty-one

Ceanna

"Mommy Ce, can Tater Bug stay with us forever?" Jalisa asked.

"I would love for Tater Bug to stay with us forever," I smiled. The kids came out of the room from playing, and that meant they were hungry.

"Mommy Ce, is the food ready yet? We're hungry!" Tater Bug and Jalisa asked.

"Yes, almost, my lovebugs." I smiled at them.

"Jalisa, baby girl, come here for a minute!" Barbara Jean yelled from the back.

"Coming. Tater Bug, I'll be right back." Jalisa ran down the hallway.

I turned the stove to low, walked over to where Tater Bug was, and grabbed his hand. "Tater Bug, come sit with me for a minute." We walked over to the sofa, and he sat down next to me.

I took in all his features. He was the spitting image of his father. They shared the same long eyelashes, perfectly arched eyebrows, oval-shaped face, high cheekbones with dimples, beautiful dark skin, long, wavy, dark hair, and these big beautiful brown eyes.

"Avantae, I wanted to talk to you for a minute, baby. I want you to know that even though you have a mother, you're welcome here. You can always come and talk to me. I know you aren't my son, but I will never treat you differently. I love you, and you can stay here as long as you want," I smiled.

"Really?" His little face lit up.

"Yes, baby, really. I enjoy you here, baby, and you're about to be a big brother soon." I rubbed my belly, and he laughed when one of the twins kicked.

"Mommy Ce, I'm going to be the best brother in the world. I can't boss Jalisa around 'cause she'll beat me up. She thinks she's the boss of me, but I just let her have her way. Daddy say never argue with women 'cause it ain't no point, and they crazy anyway," he shrugged.

"Huh? Your daddy is something else." I shook my head. "Well, baby, the food will be ready soon. Go wash your hands and get ready. Is your room clean?" I asked.

"Yes, ma'am." He headed toward the back. Then he ran back and gave me a big hug and a kiss on the cheek. I swear that my heart melted.

I was about to get up when a sharp pain hit me. It brought tears to my eyes. One of the twins was definitely in there playing and hit a nerve.

Boom Tat Boom Boom.

"It's your girl Keisha at your door. I'm coming through with Janair, so open up this damn door." Keisha knocked and rapped loudly on the front door.

I slowly stood up and wobbled over toward the door giggling and shaking my head. "So what, you're a rapper now?" I laughed, questioning Keisha as soon as I opened the door.

"Well, hell, a bish might as well be. Shit, all you need these days is a fiyah beat and a dance routine, and you'll be a star." We all laughed as Keisha danced.

"Hey, boo!" I hugged Janair. "Oh, look at my little pudding." I took the baby out of Janair's arms and began hugging and kissing all over her.

"Wait a minute. Pause. Keisha, where is Asia at?" I asked.

"Oh, girl, please don't gas Keisha up. Hunny, you don't even want to know," Janair waved her hand.

"What the hell happened?"

"Girl, Asia's been tripping lately, Ce. I'm tryin'a get away from this crazy bitch. Do you know she pulled a Donte and tapped my phone by putting a tracking device on my car?" Keisha said while using her hands.

"What? See, that's that—oh shit. Hold on! My damn corn bread!" I yelled, wobbling to the kitchen with the ladies following and taking a seat at the bar.

"You gon' eat yo' corn bread?" Janair joked, causing us to laugh.

"Keisha, my bad. What happened next?" I asked as I stood in front of the bar.

Keisha was a hard person to follow when she spoke. She was an extra long-winded person. *Lawd, get to the story already,* I screamed internally. I guess I made a facial expression because Janair smirked at me.

"So, you know, me and WyKeith has been mad chilling. I went over to his place yesterday and retwisted his dreads. Lo and behold, Asia comes banging on the door. She caused a big scene and everything. Ce, I keep telling her that we can be friends, but she's not trying to hear that shit. We just had a big blowup this morning because WyKeith called my phone. Asia ended up leaving, and I don't know where her ass is."

The doorbell rang. From the television screen, I could see that it was Asia. Keisha sucked her teeth loudly as Janair and I laughed. "Keisha, gon' and answer the door for your boo," I smiled, being messy.

Keisha got up and opened the door. She quickly turned around and came back to sit down, not even acknowledging Asia.

"Hey, Asia, boo, we're in here!" I yelled. Asia came and gave me a hug. She brought me a bouquet of beautiful roses and an MK purse.

"Awww, boo, that's so sweet of you. Thank you so much!" I teared up.

"You're welcome, love! I haven't seen you in a while, boo, and this house is absolutely beautiful." She took a seat next to Keisha.

"Thank you! Can y'all believe Avantae did all of this himself?" I placed the flowers in a vase with water.

"I can, boo! Avantae loves him some Ceanna," Janair smiled.

The ladies and I continued to joke a little while longer. The air was thick between Keisha and Asia. They barely acknowledged each other, and I could tell Asia was a little hurt. The steaks weren't as tender as I liked, so I left them in the oven a little longer.

"Boo, I'm going to go chop it up with Mama Barbara Jean and the kids awhile until the food is ready," Keisha informed us.

"Okay! Oh, Janair, you can bring the baby back here and place her in the crib if you want," I offered to Janair.

"Oh yes, boo, that would be great," Janair replied as she, Asia, and I headed toward the twins' room.

Janair laid the baby down, and I took a seat in my rocking chair. Asia closed the door and came to sit on the floor and Janair did the same thing.

"Ceanna, I don't know anymore," Asia teared up.

Janair reached over and gave her a hug. A lonely tear slipped from my left eye. I love my friends, and I hate seeing them at odds.

"I'm sorry, boo! What's going on, Asia?" I asked.

"Keisha is cheating on me with WyKeith. It took me a minute to figure it out, but she is in love with the nigga. I love Keisha, but I know she can't fully accept this lifestyle.

I was just something to do. I feel so used and hurt. I haven't loved anyone the way I love Keisha. It hurts when you love someone, and they don't love you back," she cried.

"Asia, you know I know the pain you're feeling, but things *will* get better. Sometimes you've got to let people go. I believe you'll find love, Asia, and when you do, that person won't be ashamed of you or the lifestyle. You're beautiful, Asia! Hell, if I was into girls, I would flaunt your pretty ass around." I made Asia laugh.

"Thank you, Ceanna, and you too, Janair. I know you don't know us all that well, but from the moment I met you, you were really sweet," Asia smiled.

"I agree, Janair! I'm thankful to have met you and Semaj. You two are our family now."

"Thank y'all. You know my cousin Mya is just like your cousin Mia Symone. She hurt me so bad, but just like Avantae, Semaj showed me how to love again. Asia, you'll find your happy place."

"So, Asia, have you been spending time with Gina and Jaceyon?" I asked.

"Here and there. I talked to Gina earlier briefly, and Jaceyon hates me and feels I'm an enemy. Gina is more so focused on you and Jalisa. I thought at one point we would build, but I'm not going to allow them to discuss you. You're my family and my best friend, Ceanna. You've been through enough, and I'm tired of people plotting on you and trying to take from you. Enough is enough. Truthfully, you and Keisha are all I have. Tonya is gone, and even though Mia Symone is my sister, she showed us all who she is, so I don't trust her."

"Well, I love you, Asia, and I'm very proud of you. Thank you for all you do for me; thank you for never backstabbing me, and thank you for always being you."

"So, Ceanna, are you ready?" Janair asked.

"No. Honestly, I have no clue what to do. I'm scared as hell." Asia and Janair busted out laughing.

"Girl, your facial expressions kill me," Janair laughed. "Don't worry. Later, you're going to get all the training you need. We're going to give little fat mama a bath, changed her diaper, and feed her. I got you, girlie," Janair smiled.

"Can we eat now?" Jalisa and Tater Bug knocked on the door.

"Oh, Lawd, hunny, these kids," I laughed, and we all headed toward the front.

"Jalisa, you and Tater Bug wash y'all's hands and set the table!" I yelled.

"Yes, ma'am," the kids stated and ran to the bathroom to wash their little hands.

Everyone sat at the table. Jalisa and Tater Bug placed the items on the table that I put out. Once all the food was on the table, we said grace and began to eat.

"Ceanna, girl, this shit's so good. All right, keep on and Avantae's ass gone be slim thick," Keisha laughed.

Ding dong.

We all stopped eating and looked at each other. I stood up and looked at the monitor. I shook my head when I saw WyKeith standing on the porch. *Damn, here we go.*

Chapter Twenty-two

Ceanna

"I'm just finna go. Y'all go ahead and enjoy y'all's dinner." Tears ran down Asia's face.

I didn't know what to say. I looked at Keisha, and she diverted her eyes. Tonight was supposed to be about us girls, and I didn't want Asia to leave. It was pouring rain outside.

"Asia, please stay for me," I pouted.

Asia stood up and hurried to the restroom. Janair followed her. I walked over to the front door and let WyKeith in. I normally don't do shit like this, but I know WyKeith was here for two reasons. One being Avantae sent him to watch the house and make sure we were okay, and the second reason being Keisha. Truthfully, I was in an awkward-ass situation. I just prayed we could all act like adults. After all, we had kids here.

"Hey, WyKeith!" I greeted, and WyKeith kissed me on the cheek.

"Hey, Queen! What's popping? It smells good as fuck in here," he smiled, rubbing his stomach.

Booom! Lightning struck, and I jumped.

"All, hell, nawl, nigga, get yo' ass on in here," I laughed, pulling him in the house.

"Please leave your shoes there. There's some brand-new socks in the bin." I pointed toward the closet.

"Everybody, look who's here," I announced. Jalisa and Tater Bug ran and gave him a hug.

"Uncle WyKeith, can we play games later?" the kids asked.

"Y'all let the man breathe and go finish eating," I laughed.

"Gon' on and have a seat, WyKeith. Y'all think y'all asses is slick. I know Avantae and Semaj told you to come over here to watch us." I handed him a plate of warm food.

"I plead the Fifth," he laughed.

WyKeith and Keisha were giggling and in their own little world at the table. Mama Barbara Jean and I looked at each other, and I shrugged. Hell, what am I supposed to say or do?

I joined Janair and Asia in the restroom. I felt bad for Asia. She was crying so hard, and I could tell she really loved Keisha.

"Ceanna, I think it's best if I leave. I'm sorry. I didn't mean to ruin your night, but, girl, I just can't be here with him here. I hate him!" Asia cried.

"I understand, but can you at least wait until the rains calms down? I don't want you driving in that," I said, concerned.

"Yes, I'll wait." She wiped away her tears.

"Let's go eat, and, Asia, don't let this steal your joy." Janair hugged her.

We all three headed back toward the dining area, but once Asia saw Keisha and WyKeith laughing, she lost it.

"Fuck y'all!" she yelled.

"Aw shit. Kids, come on; let's go to your room!" Janair yelled getting Jalisa and Tater Bug.

"Asia, calm down. WyKeith and I are just friends." Keisha stood up.

"Just friends? Keisha, don't insult my fucking intelligence!" she yelled.

"Asia, I've been telling you for months now that I didn't love you like that. I don't want to be in a relationship with you," Keisha expressed.

"So just like that, Keisha, after *everything?*" Asia broke down crying.

"Asia, I thank you for being a good friend. I do, but I'm not a lesbian, and I'm not okay being with you," Keisha reasoned.

"I was there for you, Keisha, when you had nobody. I loved Zylan like he was my own, you fucking bitch!" she screamed.

"Asia," WyKeith called, and I shook my head. He should have just shut the hell up.

"Oh, fuck off, WyKeith. You knew she was my bitch, and you just had to step in. Why the fuck are you here?" Asia charged at him.

"Okay, Asia, I get it that you're hurt. WyKeith has nothing to do with this. It's me! I've been telling you over and over again, but you just seem to not get it. Look, Asia, you're a good friend, and I love you as a friend, but I just can't do this."

"You didn't say that shit last night when I ate that pretty pussy of yours, now, did you?" Asia insulted her.

"Asia, did I *let* you or did you *take* it? See, that's the difference."

"I think it's best if I go." Asia stood and rushed to the living room.

I wobbled behind her trying to convince her to wait for the weather to clear, but that was a big mistake. Next thing I knew, Asia ran back to the kitchen and started pounding on Keisha. Poor Keisha always getting her ass whooped.

"Bitch, you thought I was going to just let that slick shit you just said slide?" *Whap!* "You got me"—*Whap!*— "fucked up"—*Whap!*—"bitch!"

"Get the fuck off of me." Asia fought with WyKeith who now had her in a bear hug.

Keisha stood up, holding her bloody nose, and then charged at Asia. WyKeith let go of Asia so it would be a fair fight. Barbara Jean just sipped on her wine watching the shit show.

"Ceanna, sit yo' ass down and don't say shit. If something happens to my grandbabies, I'm killing everybody." She continued to sip.

"WyKeith, do something!" I yelled.

"Man, Ceanna, damn, I ain't no ref and shit." He laughed, and then finally broke the ladies up.

"Bitch, you just wait, ho!" Keisha yelled.

"Yeah, we'll see!" Asia yelled back.

"Ceanna, I'm out of this bitch." Asia ran out the front door jumping into her car.

Barbara Jean went to go check on the children. Janair came from the back and immediately grabbed a towel and ice cubes. "Damn, Keisha." Janair held the towel to Keisha's busted lip while Keisha held her head back.

I just sat down at the table and continued eating. I was happy the dining area was huge because at least our food wasn't disturbed.

"Janair, watch out, ma, I got her." WyKeith lifted Keisha's body and took her to the bathroom.

Janair and I just shook our heads. I laughed when her ass picked up her fork and started eating too. "Shit, bish, I was not about to let this good-ass meal go to waste. Hell, they play too damn much. I'm hungry as hell. Ain't nobody got time for that extra shit." We laughed.

I finished my food and joked with Janair awhile. After I was done, I went to go check on the children. I smiled when I saw those two knocked out. Barbara Jean took little Tater Bug's clothing off and placed on his ninja turtle shorts and night tee. She tucked him in and did the same with Jalisa.

"Baby, I'm tired. I'll be in my room lying down if you need me." Barbara Jean kissed me on the cheek.

"Good night, Mama," I closed her door.

I could faintly here Keisha and WyKeith as they talked in the bathroom. I left them alone and went back toward the kitchen area. Janair had put up the leftover food and cleaned the kitchen and dining area.

"Awww, boo, thank you," I smiled.

"No problem. Besides, it's time to have infant class 'cause little mama is going to be up in a few."

Janair was so gentle and patient with her daughter. She taught me how to bathe the baby, change a diaper again, and showed me the proper way to breast-feed.

We laughed and caught up on more girl time until the baby fell asleep. I pulled out a queen-size cot and blanket set that Avantae had bought for guests. Janair and I set it up in the baby's room. I didn't mind her sleeping in this room one bit.

WyKeith and Keisha finally came out of the bathroom. Keisha had changed into her night clothing, and I could tell she showered due to her wet, curly hair.

"WyKeith, you might as well stay too. The guest room is down the hall. Here is a white tee and some sweats."

We sat in the living room, and Janair came to join us. We all talked about the incident that just happened. Keisha kept apologizing and said she was sad the way things went down. Asia was our sister, and we would get through this.

As we continued to talk, my phone went off. It was after two in the morning, so I knew it was my baby. We were all wide awake and couldn't wait to hear about his performance. I didn't even look at the caller ID. I was just happy to hear from my man. I placed the phone on speaker.

"Baby, I miss you!" I screamed excitedly.

"Wrong, bitch!"

Click. The caller hung up.

"Nawl, bitch!" I yelled out loud, star sixty-nining the number back. I was about to go ham when moments later a video attachment came to my phone.

"*Avantae, I'm coming.*" I see Zaria riding Avantae's dick. "*Hey, Ceanna, bitch, your man is in Dallas with me. Kiss my Tater Bug for me.*" Zaria smiled into the phone.

I dropped the phone as hot tears ran down my face. I felt like I was having déjà vu all over again. Janair came and hugged me. Keisha picked up the phone and began investigating the video.

"Ceanna, this shit is staged. Look," Keisha pointed to the screen.

"Do you see what I see? Avantae is motionless. His eyes are closed, and his pants and shoes are still on. Look at his hands. They are nowhere near this ho. I bet her ass drugged him."

"Wait a damn minute. Let me see that phone." Janair grabbed the phone from Keisha.

"Ceanna, this is a chick name Tasha. I met her once at the studio. Semaj introduced her as a new upcoming singer. He told me he was working on a single for Avantae and was going to let Tasha sing the hook. I bet that bitch Kwency has something to do with this. Semaj loves you guys like family, so I'm positive this shit is a setup. Trust your man, Ceanna. Avantae would never do no shit like this to you."

"She's right, Ceanna! You *are* Avantae's world. That nigga was ruthless back in the gap with my brother, but now the nigga is levelheaded and family oriented. Ain't no way my nigga would throw away what y'all building for these hoes out here. The nigga is official," WyKeith confirmed.

"These hoes are so disrespectful. *Uuuugh!* So this bitch Zaria plotted this shit out because Avantae don't want her? Bitch, I can't!" Keisha yelled.

"I think I just need to go lie down. I don't feel too good." I stood and left the room.

Zaria had crossed the line. I don't know why everyone wanted to test me. I'm kind and nice because I don't see a reason to frown or be mean, but don't get it twisted. I am the seed of a ruthless nigga named Calvin Black.

Chapter Twenty-three

Mia Symone

My phone had finally sounded off, and the message I had been waiting for came through. Ceanna sent me a text message, and it read:

Mia Symone, I really hope you get your life together. I don't hate you for what you did, and I forgive you for me, but if it wasn't for your son, I wouldn't even speak to you or help you. Now that I'm a mother, no matter how hurt I am, I can't have your son struggling. Go to the bank on West Ninth Street and ask for Peggy. There is a box for you. In the box is a card. It has $150,000 in it. There are also keys to a vehicle and keys to a home in San Antonio. The vehicle is at the home. Don't worry about shit here; just get there. Call 534.631.7999. The number is to Pablo. He'll drive you to the bank and San Antonio. Take care of yourself, Mia Symone, and I'll contact you whenever I'm ready. I won't be giving you shit else, so make the money count and get your shit together.

I immediately replied:

Thank you, Ceanna! I know this don't mean shit to you, but I do love you and miss you so much. I pray one day you'll open your heart back to me. I'm sorry!

I wiped my face after sending the text. I closed my phone and did something I never do, and that is pray. I'm so lost, but I have to be a better person for my son. This time I won't let Ceanna down.

After I finished praying, I packed a bag for my son and a bag for myself. I dressed in comfortable clothing, and I didn't worry about getting pretty, which was new.

My son was sleeping peacefully, and I knew I had to make my move. The house was quiet; no one else was home. Matter of fact, Jaceyon hadn't returned, and Gina had been in and out.

I had a bad feeling, and I knew it was time for me to leave. I looked out the blinds relieved Gina's and Jaceyon's vehicles were still gone. I hurried and called Pablo. He told me he would be there in ten minutes.

I decided to wait out in the back of the house. That way, if Gina or Jaceyon came home, I could slip through the side gate without been seen.

Little Jaceyon didn't wake up at all, and I was thankful for that. I placed the bags on the ground on the side of the house and sat on the ground with my baby.

As I waited, I attempted to call Asia, but I only got her voice mail. I had this funny feeling inside that I couldn't explain. It was weird for Asia to not answer, return my call, or text back. I hadn't heard from her since early Saturday when she and Keisha got into it.

Although Asia and I weren't as close, I was surprised when she called me crying, opening up about her and Keisha's relationship. She was so heartbroken, and I felt bad for her.

I had never taken the time to see the damage cheating and lying does to the innocent person in the relationship. Maybe I just forgot the pain. After Rodrick, I became coldhearted and heartless. I never wanted to feel the type of pain Asia was feeling.

Who am I kidding, though, because I'm feeling it now? I realize no matter how coldhearted a female thinks she is, we can't change how we're built. We are emotional, and it just takes the right nigga to break you down.

I'm feeling that now. Jaceyon hurt me so bad. The way he beat and raped me took me back to a darker time in my life. Honestly, I guess I never felt worthy, and Ceanna was right. What those boys did to me was too horrible to mention. I thought I was over that, but then it happened again and again, until I had nothing left.

My cell phone rang, and I saw that it was Pablo. I stood with my son in one arm and placed two bags on the other arm. Pablo saw me struggling and got out of his vehicle to grab the bags. He was handsome, but I made sure to keep my conversation short and divert my eyes. I sat in the backseat and lowered myself. I didn't want to take the chance of being seen.

After the bank, we were finally on our way to San Antonio. Jaceyon called eight times threatening to kill me if I didn't bring his son back. I finally placed his number on block and made a mental note to get a new phone and number. I must have drifted off to sleep because the next thing I knew, Pablo was gently shaking my leg.

"Señorita Mia! We're here."

Pablo helped me with my bags in the home and then left. I laid my son on the teal leather love seat and made my way around the house. It was a flat-level, three-bedroom home, open-floor concept, cherry wood floors, beautiful tan walls that were decorated with mirrors, beautiful artwork, and candle sconces. The kitchen had beautiful gray and black granite countertops, gray with black-trimmed cabinets, and stainless steel appliances. The living room was large. It had a large flat-screen TV, black TV stand, teal love seat, sofa, and two matching chairs. The throw pillows were gray and black. Each room had its own color theme. It was cozy enough for my son and me.

Ceanna must have just been there or had someone come there because the refrigerator was fully stocked with everything I needed.

Little Jaceyon began to cry, and I went to tend to my son. I removed my shirt and bra and began to breast-feed him. He stared at me with his big green eyes.

"I promise to be better for you, Jace. I love you, and I'll never leave you. Thank you for choosing me. You make me feel a love I never felt before," I cried.

Holding my son in my arms made me want to be a better woman. I didn't know where to start, though. For the longest, I've used men to front my lifestyle. Maybe I could get back into doing hair and even open up my own salon like Tonya had. I don't know. Maybe. First, I had to get off this unwanted weight. I didn't see how big women did it. I hated the way I looked.

I picked up my phone again and stared at the few contacts I had. I kinda of missed my cell mate. At least I had someone to laugh and joke with. It was too quiet, and it was starting to make me a little uneasy. I came across Ceanna's number and texted her.

Hey, Ceanna! I just want to thank you again for all you have done. It was hell at Gina's. You have no idea the pain I endured there. You came through for me as you always do. I would do anything to prove to you that I can change. You are all I have. I'm going to get my life together, and I pray that you don't completely shut me out. I love you, Ceanna, and thank you again. The house is very lovely. Good night!

I knew Ceanna wasn't going to text back, so I placed my phone on the charger and rocked baby Jace to sleep. Once he fell into a comfortable sleep, I went to take a nice long, steamy shower. As the warm water ran down my body, I began to think of ways that I was going to get even with Jaceyon. I wasn't going to let him get away after all the pain and hurt he put me through.

As if Jaceyon could read my thoughts, my phone rang loudly through the house. I hurried and jumped out of the shower trying to get to it before the phone went to voice mail. I was hoping the call was from Ceanna, but I was wrong. I didn't recognize the number, but I answered it anyway.

"Mia Symone, where the fuck are you with my son, bitch?" Jaceyon roared through the phone.

"We are gone, and you will *never* see us again," I screamed into the phone.

"What, bitch? Do you think I won't find you?" he asked.

"You can come looking for me all you want, Jaceyon, but I will never come running back to you, nigga. Matter of fact, if I were you, I would watch my back. I'm coming for you, Jaceyon, when you least expect it. I'm going to murder you, nigga!" I yelled.

"Bitch, are you threatening me?" he yelled back.

"Jaceyon, that's not a threat. It's a promise!" I yelled and hung up.

Jaceyon continued to call my phone over and over again. I placed the phone on silent and tended to baby Jace who was now wide awake thanks to Jaceyon. I think the baby could sense my anger because he became very cranky and wouldn't stop crying.

I was so upset, and I didn't want to take it out on the baby. Maybe my mom was right, and I ain't cut out for this shit. I laid the crying baby, who was now screaming, down on the sofa and walked away. I couldn't take it right now, and I suddenly understood how a mother could go postal and lose it. Calming myself down, I looked over at my child and immediately broke down crying.

"Mia Symone, you're not your mother, and you can change. You can love that little boy," I told myself. I picked up my son and began singing my aunt's favorite song. "*With all my heart, I love you, baby. Stay with me, and you will see . . .*" I sang Anita Baker's "Sweet Love" song. He began to calm down, and he stared at me as I sang.

I smiled back at my son, and my heart began to get overwhelmed with love, thinking of my aunt, Cynthia. She was the sweetest woman, and she treated me as if I were her own. I know she's so disappointed in how I've turned out. I can change, though, and I have to make things right.

Shaking my head, I thought of my cruel actions toward Ceanna. I didn't have to trash her designs the way I did. That was cold and vindictive. Maybe, though, if I am allowed to help, I can call Myriah from Ceanna's boutique. There is so much to do for the upcoming fashion show, and if allowed, I will help. I'll do anything to gain Ceanna's trust back.

Chapter Twenty-four

Jaceyon

"You ready, my nigga?" I asked Rick, who was sweating bullets. I looked over at him and began to have second thoughts. Maybe I should have just done this on my own. That's how I'm caught up now because I involved Mia Symone in my dirty work last time.

"Nawl, my nigga, I ain't really feeling this shit. What if we get caught? You know Avantae was big in this shit, so I'm sure his place is wired," he replied, nervously speaking with his hands.

"Look, nigga, there's money in this house, and as far as Keisha goes, that bitch stole from me. I'm just taking back what's mine. Are you in or not?" I questioned, placing on my black gloves and pulling the mask over my face. I didn't have time for the extra shit he was speaking. Avantae bleeds just like the next nigga.

"Fuck it, let's go!" Rick opened the car door and grabbed the two empty duffle bags.

The night was messy. It was pouring down rain and thundering. I'm happy Rick came along because he knew how to disable the home alarm system.

As soon as we entered, I began spraying the cameras posted around. I knew Avantae had a home system set up, but I couldn't find the main system the cameras were hooked to. We searched around and grabbed anything we could find. I frowned when I saw Ceanna's pictures sprawled around his home. "This nigga is really obsessed with my bitch," I fussed aloud while I grabbed one of her pictures off the wall.

I made it to the back of the home and began to grab extra shit, including a watch his father gave him. I then pushed a door back that led to the underground room.

"My nigga, in here!" I yelled out to Rick.

My mouth fell open in shock. It was like a candy store full of shit in there. We began stacking bullets and guns. I couldn't find the cash right off, but I continued to search. I pushed another secret door and smiled when I saw the cash.

Suddenly, Rick and I froze when the lights came on. The clicking of a gun scared us shitless. We looked around but didn't see anyone. Instantly, four red laser lights were on Rick. A light was to his head, heart, abdomen, and groin. A wave of panic came over me. I didn't plan on dying tonight, but fuck it, if it's my time, I'm going out like a G.

We stood still afraid to make any sudden movement. My eyes quickly scanned the room. There was no movement or person in sight. I finally spotted a semiautomatic. Rick must have hit a trigger line from where he was standing. Before I could warn him, the gun went off. *Tat! Tat! Tat! Tat!*

My eyes widened as Rick's blood spattered on me. *Thump!* His body dropped and hit the hardwood floor. "Fuck!" I yelled. I wasn't leaving without the cash. I searched my own body for the laser lights, and when I noticed I was clear, I quickly grabbed the money from the hidden spot. There had to be about three hundred to five hundred thousand if I was guessing right.

As I filled the bag, I noticed something white that caught my eye. "Bin-fucking-go!" I yelled, excited at the ten bricks I spotted. "Yo' boy 'bout to be on," I boasted.

I made my way back up to the front careful not to set off any more triggers. I wanted to go back and grabbed the bag Rick had, but I couldn't take any chances. As soon as I was about to leave the house, the doorbell rang. My heart dropped.

"Ayo, Tae, it's me, man, Elijah. I got you and Ceanna's rides out front. Fuck, it's raining harder than a bitch out here."

Elijah knocked a couple of more times and then left, or so I thought. He began unloading the vehicles in Avantae's driveway. I was stuck in this nigga's home for another thirty minutes.

Sweat poured down my face under the mask as I kept my eyes trained on and my gun aimed at the front door. Elijah finally left; then it dawned on me that I didn't have Rick's car keys. I couldn't go back down there. It was too dangerous. And I couldn't risk walking or being seen. Then that's when it hit me. I still had Ceanna's key to her truck on my key ring.

Once the coast was clear, I unlocked her truck and jumped in. Her truck was nice and looked as though it had a makeover. I had to think fast because I couldn't go back to the hood, at least not with her truck. Pulling over to the side of the road, I called my mother to meet me at an abandoned car wash.

"Jaceyon, what the fuck is going on, and what's in that duffle bag?" she asked as soon as I entered her vehicle.

"It went all bad, Mom. Let's get the fuck out of here!" I yelled, removing my mask.

"Where are we going?"

"Take me to Auntie's old abandoned home."

"Okay."

Once we entered the home, I looked around and became overwhelmed with emotions. I missed my aunt. Her death was unexpected.

"Jace, tell me what happened," my mother begged as she took a seat next to me on the dusty black leather sofa.

"Shit went all wrong, Ma. Rick and I went to go rob Avantae. Everything was going smoothly, but Avantae had some type of trap, and I guess Rick triggered it. All of a sudden, a gun went off, instantly killing Rick. His body is still there. I left the nigga and made off with cash and ten keys."

"So what are you going to do now?"

"Shit, I was about to hit Keisha next, before Avantae got back and shit got crazy. You down?" I asked with raised eyebrows.

"Fuck, yes, I'm down; let's go!" She stood from the sofa. We hid the cash and drugs and made our way to Keisha and Asia's home.

"Asia ain't here. She's with Ceanna. I spoke to her earlier," my mother said.

"Cool, come on."

With my mother as the lookout, I crept around the back of the home. When I finally made it in, I called my mother's phone and told her the coast was clear. She joined me in the house, and I began to touch the walls to feel for softness and texture that differed from the other walls. I knew she had a trap wall somewhere. Being married to Donte, she had to have learned something.

"Bingo!" I yelled.

My mother and I pushed a wall back and spotted the money. I ran into the kitchen and grabbed a trash bag but was halted when the front door opened. I gave a silent signal to my mother, and she hid behind the wall, slowly closing the hidden wall door. I tried to hide but wasn't quick enough. The light came on, and Asia and I stared at each other.

"Ah!" she screamed and held her chest. Her makeup was smeared, and it looked as though she had been crying.

"Jaceyon, what the fuck are you doing in here?" She came charging at me when my mother exited from behind the wall with her gun.

"Stop!" my mother yelled, cocking her gun.

Asia turned around with tears in her eyes. She walked with her hands up and took a seat at the dining table. She stared at my mother and me with disbelief and disappointment.

"So you're going to kill me now, Gina? Didn't you do that already when you brought me into this world, a born heroin addict and left me for dead in a Dumpster? Then you rob us too?" Her eyes turned to slits.

"Asia, this has nothing to do with you. Now you can just walk away and act like none of this happened," our mother said.

"My loyalty is to my friends and Ceanna."

Pfff! I shot Asia in the head.

"No!" my mother cried.

"Ma, I had to do it. She was going to rat us out. You heard her say her loyalty was to them. Now snap out of it and let's get what we came for and get the fuck out of here!" I said.

We bagged the money and were on our way out the back door. "Wait, Jace, let me just say good-bye." My mother cried and went to kiss Asia on the side of her face.

"My sweet baby! I'm so sorry!" she cried. "Wait, Jace! We can't just leave her like this," my mother said, grabbed my arm.

"We got to get the fuck out of here!" I yelled.

"Jace, I can't leave her. At least help me put her behind the wall," she cried.

"Argh!" I stared at my mother for a moment. I was beyond pissed. Wasn't shit going right for me tonight.

"Come on, Ma, but we got to hurry."

I set the bag of money on the counter and slid the wall back. We struggled while we placed Asia's body behind the wall. I took one last look at Asia and shook my head. She was my sister, a sister I never knew I had. She was a beautiful girl, but my heart was calloused, and I couldn't feel for a stranger. The bitch was the enemy, and she would have told Ceanna the first chance she got. *Rest easy, Asia!* I thought.

Just when we finally closed the door to the wall and were on our way out the back door, the doorbell rang.

Ding dong. Knock, knock, knock.

"Asia, it's me, MeMe. Open up. It's raining hard out here." MeMe knocked again.

"Fuck!" I whispered. My mother and I looked at each other with wide eyes.

I opened the back door and heard the fence open. Fuck, I had to think fast. My mother and I eased back into the house and hid in the closet. MeMe came in through the back and began turning on the lights.

"Asia, where you at, babe? I told you I was coming and would be over."

"Oh my God! Is that blood? Asia, Asia, where are you?" MeMe shouted in a panicked voice. I came out of the closet and cocked my gun. If need be, she can join Asia too.

"Ah!" MeMe screamed. "Jaceyon, please don't kill me. I promise I won't say anything. Just tell me where my friend is," she cried.

I was about to answer her when a thrumming sound was heard coming from behind the wall. It caught my attention leaving me confused. Panic rose in me. *I know damn well I killed Asia. There is no way she could be alive. I shot the bitch in the dome,* I silently fussed.

MeMe ran to where the sound was coming from and pulled out her phone. I knew I should have killed her, but

I saw that as my opportunity to hurry up and escape.

"Ma, come on!" I yelled. My mother and I made a run toward the front door. The coast was clear, and we made a smooth exit.

"Jaceyon, you should have killed her!" my mother yelled as we drove away.

"We had to get the fuck out of there. We're going to have to get ghost. I'll go back to Auntie's house for the drugs and money another time, but right now, we got to leave."

"And go where? Shit? What about clothing?" my mother cried.

"Ma, we got bread. We'll just have to buy clothing and shit later." I headed toward I-35 North.

Chapter Twenty-five

Avantae

"Mmmmmm, Ceanna," I moaned.

I was dreaming that Ceanna was giving me some head. It felt a little different, not like how Ceanna normally gave me head; nevertheless, it still felt good.

"You like that, baby?" I heard Zaria's voice.

I tried to move and wake up, but my body felt heavy, and for some reason, my motor skills were off. I was finally able to open my eyes a little bit. The sun beamed through the folds of the hotel curtains, and it had my vision a little blurry.

I sat up slowly and noticed Zaria's lips go around my head. I weakly attempted to push her off of me when I lost my balance and fell off the bed.

"Oh my God! Avantae, are you okay, baby?" Zaria asked.

My legs and body were so weak. I lay there for a second and tried to recollect my thoughts. I was drawing a blank. I had this horrible headache, and my mouth was dry.

"Baby, let me help you," Zaria said, reaching for my arms. She was butt-ass naked.

I stared at her with wide eyes and wondered what the fuck happened last night. I noticed dried up come and white residue on my manhood. *God, please tell me I didn't fuck this broad,* I silently thought. As if Zaria could read my thoughts, she smiled at me.

"Last night was so good, baby daddy. I've missed you all these years." She squatted down and tried to lower her womanhood on my lower half.

"Bitch, get the fuck off me. Ain't no fucking way I fucked you willingly. What, ho, you had to drug me for some dick? You desperate junkie!" I yelled as I tried to lift myself up from the floor. I felt something hard. It was my cell phone.

While Zaria was yelling back at me, I quickly pressed one on my phone. It was programed to Ceanna's number. I was going to let Ceanna hear this shit for herself so she'd know I ain't on no bullshit.

"Nigga, yeah, and so what I drugged you, Tae? It got your attention. I'm sick of you ignoring me for Ceanna like I ain't shit. *I* was supposed to be your wife, Avantae, *me*. Then you take my son from me and put your hands on me!" she screamed while she hit her chest.

"Zaria, you foul as fuck for this. You need help! I can't believe you drugged me and been planning this shit all along. No wonder you kept canceling on a nigga every time we were supposed to meet at the studio, telling people your name is Tasha and shit. You're fucked up."

"No, *you're* fucked up, and your mama too. The bitch got me fired from my job, but I got something for her ass too, bitch nigga!" she yelled.

"I don't know when, Zaria, it might not be today or tomorrow, but I promise your time is up. I'm going to take my son and raise him right. You fucked up, Zaria. I don't know what kind of niggas you've been fucking with these last five years, but don't let the fact that I'm no longer in the streets make you forget how much of a savage nigga I am. I advise you to leave this room and don't look back." I stared at her with murder in my eyes.

Zaria looked at me terrified and began to back up. She didn't say anything else. She hurried out of the room taking heed to what I just said. I struggled to get up.

"Ceanna!" I yelled through the phone.

"Tae, I am here," she whispered.

"Did you hear everything?" I asked.

"Tae, can you just come home?" she cried.

"Baby, I am so sorry. I promise I didn't know about none of it."

"I know. I've been calling you all morning. Zaria sent a video last night of her sucking you off and riding you. She sent it to me and even had a message attached. Now I'm going to say this one time. When I drop these babies, her ass is mine and don't try to save that ho. It ain't gon' be today or tomorrow, but I *will* be reaching out and touching that ho," she expressed.

"No, you will not because I already warned her."

"And I'm telling you!" she yelled. "Now get your ass home now. Shit, all I want is a peaceful night of sleep. Got damn! See you later, and I love you." She hung up.

I stumbled around the room trying to find my bag so I could shower. "Got damn," I fussed. My balance was off. I finally made it to the restroom and looked at myself in the mirror. I looked like shit. I had bags under my eyes. My long hair was matted, and I needed to groom myself.

The shower brought me back to life. I finally could see and get my wits about me. I'm still confused and can't remember much after drinking in the Jack in the Box drive-through. "Oh shit!" I yelled out. That's when it hit me. Zaria had to have put something in my bottle. Everyone knew Patrón was my favorite liquor.

I had just slipped my shirt over my head when there was a knock at my door. I grabbed my piece out of my bag that I always carried and went to the door, ready for anything to pop off.

"My nigga, it's me, fam!" Semaj yelled through the door.

"Man, say!" I yelled, as I opened the door and allowed him in.

"My nigga, what the fuck just happened? I know this bitch didn't! Janair just called me telling me Zaria sent a video to Ceanna's phone of her sucking you off and shit. I can't believe this shit. Man, my nigga, I feel so played. I've been having music sessions with Tasha for damn near three months. No wonder she could never seem to meet up to go over the song with you. I can't believe she set this up the entire time," Semaj spoke fast while pacing the room.

"Now Janair's all pissed at me too because Kwency's here, and I didn't even tell her. I was moving so fast, man." He took a seat in a nearby chair and began rubbing his hands over his head. He damn near looked like he was about to cry.

"Man, I can't lose Janair behind this. Last night I was so faded on the drink. I went to bed. I haven't even seen or talked to Kwency," Semaj said.

"Fam, this ain't your fault. Truthfully, I should have gone with my first mind and called Ceanna to let her know what was going on. Honestly, though, I didn't think Zaria would stoop this low, yo. She drugged my Patrón bottle and had a key to my room. I don't know what the fuck happened last night. I was out of it. Don't worry about Janair. I'll talk to her, and from now on, it'll be best to take the ladies with us."

"Yeah, you're right about that. You ready to go, fam?" Semaj asked.

"Hell, yeah. Ceanna yelled at my ass and told me to bring my ass home now." I laughed. Ceanna didn't play with my ass.

As we left the room, Semaj spotted Kwency and Zaria walking down the hall. He dropped his bags and ran full speed ahead.

"My nigga, let that shit go!" I yelled as I ran after him.

"Bitch, I ought to fuck you up. You can forget being my assistant, Kwency!" Semaj yelled as he hemmed Kwency up.

Kwency began to cry and plead with him. "It wasn't me, Semaj. It was all Zaria," she said.

"How you going to lie on me like that, Kwency? *You* set this all up. Just like you did my makeup to make it look like Avantae beat me up so we could turn him in. All of this was *you*, Kwency. I should have never listened to you. Now I will never get my son back," Zaria cried.

Semaj let Kwency go, and both of us looked at each other in disbelief. Was this bitch Zaria serious? So she *really* took battered pictures to try to frame me? "Yo, I don't even know who this chick is anymore." I shook my head in disgust at both of them.

Semaj walked off and went to get his bags, and I just stared at Zaria. "Here is the money from last night. It's ten bands. I *never* want to see you or hear from you again. Tater Bug is staying with me. You need to get off that shit, Zaria, and get your shit together. I don't give a fuck what you do, but if I ever see you again, it's a wrap, and, Kwency, you sad, ma." With that, Semaj and I walked off.

"Semaj!" Kwency yelled, crying.

"Bitch, this is all *your* fault!" Zaria yelled at her. The two women began to fight in the hallway.

Semaj and I just looked back, shook our heads, and continued to walk. I had to get back home to my woman. This shit is crazy!

Chapter Twenty-six

Zaria

After Kwency and I fought, I went back to my hotel room. I called the front desk to inform them that I would be staying an additional two nights.

I cringed at my appearance. I had a busted lip and a black eye. I washed the makeup from my face and called room service. I asked for a bucket of ice, and I ordered me a big meal off the menu. I didn't plan on showing my face at all.

Nursing my eye and lip, I sat in a nearby chair. I felt lost without my son. I wish I could be that strong black woman, but I never had an example of what that was. I've lost my way.

I've struggled a long time in life. Validation and acceptance was something I needed. The drugs helped numb feelings I didn't want to feel. Now, due to my reckless behavior, I was alone and had nowhere to go. I didn't know anyone here, and ten grand was not going to get me far.

All of my things were at my mother's house, but I refused to go back there. Besides, on Kwency's dime, I tried to buy up the entire mall. I had boots, sandals, flip-flops, heels, Jordans, purses, perfume, jewelry, a MAC makeup collection, sexy undergarments, and at least twenty or more outfits. She didn't complain once, and if I knew that bitch was going to throw me under the bus the way she did, I would have got her for more.

I attempted to call Rick. I was done with the bull-shit, and the look Avantae gave me earlier, I knew he would make good on his promise. I needed to get my shit together, and after last night, singing on the stage touched something in me.

The way the crowd went wild let me know I'm supposed to be a star. The problem now is, how will I ever get there? My meal ticket with Kwency and Semaj was gone.

"Rick, I've been calling you over and over. Why aren't you answering? Look, I was calling to pull out on the deal. I don't want to press charges on Avantae. The photos were staged with makeup to create the bruises. Avantae never beat me the way I claimed. I lied! As far as his mother, I lied about that too. I don't know anything about the insulin or Samuel's death. I don't want any part of this anymore." I hung up. I called Mia Symone next.

"Hey, Za, what's up?" Mia Symone answered.

"Nothing much, girl. I'm in Dallas," I told her.

"In Dallas? What's up there?" she asked.

"I had a performance, but the shit went all wrong. I called myself trying to set Avantae up with Kwency, and she flanked on me. Me and that bitch fought and everything. Avantae threatened me and told me I can't come back to Austin or he'll basically kill me, and that bitch Ceanna has my son," I cried.

"Well, Za, take it from me, you'll never win bringing misery to other people. Maybe you caused this on yourself. Perhaps it's time to sit back and do some self-reflecting. God knows I am," she sighed.

"What's gotten into you? You're different now, Mia Symone. The Mia Symone I know would be plotting and scheming by now," I said, shocked.

"Bitch, jail got into me, and shit, if that ain't enough, try a baby. I lost everything behind a man that never gave a fuck about me, and you know what's funny?

The same person I wronged and did dirty to is the only person who has my back. I should have never ever fucked with Jaceyon. Ceanna never did nothing to me. I let my jealousy take over, and I tried to bring harm to my own cousin. In the end, Jaceyon beat, raped me, and treated me like I wasn't shit. Ceanna came through for me, my son, and got me the fuck away from there. So stop while you're ahead, Zaria," Mia Symone cried.

"Where are you, Mia Symone?" I asked.

"I'm in San Antonio now."

"Can I come there for a few days?"

"I don't think that's a good idea. Besides, you hate my cousin, and I am not trying to bring any more bullshit her way."

"I understand," I said, discouraged.

"Well, hey, I gotta go now, Zaria. Take care of yourself and get your shit together," she urged and hung up.

I sat there confused. When did Mia Symone get so holy? The Mia Symone I knew never gave a fuck about nobody but herself, and now, she was all for Ceanna. I was beginning to feel lost and alone. I wished I hadn't met any of these people. I sat in the chair a little longer and cried my heart out.

I remember the roofies Kwency gave me and perked up. I decided to take a nice bubble bath, eat the food I ordered, and made me a nice drink. Afterward, I turned the television to the ID channel. *I (Almost) Got Away with It* was showing, and it piqued my interest. I lay in bed with my drink and took two of the roofies.

Day two came so fast. I hadn't done anything but sleep. I was a stinky mess. Checkout time was in two hours, and I struggled around the room. I wasn't going to make it, and I needed another day or two for this shit to wear off. I called the front desk and went ahead and booked three additional nights.

By the next day, I had a hunger pain so deep. I was still a little weak, but it was time to get my shit in order. Viewing the menu, I ordered up a meal for at least four people. I planned to eat every last drop too, and I did just that. I ate until I was sick.

I finally showered and got back in bed. My phone was dry, and that saddened me. *Sigh*. It was time for me to sink or swim I thought as I began surfing my phone for jobs.

Job searching was discouraging. I just couldn't see myself working a nine to five. That shit is for the birds. I needed something, though, and I couldn't stay in this room forever. Jumping up, I decided to head out to the club Avantae and I performed at. I didn't know what to expect but thought maybe someone would recognize me.

The club was loud and smoky. I could barely see as I made my way to the bar. Out of nowhere, I heard my false name being called.

"Tasha, right?" this nice, tall, handsome guy asked. I checked out his appearance, and he was all right. He wasn't Avantae, but he would do.

"Yes, hi. I'm sorry, do I know you?" I asked, nursing a drink the bartender passed me.

"Hi, my bad. My name is Mondre, but my friends call me Dre. I'm a producer here in Dallas, and I really enjoyed your performance the other night. I'm also the one who paid you guys Saturday night," he winked and extended his hand to mine.

"Oh, wow! Thank you so much, Dre! That means a lot." I smiled, thinking of ways I could get this nigga for his bread. He was a sucka-ass dude.

"So what's up? Are you signed? You got a manager or looking to get back in the studio?" he asked.

"None of the above. Matter of a fact, shit is all wrong, Dre, and, truthfully, I'm doing bad with nowhere to go. I have a hotel room for two more nights, and after that, I don't know what I'm going to do." I sadly smiled while I looked into his eyes.

"Well, shit, ma, I know you don't know me, but I've got an extra bedroom, and you could crash at my place until you get on your feet. I've got to get you in the studio, yo. Your voice is beautiful."

Dre and I danced the night away. We had a lot of sexual tension between us, and I liked his vibe. "Ma, let's get out of here and get us some food!" he yelled over the music.

He took me to IHOP. We laughed and got to know each other a little better. He was funny as hell, and although I just met him, I felt comfortable around him.

"I ain't gon' lie; I'm digging the fuck outta you." He licked his lips, and I blushed. "Can I ask you something?"

"Sure, Dre."

"What happened to your face? I can see through the heavy makeup the flaws you trying to cover up." He frowned.

"Oh, this is nothing. I got into it with a friend, and we fought a little." I kept it short and simple.

"As long as it wasn't a nigga putting his hands on you, then we're good."

I took Dre back to my room, and we made love. His skills were okay, but I've had better. *Way* better! I drifted off to sleep, and when I woke up, Dre was gone—and so was all my money.

"What the fuck? No, no, no, no, no! Why? Please, God! I'm so fucking stupid," I screamed while I pulled my hair.

Now I didn't have anywhere to go or any money. I knew after the shit I just pulled I couldn't call Avantae, Rick wasn't answering, Mia Symone ain't messing with me, Kwency and Semaj are done with me, and I damn sho' couldn't ask my mama.

"Wait!" I wiped the tears from my face that steadily fell.

"Jaceyon!" I screamed. "He'll help me; we both have a common enemy," I spoke aloud.

My phone rang, and I ran to answer it. I didn't recognize the number. "Hello," I said in a shaky voice.

"Za, this is Jaceyon. Where are you at? Some shit done popped off. We've been hiding out, but I got to shake this spot. Are you still in Dallas?" he questioned in a rushed tone.

"Oh, thank God." I broke down crying. "Yes, I'm in Dallas. I'm stranded with nowhere to go. Avantae took my son and told me if I show my face in Austin again, he'll kill me. This my last night in this room. I have no money."

"That bitch nigga ain't gon' do shit. Say, though, my T-lady and I are coming that way. Text me the address to where you are, and, Za, you ain't heard from me. One!" He ended the call.

I didn't know what that was about, and truthfully, I didn't care. I was just happy that with the help of Jaceyon I won't be homeless and out here on these ruthless Dallas streets—or worse, having to sell my ass.

Chapter Twenty-seven

Avantae

The drive back home was quiet. Both Semaj and I were in deep thoughts. Man, I have encountered a lot of dirty shit in my life, but I swear I didn't see that shit with Zaria coming.

Zaria used to be so sweet, smart, and innocent back then. I reclined my seat, and my mind drifted to a time I tried to forget.

I walked through the hood on Twelfth Street after just serving a fiend. From a distance, I saw some niggas all circled around each other.

"Damn, shorty is bad!" one of the niggas yelled.

"Hell, yeah, look at that ass. Damn, Avantae's bitch can get this dick anytime, you feel me?" another nigga yelled excitedly.

"Her pussy feels so good," the one with the phone said. As I got closer, one of the niggas pointed at me.

"Shit, run, fam!" Many of them ran. I grabbed the nigga with the phone and placed him in a headlock.

"You fucking my bitch?" I yelled. "Nigga, start talking, or I promise I'll deliver your body to your family." I cocked my gun.

He held his phone up for me to see, and sure enough, Zaria was sucking this nigga off. I wanted to cry. My heart was shattered. I took care of Zaria, fed her, kept money in her pockets, kept her dressed, and this bitch disrespected me.

"Who did you send this video to?" I yelled angrily.

"No-no-nobody, I swear." Fear filled his eyes.

"You know you fucked up, right?"

I let the nigga go, and he kept pleading with me. I calmly walked away leaving him standing there. As I walked, I placed a phone call to have the nigga domed. No nigga will disrespect me and live to tell it.

Zaria had no clue I knew about that. I knew something was weighing on her, though, especially when she heard of the nigga's demise. I thought I could maybe forgive her, but the images of her sucking another man were a permanent fixture in my mind. She betrayed me in the worst way.

"Avantae." Semaj tapped me on the arm. "We're here, man. Come on!" Semaj sighed loudly.

I low key wanted to laugh. He acted like Janair was about to kill him, and I just didn't see baby girl as being the aggressive type. As soon as I walked through the door, Jalisa and Tater Bug came running full speed.

"Daddy!" they yelled.

"Hey, Daddy's babies." I hugged and kissed both of them.

"WyKeith, thank you for holding it down, my nigga. Good looking!" I gave WyKeith a signature hood hug ending it with a snap.

"No doubt, fam."

I looked at Keisha, and then back at WyKeith with raised eyebrows. Janair just put her hand up and shook her head.

"Where's Ceanna?" I asked.

"She's in the back, lying down," Keisha answered.

"And my T-lady?"

"She's with Ceanna," Janair answered.

"I need to talk to you," Janair said to Semaj. Semaj looked at me as if he were five years old.

"I'll be back!" I left the living room.

When I entered my bedroom, my mother was consoling Ceanna. *Damn, man! This shit is going to set us back,* I thought, upset.

"Ma, let me talk to Ceanna."

"Hi, baby! I'm glad you're home." My mother kissed me on the cheek.

When she left the room, I went and crouched in front of Ceanna on my knees. Her eyes were red and swollen from all the crying she had been doing.

"Ceanna, I don't even know what to say. I just want you to know that I would never disrespect you like that. I pray this don't make you look at me differently." I looked deep into her beautiful eyes.

"I'm so angry. I want to kill Zaria. I really do! I've got one question and don't lie. Did you perform with her on stage?"

"Yes." I hung my head.

"You know when it comes to you thinking and using common sense, you don't. Y'all men do what you can't handle. When you found out she was there, the *first* thing you should have done was call. That's what *I* would have done, Tae, because I respect you. Women are vicious, especially when they want something they can't have. I'm not mad at you for handling business and performing, but I'm pissed because you didn't tell me," she yelled.

"You're right! I should have just come home," I confessed.

"No, you should have called, and I would have told you to get your money. I know how to separate dumb shit and business," she fussed.

"Where does this leave us, baby?" I asked.

"Avantae, I never said I was leaving you. I just told you where you went wrong. I'm hurt, but I know you love me, and I do trust you. Next time, use common sense, and let me say this: Stop choosing for me. Just tell me what's up. Damn, you act like I'm unstable or some shit."

"Huh? You kinda are, though. One minute your ass is Tyson, the next, saved by a fucking angel, and the next, a deadly storm," I laughed.

"What you tryin'a say?" she laughed. I stood to hug Ceanna and gave her a kiss. I tried to go further, but Ceanna shut that shit all the way down.

"Um . . . negative! Before you run up in me, you need to get tested. Ain't no telling what that junkie bitch do to get her high. You got me fucked up!" she yelled, getting mad all over.

Ceanna's phone rang, and I studied her facial expressions as she listened to the person on the other end. When she hung up, she shook her head.

"That was Vera from the police station. They found my Tahoe at the abandoned car wash."

"Huh? How is that so when the vehicles are in Houston? Man, what the fuck?" I fumed, pulling out my phone to call Elijah.

"Ayo, Elijah, I just got a call that my wife's truck was found at the abandoned car wash. Shit ain't adding up. Start talking!" I aggressively barked.

"That can't be! I dropped both your and Ceanna's vehicles off in your driveway last night. I knocked on the door, and no one answered. I thought your vehicles would be safe in your driveway. I even called your phone twice and left you a message."

"I'ma get up with you." I hung up.

"This nigga said he dropped the vehicles off at the house last night, Ceanna. Shit ain't adding up. Elijah still got the keys."

"Jaceyon!" Ceanna yelled while shaking her head. "This nigga just don't stop. He's the only other person beside you and me who has a key. Baby, come on, let's go get my truck."

"Nawl, you rest. Me and WyKeith can handle that."

"Nawl, and I'm going the fuck outta here, Avantae! Now, let's go now!" Ceanna yelled with her fists balled. I wasn't going back and forth with her nutty ass.

Semaj and Janair said their good-byes. Semaj was smiling, so I guess their talk went well. My mother stayed behind to watch the children, and WyKeith, Keisha, Ceanna, and I piled in the rental to head to the car wash.

Keisha drove Ceanna's Tahoe with Ceanna and WyKeith, and I rode in the rental. The ladies were following us back to my old home.

I filled WyKeith in on everything that took place in Dallas, and he filled me in on the eventful night he had. I laughed thinking of Asia and Keisha fighting. Shit is crazy, yo. My phone rang out, and I saw that it was Elijah. "What'd up, though?" I asked.

"My nigga, what the fuck is going on, fam? One-timers have got your fucking house taped off and shit!" he yelled. "It's like ten of them hoes."

"What! Fuck, we coming around the corner."

As soon as I pulled up, I saw a body bag being carried out. "What the fuuuck?" I yelled and jumped out of the car. One of the officer pigs pointed at me.

"Avantae Wallace Jr.?" the one-timer asked.

"Man, who the fuck wants to know? I ain't done shit. Ayo, what the fuck is going on, yo? The *fuck* is this?" I yelled with wide eyes.

"Avantae Wallace Jr., you are under arrest for the murder of Detective Rick Miles." The pig began to handcuff me.

"Man, let me go. I ain't do shit, man!" I yelled.

"Nooooo, Avantae! That's my husband." Ceanna fought with one of the cops. She reminded me of Bird on *Soul Food*, the way she yelled and screamed at the officers.

"Get your hands off of her. WyKeith, get Ceanna and Keisha!" I yelled as the police slammed me on the ground.

"Aaaah, fuck, you bitch-ass cops always fucking with a nigga!" I yelled.

"Do you know who the fuck I am? Get your fucking hands off of me, bitch. I will shut this fucking city down!" Ceanna yelled at one of the cops. He began to back away from her.

"Avantae!" Ceanna yelled. I looked her direction and saw that she pick pocketed the same officer. Concealed in a clear bag was a phone. Ceanna smiled at me, and I knew I had a rider.

"Don't worry! I'll be down there first thing in the morning—*with* the lawyer!" she yelled.

WyKeith escorted Keisha and Ceanna back inside the Tahoe, and he got behind the wheel. I didn't know what the fuck was going on, but I know I ain't do shit.

Chapter Twenty-eight

Ceanna

Keisha and I sat in the back of my Tahoe as WyKeith drove us back to my home. I was in deep thought thinking about the events that just transpired. Truthfully, I didn't want to involve my family. Although I know they love me, they are too deadly and dangerous. I made a promise to myself once my parents died that I would cut ties with my family and love them from a distance.

I didn't want Tater Bug, Jalisa, or my children to experience street wars, bloodshed, home invasions, kidnappings, lawyers, or court arrangements. I wanted them to be free and just be children. Somehow, though, I just can't escape the streets or the dangers that lie within them.

To get Avantae out of jail, I was going to need someone powerful. I didn't want to, but I knew I was going to have to call my father's attorney and call Judge Watts to inform them of the situation. The fact that Jaceyon did all of this to get me back is crazy.

"Boo, are you okay?" Keisha asked, rubbing my stomach.

"Keisha, honestly, I'm just trying to hold shit together."

"I bet Janair thinks we're a bunch of nuts," Keisha laughed, causing me to laugh as well.

"Damn, Keisha, everywhere we go you've got to show yo' ass," I laughed.

"I'm sorry, Ceanna! I didn't mean to ruin our girls' night," Keisha expressed.

"I know, boo, but I told you that would happen."

"You did, Ce, but it's not like I haven't been real with Asia. I told her how I felt way before WyKeith and I got so deep. She just doesn't want to let go. I just hope Asia is okay. I don't want to lose her friendship, and as a friend, I love her. I'm going to give her some space for a minute."

"Have you heard from her?" I asked.

"No. I called twice, though, earlier, but she didn't answer. I'll give her about a week, and then I'll go home to talk to her."

We chatted awhile longer before we finally pulled up to the house. The kids ran out of the game room to greet us as usual, and when they didn't see Avantae, they began asking a million questions. I looked at Mama Barbara Jean and shook my head no, signaling to her that something was wrong.

"Kids, y'all go play for a while," Barbara Jean said.

"But, Grandma, we want Daddy. Where's Daddy?" the kids asked.

"Daddy had to go handle some business again out of town. He sends his love and will see you soon." I felt horrible for lying to them.

The kids seemed to sense I was lying, but they didn't ask any more questions. They turned and ran back to the game room. I felt extremely guilty because one thing my parents didn't do was keep things from me or lie about things that were going on.

I turned on the monitor to keep an eye on the children in the game room. WyKeith, Keisha, Mama, and I sat at the dining table. I pulled the plastic bag from under my breast and retrieved the phone out of the bag that I stole from the police officer. Before I powered it on, WyKeith took it from my hands.

"Hold on, Ce! Let me disable something real quick. I don't want them to trace this phone here. Naw what I mean?"

"Ceanna, baby, what's going on?" Barbara Jean asked.

"I don't know. I got a phone call stating that my vehicle was at an abandoned car wash. We left to get my vehicle and then went over to Avantae's old home. When we got there, it was surrounded by police. They were bringing a body out of the home. Some guy name Detective Rick. Anyway, they ended up arresting Avantae. I was able to pick pocket this phone from the police officer. WyKeith, will you do the honors?" I asked, pointing to the phone.

WyKeith nodded his head as he surfed through the phone. The suspense was killing me. "Damn!" WyKeith sighed.

"What?" we all asked.

"Basically, Zaria and Jaceyon were trying to set Avantae up. Mama Barbara Jean, they were even trying to get you for murder."

"Murder?" Keisha's eyes widened.

"Yeah, and I might as well gon' and tell you this, Keisha. I killed Samuel. Remember when I shared my story with you at the hospital when Zylan passed?" Barbara Jean asked.

"Yes," Keisha cried.

"Well, it was him, Keisha, and when I saw him lying in that hospital bed, I got my revenge. I never meant to hurt you, Keisha, and I'm sorry I took away someone you loved, but I had to do it," Barbara Jean said, crying.

Keisha began shedding tears. She really loved Samuel, and he treated her good. He had ended up being her child's father, and now Zylan and Samuel were gone. However, she didn't blame Barbara Jean, and she understood it. She herself knew what it was like to have a piece torn from you.

"I understand." She smiled sadly at Barbara Jean.

As those two talked more, I sat there in a daze. Something was off, and shit wasn't adding up to me. I needed to see something, so I told the guys to follow me into the panic room.

Avantae had the security system hooked up in the panic room. He had access and eyes everywhere. He even had cameras to my boutique, his shop, his home, my condo, and Tonya's condo. There were so many screens. I searched for the screens at Avantae's home and rewinded the tapes to Saturday night.

"Look," Keisha pointed at two masked gunmen.

We all stood there shocked. I couldn't confirm who the men were until one of the gunmen began spraying all the cameras. I caught a glimpse of something.

"Pause the tape. You see right there? Look." I pointed to the gunman's inner left arm.

Clear as day, Jaceyon's AK-47 with six bullets surrounding the gun tattoo showed on one of the many blind cameras he missed.

I witnessed Jaceyon steal a picture of me off of Avantae's wall. *"You my bitch, Ceanna, and will always be. I'ma kill that nigga and get back what is mine,"* he spoke as he kissed the photo of me. He even stole two watches of Avantae's; one of the watches was given to him by his father, and he stole a chain and a pair of Jordans.

"Broke-ass nigga!" Barbara Jean yelled.

"WyKeith, were there any videos on the phone too?" I asked.

"Yeah, man, Ce, but I skipped over the shit on purpose. You *don't* wanna see that."

"Let me see." I held my hand out for the phone.

"Nah, Ce, I'm telling you, it's some fuck shit on this phone," he spoke with his hands.

"Well, I wanna see too," Keisha backed me up.

"Here, mane," WyKeith sighed while passing the phone.

Keisha and Barbara Jean huddled by me. I pushed "Play," and we were all so disgusted. I shook my head in disbelief at what I saw. Although I knew Avantae had always been truthful, I didn't want to believe him when he told me Jaceyon was gay, but here it was clear as day on Rick's phone. Jaceyon was taking it up the ass.

"I told you." WyKeith came around to give me a hug.

"I'm okay; I'm just shocked and disgusted," I admitted. "I can't believe I didn't see the signs. I'm so thankful to God that he didn't give me HIV or an STD. God spared me, and in that moment, I know he loves me because he was revealing everything to me about Jaceyon."

I needed to focus my energy elsewhere so while WyKeith made a phone call, I excused myself to my bedroom. Although I didn't want to, I had to involve my family. I didn't know where Jaceyon was, and seeing how obsessed he was with me and trying to bring malice to Avantae, I had to take matters into my own hands and protect my family.

Calling my family to give orders was extremely hard. I didn't understand the Haitian Creole language or the broken English from my family. It took awhile, but once I got ahold of my cousin Leyssa Gaelle on the phone, we were able to organize a security plan for my babies, Jalisa, and Tater Bug. I didn't want this to affect them, and I wanted them to still go to school as usual. However, their safety would always be number one.

"Hey, Ce!" Keisha said, startling me while she entered my room.

"Hey, boo! Lawd, my family is crazy," I smiled.

"You don't really speak of them much."

"That's because I was always afraid of them, Key. My cousin from my mother's side, Leyssa Gaelle, is really the only one I remember that's sane. She's still deadly, though, and plus, she speaks English too."

"Well, love, everything will be okay." Keisha sat next to me on the bed and gave me a hug.

"I know that was hard seeing Jaceyon like that. I'm your friend, and I know you're not okay. I wish I could take away all of your pain, boo. It's been one thing after another, but your time of relief is coming. At least now with the detective's phone and everything that has happened, you'll be able to use this against Jaceyon, and Avantae will be able to use what Zaria has done against her to get full custody."

"What would I do without you, Key?" I asked as tears fell.

"Are *you* okay, though? I know you loved Samuel, and hearing Mama say she killed him must be hard," I said.

"I'm fine, and honestly, I don't blame her. She shared her story with me when Zylan passed. She helped me, and it was because of her, I pushed through most days. I understand! She did what she felt she had to do. Sometimes when a man violates you, it hurts you, and you are never the same. You become a prisoner in your own mind, afraid to leave the house, afraid to date, and it changes you. You find some type of comfort when they're dead," she shrugged.

"Wow, can you believe all the shit we've been through together? Bitch, you're stuck with my ass. Key, on some real shit, though, will you be my babies' godmother and look after my children if anything was to ever happen to me?" I asked seriously.

"Ce, I'd be honored. Thank you for asking me. That really touches me." We hugged.

"Oh, that's what I wanted to ask you. Are you still doing Jalisa's party?"

"Yes, next weekend, and, hopefully, Tae will be home, and everything has died down."

WyKeith and Keisha stayed over another night. I was thankful for friends like them. I didn't have to go through things alone, and that was a huge weight lifted off my shoulders.

Chapter Twenty-nine

Avantae

Man, I'm so fucking pissed off. They had me locked up downtown with these bum niggas, smelling shit and piss. I haven't been inside this shit hole in years. I felt closed in, and I didn't like being behind steel bars, with hard steel benches and a room full of musty, itchy balls, fruit-cake type of niggas.

All I know was I better be out of this bitch tomorrow. I know Ceanna and my mama sick right now.

I really tried to abide by my promise. I prayed, took a leave of absence from the streets, got my son, and became a man, but that wasn't enough, and I feel like a sucka-ass nigga mane. Niggas think I'm slipping out here, boi, but they about to see.

I should have killed Jaceyon a long time ago. This nigga has done all he can to put hell into Ceanna's and my relationship.

Stealing from me woke the beast up in me. After talking to my baby and WyKeith, I can't believe the lengths Jaceyon and Zaria went through to tear us apart.

My baby Ceanna is so strong. The strength that woman has amazes me, but I know she's tired, and she deserves peace and closure. I'm going to give that to her, and if I have to have blood on my hands to protect my family . . . I will.

I'm also starting to think letting Zaria live was a huge mistake. I know I told her to stay gone, but after sitting here, thinking about how she plotted for months on me is unbelievable. Just the way she treated my son alone angers me.

Man, I hope Jalisa and my son don't look at me differently. I really wanted to be a role model for them. I tried to keep all the street shit away from them. The last thing I want is for my son to glamorize this shit.

I must have dozed off because the next thing I remember is my name being called. God must have been on my side because once I appeared before the court, the judge was none other than Judge Watts.

Judge Watts was on Calvin's payroll back in the day, and he used to chill with my pops. When he saw me, we made direct eye contact, and I knew Ceanna had something to do with this.

Judge Watts gave his order, and before he hit the gavel, he blinked three times. He had secretly told me that he would be paying me a visit.

My bail was granted, and I was a free man for now. I walked out the doors of the courthouse, inhaling the stench of downtown Austin.

"Avantae!" I heard my baby call my name.

I smiled at Ceanna as she attempted to jog toward me. She was so damn cute in her gray jogging set and flip-flops.

"You know they couldn't keep a real nigga down," I smirked while I kissed her.

"Come on, baby! WyKeith, Keisha, and Mama are in the truck waiting." Ceanna grabbed my hand.

"Where are the kids?" I asked, paranoid.

"They're at school. It's Monday. Don't worry. I hired eyes on them. I'm no fool, and I don't know where Gina or Jaceyon is at."

"We need to get them!" I was uneasy.

"Avantae, you do know my mom's people are Haitian and Spanish, right? Trust me; they will shoot up the entire city if I order it. There are fifteen men and women on guard. Two are cafeteria workers, one works in the administration office, three are janitors, each door is guarded; then there's the hall monitor, substitute teachers. . . . Need I go on, baby?" Ceanna asked while smiling.

"All right, then, Gangster," I smiled.

I had to watch Ceanna's ass. How the fuck did she organize all of that shit for the kids just to go to school? I was impressed and turned on at the same damn time. And I was hungrier than a bitch, so we went to this Mexican restaurant run by Ceanna's Mexican cousin Elizabeth. It was a front for the cartels. A lot of trafficking came through there, but the food and drinks were so damn good. We were seated off in a more private section.

"Avantae, I did that thing, and everything is good," Keisha spoke in code letting me know the baby shower was handled.

WyKeith and Ceanna looked at both of us wondering what we were talking about. I smiled because Ceanna was so nosy.

"So what the fuck is going on, yo?" I asked everyone. The suspense was killing me.

WyKeith passed me Rick's phone. Everyone looked at me as I viewed all the information on the phone. I was heated! I couldn't believe the messages between Zaria and the detective. She even fucked the nigga a couple of times. Then she had the nerve to set my mama up too.

I almost threw up at the fucking session between Rick and Jaceyon. Here Jaceyon was trying to set me up and didn't even know he was recorded taking it up the ass. *Fuck boy, aye,* I silently thought.

"That's not all, Tae. There's more at the house on the cameras," Ceanna informed me.

"That's what's up because later, the judge and lawyer are stopping by."

"Ceanna, Jaceyon has got to go, and after seeing the shit Zaria did, I'm going to have to put a price on little mama's head too. I won't feel comfortable with them still breathing."

Ceanna was quiet, and I knew she didn't agree with what I was saying. Truth of the matter was, a lot of this shit would have been avoided if I had killed Jaceyon a long time ago. He won't stop until he kills Ceanna or finds a way to get me out of the equation for good.

"I know," Ceanna said, shocking the fuck outta me.

"I bet Jaceyon and Gina are hiding out at Cheryl's old home," Keisha blurted out of the blue.

"Why would they be there?" Ceanna asked.

"Because nobody would suspect that, and it's abandoned."

WyKeith and I looked at each other, and I knew he was thinking what I was thinking. I would give this a couple of days, and then I was putting my murder game back into motion. Jaceyon had crossed the line.

The five of us chopped it up awhile before Ceanna and I dropped Keisha and WyKeith off at our home to get their vehicles. Next, we went to get the children from school. Ceanna was right. The school was heavily guarded. To the naked eye, it appeared as though the workers were a part of the school's staff.

"See, I told you." Ceanna smiled and grabbed my hand.

"Daddyyyyy!" the kids screamed.

Hearing those words always made me smile. I was definitely a proud man and father. I laughed once the kids got into the vehicle. They damn near talked my mother's ear off. I smirked at her through the rearview mirror, and she gave me a "help me" look.

"I'm happy to have you home," Ceanna smiled.

"How are you feeling, baby?" I asked.

"I'm okay, baby, just a little tired and my feet hurt. Oh, baby, before we go home, can you stop by the store? I need to grab something real quick," she smirked.

"Sure. What is it?" I asked.

"Rubber bands." She smiled seductively.

"Y'all ain't slick," Barbara Jean yelled from the backseat.

"Damn, we can't get shit by you, huh?" Ceanna laughed.

"We ain't got to stop, though. I already got three from WyKeith." We laughed. Ceanna's ass was going to gimme that shit. I can't wait any longer.

When we arrived home, I wanted to make love to Ceanna, but I had to review the cameras first. Jaceyon had lost his mind. The nigga stole the watch my pops gave me, and just on that alone, I wanted to kill him.

Judge Watts and the lawyer Charles came over that evening. They reviewed the cameras and the information on Rick's phone.

"This shit is crazy." Watts shook his head and sipped on his Patrón.

"Unbelievable." Charles took a puff of his cigar.

Once Ceanna came and joined us, Charles and I respectfully put out our cigars. She gave me an "I know I done told yo' ass no smoking in here" look, and I smirked, knowing damn well she was not about to act a fool in front of these two powerful men.

"Ceanna, you're just as beautiful as the last time I saw you. You are the spitting image of your mother, Cynthia. Calvin would be proud," the judge beamed while giving her a kiss on the cheek. I don't know why, but I became jealous. *Ho-ass nigga,* I silently fussed.

"Judge Watts—" she said but was cut off.

"Call me Malcolm."

"Well, Malcolm, thank you, and you're too kind." She smiled at him.

"Hi, Charles! Thank you for coming." Ceanna reached to hug Charles.

"Anything for you, beautiful," the lawyer replied.

Do these niggas think I'm some clown-ass nigga right now? I mugged both of them. Ceanna smiled at me and tapped my knee. She knew I wasn't feeling they asses up on my woman.

"So let's get down to business," Ceanna smiled. "I'll go first, Charles, and get out of you men's business."

That's another thing I loved about Ceanna; she didn't crowd me or overstep her boundaries. She knew when to speak and when to speak when spoken to. She was graceful, not forceful, but had a powerful essence about her that made you listen and respect her.

"Sure, beautiful, go ahead," Charles smiled, causing me to frown.

"Well, since you have viewed the tape, clearly Jaceyon is unstable, dangerous, and, therefore, I don't want my children around him. I want the divorce processed immediately. I want a restraining order against Jaceyon for my daughter Jalisa and me. He is not to visit my shop or be anywhere near me—oh, his mama too. The home we shared was in my name. Therefore, none of the proceeds are to go to him. We have no joint property or money. We weren't married for ten years, and I don't owe that nigga shit. That's all. Oh, and I want to adopt Avantae Devin Wallace III." She smiled at me and squeezed my knee.

"Ceanna, sure, I will have that arranged! Since Watts is here, it shouldn't be an issue to get all the paperwork signed. Come by my office Friday, and I'll have everything ready for you," Charles said.

"Oh, Charles, my estates and investments, how are they?" Ceanna asked.

"Let's just say, Ceanna, you'll never be broke. Your father was a wealthy man, and your mother was very smart with how the money was invested. You, dear, are making money in your sleep," Charles expressed with his hands.

"Well, that's wonderful. Please make sure to add Jalisa and Tater Bug to my accounts as well. Once Avantae and I marry, be sure to give him my father's associates and add him to the estate. Okay, well, handsome gentlemen, let me get out of here." Ceanna hugged everyone and kissed me on the lips.

"Avantae, hurry up and get them out of here. I'm horny as hell," Ceanna whispered in my ear and licked it. My manhood shot straight up, and I had to excuse myself for a minute. Ceanna can get it now, shit.

"Gentlemen, excuse us for a moment." I left the two men alone. There was a secret camera in this room, so I wasn't worried about leaving them.

Ceanna pulled me into the hall bathroom and placed the condom on with her mouth. She began sucking my manhood taking it in her mouth whole.

"Ah, fuck, ma!" I moaned out. "Ma, I gotta feel you." Ceanna stood and leaned over the sink. I gently entered her womanhood which sucked me in like a vacuum. Her sweet nectar was made just for me.

"Mmmmmm, daddyyyyy! Yes!" Ceanna sexily moaned. Seeing her sex faces in the mirror turned me on, and I began to murder that pussy.

"Oh shit, right there, Tae. Mmmm, I love you, Avantaeee." Ceanna bounced back, causing my knees to weaken. She knew I couldn't take too much longer of her bouncing like that.

"Fuck, do that shit. Do that shit, baby! You sexy, black muthafucka. You're so fucking sexy, Ceanna." *Wham!* I slapped her ass.

"Tae, I'ma kick yo' ass. Ah, I'm coooming!" Ceanna screamed too damn loudly.

"Aaaargh," I moaned, easily pulling out of Ceanna. I threw the condom in the trash, and Ceanna turned around and smiled at me.

"I love you!" I rested my head against her forehead.

"I know, baby! Now go handle your business, with yo' jealous ass. You're cute, Avantae." She laughed, and I slapped her ass again.

"Boy!" Ceanna hit me on my arm, and I laughed.

When I got back to the room the fellas were in, they grinned at me. I knew they had heard my baby's sexual moans and my groans. I didn't care, though. Our sexual appetite had to be fed by each other.

"My bad, y'all! Now, back to the matter at hand. I want full custody of my son, and since Ceanna's divorce will be final, I need a license drawn up to marry her. Put a restraining order against Zaria too. She is not to contact my son or step on the grounds of his school," I ordered. I hated all this legal shit. I'm a hood nigga, and I prefer to dome a nigga and keep it moving. Since I have a wife now and kids, I had to move smarter.

"No problem, Avantae. I brought this. Have the mother of Zaria sign this. It states that she is giving you permission to have full custody of her grandson, and she wants no part of raising him in the absence of her daughter." Charles handed me a document.

"That shouldn't be a problem."

"With this evidence I have, Avantae, everything will be thrown out. Luckily, Jaceyon stole those keys. That way, you aren't facing a drug charge. As far as the guns—" Judge Watts said but was cut off by Charles.

"They are lost. I called in a favor for the guns to be removed from the evidence room. Technically, they have nothing on you," Charles smiled. This nigga was official. I see why Calvin kept him for years.

"Well then, Mr. Wallace, it seems as if everything is in order," Watts said.

"And my mother?" I asked.

"They can't prove anything, and they have no evidence on her, so she is good. It's also a good thing she no longer works there at the hospital. I wouldn't worry about that, though," Watts confirmed.

The gentlemen stood to leave and shook my hand on the way out. A sense of relief washed over me. Finally, I can marry Ceanna, have full custody of my son, and we can move on with our life.

Chapter Thirty

Ceanna

This morning started off just like every other school morning. I cooked breakfast, and we got the children ready for school. I gave Jalisa twenty-four invitations for her party and told her she could invite whoever she wanted.

Once the kids were situated in the school, I ran by my boutique and looked around to make sure my staff was doing their jobs. The place was really clean, and all the inventory was neatly hanging on the racks.

I said my hellos as I walked by the many customers that shopped in the store. I smiled at this beautiful, light-skinned sista. She was indecisive about two dresses she had in her hand.

"You're really beautiful!" I said to the woman.

"Wow! So are you! Hi, Ceanna, it's an honor to meet you. I love this store. I shop here all the time, and your staff is so professional and friendly," she smiled.

"That makes me happy to hear that. What's your name?" I asked.

"Brittany," she said.

"Well, Brittany, I have a fashion show coming up in about six months. I would love to have you as a model. You're stunning!"

"Really? I'd be honored," she beamed.

"Awesome, and, boo, the dresses are on me. I think you would rock the shit outta both of them," I grinned. "Grab you a pair of shoes as well. I'll let the cashier know it's on the house." I said my good-byes.

I made my way to my office and smiled at Myriah. She was one of my backups and someone I trusted to run the shop.

"Ceanna!" she screamed and jumped up to hug me.

"Heeey, boo! How are you?" I asked and then took a seat.

"Missing your crazy ass. It ain't the same around here without you, boo."

"Well, how is everything going with the girls?" I asked.

"They're great, boo. We have an excellent staff here. Everyone loves working for you, and you treat your staff so well. Thank you too for the bonus you sent me. I really needed that, Ceanna. You have no idea," she smiled.

"You're welcome, boo, and when I get back, I plan to give everyone a raise too. Coming up we'll be putting in long hours getting ready for the spring show. Anyway, well, love, I'm going to get going. There's a lady up front named Brittany. Get her information for me. She'll be one of our models for the spring show. Everything she has is on the house today. Let me go, now. Tae and Mom are in the car," I stood and gave Myriah a hug.

"Oh, Ceanna, I've been meaning to call you, but time got away. Some lady by the name of MeMe has been coming by asking for you. Here, she left her number." She handed me a piece of paper.

"Oh, okay. Did she say what it was she wanted?" I asked, puzzled. Lord knows I don't need any more craziness in my life.

"No, but she was always in a rush, and she looked worried."

I chatted a few more minutes and said my good-byes to the ladies. Outside, the cool air felt so good against my skin. My hair blew freely, and I actually felt pretty good today. As I made my way to the truck, a guy blew his horn at me and lowered his window. "You're fine as fuck. You got a nigga, ma?" he asked while licking his black-ass lips. I smiled politely and kept walking, hoping the guy would keep going, but he didn't.

I saw Avantae open the truck door getting out with his pistol. "Oh, Laaawd," I fussed loudly.

"What, nigga?" Avantae yelled, waving his gun. The guy burnt off in his truck and almost hit an elderly lady.

"Tae, do you just have to be ignorant all the time? Damn!" I fussed.

"Ceanna, don't play with me. Get yo' ass in the truck with that little-ass dress on. All you see is ass when you walk. Nawl, that dress too tight," he fussed, causing me to laugh.

"You're doing too damn much, Tae," I joked, squeezing his arm. "Anyway, I want to surprise Jalisa later around lunchtime. I ordered a bouquet of balloons and cupcakes for her classmates. We got, time, though for a round of shopping."

"She'll love that." Avantae softened up and kissed my hand.

Later, Avantae rolled his eyes in annoyance as Barbara Jean and I shopped. He was ready to go and threw a little bitch fit. I purposely ignored him and gathered more items just to make him wait longer. Hell, don't nobody say anything when Avantae be shopping for shoes and hats.

"Y'all almost done? Man, I'm hungry, and, Ceanna, all that shit in your arms you ain't getting. Your ass is too damn big. I swear you gon' make me body one of these niggas," he complained.

"Tae, shut up shit. You just ate three hours ago, and for the record, I'm grown as hell," I fussed.

We shopped another thirty minutes and then headed out to pick up Jalisa's surprise. Avantae was still sulking and complaining about being hungry. I rolled my eyes superhard at him. I never met anyone who can eat like him, and he doesn't gain a pound.

"Baby, where do you want to eat?" I asked, trying to lighten his mood.

"I want some shrimp and crabs, baby. Let's go to Red Lobster," he said and perked up.

"Okay, after we go surprise Jalisa we'll go there. Happy?" I smirked at him.

"You two are a mess. Devin, you ain't shit but a big-ass baby," his mother laughed, and Avantae tried to hide his smile.

As we walked the halls of Jalisa's school, I nodded my head at the many family members who were acting as staff to protect Jalisa and Tater Bug.

"*Knock, knock, knock,*" I sang as I knocked three times on Jalisa's classroom door. Her teacher, Ms. Deanna, opened the door and smiled at us. I spotted Jalisa and Tater Bug coloring their A, B, Cs with two other students at their table. I was grateful that both she and Tater Bug were in the same class.

I made a mental note to check on Tater Bug's progress. He started school a year later and should be in kindergarten, not Pre-K. *Zaria is so damn sorry,* I silently thought.

"Jalisa, look who's here," Ms. Deanna sang out. Jalisa looked up and ran toward Avantae, Barbara Jean, and I.

"Yay! Mommy Ce, Daddy Tae, and Grandie ma." Jalisa jumped up and down while she hugged each and every one of us.

"Class, gather around," Ms. Deanna said once Avantae set the cupcakes on the table.

The cupcakes were designed in a *Frozen*-themed princess dress. I had the bakery make Anna black, and there were twenty-four cupcakes. I even brought punch, little *Frozen* goody bags, *Frozen* napkins and plates.

Jalisa loved her balloons and gift we brought her. I asked her if she had given out her invites, and she told me yes, and that all the kids from her class were invited.

After we visited with my little princess at school, we were on our way to Red Lobster, when I received a text from Charles, my lawyer.

Ceanna, stop by the office today before four. The documents are ready.

I responded, You're the best! I'm on my way now and thank you again. ☺

"Baby, I know you're hungry, but I just received a text from the lawyer, baby, and I'm finally a free woman." I smiled as tears of joy ran down my cheeks.

"*That's* what the fuck I'm talking about! Shit, Red Lobster can wait, baby. Let's go get them papers," Avantae sang in Usher's voice.

My heart felt like it was about to burst with joy. In my hands, I held my divorce decree, full custody paperwork for little Avantae, and restraining orders for both Zaria and Jaceyon. All my affairs were finally in order, and I felt so free now that Jaceyon and I are completely over.

I took a picture of the documents before me and shot Jaceyon a text message. Nobody had seen or heard from him. However, I wanted him to know that he and I were done.

Attached to the text message are legal documents. We are now divorced. You have no rights to any of my shit. Jalisa and these twins are off-limits to you, and there is a restraining order against you as well. You fucked up, Jaceyon, big time. We could have settled this like mature adults, but, nawl, you couldn't do that. Take care of yourself!

"Baby, who you texting?" Avantae asked. I was so preoccupied with my text that I hadn't even noticed that we weren't moving from the lawyer's office.

"Jaceyon, letting him know we are finally divorced and to stay away." I looked up and locked eyes with Avantae. A wide grin plastered on his face.

"Can I make you a Wallace now?" he asked while kissing my left hand.

"I would be honored," I smiled.

"Say no more! How much time do we have before we go back to the school to get the kids?" he asked.

"Two hours," his mother answered.

"Okay, cool. I'ma shoot by Zaria's mama's house real quick to give her this legal document. Tater Bug is officially in my full custody." I squeezed his hand.

I loved when my man was happy. Getting custody of his son was a huge burden lifted off of his shoulders. He was an excellent father, and I'd decided that I was going to give these twins his last name too. He'd been there from day one.

While Avantae was in Zaria's mother's home, a text came through from Jaceyon. I sighed deeply not wanting to deal with his foolishness. I knew he was going to flip when he saw we were done. I just wanted Jaceyon to leave me alone for good.

Ceanna, yeah, we will see. It's till death do us part in this bitch, and you can't just toss me away. I'll kill you before I let that nigga wife you. If I were you, I'd watch my back. This shit is far from over. You'll see!

"Is this nigga threatening me?" I yelled.

"What's wrong?" Barbara Jean asked.

"Mama, look." I showed her the text Jaceyon sent me.

"Don't even trip. That nigga's time up anyway." She passed me back my phone.

We spotted Avantae coming toward us with a huge smile. He dapped some of the males that stood around as he made his way back to the truck. When he entered, he noticed the expression on my face, and his smile turned into concern.

"What's up, baby? You okay?" he asked.

I passed him my phone, and he read the text Jaceyon sent. His nostrils flared in anger when a second text came through.

"What it say?" I asked curiously.

"This fuck boy sent a picture of his diseased, sick, shitty-ass dick saying you'll never forget him!" Avantae yelled.

"Oh yeah? Let me see my phone." I took the phone from Avantae.

Jaceyon, sweetie, your idle threats don't mean shit to me. As far as your dick, we all know you take it up the ass. Rick recorded you. You even framed Boog to hide your little secrets with yo' shitty-dick ass.

I passed the phone back to Avantae, and he read my response. He laughed loudly and shook his head. "Ma, we still got a lot of time. Let's just go back home until it's time to pick the kids up. I need to go to San Marcos later, so we'll eat there."

"You two have at it. I'm tired and need a nap," Barbara Jean said.

"Me too," I yawned.

I went straight to bed once we got home. I was sleepy and exhausted. My bed felt so comfortable and cozy. I closed my eyes and sleep quickly took over me.

Avantae came to wake me when it was time to get the children from school, but I was too tired, and my energy was low. I couldn't seem to open my eyes, so I asked him if he could get Jalisa's cake, decorations, and the order I placed at Party City.

It seemed like minutes later when I heard, "Mommy Ce, Mommy Ce, Daddy Tae said wake up and come in the living room. He has a huge surprise for you," Jalisa and Tater Bug said while shaking me. It was well after eight in the evening.

"Okayyyyy, I'm coming," I moaned.

I went to the restroom to handle my oral hygiene and washed my face. As I was walked down the hallway, I could hear voices other than the ones who lived here. *Oh Lordt, what does this boy got up his sleeve?* I smiled to myself.

When I walked in the living room, I started sobbing, doing that ugly cry. There were purple and white rose petals in a heart shape with candles lit everywhere. Present were WyKeith, Keisha, Vera, who was my mother's friend, Myriah from my shop, Elijah, Mama Barbara Jean, the kids, Janair, and Semaj. The only one missing was Asia, but I figured she was still upset.

Avantae walked in front of me and grabbed my hand; then he walked me in the center of the rose petals heart. My heart began to thump loudly once he got down on one knee.

"What?" I burst out crying. "Yeeees, Avantae!"

"You've got to let him ask you, Ceanna!" Keisha yelled out, causing everyone to laugh, including myself. Avantae looked at me and pulled out the most beautiful ring I had ever seen.

"Ceanna, you know I'm a hood nigga. I didn't know much about being a man or even how to love a woman until I met you. You showed me what it means to love someone unconditionally. You made me whole. All I knew was pushing weight. I never thought I would run a successful business or be a father, but you saw that in me. You're special! I was a broken nigga, I mean, man, with no future. My heart was dark and cloudy. You're my light, and you bring me peace. I crave you, and I need you. Will you walk with me and ride with me forever? Will you do me the honor of being my wife?" Avantae asked as tears fell from his loving eyes.

"Avantaeeeee!" I sobbed. I wanted to give a beautiful speech back, but I was so choked up. "Yeeees!" I cried and nodded my head. There wasn't a dry eye in the room.

Avantae stood up, and I fell into his arms. I cried so hard. The love he had for me has restored my inner peace. He has helped heal me and brought me back to my worth. He gave me a love of my own and showed me my inner beauty. I never thought in a million years I would be here.

"I'll never hurt you," he whispered in my ear.

"I love you, Avantae, and thank you." I looked up at him and kissed him.

"WyKeith, are you taking notes?" Keisha asked, causing everybody to laugh.

"Aye, Tae, look what you done started," WyKeith joked.

"Ohhhh, Ce, let me see this ring," Janair said as she, Keisha, Myriah, Mama, Vera, and the kids gathered around me. All you could hear was *"ooohs"* and *"aaaahs."*

To complete the night, the fellas gathered in the back-yard and BBQ'd for us ladies. It was such a beautiful night, and I was happy I had help with all the goody bags for Jalisa's party.

"Ceanna, your mother would be so proud," Vera said, tearing up and hugging me.

"I miss her so much!" I bit my lip to stop from crying.

"Thank you all! I love each and every one of you. I know my moody ass has not been easy to deal with, but to have you here with me means so much to me. I can't believe I'm getting married. Aaaah!" I hid my face because I couldn't hold it any longer. The waterworks came on down. All the ladies gathered around me and gave me a big hug. I wanted this feeling to last forever.

Chapter Thirty-one

Avantae

My cell phone rang loudly. I hurried and jumped up to answer it. Ceanna had been going ham on my ass, especially when woken out of her sleep. I had been expecting a call from the lab. Yesterday while the kids and I were in San Marcos, I stopped by a lab and got tested. I wasn't about to be making love to Ceanna with cheap-ass rubbers. I needed to feel her, so I made sure to get tested, and I paid the tech a nice amount of money to get speedy results.

"Hello," I answered in a rushed tone.

"Mr. Wallace, this in Donisha from Lab Corp. I was calling you to let you know your test results all came back negative. I mailed a copy to your home address as well," she confirmed.

"Thank you!" I hung up.

Ceanna was sleeping so peacefully, but I was about to wake her little pretty ass up. I wanted to laugh out loud at the way Ceanna was sleeping. She had her fists balled up ready. Her mouth was wide open, and her hair rag was dangling to the side.

Her ass was sleeping too good, and I couldn't help but to mess with her. I took my fingers and lightly brushed them over her arm. She slapped the shit out of her arm thinking something was crawling on her. Boiiiiii, that shit was funny as hell. I couldn't hold my laugh.

"*Uuuugh,* you play too damn much, Avantae." Ceanna woke up. "Leave me alone," she whined.

"I got my test results, and I'm clean. I need that thang," I laughed, while I rubbed Ceanna's booty.

"Gon' on somewhere. Damn, I was sleeping good," she fussed.

"Fuck all that, Ceanna. Look at my shit! It's brick hard." I rubbed it against her ass. Then I started licking Ceanna's ear, knowing that would turn her on.

"Mmm, put it away. I'm so . . . mmm," she moaned and then opened her legs.

I gently slide between her legs and felt I was in heaven. I could never get tired of being in her warmth. After our love session, I wiped Ceanna and took a quick shower. Today was going to be a busy day with Jalisa's birthday party.

While Ceanna continued to sleep, I rolled up a blunt and went outside on the back porch. Moments later, my mother joined me. She kissed the side of my head and took a seat. I respectfully put out my blunt.

"Ma, how you feeling?" I asked.

"Baby, I'm doing okay. The meds make me sick, but other than that I can't complain." She smiled.

"Are you happy? I never asked you what you wanted. I guess when I reunited with you, I just wanted to protect you and give you everything. I just moved you in here making you give up that apartment and job." I reflected on how selfish I might have been.

"Avantae, I'm more than happy. *You* make me happy, son. Just seeing the man you have become warms my heart. You're nothing like your father was." She looked away.

"Were you happy with him?" I asked.

"Yes and no. I'll tell you a story. My mother was a Cuban immigrant who fell in love with a black married man. My life was a struggle, and we were very poor. I met your father while working at a fast-food restaurant. Those were the happiest days of my life. Your father meant the world to me. In the beginning, it was just he and I. Two poor, working people who were in the struggle together, but the love was so pure. Then we had you, and, baby, you were the love of my world; you still are. You were such a joy to us, Avantae. Things were good. Most nights we had chicken, but we ate, had a roof over our head, and clothing on our backs.

"Then it all changed. Your father began a brief affair with Cheryl. I did what my mother did and ignored the obvious. I played like I didn't know, and I never said a word to him about it. I hid my tears and pain. Your father began to change. All of a sudden, he wanted more and wanted to be something he wasn't. He hooked up with Teddy, and the next thing you know, the cars, women, money, and disrespect came. Sure, he took great care of us, and we were living big, but he forgot to protect us.

"I knew I was expecting, but your father was never around long enough to share the exciting news. That night when those men broke in our home, your father was with his mistress. That was the worst night of my life. The only thing I had left in me was my unborn child. I needed your father more than ever then, but once he found out I was raped and given HIV, he turned his back on me and made me abort my child. I died that day. Something in me broke, and I couldn't piece it back together.

"Can you believe I hated drugs and what your father did for a living? Whoever would have thought that those same drugs would be my best friend? I was lost in a world of pain, and I couldn't find my way. Then when your father took you away and left me, I had nothing else to live for. I had a hatred for your father so deep at one point. I learned about Donte years ago. It took time, baby, for me to let go of the anger and pain, but my love for your father never faded." She smiled.

"You're so strong! That's what I love about you. I think that's why I love Ceanna so much. She reminds me of you. Your grace, love, kindness, and raw truth are commendable to me. I love you, Ma, and I'm so sorry you went through that. For so long I felt I failed you. I didn't protect you, and I felt unworthy of love. I dreamed about you for years. I didn't know where you were or if you were alive. I used to tell myself you were dead. I used to wonder if you ate and if you were safe. Pops talked about you often, and truthfully, Gina wasn't shit, and he knew that. You are rare and the apple of my eye. To see you healthy warms my heart. I need you more than you know, and I love you." I shed tears. My mama was my heart.

"I love you too, son, and thank you for not questioning me about killing Samuel. I know you know I killed him."

"I had to let you handle him. I couldn't figure out what it was about the nigga I didn't trust. That night was blurry, but there was something about the nigga I never trusted. Then one day the shit hit me like a ton of bricks. It was him! I was going to kill his ass, but Jaceyon shot me. When I heard the news of him being dead, I knew you murked that nigga." I smiled.

"What do you have planned for today?" I asked, changing the subject.

"Well, I'm going to meet up with Keisha, and we're going to set the venue up for Jalisa's party for later on, and then go do some shopping for the baby shower. I'm so excited, Devin, to hold my little grandbabies. Boy, and make sure you give Ceanna some time to heal before you put another one in her," she laughed.

"I can't promise that," I chuckled and kissed her on the cheek.

"Are you hungry?" she asked.

"Man, I thought you would never ask," I joked.

"Boy, come on here. I still got another hour or so before I leave."

"You're going to have to teach me how to cook. I know Ceanna won't be able to do too much after she has the babies, and it's going to be on me to help her as much as I can."

"That won't be a problem, baby. I love the way you cater to Ceanna and take care of her. You're a good man, baby. That was a beautiful ring you gave her, and I can't wait for the wedding too. Do you guys have a date in mind yet?" she asked, placing on an apron.

"Not yet, but I was thinking maybe on Ceanna's mom's birthday on something like that. I'll let her pick the date. You know I don't be knowing about all that. I just hope she lets me pick a color or two," I chuckled.

"Well, you know you probably won't win that round because whatever Ceanna does, you know purple will be incorporated," she said with a smile. "Now, come on and let's cook before the kiddos wake up."

As I cooked with my mother, a sense of peace came over me. When I was younger, I used to help her around the kitchen, and that's how we would bond and spend some of our time. I loved this woman, and I hated that we spent so many years apart from each other. I vowed to make up our time and grow stronger every day.

I hadn't told Ceanna or my mother yet, but I signed up for some HIV education classes. I didn't know too much about the disease, but I wanted to educate myself. Maybe in the near future, Ceanna and I can put together something for HIV/AIDS awareness. We have the means to do so, and we can help push the cause and educate our youth.

"Breakfast! Yayyyyyy, I'm hungry," the kids said excitedly. They had just woken up.

"Daddy, please don't mess up the food, 'cause I'm so sorry, Daddy, but you can't cook like Mommy Ce and Grandie ma," Jalisa joked, causing us to laugh.

"Girl, I go hard in the kitchen. *I'm* the one who taught Ceanna how to cook," I smirked.

"Yeah, right, Daddy. You burned the bacon last time and almost set the house on fire trying to cook pancakes," Tater Bug joked, and we all laughed.

"Yeah, okay, I see now we going to have to have a cooking battle."

"And you will loseeeeeee," Jalisa added, laughing.

"Man, whatever, girl; go wake up Ceanna."

"I'm up! Ooh, hell, nawl. Avantae, *you're* cooking?" Ceanna asked with a frown, causing all of us to laugh.

"Yes, I am, and as you can see, it ain't watermelon or cereal, nor did I burn the kitchen down," I beamed.

"Now gon' and sit down, Queen, and take yo' badass kids with you."

"Who's bad?" Tater Bug yelled out moonwalking to the table.

"Say, man," I laughed so damn hard, "these kids are fucking crazy, yo."

My mother, Ceanna, and the kids sat at the table and continued to talk shit. That's all right. This breakfast is about to go hard in the paint.

"Todayyyyy!" Jalisa yelled out, causing me to laugh again. She's a bossy little thang. I hurried and set everyone's plate in front of them starting with Ceanna's.

"Tater Bug, what you think? It looks good, right?" Jalisa questioned, looking at Tater Bug, and then they both inspected the food.

"Yeah! Daddy, you did all right. It still ain't Mommy Ce's cooking, though." Tater Bug laughed, and he and Jalisa gave each other a high five.

Little chumps, I silently thought. I sat down with my crew at the table, and Jalisa led us in prayer.

"Dear Lordt! Thank you for this food we're about to receive. Thank you for my people and the many laughs we have. Oh, and, Lordt, it's my birthday, so I pray Daddy Tae's food is good. Ameeeen, Lordt!" she sang.

"Maaaan!" I laughed, causing Jalisa to laugh. "Ceanna, she has been around yo' crazy ass too long. She's saying 'Lordt' now." We all howled, then we finished eating, and my mother left to go meet up with Keisha.

"Kids, y'all clean the kitchen," Ceanna told them.

"Yes, ma'am," they replied, and I smiled. I loved the respect they had for Ceanna.

Ceanna and I sat in the living room. She propped her swollen feet on my lap, and I began massaging them for her. I stared at my woman, happy she chose me of all niggas.

"What you thinking about, handsome?" Ceanna asked while smiling.

"Just you, love. I'm thinking how I'm the luckiest nigga right now," I smiled. "How are you feeling?" I asked and then rubbed my baby's big round belly.

"I'm really uncomfortable. It hurts a lot to do too much. My back pulls a lot, I'm out of breath a lot, and my feet always hurt. After today, baby, I think I need to be still. I don't know how much longer these babies will hold. A lot of it has to do with my weight too," she admitted.

"I'ma help you as much as I can. Gimme me the information for the fashion show too. We gonna make this shit pop this year. I got you. I know you been a little down about the weight you've gained, but we will work out together, and if it means anything, baby, I think you're beautiful the way you are," I smiled.

"You know me, huh? Yeah, I have been stressing about the show. Myriah is good, but you know I'm sensitive about my shit. Can't nobody see your vision the way you do, and I been wondering how will being a new mother fit into all of it. To be honest, Tae, I have been down about my size. This extra weight is too much, and I feel so heavy, not like before. I definitely have to get fit, especially if I'm planning on giving you another baby or two," she smiled.

"Ma, you already know I'm knocking you up. You can forget about waiting six weeks and shit. Hell, nah, I can't go a day without your shit. I'm addicted, baby."

Ding dong, ding dong.

"Tae, are you expecting anybody?" Ceanna asked.

"Oh yeah, that's Julia. She came to teach us things about the babies." I stood, getting off the sofa.

"Tater Bug and Jalisa, do Daddy a favor and bring five of the yoga mats in the living room!" I yelled.

Julia gave us a lot of information. We had fun learning breathing techniques and different fun activities. She also showed us how to change diapers, feed, and burp the babies. The kids also had fun too and had a lot of questions. Julia stayed about an hour and a half before she left.

Ceanna did Jalisa's hair really pretty, and she braided Tater Bug's hair. I had a new idea for my long mane and asked my baby to twist me up. Once my little princess was dressed and ready, I pulled her on the back patio to have a private talk with her.

"Jalisa, baby, I want you to know that I love you, baby, and I'm proud of you. You're my little princess, and I promise to always love, guide, respect, and protect you. I want you to know, baby, that you can always come to me. Never be afraid to talk to me. I know I'm not your real father, but I promised your mother that I would raise you up as my own. Today is your special day. I want you to enjoy yourself, baby. I love you, baby girl." I pulled out a gold necklace that read *Daddy's girl* and placed it around her neck. Tears fell from my eyes, and Jalisa wiped them.

"Thank you, Daddy, and I love you too," she cried, and then whispered, "I won't tell nobody that you're out here crying." We laughed and headed back inside.

Ceanna beamed at me with joy and mouthed, "*She loves you.*" We piled into my truck and headed to celebrate baby girl's big day.

Chapter Thirty-two

Ceanna

The party was so good, and I enjoyed seeing Avantae play with all the children. I'm so thankful Keisha and Mama set the venue up because I've been having some slight pain on and off today.

"Hey, boo! You good?" Janair asked, taking a seat next to me. I guess she noticed me frowning.

"Girl, yes, it's just one of the twins is lying in the wrong spot. I'm so uncomfortable." I rubbed my stomach.

"Well, it's almost that time, and you probably should relax after tonight," she smiled.

"Yeah, you're right about that. I'm so nervous to become a mother."

"Your facial expressions are funny as hell, but, Ce, you're going to be a wonderful mother. It comes so natural to you. You're such a loving person and a real woman. You know most women would have turned their backs on Tater Bug. You took him in and never even blinked, and the way you love Jalisa, I mean, oh my God." She smiled.

"Thanks, J! I really appreciate your friendship. It means a lot. I'm happy I met you. I know you probably think we're a bunch of goons and nuts," I laughed.

"Honestly, Ce, I think it's commendable how you steered Avantae away from the streets. You could easily be a queen-pin and picked up where your daddy left off. *Whew,* Calvin was *that* nigga." We both laughed.

"Baby, what's up with Asia? I mean, I know baby girl's hurt over Keisha, but, damn, ain't like her to not answer the phone or be at important shit. Key said she hasn't been home, and she's been staying at WyKeith's to avoid Asia, but we need to stop by there and check on her. Something ain't sitting right," Avantae said with a worried look on his face as he came, sat, and joined our conversation.

"I was just thinking that."

I kept yawning the entire time of the party. My energy level had been so low, and all I wanted to do was sleep and eat. The kids were having a blast, though. There had to be at least thirty kids in attendance. I was excited to see Tamara and her four children. She apologized for Zaria's behavior, but I wasn't mad at her. Tamara had always been very kind to me, and Tonya spoke highly of her.

I didn't think that Melody and Tyler's mother, Ms. Perry, would show, but when she walked in, the biggest smile formed on my face. Donte's twin daughters, Marcus Jr., and little Courtney were dressed supercute. I smiled, knowing Avantae had something to do with this.

"Ms. Perry, thank you for bringing all of the children to Jalisa's birthday party. You may stay if you'd like. If not, I'll have Avantae drop the kids off later this evening," I said politely.

"Hell, nawl. I won't be staying with that bitch Keisha here. At least you're a real bitch, Ceanna, and I can respect you for seeing the bigger picture. Keisha's ass, on the other hand, acts like she's too good to see about Donte's daughters! She's *still* his wife," she yelled a little too loudly.

"Well, okay! I'll be sure to drop them off before eight tonight," I half smiled. This bitch is on one. *Not today, Ceanna, not today. How the fuck are you mad at Keisha*

*when your daughter Tyler was Donte's side bitch? She
betta gon' on with that bullshit. The only reason I invited
them is because Avantae is their uncle, and Jalisa hadn't
seen Courtney and Marcus in a while. Bitch betta act
like she know. Calm down, Ceanna,* I coached myself.

"Bye," she said and rudely walked away.

If these kids weren't standing there looking at me, I
swear I would have told her ass where to go. She got this
round, but I bet she wouldn't get none 'notha time.

"Jalisa!" I yelled her name among the playful, rowdy
children.

"Yes, Mommy Ce? Oh my God! Marcus, Courtney!"
Jalisa yelled while running toward them. The trio hugged,
jumping up and down, and I couldn't help but shed tears.
My emotional ass was always crying.

"I missed y'all so much. You got to meet my brother
Tater Bug," Jalisa sang while grabbing Marcus and
Courtney's hands. She turned to run off, and then came
back.

"Y'all can come too. I'm Jalisa, and it's my birthday.
We're partying hard in there. Come on," Jalisa told the
twin girls. I just laughed at her. Jalisa had my personality
to a tee. She was so friendly and made friends easily.

I spotted Elijah, Semaj, WyKeith, and Avantae playing
a game of pool and drinking a beer. I laughed because
adults will always have fun even if it's a kid's party.

I shook my head and began to walk back over to the
table occupied by Janair, Vera, Mama Barbara Jean, and
Tamara. I didn't see Keisha and thought maybe she went
to the bathroom. I headed that way.

"Key, are you in here?" I yelled.

"Yeah," she moaned.

"You okay?" I asked, knocking on her stall. Keisha
opened the door with tears in her eyes.

"What's wrong, boo?"

She was silent for a moment, and then extended her hand. She had a pregnancy test. I took it out of her hand and instantly threw my hand up over my mouth.

"Key, for real? I'm going to be an auntie? Does WyKeith know?" I asked in shock.

"No, and I never meant for this to happen. Ce, I never meant to hurt Asia the way I did, and I feel horrible. I mean, I'm feeling WyKeith, but I never meant to break her heart. I can't even face Asia right now . . . and then for her to find out I'm pregnant too would kill her. I don't know what I'ma do, Ce. I can't have this baby. It's too soon, and I barely know the nigga. I'm all over the place, and then when that bitch Ms. Perry walked in with Donte's girls . . . I couldn't take it," she vented.

"No judgments, and whatever you decide to do about the baby, I'm here. As far as Asia, I don't know what to say, Key. Nobody has heard from her. We need to go by there and check on her. I just hate y'all fought. WyKeith is cool and all, but niggas don't be letting females come in between them. We need to adapt that mind-set too. We've been friends for too damn long. Ain't no breaking up in this bitch."

"You're right. I should have never lasted as long as I did with Asia and maybe getting a house was like too real for her. The way she sees me I just don't see her that way." Keisha shrugged.

"You think yo' ass slick, though, Key. You've been jumping on that wood of WyKeith's," I laughed.

"*Whew,* that man got what make you wanna come home early and act right dick. I be like, 'yes, sir' in this bitch. What a sista gotta do?" she laughed, and then we hugged.

"Love you, boo, and it'll be okay." We locked arms heading out of the bathroom, and Avantae's ass almost fell in the bathroom once we opened the door.

"*Uuuugh!* Tae, you're so damn nosy. Don't say shit." Key punched him in the arm, and we all laughed.

"Man, chill out, Ms. Eastside Thugga. I was coming to get Ceanna so we can cut the cake and open the gifts. These badass kids are driving me crazy, yo," he laughed.

"Tae, yo' ass can't even lie right." I snickered, and we all headed back to the party room.

Chapter Thirty-three

Ceanna

After I dropped the kids off at school, I stopped by WyKeith's house to pick up Keisha. She had set up a doctor's appointment and wanted me to go with her.

"Ceanna, slide on over. Avantae just called my ass going in about how he don't want you driving," Keisha laughed as soon as she made it to the vehicle.

"Ugh, he gets on my nerves with that shit. I'm pregnant, *not* handicapped." I chuckled while sliding over to the passenger side.

"How are you feeling, baby mama?" I asked Keisha.

"I don't know, Ce. WyKeith confessed that he loved me earlier," she smiled.

"Well, babe, that's beautiful, and I'm happy for you, Key. Did you tell him yet?"

"No, I'm scared, Ce. What if he doesn't want kids or something? Plus, you know he still dabbles in that life," she sighed.

"Well, boo, just tell him. WyKeith seems like a stand-up guy, Key. If not, you know my niece or nephew ain't going to hurt for shit," I smiled.

We finally made it to the doctor's office. Keisha and I were both shocked that she was already sixteen weeks. She wasn't showing at all.

"I *knew* your ass been riding that dick!" I yelled, causing Keisha to bust out laughing.

"Oh my God, Ce, I didn't even know I was pregnant all this time."

She put her clothing on and grabbed her sonogram photo. She couldn't stop crying and looking at the images of her love-on-top baby.

We made it back to my vehicle when my phone rang. I didn't recognize the number, but I had this nagging feeling to answer the phone.

"Hello," I answered.

"Hi, may I speak to Ceanna, please?" a female voice asked.

"Yes, this is she. How may I help you?" I frowned.

"Ceanna, hi. My name is MeMe. I've been trying to reach you at the boutique. I went through Asia's phone and found your number."

"Okay, is there something I can help you with?" I asked, getting pissed off. She was doing too much trying to reach me. I had no clue who this chick was.

"Asia was shot last Saturday and is in a coma. Jaceyon and his mother did this to her. The doctors are talking about pulling the plug. I don't know what to do. Can you please come to the hospital? I'm at Brack, room 243," she sobbed uncontrollably into the phone.

"Oh my God! Nooooo!" I dropped my phone sobbing.

"Ceanna, what's wrong?" Keisha began panicking. She picked up my phone and began crying her eyes out as MeMe informed her of Asia's condition.

Keisha and I cried and held each other. Asia was our sister and friend. I couldn't believe Jaceyon would do this. "I'm soooo sorry! I'm soooo sorry!" Keisha cried.

"I've got to call Avantae." I sobbed while dialing his number. The phone rang twice before he answered.

"Hey, brown sugar, are you and Keisha enjoying y'all selves?" he asked in a cheerful tone.

"Taeeeeeeee, Ja-Ja-Jaceyon shot Asiaaaaaaa! She's in a coma, and the doctors want to pull the plug!" I cried hard into the phone.

"Man, what the *fuck!* Where are you at, ma?" he asked in a rushed tone. I could tell he was running through the house.

"We're on our way to Brack," I cried as Keisha began driving.

"I'm on my way. I'ma hit WyKeith too. Love you, baby."

"'K, and love you too."

I sat in the passenger seat silently crying with my eyes closed. I'm so tired of everything. I can't believe Jaceyon would hurt me this way. He knows how much I love Asia. I don't know who he is anymore.

We were almost at the hospital, and it was only right that I called Mia Symone and informed her of what was going on. I dialed her number, and she answered on the fourth ring.

"Hi, Ceanna," she nervously answered.

"Mia Symone, something bad has happened to Asia. Jaceyon shot her, and the doctors are wanting to pull the plug on her. We're at Brack."

"What! Nooooo! My sister! Are you telling me she's going to die?" Mia Symone cried.

"Yeeees!" I cried.

"I'm on my wayyyy!" she sobbed, hanging up the phone.

Keisha and I looked at each other when we arrived at the hospital. Neither one of us wanted to get out of the vehicle. We hugged each for a long time and finally got out of the truck. We held hands as we walked down the halls of the hospital. When we made it to the room Asia was in, we paused.

"Ceanna, I can't do this," Keisha cried.

"I know, Keisha, but we have to." I wiped her tears.

"You're always so strong, Ceanna," she cried.

"I have to be, Keisha, I don't know how else to be. I know we'll get through this, though, together," I sadly smiled.

I opened the room door, and my heart felt like it was about to burst wide open. Asia had a bandage around her head and tubes connected to her. I spotted a girl crying in the corner that I assumed was MeMe.

Keisha cried while she grabbed Asia's hand. I leaned over and gave Asia a kiss on her cheek. Her face was so swollen, and she looked so fragile lying there. Moments later, Avantae, Barbara Jean, and WyKeith walked in the room. Their reaction was the same as ours was moments earlier. There wasn't a dry eye in the room.

"Ma, what happened?" Avantae asked MeMe who had her head in her hands. She looked up as silent tears ran down her face and made eye contact with each one of us.

"My name is MeMe, and I'm a friend of Asia's. She called me last Saturday and asked me if I could meet her over at the house. She was crying extremely hard and told me she had just gotten in a fistfight. It was raining so hard, and I kept begging her to pull over. She kept saying she lost the love of her life and how she wanted to die. I told her I would be over in ten minutes. That was the last thing I said to her. When I got to the house, I knocked and rang the doorbell. *'Asia, let me in. It's raining so hard,'* I kept saying. I knew she was home because her car was out front.

"The fence was slightly opened, so I came around back. I turned the back doorknob, and it wasn't locked. I began turning on the lights calling Asia's name, and she didn't answer. When I made it toward the dining area, I saw blood everywhere. That's when Jaceyon came out pointing a gun at me. In his hands, he had a black trash bag. He was about to shoot me when a noise came from behind the wall. It was Asia. He shot her and threw her body behind the wall. I ran over to the wall and found Asia shot with a bullet in her head. Jaceyon and his mother left, and I called 911. The bullet went straight through!" she cried out.

"I appreciate you calling us and taking care of our friend this entire time," Avantae said as he hugged MeMe. The door opened, getting all of our attention. In walked an older African American woman.

"Hello! Have you all made a decision?" she asked, and that pissed me off. Avantae saw my facial expression and stepped in.

"Uh, Doc, no disrespect, but this is our sister, and we don't even know what the fuck is going on."

"The bullet went clean through. However, Asia lost a lot of blood. Her brain keeps swelling, and we have performed three operations this week. *If* she wakes up, she will be severely brain damaged. She won't remember you, and she will be a shell of who she used to be. My best advice to you all is to pull the plug. There is nothing more we can do for her," the doctor said with no emotion, as if she was numb and had delivered this news too often.

"Doc, let us have a minute," Avantae said, and the doctor exited the room.

"What if she wakes up? What if we can help her remember us? Tae, I don't want to pull the plug," I cried.

"Ceanna, what if she doesn't, though?" WyKeith asked.

"WyKeith, we can't just *kill* her like that," Keisha cried.

"Asia won't be the Asia we know. Do you *really* want her to walk around other than herself?" Avantae asked.

"Look, her hand just moved, Tae!" I yelled.

"Ceanna, it's a reflex."

"No, I saw it too, Tae." Keisha ran over to whisper in Asia's ear. "Asia, if you're alive in there, we need you to wake up and give us a sign. If you can hear me, move your hand. I'm sorry, Asia! I do love you. You're my sister and one of my best friends. I never meant to hurt you, and I pray you can forgive me," Keisha cried and buried her head on Asia's arm.

"Oh my God, her hand just moved!" Mama Barbara Jean yelled.

"I told you," I sobbed into Avantae's chest. I was not pulling the plug on my sister. I refused.

Just as Avantae was about to answer, Asia began violently jerking. Keisha ran into the hall and hollered for the doctors. Three doctors came in and ordered us all to step in the hallway.

A heavy feeling engulfed us. We all knew Asia was gone. As we hugged each other, cried and waited, I heard my name called in a high-pitched voice. It was Mia Symone rushing toward us with her son in her arms.

"Ceanna, where is she, where's Asia?" Mia Symone cried.

I didn't get a chance to answer. The three doctors stepped out of the room and delivered the saddest news ever. Asia was gone forever.

Chapter Thirty-four

Avantae

I can't explain the hole I felt in my heart. Asia was like my sister. She was so cool and down-to-earth. I can't believe Jaceyon killed her like that. I am *done* playing with this nigga.

I had my mother go pick up the kids while Keisha, Ceanna, MeMe, and Mia Symone stayed at the hospital. I gave WyKeith the signal, and I was about to fuck Jaceyon's world up.

WyKeith and I left the hospital and headed over to Jaceyon's aunt Cheryl's abandoned home. She stayed ducked off away from others, which was good for us. I knew Jaceyon and Gina weren't going to be there, but I had a gut feeling that my shit that Jaceyon stole was there.

I kicked in Cheryl's back door going through the home and ripped that bitch to pieces. In the back of the closet, I spotted a duffle bag. I opened it and—*bingo!* My ten keys and money were in the bag.

"Bitch-ass nigga!" I yelled. I called Jaceyon's phone, and he answered, breathing through the phone.

"Nigga, you killed my sister Asia and had the nerve to rob me and steal my shit, you bitch-ass nigga. I'm at Cheryl's house now, ho, and I found my money and bricks. I'ma burn this muthafukka down and Gina's home too, you bitch," I laughed.

"Bitch nigga, try me!" Jaceyon yelled.

"I already did, and by the way, I got the tape of you getting it took up the ass by Rick. That nigga recorded you, bitch," I laughed and hung up.

I kept trashing Cheryl's home and paused when I came across a journal. I opened it up, briefly scanning the pages. This ho was obsessed with my father and seeking revenge. I placed the journal behind my back and took the gasoline can from the kitchen.

WyKeith and I began dousing gasoline everywhere. We made it to the back door, and I flicked three matches. The home began to engulf in flames. We ran to the truck and dipped off. I wanted Jaceyon to come see me.

WyKeith and I went to Ceanna's old condo to devise up a plan. I already knew I wouldn't be making it home to Ceanna tonight, but I had eyes everywhere, and my family was protected.

As WyKeith and I went back and forth, Ceanna called me crying her eyes out. I thought she was still upset about Asia, but once Ceanna sent me a photo message, the beast in me was now fully awake.

"Yo, blood, you good?" WyKeith asked.

"My nigga, look what this ho-ass nigga did," I stated, showing Wykeith the photo.

"That's some disrespectful-ass shit, blood. I'm ready to dome this nigga, son. Just give me the fucking word."

"I can't believe this nigga would scoop this low to fuck up baby's parents' headstones like that. Calvin's death anniversary is next month, and that's fucked up, yo." I sighed and sat back on the sectional.

"So what you wanna do?" WyKeith asked as he removed the rubber band from his dreads.

"First, we got to find this nigga. It's still early, so we got to move at night. Shit is crazy, fam."

"You know, I still ain't found the bitch who set my brother up to get killed. The shit fucks with me every day," WyKeith changed the subject and fired up a blunt.

"Your brother was a real nigga. When I heard he was killed, I ended up killing one of the niggas who was in on the robbery." I shook my head at the memory.

"My brother spoke highly of you, and I know it was you that looked after his wife and children. Them niggas took all my brother's bread too. At the time, I was trying to come up in the game, and my paper wasn't nearly as long as my brother's."

"I couldn't let Karlie and the kids be out like that. The feds took the rest of the shit from Karlie. They left them with nothing, and my nigga didn't have life insurance or nothing. I'm proud of little mama, though," I smiled.

"I am too, my nigga. Shorty's doing really good. She's still holding down her job, and the kids are doing really good. My nephew be fucking them boys up on the field. Matter of fact, the LBJ and Reagan's game is next month. Are you down to go?" he asked.

"Hell, yeah!"

"Jaguars!" we both yelled and high-fived.

"Not to get off subject, you know Keisha's my sister, and I ain't a nigga to be in the next man's business, but, bro, keep a hunnid. Are you still fucking with Shawanda?" I asked, inhaling the weed.

"We're still married, but we ain't fucking with each other. We haven't been together in a year. But on some real shit, I didn't know Mia Symone was yo' people. Back in the gap, I used to knock that off." He shook his head.

"Man, say, dig these blues, my nigga. I hit her one time and quit. Her shit was so foul, and shorty burned me with two STDs!" I yelled.

"What the fuck? Hell, nawl. Does Ceanna know?" he asked, shocked.

"Yeah, I told her. On some real shit, though, bro, if you're serious about Keisha tell her about Shawanda and the situation. I almost lost Ceanna behind *not* telling her about Zaria and my son."

"I hear you, my nigga."

WyKeith and I chopped it up for hours. Night finally came, and we decided to hit a strip club. Strips clubs were good places to conduct business and catch niggas slipping.

I was about to make Jaceyon pay for everything. My wife will no longer shed any more tears over him. He should have approached the situation like a man and chucked up his losses for fucking up.

I hit up former street runners that I knew I could trust. With me at the strip club was Wykeith, Elijah, and my nigga Tam. We were all sitting around in the back of the club at a table.

My phone rang, and it was Mia Symone. She hit me with some vital information on the whereabouts of Jaceyon. She informed me of a hotel Jaceyon was holing up in and the room number. I let my crew know what she said, and Tam informed me that one of his little mamas named Sonya worked at the hotel.

Sonya gave Tam a quick blueprint of the hotel. She informed him where the cameras were located and where all the blind spots were. We headed over to the hotel, and I parked behind two of the Dumpsters that were side by side to each other.

Sonya met us by the Dumpsters and gave Tam the room key to room 264. I waited in the truck with Elijah while WyKeith and Tam took the stairwell to Jaceyon's room.

After ten minutes of waiting, Tam and WyKeith walked out with Gina. She was terrified but knew not to make a scene. To the naked eye, it appeared as two were a couple and the third man was a friend. They ordered Gina in the truck, and I pulled off.

"Avantae, what's going on?" Gina cried.

"Gina, your time is up, and so is Jaceyon's. He killed my sister Asia and brought malice to my wife. I heard you were with him. Where's Jaceyon?" I asked in an aggressive tone.

"I don't know, Tae," she cried and hung her head.

"Okay, I see you wanna play loaded." I turned up the music.

I continued to drive another forty minutes deep into the dirt roads of Gonzales, Texas. I had a hidden shack that nobody knew about except my old friend Jesús. He was a Mexican cartel leader.

The guys brought Gina into the shack and tied her to a chair. Snot dripped from her nose as she continued to sob. It's sad it had to come to this.

When Gina was married to my father, she used to treat a young nigga as her own. My beef wasn't with her, but I also didn't care for the way she treated Ceanna. She was a bitter old woman who was always trying to run game on someone. Since her son had malice in his heart toward Ceanna, I couldn't trust her either. She was the enemy.

I began videotaping Gina. I had a message for Jaceyon. "You thought I was playing with you, fuck boy?" I turned the video toward his mother.

"You see that, Jaceyon? I caught you slipping, bitch. Say hello, Gina," I smiled.

"Jaceyon, please help me!" she cried.

"Never disrespect a nigga of my caliber. Pull the trigger, my nigga," I gave WyKeith the go-ahead.

Gina's blood and brain matter spattered everywhere. Her head leaned downward with her eyes wide open.

"Rest easy, Gina." I stopped the video.

"Jesús!" I yelled into the phone after dialing his number.

"Halo, Avantae."

"Call the cleanup crew and dispose of this bitch. GL0244."
I gave Jesús the location in a secret code and hung up.

"Let's ride, my niggas," I told Elijah, WyKeith, and Tam.
Leaving Gina's lifeless body behind, these muthafuckas
will put some respect on my name.

Chapter Thirty-five

Jaceyon

We had a couple of pit stops at different hotels before we actually made it to Dallas. The days were long and draining, but I had to tread lightly. As my mother slept, my thoughts drifted consistently to Ceanna. My heart felt like it was going to stop at any moment.

Damn, I can't believe I shot Asia. I didn't want to, but I knew she would run back and tell Ceanna what we had done. I couldn't take that risk. It doesn't matter, though, because my mother was right. I should have killed MeMe as well.

We made it to Zaria's room and crashed for the night. Zaria was able to get me a cot to sleep on. I tossed and turned thinking about my next move. I had been moving too sloppy lately.

As I lay on the cot, I thought about the money I had on me. If Keisha hadn't spent any of the money from the trap that she stole, then it should be four hundred thousand in the trash bag. With that and the money at Aunt's abandoned house and the bricks, I should be on in no time.

I grabbed my phone and began going through my Facebook. I guess Ceanna forgot I was her friend on there. I jumped on her page and continued to scroll it when something caught my eye that broke my heart.

Ceanna put together a video of her and Avantae. The last photo on the video was a picture of the ring he had given her with the caption, "I said yes."

Damn, Ceanna wasted no time with that nigga. She just sent me the divorce decree along with other documents. Can she *really* be that coldhearted?

As Zaria and my mother slept, I shed tears that I had been holding in. I really missed my wife, and it's killin' me that Ceanna won't even speak to me. I tried to be civil in the beginning and talk things out, but she wasn't trying to hear shit.

I don't know why, but I kept scrolling her page and anger rose in me once I saw Jalisa in many photos. I can't believe I forgot her birthday. Avantae took over my family. He had replaced me in every single way. That shit was not fair at all, and I'm really disappointed in Ceanna. I thought she was a real-ass female, but she just like the rest of these hoes out here.

I know I was a dog-ass nigga, but, damn it, I took care of home. Ceanna didn't want for shit. I always did little nice shit for her. I mean, damn, what nigga don't cheat or fall short? She wanna just throw a nigga to the side like that.

My head is so fucked up. I can't believe that ho-ass nigga Rick recorded me. Something told me to walk away, but he had news I needed. Now, my business is all on Front Street. I never wanted Ceanna to know that side of me. I rid myself of those demons long ago, or, at least, I thought so. The knocking on the door woke me the next morning. I didn't even know that I was asleep.

"Housekeeping," the maid said, entering the room. "Oh, I'm sorry, you no stay another day?" the maid asked in broken English.

"What time is it?" I asked. I could hear my mother snoring.

"It's eleven in da morning, sir," she replied.

I asked the maid to give me twenty minutes. She nodded her head and left. I sat up on the cot trying to get my bearings together. I had a huge headache. I stood while stretching and made my way to the restroom. Zaria was nowhere in sight, but I thought maybe she went to go get her some breakfast.

As I was using the bathroom, I noticed that everything was bare; even the countertops that contained all of Zaria's makeup and hygiene products were empty. I opened the shower curtain, and nothing.

I finished urinating with suspicion rising in me. I opened the bathroom door and went into the closet where I had stashed the money. My shit was gone, along with my fucking car keys.

"That bitch!" I yelled while flipping the flat-screen TV that was on the dresser.

"What-what's going on?" My mother woke up dazed.

"Zaria stole the money and my fucking car keys!" I yelled. "Get the fuck up. We've gotta get the fuck outta here."

My mother and I caught a cab to the bus station, where we booked a one-way Megabus ticket to Austin for twenty-five dollars each. My mother only had $100 to her name. Luckily, I took twelve grand out of the bag and placed it in my sweat pockets. I was thankful Zaria didn't look in them.

Due to the many stops, we didn't get to Austin until nighttime. I had to move smart and stay under the radar. I got my mother and me a hotel for a couple of nights while I plotted things out. One thing I knew for sure was that Zaria would come back to Austin. She wouldn't skip town without her son or at least attempt to get him. I'm going to murk that bitch when I find her.

The good thing is I got money and ten bricks at Aunt's house. In the morning, I'm going to cop a cash car to get us around in until we can make it back to the hood safely.

My mind was so fucking stressed. I don't have the means to go up against Avantae if a street war started. Damn, I should have gone back to get the bag Rick had.

"Jaceyon, baby, it's been a long day. Why don't you get some rest?" my mother stated.

"You're right. My mind is so fucked up. I gotta kill this nigga Avantae. It's the only way, and if Ceanna gets in my way, she can get it too."

"Do you know where she's having the twins at? She's close to delivery. Maybe we can steal the twins or get one of them at least. We can use them as bait," my mother suggested.

"That ain't a bad idea." I rubbed my head.

As I lay in bed, I thought of ways to slowly break Avantae down. The way to a man's heart is through either his bitch, children, mother, or money. Any one of them sounds like a winner in my eyes, especially his mother. Sleep took over me quickly. I woke up to the smell of breakfast. My mother had got us breakfast from down the street.

After eating, I showered and put back on the same clothes. I had to run errands, so I gave my mother a little money to get her some clothing.

I caught a cab to drive me to a cash car lot, where I spotted a dark blue 2004 Chevy Impala with tint. After paying three grand, the vehicle was mine.

As I cruised the streets of Austin, I smiled. I'm about to be on real soon, and niggas will be bowing down to me. A devious thought came to my mind, and I swung by Dollar General. I wanted Ceanna to pay for posting that video, so I'm going to hurt her where it hurts the most.

Pulling up to the graveyard, I parked and searched the grounds for Cynthia and Calvin Black's name. "*Bingo!*" I yelled, making my way toward their headstones. Excitement filled me as I shook the bottle of red metallic spray paint. *Shoooo, shoooo, shoooo, shoooo.* I painted over and over on both Calvin's and Cynthia's headstones. *"'Til Death Do Us Part, Ceanna,"* I wrote and laughed.

I stood back and admired my handiwork. The paint settled nicely. I pulled my phone out to snap photos. Since Ceanna wants to play, she can choke on her tears and grieve over her dead parents.

Avantae's name popped up on my screen. That nigga got me for my shit. I hung up the phone and drove back to the hotel.

My T-lady had already beaten me back to the hotel. "Did you get the money?" she asked excitedly.

"No, Avantae's got my shit!" I yelled.

My mother stared at me for a long time not saying a word. I knew she was judging me and looking at me as if I were weak. I failed her, and Avantae won. She turned her back to me and sat down to turn on the TV.

"Breaking news: This is Selena Gore reporting live from KVUE. This is just in. As you can see, firefighters are trying to quickly put out the flames. Now, this isn't confirmed yet, but firefighters are saying this fire was deliberately set. A neighbor walking her dog spotted a big cloud of black smoke, dialed 911, and firefighters immediately responded. No bodies were found as of yet. We'll bring you more live coverage as the story develops. This is Selena reporting live. Back to you, Tommy."

All the wind I had was knocked out of me. I was defeated, broke, divorced, and soon, I'll be a wanted man. I couldn't take the stares any longer from my mother, so I left the hotel room and drove around until the wee hours in the morning. I was fucked up from drinking Everclear and really needed to just go lie down.

When I made it back to my hotel room, I noticed that my mother was gone. I thought maybe she went to the lobby because her wallet and wig were still lying on the dresser. She never goes anywhere without either. Honestly, I was kinda happy she was gone. I didn't like the vibe she was giving me.

I lay down on the bed and was about to close my eyes when my phone sounded off. I noticed it was Avantae's ho ass with an attachment video. Watching it, I burst out crying. That nigga killed my mama.

I jumped up and grabbed what I could find. I knew I had to leave the hotel. Avantae knew where I was, and if he did that to my mama, then I knew he'll do even more to me. I've got to get the fuck outta Dodge.

Chapter Thirty-six

Zaria

The way Jaceyon and Gina looked when they entered my room made me think that maybe hooking up with them was a mistake. I lay in that bed next to Gina as she slept. All I could think about was all the shit that had happened. I saw the light brightening up the room, and I knew that Jaceyon was still awake. I kept my eyes closed, and played like I was asleep, all the while thinking what the fuck I was going to do now. I lost the man I loved to this whale a bitch Ceanna, my son had been taken, Mondre stole my money, and now these two slim, grimy people are in my room. Oh, I forgot to mention being broke too.

The way I saw it, I had two options: either depend on Jaceyon and his mama, or steal that bag I saw him place in the closet. Let's just say the last choice won. I refused to be broke, homeless, using a nigga, or selling my body. Not happening!

I heard Jaceyon's sorry ass crying over Ceanna. I mean, good gawd, what the fuck did these niggas see in her? They worshiped her, and all I saw was a big, black female. Wasn't shit special about her. Okay, so she had a big booty—big deal. Her daddy was that nigga back in the day—big deeeaaal. Her hair was long, and she had gray eyes that changed colors. That shit wasn't special. Any bitch could buy contacts or an ass. I was tryin'a figure out how these niggas were so weak behind her ass. *Uuuugh!*

Anyway, I rolled my eyes for the millionth time as Jaceyon cried in the dark for hours. Even though I didn't like Ceanna, what Jaceyon had done is unacceptable. I wouldn't take his ass back either, but he's doing too much. Finally, the nigga drifted off to sleep, and I carefully got up and quickly made my move. I'm so happy all my shit was still packed, and I never took shit out of the bags. Other than my hygiene products, all my belongings were packed and ready to go.

Jaceyon and his mother were snoring. An evil laugh escaped as I thought of them waking up to see that I was gone with their shit. I grabbed the car keys, Jaceyon's pistol, and made my great escape. The shit was too easy.

Remembering the route to the club, I made my way there. The clubs closed at 2:30 a.m., and I made it just in time as I saw people exiting the club. I waited, and as soon as I saw Mondre—*Pow, pow, pow, pow*. I shot him. People ran screaming and hauling ass out of the parking lot. You couldn't tell where the shots were coming from. I pulled off smoothly as if nothing happened.

Soon, I pulled over by a dimly lit gas station and spotted a vehicle parked over to the side. Surveying the area, I hopped out of Jaceyon's ride and grabbed a screwdriver out of his glove compartment. I hurriedly switched license plates just in case Jaceyon reported his vehicle stolen.

Jumping back in the truck I made my way to I-35 South. I was going back to get my son. I blasted the music, trying to stay awake. I was so tired of driving and thought about pulling over numerous times, but I couldn't go to sleep just yet.

Finally, I made it to the outskirts of Austin and stopped in Round Rock. Although I changed Jaceyon's plates, the hood and everyone knew his truck. I couldn't chance it, so I pulled over and grabbed my suitcase.

"Fuck! Think think think!" I yelled aloud.

I got back in the truck and got back on I-35 North. Coming back this way was a huge mistake. I've got to get out of Texas altogether and come up with a plan to get Tater Bug later.

I drove and drove and drove for hours until my eyes began to fail me. I was tired, and I didn't know where I was. I checked into a motel and was out.

Late the next morning, I checked out and continued on the route I was taking. I stopped every three hours, stretched, and filled up on gas. I finally landed in Atlanta and thought that would be a great place to start over. I counted the money in the bag and jumped with joy when I learned I had close to four hundred thousand. I had never had that much money in my entire life!

Thinking smart, I found me a realtor and bought me a nice condo. I also got rid of Jaceyon's truck and bought my own nice little ride. I was riding high and living on top of the world. Finally! The only thing I was missing was my son. I planned to get him back one day, and when I did, it would be when Avantae and Ceanna least expected it. For now, though, I was going to enjoy this money and try to get on somebody's track.

Chapter Thirty-seven

Mia Symone

Once the initial shock of Asia's passing settled, things were really awkward between us all. WyKeith and Avantae barely acknowledged me, but they both hugged Keisha and Ceanna. I had no one to console me through my pain. I admit even in this tragic situation, I was soaking in jealousy.

I watched as the guys catered to their women. Even though Keisha and I barely got along, I must give it to her. She looked good. Her dark skin looked good against the 1B/350 Chinese cut banged bob. Her black matte lipstick gave her a grown and sexy feel. Her body is sick with it in an all-black jumpsuit, and I was digging her white and black sandals that showed off her perfect black gelled polish toes. She's was glowing, and the way she was wrapped tightly in WyKeith's embrace, I could tell she was a woman in love.

Ceanna and Avantae were just as cute as ever. He made Ceanna happy. Looking on at the two, my heart tugged a little when I noticed the huge cluster diamond rock on Ceanna's finger. I wondered how he proposed and who all was there. Did they celebrate? Did they go somewhere? When did he ask? The questions swirled in my head. I hated we aren't close anymore, and I hated I no longer have that bond with Ceanna. I missed my cousin!

Ceanna was so beautiful. I'd always loved her long, naturally curly mane. It was pretty, and her hair always smelled good. She's put on extra weight, but she looked adorable. Her solid purple maxidress was hugging her in the right places. Her ass had grown bigger, and you couldn't help but stare at it. My eyes widened when I saw my cousin's feet. They were so swollen, and they looked painful.

I diverted my eyes from WyKeith and Avantae. In this moment, I felt very small and just wanted to disappear. I've slept with both of them before. I guess it's not cute being a ho when you can't seem to shake away all your naked skeletons.

Once the guys and Avantae's mother left, we ladies stayed behind. The vibe was messed up. Ceanna and Keisha were cliqued up, and MeMe was just weird to me. Keisha kept giving me side eyes and evil glares the entire time. It's always the bitches that can't bust a grape and always getting they ass whipped that throws the most unnecessary shade. It's like they asking for the ass whooping. She had better be happy I'm changing!

I stayed off to myself with my son in my arms. I had to use the restroom really badly, and I didn't want to take my son in a hospital restroom. I stood and went over to where Keisha and Ceanna were sitting. Keisha placed her hands on her hips. She was giving way too much attitude. I expected that from my cousin but unlike Keisha, Ceanna was chilled.

"Ceanna, I know this is awkward, but I really need to use the bathroom. Can you please hold my son?" I asked, extending my baby to her. Ceanna looked at me, then at my child, and then back at me.

"Sure," she smiled.

"Thank-thank you." I nervously smiled back and turned to walk off.

"He's so beautiful," I heard Ceanna tell Keisha.

My heart was filled with joy. My cousin is such a sweet person. I'm happy she doesn't treat my son poorly or differently because of my hurtful actions toward her. I'm hoping Ceanna will invite me back into her life. Maybe this is a start.

Once I made my way back over to Ceanna, I decided to clear the negative energy in the room. I started this beef with all of us. Truthfully, Keisha had every right to feel the way she felt. What I did to her was dirty. Although Donte is her husband and he cheats with everyone, the fact that I have known Keisha and worked with her at one point at Tonya's salon, I should have had more respect for her as a woman.

"Keisha, I want to apologize to you for my part. I should have never slept with your husband. I had no right to do that. I'm growing as a person, and I'm trying to correct all my wrongs. I know you may not believe me or even may not accept my apology, but I just wanted to be woman enough for once in my life and say I'm sorry to you," I said while looking at her.

"Mia Symone, you can save all of that. I just don't like you nor do I respect you. However, I appreciate you for saying that, but it don't matter. I'm not even mad at you. Donte ain't shit and never was. That nigga cheated and dogged me the entire time we were married. I thank you and every other female. Y'all showed me who he really was, and it's a shame I had to fight so many bitches behind Donte's worthless ass. As far as you're concerned, it ain't no beef at all. I just don't respect you or trust you. However, I can be cordial and stop acting like a bitch toward you every time I see you. That ain't even necessary. Your son is beautiful, by the way," she looked over at him still in Ceanna's arms.

"How are you liking the home and San Antonio?" Ceanna asked, looking down at my son.

"I love it! It's so peaceful, and the people are friendly there. Thank you, Ceanna, for everything," I smiled.

"That's what family does. Besides, Jaceyon ain't shit. I ain't about to be harping on what y'all did in my spirit like that. Ain't no sense in being mad. I don't want his ass, and even if you decide to be with him, Mia, I wouldn't even care. When I say I'm over Jaceyon, that's what I mean."

"You don't have to worry about that. I learned my lesson. Besides, I will never be happy bringing misery to other people."

The funeral home finally came to pick up Asia's body and another weird moment of silence filled the air. I didn't know what else to say to Keisha or Ceanna. It's not like I could laugh with them or ask any questions about their life. I truly felt out of place, and I was ready to leave.

"Mia Symone, please stay in town. I'll call you in a day or two," Ceanna said and handed me back my child.

I checked into a new hotel off of 290 East. It was pretty decent and cozy. Little Jace became very fussy. I bathed him, fed him, and put him to sleep. It was very lonely being a single mother. I had no girlfriends or adults to talk to, and men were out of the question.

I thought about Asia mostly, and I cried the entire night. I really didn't have a lot of time to bond with Asia the way I would have liked. When we found out we were sisters, it was really weird for us both. We didn't have a clear understanding of our parents' past. My mother never talked about my father. I just know she had a hatred for Gina. I got bit and pieces from Gina, but there were still pieces that I felt were missing. We were all connected in some sort of way.

Asia struggled with the fact that I was her sister. I would have too because, let's face it, my track record is horrible. However, I always appreciated Asia, because she came through for me more than once.

Honestly, I don't know why Ceanna wanted me to wait around. I felt like the outsider. I'm happy Ceanna called me, but it's not like I can cry and grieve with her. Besides, I saw the looks everyone kept giving me, and, truthfully, I don't blame them.

Keisha hated my guts, and she had every reason to. I just hoped she didn't come for me at all again, because then, I'd have to hurt her feelings. I meant what I said earlier. I didn't have the right to bed her husband, Donte, the way I had, but at the same time, she sure knew how to pick these niggas.

I'll let you in on a little secret. WyKeith ain't shit either; at least he wasn't back in the day. I used to bounce all on that dick back then.

When WyKeith saw me, he hurried and left with Avantae, avoiding eye contact. He's married to this chick name Shawanda, and if I'm not mistaken, he still is. She's some ghetto-ass bird from San Antonio. That ain't my business, though. Like I said, maybe he's changed.

Besides all of that, I just don't belong in the circle, and, truthfully, I'm tired of begging for forgiveness. I fucked up. What more can I say? I know one thing, though, I am not about to keep apologizing over and over.

I'm surprised Ceanna asked me to stay in the city. I didn't know what for when nobody likes me or even speaks to me, but I agreed. I was tired anyway and didn't feel like driving back to San Antonio.

I woke up around 3:00 a.m. dying of thirst. Little Jace was sleeping peacefully, and I didn't want to move him. I spotted the bucket for ice on the dresser, grabbed my room key card, and made my way to the second floor where the ice machine was.

I was a little winded from the long hallways. The ice machine was at the end of the hall. Due to the many hotel rooms, as soon as you stepped off the elevator you had to make three right turns just to get to the machine.

Turning on the last right hallway, I spotted Gina getting ice at the end of the hall. I ducked back behind the corner and peeked around the wall. I watched as she finished getting her ice.

Gina returned to room 264. I smiled because her room was by the stairwell. I figured that she had to be here hiding out. So much shit was going down between Avantae and Jaceyon, so my assumptions were right.

My plan had always been to kill Jaceyon for what he did to me, but hurting his mother is definitely not a bad idea. From memory, I blocked my number and dialed Avantae's number. He was in kill mode, and if the beast is awakened in Avantae, then I know he isn't home yet, and he's somewhere ready to fuck some shit up.

"Who the fuck is this?" Avantae answered his phone. I could hear bitches in the background and instantly knew he was at a strip club.

"Avantae, this is Mia Symone. Listen, don't hang up. I got some information you may want to hear," I whispered.

"Speak!" he said like a boss.

"Listen, Jaceyon and his mother are at the new hotel on 290 East. They're in room 264, the last room at the end of the hall by the stairwell."

"Ayo, WyKeith, Tam, and Elijah, let's go get this fuck boy. Mia Symone, good lookin' out, ma, and stay around in the city. Ceanna wants you there for the birth of the twins, and you're invited to the baby shower. One!" He hung up.

I hurried back to my room forgetting about the ice. I smiled, knowing that victory was on my side. Wow! Avantae had never before spoken kindly to me. Maybe things will turn over for me after all.

Chapter Thirty-eight

Ceanna

"Mommy Ce," the kids said while trying to wake me.

These last few days I've been really sad and withdrawn. I didn't mean to take it out on anyone, but I'm so tired of being strong all the time. I just wish I could withdraw into a shell. It's been hell for me, and honestly, I wanted to just run away from it all. On top of that, I've been in a lot of pain.

I stayed up the night before and ordered new head-stones for my parents. With all Jaceyon had done, messing over my parents' grave site was the ultimate. I now see what Avantae was saying about him all along. He wasn't going to stop, and I had a bad feeling in the pit of my soul that things were only going to get worse.

"Yes, babies," I moaned with my eyes closed.

"Daddy Tae told us to bring you this. He said get ready. Everyone is here waiting on you," they said, laying something soft over my body.

"Waiting on me for what?" I asked with my eyes still closed.

"He said don't tell you, but to get ready," Tater Bug answered.

I opened my eyes and took in the children's appearance. They were both dressed in white. I didn't know what was going on, but I got up, quickly showered, and lightly applied a little makeup. I pulled the white sleeveless maxidress over my head that the children brought me and place my swollen feet in some flats. I wasn't feeling good today, and, honestly, I just wanted more rest.

When I made it to the front, the entire crew was there including MeMe, Mia Symone, Elijah, and his beautiful wife, Ashley. Everyone was dressed in white. It truly was a beautiful sight to see the different shades of black beautiful skin tones against the white clothing.

Avantae walked toward me and gave me a kiss. "You look absolutely beautiful." He smiled and then cupped my belly with both hands.

"Thank you, baby, so do you, my king. What's going on, baby?" I asked.

"I called everyone here, baby, so we can celebrate Asia. I have a van outside that's going to take us to Lake Travis. I have a boat waiting. WyKeith and Keisha are going to cook us all a nice meal too." He smiled. I couldn't do anything but wrap my arms around Avantae and cry.

Avantae was so thoughtful and always took care of my heart. He saw me and understood me. For Avantae to set this up meant the world to me. I missed my friend so much it hurts. I blamed myself. Maybe I should have followed her and stopped her from leaving. I don't know, but I just felt guilty.

I was so confused! I just don't understand why Jaceyon would hurt me this way. He took away my sister, and then shit on my parents' headstone. I can't take too much more.

"*Ssshhhh*, we're gonna get through this, I promise," Avantae said, rubbing my back.

"Taeeee, I miss her and Tonya so muuuch!" I began to break all the way down.

"Mommy Ce, don't cry! Remember, roses are red, violets are blue, but as long as I touch my heart, I'll always have you," Jalisa sang and hugged my leg.

"Oh, Jalisa! I love you, baby!" I cried, letting go of Avantae and hugging her.

I looked up and locked eyes with Mia Symone. She stared at me as she shed tears. Looking at her was as if time had stopped. It was as if she and I were the only people in the room. I don't even remember moving, but something special happened. She and I hugged.

It felt good to hug Mia Symone. Who would have thought that I would be here? I forgave her wholeheartedly, and I was no longer angry. I composed myself and smiled at her. I kissed her son and said something I never thought I would.

"Tater Bug and Jalisa, come here." Both of the children ran to me. They stood on both sides of me and looked up.

"I want you to meet your brother. This here is baby Jace." I pointed at the baby. Little Jace began to yawn and stretch in Mia Symone's arms. He then opened his big green eyes.

"He's so pretty! I see now I'ma be in a lot of fights 'cause I already got to tell them girls Tater Bug ain't marriage material, and now I have a brother with green eyes," Jalisa sang while she hit her forehead with an open palm. Everyone in the room laughed so hard at her dramatic expression.

"Yeeees, another boy, 'cause Jalisa is bossy and crazy sometimes. Daddy, she's really crazyyyy. Not crazy like Mommy Ce, but another level of crazy," Tater Bug said while using his hands. I looked at Avantae, and he gave Tater Bug a look like *change the subject, little bro*. We all laughed at those two kids.

I walked back over to my handsome man, and he swallowed me in his long arms. I always felt so protected in Tae's embrace. His tall, slender body always gave me comfort.

The boat ride on the lake made me feel so free. I broke away from everyone and went to the back of the boat where I stared at the beautiful clear water. I could see the fish below swimming in their own little world. The wind lightly blew against my skin, blowing my long, curly hair. At this moment, I felt at peace. I smiled, thinking of Asia. I remember when I met her at HT.

I had just come from my African American Studies class. I was about to place my key in the keyhole when I heard a girl screaming "oh nooooo." Me being me, I crept down the hallway. The girl's room door was open, and a cloud of smoke could be seen. I could see her running about in a wife beater and black boy shorts. She had flour in her hair and on her face. She turned on her fans and opened the window.

"Oh nooooo! Shit, I can't cook for shit!" she yelled.

I couldn't hold my laughter in as I watched her throw whatever she was cooking in the skillet under running water in the sink. From where I was standing looking in, the kitchen was a mess, and all you saw was smoke. The skillet made a loud sizzle sound, and I laughed so loud when she threw the damn skillet in the sink, that I scared her.

"You scared the shit outta me." She jumped and then busted out laughing. "Hi, I'm Asia, and as you can see, my ass can't cook for shit." She laughed and shook her head.

I stared at her for a moment and was literally taken aback by her beauty. She was of average height, with this milky, vanilla, light skin. Her hair was very curly, with fall colors of light browns, plus a hue of red and orange. Her eyes were striking to me. They were gray and resembled mine but were a lighter gray. She reminded me of my dad's grandmother who was killed along with my grandfather in a street war with the Cubans.

"Hi, I'm Ceanna, and it's nice to meet you. I'm in 3H down the hall. As far as the cooking goes, don't worry. I'll teach you. You can't be no worse than my friend Keisha used to be. She tried cooking fried chicken like scrambled eggs and almost burnt down our room. Now she can cook her ass off," I laughed.

"Well, don't laugh, but that's exactly what I did." We both fell out laughing at that.

That was the beginning of our friendship. Funny how later we found out that we really were related, and that my uncle Carlos, Mia Symone's father, was actually her father too. I'm always so shocked how that happened.

"Hey, beautiful, what are you out here doing? I had to come check on my baby," Avantae whispered in my ear, wrapping his arms around me.

"I was thinking about Asia and the first time we met. Tae, do you know this fool was trying to fry chicken like scrambled eggs? She didn't have enough grease and almost burnt some shit down." I laughed while leaning my head against his chest.

"Are you okay, though, baby?" he asked. "You never have to pretend with me. Look at me, baby, and talk to me." I turned around to look at him.

"Sometimes I wonder what I've done to deserve so much pain and cruelty. I can see if I've done wrong to people, but it's like I never catch a break. I lost my father, mother, first son, Zylan, Tonya, Asia, and ended up marrying a fuck nigga who cheated on me and disrespected me; then my ex, Marcus, tried to rape me. On top of all of that, Jaceyon shit on my parents' graves, and my aunt

Monica turned on me. I can't even break all the way down, Tae, because I fear I won't come back," I cried.

"You can come back, baby, and I see you do that every day. Sometimes in life, baby, we go through shit. It builds character. I love your strength, baby, and I would never look at you as weak if you need to break down. That's what I'm here for, Ce. We're gonna get through this together. Never will Jaceyon, his mother, or Zaria ever be able to bring this family malice again," he said, wiping my tears.

"Thank you, baby." I placed two kisses on his neck.

"Ceanna, I don't know why you fucking playing and shit. Keep on, girl, and we finna get down right *here*. You feel that, girl?" Avantae poked my belly with his ready manhood.

"Tae, you're a mess. Come on, let's go to the bathroom. I might not be able to sexually please you one way, but my mouth is working just fine." I led the way back inside the boat. *Whap!*

"Look at how that ass shakes. That ass right there," he mocked Mystikal.

"You got one mo' time to hit my ass that hard. That shit hurts."

"Heeell, yeah! I'm sho' gonna put some more babies in you. That ass is phat as fuck." *Whap! Whap! Whap!* Avantae hit it three more times.

"You know what? I'ma twist yo' right ball, just wait," I pointed at him.

"Nah, Ce, I'm good on the head right now. Yo' ass don't play fair. Throwing ice-cold water and shit on a nigga 'cause I farted. Who don't fart? Hell, I just did." Avantae rubbed his stomach.

"Tae, *uuuugh,* and you did a silent one too. That shit's in my mouth now. Don't even come in here with everyone else. You just rude, and your farts are disrespectful shit."

I frowned while holding my nose with one hand and fanning the air with the other hand.

"Girl, move. I'm going up in there." Avantae opened the sliding door that led into the inside of the boat.

"Avantae, hell, nawl!" Keisha yelled from the kitchen of the boat.

"Man, girl, gon' on. You can't even smell from over there," he laughed.

"Nawl, my nigga, you foul," Elijah held his nose.

"Daddy Tae, you stink so badly. Mommy Ce, how do you do it?" Jalisa yelled while being dramatic.

"She throws ice-cold water on that ass," Janair said, making us all burst into laughter.

We all ate a nice home cooked dinner. Keisha and WyKeith prepared a nice salad with walnuts, candy-coated pecans, cucumbers, apples, and strawberries. They dressed the salad with a Raspberry Vinaigrette salad dressing. They prepared a honey glaze with butter and garlic shrimp, chicken, and a fully loaded baked potato. The guys drank heavier liquor while the females preferred wine and margaritas. I also had a glass of wine since my doctor gave me the okay. The kids, of course, had juice, and for dessert, Keisha spoiled us with a caramel cheesecake.

The food was absolutely delicious. I smiled, admiring how good Keisha and WyKeith worked in the kitchen together. He was so loving toward her, and I could tell she was truly happy.

Ding ding ding.

"This toast is to Ceanna and Avantae. I just want to say thank you for forgiving me. I don't know what I would do without you," Mia Symone said as tears fell.

Everyone looked at Avantae, and then me. That was some awkward shit, but, hell, I'm over it. I started clapping. I don't know why, but I did. Everyone looked confused but clapped as well. *Maybe it's the wine.*

"Mia Symone, you stepped up and came through when it mattered. Like Ceanna said, you're family," Avantae spoke.

"*Bbbbbllllrrrrgggghh, bbbbbbllllllrrrrrggggh!*" Keisha began vomiting.

"Pass the trash can, my nigga!" WyKeith yelled urgently to Semaj.

"Oh my God, Key, are you o—" I asked, but Keisha vomited again.

"*Blurghhhhhhhhhhhhhh!*"

"Baby, are you sick? Come on, baby, let's clean you up," WyKeith said, walking Keisha to the bathroom. Janair and Mia Symone began cleaning up the vomit, and I'm just happy I was done eating.

"Ayo, baby, we finna go on the back deck. When y'all are done, come out here. I got something for you, MeMe, Keisha, and Mia Symone," Avantae said, holding a lot of balloons in his hand. I nodded and stayed seated in my chair. I was in so much pain. The rubbing of my belly that Barbara Jean gave me was soothing.

Ten minutes later, Keisha and WyKeith came out of the restroom. She looked at me blinking four times. That was our girl signal code of communication. She silently told me WyKeith knew she was pregnant.

We all went up the four stairs that led to the back deck, and I almost fell out. Avantae was such an amazing man. On the deck, he had white rose petals, a large photo of Asia, Tonya, Mia Symone, Keisha, and me.

Mia Symone, Keisha, MeMe, and I joined hands. I couldn't stop crying. Just seeing how happy we all were in the photo told my spirit that forgiving Mia Symone was the right thing to do.

"I know we can't bring Asia back. How she died was fucked up, and I promise everything will be handled. I brought everyone here so we can celebrate her. Asia was so cool, sweet, and most of all, trustworthy. I always respected Asia for how she carried herself. I brought everyone a white balloon and a marker. That way, before we release the balloons, you can write her a message. Ceanna, MeMe, Mia Symone, and Keisha, I also got y'all these." Avantae passed each one of us an urn. He had gotten us all of our favorite colors ranging from a wild orchid purple, hunter green, hot pink, and ocean blue. I kissed mine and ran my fingers over the lettering. *"In loving memory of Asia Monecia Black."*

The urn was so beautiful. I was amazed at how Avantae got us our own. I didn't even know you could do that, but I guess with money, you can do whatever you want. I took a seat next to Jalisa on a side bench.

"Mommy Ce, is Auntie Asia with Mommy?" she innocently asked.

"Yes, baby, she is. Would you like to write a letter to Auntie Asia and your mom Tonya?" I asked while pushing Jalisa's hair from her face. She had hair like Asia and an olive complexion. She was such a beautiful little girl.

"Yes," Jalisa sadly nodded her head. She then started crying.

As if Avantae could sense her tears, he stopped his conversation with the guys and came over. He scooped her into his arms, and she buried her head in the crease of his neck. He calmed her down as he always did and placed a smile back on her face. The two of them began writing on her balloons.

"Mommy Ce, would you be mad at me if I sent one up for my mommy?" Little Avantae asked while coming to take a seat next to me. I looked over at Avantae, and then back at Tater Bug.

"I would never be mad at you. Here, baby, let's tell Zaria that you love her." Tater Bug shook his head no and wrote: *"Bye, Mama, I have a new mama now, and she loves me.*" He had a little work to do as far as spelling; nevertheless, I was shocked.

I took the marker from little Avantae and began to write a message to my sister Asia. "*I love you, Asia! I'm so sorry this happened to you. I will always carry you in my heart.*" I then kissed the balloon leaving my full lip print.

"Everybody, before we send our balloons up, I have an announcement," WyKeith said, getting all of our attention.

"They say when a loved one passes, a new life is created. So, today, let's celebrate Asia *and* a new life. My baby Keisha and I are expecting," he smiled.

"*Ohhhhs, aaaahs, congratulations, that's what's up, my nigga, and yayyyy*" echoed throughout the boat. We then held our balloons up and on the count of three released them.

"We love you, Asia!" we all said.

"Oh, everybody, before I forget, please clear your schedule for Saturday," Avantae announced and every-one acknowledged what he asked.

We stayed a little longer on the boat enjoying each other. The ladies and I vibed with each other, and I even got to know Elijah's wife, Ashley, a little better. She was really cool and down-to-earth. I could see myself hanging with her.

Avantae came over and announced that we needed to leave because he had a surprise for me. We all cleaned up, packed up, and headed toward the van.

"Ceanna, we're almost there, so I've got to cover your eyes." He placed a blindfold on me.

I felt crazy as hell being blindfolded in a van full of people. The van started to rock, and I could feel bumps in the road. *Oh, Lawd, what's this boy got up his sleeve? I* silently thought.

"Okay, baby, we're here. Give me your hand, baby, and I'ma lead you." Avantae took my hand.

We walked a little distance, and I wondered where we were. I could hear Jalisa and Tater Bug's excitement as we got closer. We suddenly stopped, and Avantae untied the blindfold.

"Surprise!" everyone yelled.

"What!" I fell to my knees crouching in front of my mom and dad's graves.

"Thank you!" I sobbed. Avantae had restored my parents' grave site. Fresh flowers were placed by both of the new headstones.

As I cried, the kids came and hugged me. I held both of them, rocking back and forth. I missed my parents so much.

Chapter Thirty-nine

Avantae

Another week had gone by, and I had been trying to track Jaceyon down. I couldn't seem to find this nigga. I was really uneasy with him still lurking around. I've put everyone on alert for him, even placing a million-dollar bounty on his head. It shouldn't be *this* hard to find him.

The light snores I heard from Ceanna lying next to me placed me at peace. I just wanted to make my baby happy. Seeing her face the other day at her parents' grave site almost broke a nigga down. I can't believe Jaceyon was doing all he could to hurt her. It's mind-boggling.

I couldn't sleep so I got up and gently closed the door, careful not to wake Ceanna. I checked on the kids, and then made my way to the living area. The yoga mats were still there, so I decided to mediate.

Meditation had really been helping me change. It brought about an inner peace. I could think clearer and better calculate my moves. It also made me think of my mistakes and how to be better.

As I sat meditating, I began to think of the streets. No matter how much I tried to turn away, something seemed to pull me back. I was conflicted! On the one hand, I loved this journey of the family man, but on the other hand, I felt niggas were testing me.

I heard my phone ringing from the kitchen table and got up to go answer it. It was three in the morning, so I wondered who this could be. My heart began thumping hard when I saw Tam's name on my screen.

"What's the word, my nigga?" I asked.

"Yo, nigga, meet me at the trap in the Del. I'm following Elijah. He has the package with him, and we're taking that package there. You know what it is?" He hung up. He had just told me in code he had Jaceyon.

I already had on my sweats and a black tee, so I slipped on some socks and my Js. Then I checked my clips and made sure my guns were ready, grabbed my keys, and set the house alarm.

Del Valley was a ten-minute drive from Manor. I arrived in no time to the trap. I had made up my mind that I wasn't going to kill Jaceyon there. It would be too easy to trace it back to me. I looked around before I got out of my vehicle and was confused when I didn't see Elijah's vehicle.

"What's up, Tae?" Tam dabbed me up as soon as I walked into the trap.

"What's up, fam? Where's Elijah?" I asked, confused.

"That nigga changed his mind and let Jaceyon go," he said.

"Nigga, the fuck you just say to me? You let that ho-ass nigga get away?" I yelled. I was pissed off. I turned my back walking away from the nigga. I wanted to body this nigga for wasting my time. I began to inspect the trap house and walked farther in.

Pow! Pow! Pow!

I turned around in shock. Elijah had his gun pointed at Tam shooting the nigga over and over again.

"Ayo, what the fuck just happened?" I yelled, still in shock.

"The nigga was about to kill you, my nigga. This ho-ass nigga signaled for me to pull over. I got out of the vehicle and walked to the driver's side to see what was up, and the nigga shot me three times, then burnt off. Luckily, I put my vest on tonight. I figured that nigga was on some funny shit, and I had a feeling he was going to come here!" Elijah yelled. "I pulled up just in time. My nigga, I don't know what I would have done if I had lost you," Elijah expressed, breaking down.

"Family, I'm Gucci because of you. Thank you, my nigga, for having my back. I can't believe this ho-ass nigga was trying to off me like that. He lied and said he had the ho-ass nigga Jaceyon," I yelled, kicking the dead nigga in the head.

"Is that what he told you? This nigga told me you wanted us to meet you at the trap in the Del. You didn't touch anything, did you?" Elijah asked.

"Nawl, G!"

"Let's burn this muthafucka down then." Elijah struck a match.

We left the trap house burning and drove over to my old house. Elijah was holding his chest, and I knew from the impact he was in pain. I hit up Jennifer, a chick who's an RN. I kept her on payroll just for times like these.

Jennifer came over with pain medication and checked Elijah out. Under the vest, his light skin was bruised pretty badly from the impact of the bullets. Jennifer worked quickly and was out of our hair in no time.

"You good, my nigga?" I asked.

"Man, that ho-ass nigga got me, fam. He caught me slipping."

"Damn, man, I'm sorry this happened. I can't believe this nigga was about to dome me. This nigga and I go way back since freshman year. I've been sitting here trying to think what I did to this nigga to make him turn on me like that," I spoke with my hands, still in shock.

"Your position, family. See, you've been outta the streets for a minute, Tae, while this nigga Tam has been rising. He probably was afraid you were going to come back and take over, not even knowing that these streets have been yours for a minute. Niggas respect you out here. Tam didn't get that type of respect. Me, though? I never wanted that type of position. I was just trying to come up and make a way for my wife and children. Shit is hard, fam, and we doing bad," he said despondently.

"My nigga, why I'm I *just* hearing about this? We've been brothers forever, and you could have come to me."

"I didn't want you to think I was this lame-ass nigga. I ain't a drug dealer like that. I'll kill a nigga, but I can't push no weight. I ain't made for that shit. When you were in the game, I rode for you because you're my brother. I would have died for you, so I stayed ready. You kept my pockets nice, but once you left the game, I didn't have shit to fall back on. I've been working at this bullshit-ass city job, making fourteen dollars an hour with a family of six. I can't win, and my wife steady riding my back because I can't afford the shit I used to," he sighed.

"Well, say, man, dig these blues. Either way, you gonna be straight, my nigga; don't worry. Are you good to drive? I've got to get back to my family. You know tomorrow is going to be a long day with the baby shower and all. I hope y'all are coming."

"I'm good, man, and thanks, man. You're a good nigga, Avantae, and I appreciate you. We're going to be there for sure. My wife really likes Ceanna too." Elijah slowly stood.

"Yeah, Ce likes her too. Shit, though, as far as your job is concerned, why don't you just come back and work for me? I've got a shoe store, the clothing store for men next to Ceanna's boutique, the barbershop, and you know I'm working on this music shit. I can always use someone to run the store, and you're a trustworthy, hardworking nigga. Give it some thought and let me know. Either way, my nigga, you and your family are going to be straight. What does Ashley do? Shit, Keisha about to open the salon again too, and Ceanna keeps staff as well. Plus, you know we got that fashion show coming up."

"Shit, Ashley has been trying to start a day care service. She can't work because we can't afford child care. For three children they want twenty seven hundred. Hell, that's more than a nigga makes. I know she can do hair, though. She keeps hers nicely done and my daughters' hair. She would love an opportunity. I know she's tired of being stuck at home."

"Well, does she have an education or license for the day care? My nigga, we can get that shit popping now." New businesses always excited me.

"As a matter of fact, she does."

"Well, say no more! We finna get little mama right," I smiled.

"That's what's up and good looking."

As I drove back to my home, I was extremely disappointed. I had gotten my hopes high that Jaceyon would be taken care of. I kept having this nagging feeling that something bad was going to happen, and I couldn't rest. I was looking over my shoulder all the time, and I was afraid to let my family out of my sight. I know sometimes everyone thinks I'm smothering them, but I'm just being careful. I grew up with Jaceyon, and I know how dangerous he can be. When he can't have his way, he goes to extreme measures.

I checked the perimeter of the home, peeked in on my mother and kids, set the alarm, and went to shower. I made sure to take a shower with Ceanna's favorite scent. I needed a release, and I needed to feel her warmth.

Chapter Forty

Ceanna

"Wake up, ma!" Avantae nudged me lightly with his left hand while he placed a food tray down on the nightstand with his right.

"Umm, baby, you smell so good," I moaned while I kissed Avantae on the lips. His cologne was exciting me all over again.

"Thank you, baby! I'ma dip out, but get ready. Keisha will be here in an hour to get you. I made you some turkey bacon, French toast, eggs, and I know you love watermelon any time of the day," he laughed.

"Ahh, shit now! I see those cooking classes Mama's been giving you is paying off. Baby, where are kids and Mama at? It's too quiet around here."

"The kids are with Janair and Semaj, and Mama is in the front waiting on me. Don't ask no mo' questions, Ce. You're so nosy. Now I see where Jalisa gets that from," he laughed.

"Whatever, Tae! You, your mama, Keisha, Janair, Tater Bug, and even Jalisa's little ass is acting *really* funny. You know how I am, baby. I need to know," I fake pouted and smiled.

"Little nosy ass! Just know today is all about you, baby. Keisha even brought you an outfit to match the colors for today." He placed a bag on the bed. Avantae kissed me one last time and headed out of the bedroom.

"Be ready!" He poked his head back in and then left.

I ate my food enjoying every bit of it. Avantae had come a long way. Cooking was never really his thing. Well, let me say regular stuff, 'cause Avantae could barbecue and grill his ass off. He also made this special barbecue sauce that was to die for.

It was a little after eleven in the morning, and I can't believe I slept that long. If Avantae hadn't have woken me up, I would probably still be asleep. I was so tired lately and very sore. I had been keeping Cherrika Jones, my doctor, on standby.

"What Keisha done brought me?" I spoke aloud to myself while searching through the bag. I pulled out a really pretty, long, purple and white maxidress with cute little Gucci purple flip-flops. *Aaaaw, my boo sho' know how to make a girl feel special.*

After showering, I sat at my all-black Hokku Designs Katella Vanity Set. There, I lightly applied MAC NW47 Pro Longwear Foundation, coordinated with a warm purple eyeshadow, and gave my long lashes instant volume with a black Zac Posen mascara. I pencil styled my eyebrows by finishing it with a brow finisher, and lastly, I enhanced my big juicy lips with a courting seduction lipstick.

I smiled at my appearance. My pregnancy had been a very difficult one, oftentimes leaving me very self-conscious. Countless times, I watched as Avantae worked out rebuilding his strength from being shot. I envied his toned body and knew that he had plenty of women at his disposal. Although he would remind me of how beautiful I was to him, it did little for my self-esteem at times.

While pregnant, I had put on an extra fifty pounds. It was very hard for me to do normal activities. Something as simple as showering would tire me easily. My legs and feet stayed swollen, I often stayed tired, moody, and sore, not to mention the changes with my skin. My skin was very dry some days, oily other days, leaving pimples and hair bumps to make appearances on my once-flawless skin.

As I continued to beautify myself, I removed the bonnet off my head and began unrolling the flexi rods. Once all of the flexi rods were removed, I took a little oil sheen and lightly sprayed the curls. Next, I began separating the curls until I had a completely full curlicue curl pattern going on.

I stood up and admired myself in the full-length mirror. I was ready to drop any day now, and the way I was feeling, Lord knows I was ready. "Y'all mama is the shit!" I yelled out while I rubbed my belly.

Today, I felt really alive, refreshed, and I was excited to see what Avantae and Keisha had up their sleeves. I began humming along to the soulful lyrics of "Let It Burn" by Jazmine Sullivan playing from the Pandora station off my iPhone.

"That's my shit!" I hollered out to no one in particular.

Honk, honk, honk!

"Damn, shit already? Keisha's ass ain't never on time, and all of a sudden, she wanna be extra today?" I yelled.

I hurried and threw on my bra, put on my Spanx, and threw my flowing purple and white maxidress over my head. I was sweating, mad as hell, and cussing at the same damn time.

"Where's my shit?" I yelled out, wanting to cry.

Hell, I couldn't find my damn purse. I burst out laughing when I saw my Gucci purse on the damn bed. *Lawd, I'm losing my mind.* I sprayed my Jimmy Choo perfume, quickly applied lotion, threw my wallet in my purse, slid my feet into my cute Gucci flip-flops, and grabbed my keys.

Honk, honk, honk!

"Hurry up, Ceanna, or we gonna be late, shit!" Keisha yelled.

"Damn, Keisha I'm coming. Why don't you just wake up the entire neighborhood?" I fussed while practically jogging to her car.

"Well, don't you look adorable," she said as soon as I sat down in her vehicle. "Hi, Auntie's babies," she cooed while rubbing my stomach.

"Really? Hunny, I feel like a big-ass whale. I can't wait to drop these kids. I feel and look a mess; but as you asked, I am dressed. Where are we going anyway? Everybody's acting all secretive and suspect," I said, raising my eyebrows at her.

"Girl, boo, no, you don't! Who looks a mess is your cousin Mia Symone. Sorry, I had to say it. That weight on her, hunny—nah," Keisha shook her head, and I just laughed.

"She has gained at least fifty pounds. I've never seen her that big in my entire life," I admitted.

"So how have you been feeling, Ce? You're my girl and all, so you don't have to put on with me." Keisha looked at me with concern. By her taking her eyes off the road, she hit a big-ass pothole.

"Got damn, Keisha. You tryin'a make me go into early labor?" I laughed while holding my stomach.

"My bad!" Keisha chuckled.

"Key, honestly, I never thought I would ever love again. Jaceyon really hurt me so badly; not only him but Marcus too. I was really hurt by their actions. So hurt to the point I tried to push Avantae away. I felt so broken inside. Today, though, I feel so alive and free. I'm in love and so happy, Key," I smiled.

"That makes me so happy. I love you, Ce, and I don't know what I'd do without you. You deserve happiness and love. Avantae is really a good man and person. He called me every single day when Zylan passed. He made

sure I was good. He's always so protective, Ce, and
Avantae really helped me kick my drug habit. I mean, I
still smoke dro and drink my little chocolate ass off, but
that hard shit I kicked. Avantae talks about you all the
time, even before you gave him a chance. Don't even get
me started on when you stopped talking to him recently.
Po' baby didn't know what to do with himself," she smiled.

"That boy is so crazy. Sometimes, Key, you've got to
let these niggas know that you not finna play these little
games. He found out real quick too. Avantae really is a
good person. I'm so proud of the man he has become. I'm
happy Avantae walked with me through the storm. He
never gave up on me. I love that man so much!"

"So are you ready?" she asked while rubbing my belly.

"Hell, yeah! I don't think I'ma make it too much longer.
Hunny, I got my doctor on standby. These babies act like
they want to come soon. Hunny, I can't wait." I took a
deep breath.

"The question is, baby mama, are *you* ready? Wait,
though! Oh my God, so what did WyKeith say when you
told him about the baby?" I asked excitedly.

"Girl, so I kept on vomiting in the bathroom for like five
minutes. I was so weak. When I was done, I stood up and
washed my mouth out. WyKeith was standing behind me,
and then, girl, he wrapped his arms around my stomach
and began rubbing it. I looked at him through the mirror
shedding tears, and WyKeith just smiled at me. He told
me he loved me and that he was excited." She smiled so
big.

"Aaaaw, that's so adorable, Key. I really like WyKeith.
Where the hell are we going? Yo' ass hitting every damn
pothole. Yo' ass can't drive, damn," I laughed while
holding my stomach.

"We're almost there, Ce. Damn, your ass is so crazy all
the time. On some real shit, though, Ceanna, I'm tryin'a

figure out why Mia Symone is still around. That ho ain't changed. Do you know WyKeith even had sex with her back in the day? Sho' did, he told me." Keisha shook her head.

"What, bish? Naw! Damn, Mia! Who *hasn't* she slept with? So here's the thing. I know Mia Symone is a ho, but I promise she wasn't always that way. Ever since we were little, she was always searching for something. She was the sweetest girl until our ninth-grade year. Mia Symone was gang-raped by eight boys. My aunt didn't believe her. She had even gotten pregnant, and my aunt made her give the baby up for adoption. My mother tried to get the baby back, but it was a closed adoption. After that, Mia Symone was never the same. She and I had always been close, but the older we got, she began to ho herself out. Boiiii, I used to whip hoes' asses behind her. What she did is unforgivable, but I could never hate that baby. Those eyes of his touched something in me, and I loved him. How, Key, I don't know, but I do. I don't trust her like that, but she's family too. Other than you guys, I don't know my family. I mean, I know where they are, but I try to stay away from them. They're a bunch of goons, killers, and some mo' shit," I reasoned.

"Well, that ain't no excuse to be no ho."

I didn't have a comeback, nor was I about to sit up and defend Mia Symone. The truth is, she had done a lot of dirty shit.

Keisha drove another ten minutes before we pulled up to this beautiful venue. It was packed with a lot of vehicles.

"Girl, what did you and Tae do?" I asked, smiling.

"You'll see, come on," she said.

We walked into the venue and out of nowhere, everyone yelled "Surprise!" I looked among the beautiful crowd of people and couldn't help but shed tears. There had to have been over sixty people there. I covered my head with my hands, continuing to cry tears of joy. Avantae came and wrapped his long arms around me. "*Aaaaw,*" the crowd sang in unison.

The decorations were so beautiful. Keisha had violet purple, wild orchid, and gold balloons everywhere. The table decorations were extremely lovely. The vases had wild orchids and rose petals with a floating gold candle. Two goldfish were swimming around in the water. Cute favor boxes were in front of each seat. My eyes grew extremely wide when I saw five long tables filled with gifts.

Avantae placed a sash on me that read, "*My Queen.*" I smiled at him, and we took a seat by the gift table. "You see this shit, baby? WyKeith hooked us up, baby. That ain't even half of it. Earlier this morning, while you were sleeping, this nigga came through with diapers and all kinds of shit," Avantae excitedly said while he pointed at the gift table.

"Really? That's so sweet of him. Baby, how did you get all of this by me? This is so beautiful. I love it, baby. It's so beautiful in here. I love the fact that Aariah and Aaniah's names are the focal point of the decorations too. I knew your ass was up to something. I can't believe you got this by me." I looked at him.

"Oh, I got something else for you too." He licked his lips.

"Oh, Laaawd! Come on, Tae, let's walk around so I can say hey to everyone," I laughed.

"Mommy Ce! We got you good, huh?" The kids laughed while running to give me a hug.

"Y'all sho' did! You two look so adorable too. Tater Bug and Jalisa, I love y'all hair," I smiled.

"Auntie Janair took us to the hair shop, and Keisha hooked a young sista up," Jalisa said.

"Aye, aye!" the kids sang in unison. I shook my head and laughed.

"Daddy, I've got to go to the bathroom," Tater Bug said, pulling Avantae's arm.

"Ceanna, I don't see how you deal with these badass kids, man. Jalisa and Avantae's ass drive me crazy," he laughed.

I walked around for a minute to greet everyone and saw some of my employees, Avantae's employees, the crew, of course, my doctor, Vera, MeMe, Tamara, and I was shocked to see Ms. Perry. Everyone one had on something purple.

"Man, Ceanna, I already told Tae's ass don't worry about clothes and shit. You see those tables with all those gifts? The plug came through." WyKeith smiled while rubbing his hands.

"WyKeith, I really appreciate you for everything you've done for me. Thank you for being a part of our family. We love you and value you. Thank you for loving my girl, Key, too. Please don't hurt her 'cause I'll have to cut you," I laughed . . . but I was dead-ass serious.

"Naw, Ce, your ass is straight nuts. Yeah, I heard about you, and I don't want them kind of problems. You got a mean-ass right hook." We laughed.

"WyKeith, your ass is crazy. What's the food looking like, though?" I asked.

"Man, good as fuck. I had to keep Tae's ass outta the food. Man, Keisha, Mama Barbara Jean, and Ms. Vera's ass threw down, Ceanna. Come on; the food is over this way." WyKeith led me over to the other side of the room.

I hadn't seen this when I first walked in. This side of the room was so beautiful. There was a balloon arch with candy jars and painted wooden letters with the twins' name. The table was filled with flavored popcorn bags, candy apples with twin girls on them, purple cupcakes, strawberries dipped in gold and purple, Rice Krispies Treats, Oreo cookies with twins on them, purple-frosted pretzel sticks, a white chocolate fountain, and cake pops. The cake was a single sheet. It had a mother holding her stomach with the footprints of the baby kicking. It was so pretty! There was even a bar set up with all kinds of liquor. A margarita machine was even there.

Aligned along the wall were two tables filled with food. One table had appetizers of cheesy turkey taco phyllo cups with zesty lime cream, buffalo chicken skewers, deviled eggs, pineapple with sesame chicken, pesto tortilla pinwheels, meatballs, lemon pepper wings, barbeque wings, hot wings, roasted smoked salmon with mango avocado salsa cups, seafood pasta salad, cucumber bites, a creamed spinach dip, and queso with chips. Table two had spaghetti with cheese, cheese and garlic bread, sausage, broccoli/cheese casserole, greens, yams, mac/cheese casserole, brisket, shrimp, African rice, gumbo, shepherd's pie, and ziti. Everything looked amazing, and I knew it was going to be good because the women who prepared the food could cook.

The music was live, and even though I was sore and in pain, I had to go out there and show my babies and the rest of the kids how to do this cute JuJu on the beat dance. I might be big and pregnant, hunny, but fat don't stop no show, and I could drop this shit and pick it back up.

"Aye, aye, aye, go, Ceanna!" the crowd sang, and then Keisha, Janair, and some of the guys joined me and the kids on the floor.

After I was done dancing, Avantae's little jealous ass came to whisper in my ear. "Nawl, Ceanna, you can't be doing all of that. You got niggas in here looking at your ass and shit." He was serious as hell.

"Avantae, you be doing the most," I laughed, causing him to laugh. He began to draw his hand back, and I stopped him.

"Boy, if you hit my ass that hard again, I promise you we gonna have some issues," I laughed and kissed him.

"Attention, everyone! We're going to get started with our first game. I need all the men in the room to come sit at this table. So this game is called 'Name That Baby Food.' You will be blindfolded, and whoever guesses the baby food correctly wins a free getaway weekend to Kemah Island," Keisha said as she pointed at a long table.

"I know you betta get this right, Semaj!" Janair yelled out, causing us all to laugh.

The guys ate their first serving of food. I laughed so hard seeing their faces. They were eating Zucchini Broccoli Medley. *Yikes!* I know that shit was nasty.

"Y'all tryin'a kill a nigga!" Lee, one of Avantae's employees, yelled out, causing us all to holler out in laughter.

"This is that zucchini broccoli mess, and the only reason I know is because my daughter had a fit and threw it on my lip," Elijah said, and everyone laughed again.

"He woooon!" Keisha yelled, and everyone clapped.

"Hell, nawl, what's the next game? That shit was nasty. Keisha, you're *so* wrong," Semaj fussed, and the fellas all agreed.

"Okay, guys, the next game is 'Baby Bingo.' The prize is $100," Janair announced. She and Keisha were hosting the baby shower.

The games went on and on. They were a lot of fun with lots of laughter. We played all things "Baby A-Z, Baby Word Finder, How Well Do You Know the Mother/ How Well Do You Know the Father, Who Can Drink the Fastest," to "Who Can Design the Best Onesie."

I really had a great time, and the food was to die for. I tried to keep up with the kids with the cute dance routines, and even Avantae and I danced a few rounds.

"Attention, everybody, this here is Pastor Jeremiah. I asked him to come here today because as you know,

I asked Ceanna to marry me. I wanted to let her plan her day the way she wanted, but I didn't want my babies coming into the world without me being married to their mother. So, Ceanna, will you marry me here and right now, baby?" Avantae asked.

I couldn't even make it up to where Avantae was standing. I had my head in my hands sobbing uncontrollably. "Aaaaw!" the crowd sang. Avantae came over to where I was sitting, and the pastor followed him. I stood and fell into Avantae's arms.

"Yeeees!" I cried, and claps rang out throughout the building.

Pastor Jeremiah began to say the wedding vow script. "Will you, Avantae Devin Wallace Jr., have Ceanna Nicole Black to be your wife? Will you love her, comfort and keep her, and forsaking all others remain true to her, as long as you both shall live?"

"I *do!*" Avantae raised my chin to look up at him.

Pastor Jeremiah asked me to repeat after him, and I did. When pronounced husband and wife, Avantae kissed me long and passionately. For a moment, I forgot where we were. It was so special.

We signed our marriage license in front of everyone, and we even had a mini photo session. So many people came up to hug and congratulate us. The day was perfect, and I wouldn't have it any other way.

I excused myself for a moment to go to the restroom. I'm happy my dress was long because I just pissed all over myself.

"*Aaaargh, ooowww, oooowwww!*" I cried. I breathed in and out while sitting on the restroom floor. The pain was unbearable.

"Ceanna, you okay in here? You've been in here for a minute, ma," Avantae asked, coming in the restroom.

"Nooooo, Tae! I think my water just broke. *Aaaaargh!*" I doubled over in pain.

"Oh, fuuuck! What-what I'm I supposed to do?" Avantae began pacing back and forth.

"Tae, get the doctor. *Aaaaargh!*" I yelled.

"Right! Somebody help! She's in labor!" Avantae's crazy ass yelled loudly running out of the bathroom.

"Ceanna, I'm here," the doctor said, rushing into the bathroom. She began checking my cervix.

Avantae was next to the doctor, then Mama and girls came in gathering around me. They were either rubbing my head, holding my hands, or offering words of encouragement.

"Y'all ready to have these babies? She's ready, and we won't make it to the hospital in time," the doctor said.

"Tae, it hurts so badly. *Aaaaargh!*" I screamed loudly.

"Baby, I know, but you can do this, Ceanna."

"Everybody's gonna see my Va-jay-jay." I cried hard. I was so emotional and in pain.

"Boo, don't worry about that. At least you shaved," Keisha said, causing everyone to laugh.

"*Oooowww, oooowww*. Taeeeeee, I'm gonna kick your aaaass. *Oooowww!*" I yelled.

"Okay, she's ready! Come on, Ceanna, on the count of three, give me a big push. The EMS workers are on the way so don't worry. Come on, 1, 2, 3 . . ." She and the room counted.

"*Aaaaargh!*" I pushed hard.

"Come on, Ceanna. Baby, I see little mama's head!" Avantae yelled excitedly. The room was loud and filled with joy.

"Come on, Ceanna, give me another big push," the doctor ordered.

"*Aaaaaaaaaaargh!*"

"Here she comes."

"*Whaaaaaam!*"

I heard the first cry, and I began sobbing so hard. The doctor passed the baby to Janair.

"Come on, Ceanna, the other baby is ready *now*."

"Push, push, push!" everyone chanted.

"*Aaaaaaaaaargh!*" I pushed, feeling a sense of relief.

"What-what's wrong with her? Why isn't she crying? Avantaeeee!" I began sobbing, and then I heard her.

"Wha-wha—"

"*Whaaaaaaam!*"

The second baby hollered out.

"She's in here!" I heard Mia Symone yelled out to the EMS workers.

"You did it, ma! I'm so proud of you," Avantae kissed me on my forehead.

He hurried and cut the umbilical cords before the EMS workers took the babies. They placed me on a gurney in a separate truck. Keisha rode with me, and Avantae rode in the truck with the twins. They took us Seton Hospital.

Chapter Forty-one

Jaceyon

I was low-key chilling in the city of Killeen. For the longest, I had been lying low trying to figure out how I was going to kill Avantae. I can't believe he killed my mama like that.

My mama treated him as her own and cared for him even after his father was killed. *Damn, he pulled the trigger as if it was nothing.* I shook my head.

I hadn't been able to get to a barber, and my face was looking bad under my chin. Surveying the area, I stopped by a hair store. I heard this sister in the store talking loudly on her phone.

"Yeah, girl, I'm so excited. Myriah called me from Ceanna's boutique, and we'll be starting practice soon. Oh my God, you should see her twins too. They are absolutely beautiful. She had them yesterday. Can you believe she and Avantae married yesterday at her baby shower, and then she went into labor? She was so surprised to see me as her nurse. She truly is a sweetheart. Oh yeah, come up to Seton tonight. I'll be working on the private wing, but you can come get the application. Well, all right; bye, girl."

That's black women's downfall. Either they talk too damn loud or too damn much, I silently thought. I followed her briefly, thinking of what I was going to say to her. She wasn't my type by any means, but she was pretty for a big girl. She was light-skinned with dark brown eyes and a short hairdo. I admit she wasn't Ceanna, but she was the only inside I had right now.

Avantae placed a million-dollar bounty on my head. I couldn't move the way I needed to, and I couldn't get far on the seven grand that I had left to my name. Luckily, the nigga Tam gave me another pistol and gave me one of his stash spots to lie my head in. He was supposed to kill Avantae, and the plan was for us to take over again, but I ain't heard from that nigga, so I know he's leaking somewhere.

I stared at the woman for a few moments, picking up on her vibe. I could tell she was single, had low self-esteem, was looking for a man to love her, and she didn't have kids. I was an expert at reading women. That's how I picked my prey. When she went to place her items on the counter, I quickly made my move.

"Add her items to mine. I got you, beautiful," I smiled.

"Oh, wow, thank you! That's so kind of you." She smiled back. I saw her checking me out. I'm not cocky, but I know I'm one fine-ass nigga with a big dick to match.

"You're welcome, beautiful. What's your name?" I asked.

"Brittany." She grabbed her items, and I grabbed mine. We continued our conversation outside.

"I'm David, by the way. This may sound a little too forward, but I really would like to get to know you. Have you eaten? May I treat you to breakfast?" I smiled. Fat women love to eat.

"Wow, I can't remember the last time a guy has asked me out. I'm flattered," she smiled. She stared at me for a moment.

"Sure, I'll follow you." She smiled, and that was too easy.

"I'm not from around this area. I just moved here from Dallas, so what do you suggest?" I asked.

"Oh, really? Well, what if I just cook for you instead?" she asked while texting on her phone.

"Really? Are you sure?"

"Yeah, why not? Besides, that way, I can change and be more comfortable. I've been caring for newborn babies all night, and I just got off."

"Okay. Well, cool, beautiful. I'll follow you."

I jumped in my whip, following Brittany. I laughed to myself thinking how easy this shit was. Brittany kept driving a ways out. We finally pulled up to this nice home that was in a more secluded area. She had some big land that was surrounded by large trees everywhere. I parked on the side of her Kia Sportage and had gotten out the same time as she did.

Brittany's home was bare but clean and still nice. She had the typical black leather furniture with a flat screen and TV stand. It didn't really look as if anyone stayed there often, but with her being an RN, I would expect that.

"Well, go ahead, David, and make yourself comfortable. I'm going to change and start cooking." She smiled and then disappeared.

I began flipping through her channels and settled on *The Barbershop*. Brittany came back out changing into jogging pants and a wife beater. I wanted to frown, but I smiled and told her she looked nice.

As she cooked, I came and sat at the dining table. We laughed and made small talk. She was really funny, and I was actually starting to like her personality. I took a bite of her food and sipped down my apple juice. Suddenly, Brittany's mood changed, and she put me on alert.

"So, Jaceyon, let's stop the bullshit. Your time is up," she laughed.

Immediately, the room began to spin. I saw Brittany picking up her phone, and the last thing I heard was . . . *"Avantae, I got him."*

Splash! "Wake up, nigga!" Avantae threw cold water on me.

I tried to catch my breath; then I was hit with a chain, causing me to scream out in pain. "*Aaaargh!*" My feet were taped to the chair, my mouth was taped shut, and my hands were taped behind my back.

"You wanted my life, you bitch-ass nigga." *Whip!* "You tried to bring malice to my wife." *Whip!* "You stole my watch my daddy gave me." *Whip!* "Ho." *Whip!* "Dick in the booty" *Whip!* "Ass nigga" *Whip! Whip! Whip!*

I passed out from the pain. Avantae was like a raging pit bull. *Whap! Whap! Whap! Whap!* He punched me over and over in the face, causing my nose to break. I could taste the blood forming in my mouth. Then he ripped the tape off my mouth.

"You got any last words, nigga?" he yelled, and I spit the blood in his face. Avantae took a rag from his back pocket and wiped off the blood. He threw his head back laughing in an evil way. The front door opened and in walked four Mexican men. I instantly knew they were the cartel. Just then, I pissed on myself.

"Ayo, Jesús! Just in fucking time. I was about to murk this nigga myself. He's all yours!" Avantae laughed.

"Halo, Jasion," the leader Jesús said in a heavy accent.

"Chu fuck with my friend, chu fuck with me. Chu belong to the cartel now. Chu will pay. Gather him!" he yelled, and the other three Mexican men grabbed me.

"Pleaseeeee, Avantae! I'm your brother, man. I'm sorry! Don't do this, man!" I yelled before I was knocked out cold.

I woke up hours later in the back of a truck. There were three other men lying there. We all had been beaten. I was the only nigga. The truck stopped, and the door opened. We were ordered out and stripped butt-ass naked.

"Tis one first," a fat Mexican man said while he pointed at me.

Two men grabbed me. It appeared as if we were in a jungle of some sort, out in the middle of nowhere. The wooden fence in front of us opened, and my eyes grew wide when I saw big-ass alligators aggressively floating in the water.

"Ho-ass bitch, let me go." I fought with the men and got free. I took off running . . . only to catch a bullet in the right calf.

"Aaaah, fuuuck!" I fell, rolling on the ground. I saw the Mexican coming at me and attempted to run again. *Pow! Pow! Pow!* I was shot over and over again. That was it. I was done. Darkness took over me. A nigga had a good run while it lasted.

Chapter Forty-two

Avantae

As soon as I got to the hospital, I made sure to secure the floor. Ceanna had the biggest room in a secluded area of the hospital. I couldn't take any chances with my family's safety.

The twins were very healthy. I stood with Nurse Brittany and watched as she bathed and washed Aariah, who was really enjoying getting her hair washed. She kept her little gray eyes open staring at Brittany and me. I had Aaniah in my arms, and she was fast asleep. I could already tell who had my personality verses Ceanna's.

Aaniah was the calm and chilled baby, while Aariah was the feisty one. They were so beautiful, and even though the girls were identical twins, you could tell them apart. Aaniah had a beauty mark by her lip, her eyes were also gray, but she had these extremely long, dark lashes and pouted lips like Ceanna. Aariah, on the other hand, had a beauty mark by her right eye, and she had dimples.

Ceanna was finally brought back to the room. Due to pushing so hard and the natural birth of two babies, she tore too much and had to be sewn up.

She was knocked out, and since Aaniah was already asleep, and I had Brittany to help me, I left her alone. I know my baby was tired, and I was so proud of her. She gave me the two biggest gifts today. First, by becoming my wife, and second, giving birth to my daughters. Seeing my babies being born touched something in me. It was such an amazing sight to see.

"There you go, little one. We're all done," Brittany said, drying the baby off. She yawned and closed her little eyes.

"Mmmmm," I heard Ceanna moan.

"Baby, I'm here!" I ran over to her with the baby in my arms.

Sssssss, Ceanna moaned while sitting up and reaching for the baby. A flow of tears began to roll down her cheeks.

"She's so pretty, Tae!" Ceanna said while kissing the baby all over. Aaniah began to stir in her arms and started moving her mouth.

"Looks like somebody is hungry." Hold her a minute, Tae. Ceanna pulled out her right breast. Aaniah latched on quickly, and I smiled. I can't describe how a nigga was feeling right now.

"Here's the other little beauty right here," the nurse said, walking over to the bed.

"Oh, wow, you're a nurse? I never forget a beautiful face." Ceanna smiled.

"Yes, and, hi, Ceanna," Brittany beamed.

"Tae, this is our new model for the fall show," Ceanna said.

"Nice to meet you! Listen, Brittany, this wing is secure, and I like your vibe. I need you to watch after my wife and girls until they're ready to be discharged. I'll pay you a thousand dollars for every additional hour you stay."

"Oh, wow, sure! I mean, I do have to leave in the morning for a few hours, but I'll be right back," she assured us.

"May I ask why you're in this area? Is something wrong?" she asked.

"My ex-husband Jaceyon is out to bring harm to my family. He has disappeared, and we can't find him. We've got to be safe," Ceanna explained.

"I agree. Do you have a photo of what he looks like?" she asked. I took my phone to show her a photo.

After a while, the entire crew showed up with food and flowers. Brittany got everybody chairs, and we all camped out in the room. The kids enjoyed seeing their sisters and damn near cried when they had to leave. I had WyKeith and Keisha stay at the house with my mom and the kids while I stayed at the hospital with Ceanna. The babies' beds were in the room with us, and Brittany brought me a comfortable-ass reclining chair.

"How's my favorite couple this evening?" the doctor asked, coming through the door.

"Hi, Cherrika," Ceanna said, giving her a hug.

"What's up, Doc?" I hugged her.

"Ceanna, you did good, baby. I sure didn't think we would have the babies at the center on the floor," she laughed.

"Me either," Ceanna chuckled.

"Avantae, you should have seen your face," the doctor said.

"Maaaan, say, I didn't know what the fuck to do." We all laughed.

"Well, baby girl, we're going to keep you guys tonight and tomorrow night. Your blood pressure and swelling are bothering me some, so we've got to get it down. I'm going to get out of here, but I won't be far at all. The guards are on the door, love." She kissed Ceanna's forehead and kissed the twins.

"Oh, Avantae, give my girl six weeks, okayyyyy?" she laughed and exited the room.

The twins woke up on and off throughout the night. Ceanna and I switched off back and forth. I was so in love and dog tired.

"Hey, Avantae, I've got to run. I'll be back. Breakfast should be up shortly." Brittany tapped me on my shoulder. I must've dozed off.

While the twins and Ceanna slept, I took that as my opportunity to shower. WyKeith and Keisha brought us a bag yesterday before they came with the kids.

I pulled out a pair of white socks, a long black tee, gray sweats, and grabbed my hygiene products. Then I ran the water in the shower making it hot and stepped in it.

"Aaaah," I moaned. The twenty-minute shower felt so good.

"*Whaaaaaam!*"

I heard one of the twins and hurried out of the shower. I quickly dried off and wrapped a towel around me.

"Hey, little mama; it's okay." I picked up Riah and began rocking her back and forth. I noticed she was wet, so I decided to just go ahead and give her a little bath. She smiled and looked at me the entire time. I think she liked my little rap song I was rapping to her.

"Tae, what you over there doing?" Ceanna asked while smiling.

"Giving my Riah a bath, and baby girl is loving it." I smiled.

"You're such a good daddy. Uh-oh, looks like Niah is next," she said.

I dried Riah and wrapped her up; then I passed her to Ceanna and grabbed Niah. I did the same thing with her as I did with Riah. After the twins were bathed, fed, and dressed, they fell quickly back to sleep. Next, I helped Ceanna with her hygiene. She was my baby, and I didn't mind helping her with her feminine areas.

My phone rang, and I noticed it was Brittany. I had given her my number so that she could keep me informed. "What's up, Brittany?" I asked while I washed Ceanna's back. I placed her on speakerphone.

"Avantae, you'll never believe this, but Jaceyon is in Killeen. The nigga is following me now."

"Text me the address, and good looking out, ma. I appreciate you. Hold him off, drug him, or whatever you got to do, but don't let that nigga outta your sight." I hung up. My phone immediately went off with a text from Brittany. I shot Jesús a text to let him know it was time.

"Baby, the girls, Mama, and the kids are on their way here. I gotta go handle this nigga," I said as I helped Ceanna dry off.

"Go handle your business, baby, and come back to us. We love you!" She kissed me.

"Love you too. Don't eat that nasty-ass food. Mama cooked for you. You need anything, baby, when I get back?"

"Yes, Tae, can you please buy me some XL Depends for women? I'm bleeding too heavy, and these little-ass hospital pads is not it."

"Uh . . . okay. Where do I get them?" I asked and frowned, confused. *The fuck!*

"Just ask the store clerk. They'll know, baby," she laughed.

I hurried out of the hospital and jumped in my ride. Killeen was an hour away, but I made it there in thirty minutes. It seemed like I couldn't get there fast enough. I hit Brittany's phone letting her know I was there. She came and opened the door for me.

"He's in here, Avantae," she pointed. Jaceyon was laid out on the floor.

"Good looking. Are you good?" I asked.

"Yes, I'm good. Now, I can get the hell outta here," she laughed.

"No doubt, and I appreciate you. I'll hit you up with some ends too."

I placed a chair in the middle of the living room and lifted the heavy nigga. I struggled at first cause he was dead weight. With the duct tape, I began taping this nigga's legs and hands behind his back. My plan was vicious. I sold this nigga to the cartel. He belonged to them now. That didn't stop me from whopping his ass, though.

Splash! I took a bucket of ice-cold water and threw it on him. He instantly woke up. Then I took a chain I had in my truck and wrapped it around my hand. I struck him over and over again leaving open wounds on his body. He began bleeding and jerking his body with every strike. I removed the tape, and the nigga disrespectfully spit in my face, sending me into overdrive. I was happy Jesús came when he did, or else I would have killed that nigga.

"Avantae, chu good here my friend," Jesús smiled, telling me to leave. I walked out of the home feeling relieved. Finally, my baby and family can rest.

Epilogue

Avantae

One year later

I know y'all didn't think I was going to leave y'all hanging like that. Man, I'm the happiest man in the world right now. Ceanna just gave me a son, Amair Devin Wallace, and we're stronger than ever. Jalisa and Tater Bug are doing wonderful as well and still driving me crazy as hell. My mother is still the apple of my eye, and she's still doing well. Oh, and me yo' boiiii doing big things, aye. Dig these blues! I got a new shoe line, my mixtape just dropped, and the shit has gone viral. They loving yo' boiiii. The crew is doing well. Semaj just produced a huge track for an upcoming artist, Janair is almost finished with school, and their baby girl is growing so big. Elijah and his wife Ashley opened a successful day care center. WyKeith and Keisha had a baby girl, and believe it or not, Mia Symone has really gotten her shit together. As far as Zaria, I haven't seen or heard from her, and I hope I never do. I would hate to come out of retirement.

Ceanna

Whew, it has been a ride, Laaawd knows. I'll take this ride with Tae anytime, though. I never thought I would be here. After my fashion show, I was featured in several top magazines, even opening up several boutiques around the world. Avantae and I are so blessed. However, you know that fool was not letting me wait six weeks. I got pregnant damn near a month later. That's it, though, hunny, for a while, anyway. Lawd, all these damn kids are going to drive me crazy. I hope you guys enjoyed our story. Remember to always pull together in rough times and never apart. Communication is key! Well, bye, you guys! Lawd, let me go; one of my children is in there cutting up. I bet it's Aaniah. She's *always* into things. Y'all say a prayer for ya girl.

Previous Books

The Worst Thots Ever:
A 512 Scandal Series, VOL. 1–3

Cuffed By A Savage and His Lies

Salvaging What's Left of Me, VOL. 1–2

Upcoming Books by the Author

I Was Made to Love You 2

Love Under New Management:
The Keisha and Wykeith Story

Mirros and Mascara:
The Mia Symone Story

A Broken Clock is Right Twice a Day

The Final Hour

The Lies He Told to Keep Me

and many more to come . . .

Interaction Questions

What would you do?

1. If you were, Ceanna would you have forgiven Mia Symone?
2. Would you let Jalisa spend time with Jaceyon and Gina after all they had done?
3. Would you have given Jaceyon a second chance?
4. Do you think that you would have been able to accept Avantae's child, or would that be a deal breaker?
5. How do you feel about Keisha and WyKeith's relationship?
6. Have you ever been in a situation where you no longer loved or wanted to be with the person, but they can't let you go?
7. How do you feel about mothers-in-law? Are you close to yours or at odds?
8. What are three facts about Ceanna that you think are true about the author?
9. Would you be able to raise someone's child after that individual passed away, knowing that that person had betrayed you?
10. Have you ever tried to divorce someone who has made it difficult for you?
11. Do you think Ceanna and Avantae should have waited before they became involved?

12. Who do you relate to more in this book?
13. If you were Ceanna, would you allow Jaceyon to be a part of the birthing process?
14. What's your take on Zaria?
15. Do you think WyKeith is a good man, or do you think he will break Keisha's heart?

Author's Bio

The incomparable Author Jessica Wren is known for her critically acclaimed series, The Worst Thots Ever, I Was Made To Love You: The Ceanna & Avantae Story, Cuffed By A Savage & His Lies, and now she brings you Salvaging What's Left Of Me. The author is a native of Austin, Texas. She has been penning her stories since the age of fourteen. In 2005, she received her Creative Writing Degree. In 2015, she was signed to Cole Hart Presents. In 2016, she branched off on her own and took the independent journey. In 2016, she was listed as UBAWA Top 100 Urban Authors. In 2017, she was listed as UBAWA Top 100 Urban Authors. She has released a total of seven books, one being a collaboration with twelve other women. In the collaboration "Women Withstanding All," Author Jessica Wren gets personal with her story, *There Is Life After Divorce*. In 2017, she signed with Blake Karrington Presents while continuing to release independently. This author keeps growing and perfecting her craft. Outside of writing, she loves to live life to the fullest. In her spare time, she enjoys painting, designing, planning events, traveling, and spending time with her loved ones. Stay connected with this creative raconteur.

Contact the Author

Twitter:
wren_jessica

Instagram:
authoressjessicawren

Facebook:
Jessica A. Wren

Author Page:
Books by Jessica Wren

E-mail:
authoressjessicawren@gmail.com

Web Site:
www.booksbyjessicawren.com